"One of the most tough-minded writers of the genre."
—*San Francisco Chronicle*

"America's answer to Ruth Rendell."
—*The Denver Post*

PRAISE FOR

Bone by Bone

"Ms. O'Connell gleefully invents a hothouse of . . . malice. She assigns dark secrets and strange habits to every last character in her serpentine story."   —*The New York Times*

"O'Connell specializes in stories about damaged, complex, and strong characters. [She] brings the same high standards and insight to . . . *Bone by Bone* . . . a coming of age novel, a story about families, secrets, revenge, and tolerance."   —*South Florida Sun-Sentinel*

"Intriguing, complex characters, and long-buried secrets . . . Highly recommended."   —*Library Journal*

"A deep, psychological suspense thriller."
—*Midwest Book Review*

continued . . .

Dead Famous

"O'Connell's prose—sharp, gritty, and streetwise—is in top form. Ingenious . . . O'Connell sets the standard in crime fiction." —*Publishers Weekly* (starred review)

"Mallory returns with a vengeance and in total control . . . blazingly original. Once again, O'Connell transcends the genre." —*Kirkus Reviews* (starred review)

Crime School

"Easily one of the most original and striking crime fiction protagonists to appear in the last few years . . . Multilayered, serpentine in plot . . . a rich, evocative novel."
—*St. Petersburg Times*

Shell Game

"Rich, complex, memorable . . . another superb effort from one of our most gifted writers."
—*Booklist* (starred review)

Judas Child

"Breathtakingly ambitious suspense . . . A brilliant twist . . . mesmerizing." —*Minneapolis Star Tribune*

"Her most stunning novel yet . . . more chilling, twisted, and intense with each page . . . [a] soul-shattering climax." —*Booklist* (starred review)

continued . . .

Stone Angel

"A hard-edged, brilliant, and indomitable heroine. *Stone Angel*, as much Southern novel as mystery novel, is rich in people, places, and customs vividly realized, with mordant humor, terror, and sadness." —*San Francisco Chronicle*

Killing Critics

"Darkly stylish . . . highly original . . . This is great fun."
—*Chicago Tribune*

"A tight, twisting mystery." —*Newsday*

The Man Who Cast Two Shadows

"Even more satisfying than *Mallory's Oracle*. And that's high praise indeed." —*People*

"Beautifully written." —*Harper's Bazaar*

"The suspense is excruciating." —*Detroit Free Press*

Mallory's Oracle

"Mallory is a marvelous creation." —Jonathan Kellerman

"A classic cop story . . . one of the most interesting new characters to come along in years." —John Sandford

"An author who really involves you, and makes you care." —James B. Patterson

"Wild, sly, and breathless—all the things that a good thriller ought to be." —Carl Hiaasen

TITLES BY CAROL O'CONNELL

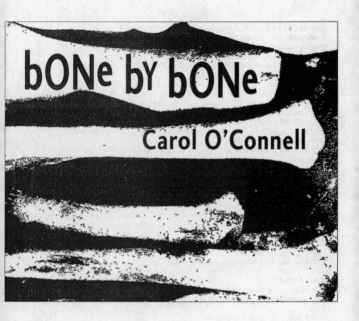

bONe bY bONe

Carol O'Connell

BERKLEY BOOKS, NEW YORK

THE BERKLEY PUBLISHING GROUP
Published by the Penguin Group
Penguin Group (USA) Inc.
375 Hudson Street, New York, New York 10014, USA
Penguin Group (Canada), 90 Eglinton Avenue East, Suite 700, Toronto, Ontario M4P 2Y3, Canada
(a division of Pearson Penguin Canada Inc.)
Penguin Books Ltd., 80 Strand, London WC2R 0RL, England
Penguin Group Ireland, 25 St. Stephen's Green, Dublin 2, Ireland (a division of Penguin Books Ltd.)
Penguin Group (Australia), 250 Camberwell Road, Camberwell, Victoria 3124, Australia
(a division of Pearson Australia Group Pty. Ltd.)
Penguin Books India Pvt. Ltd., 11 Community Centre, Panchsheel Park, New Delhi—110 017, India
Penguin Group (NZ), 67 Apollo Drive, Rosedale, North Shore 0632, New Zealand
(a division of Pearson New Zealand Ltd.)
Penguin Books (South Africa) (Pty.) Ltd., 24 Sturdee Avenue, Rosebank, Johannesburg 2196,
South Africa

Penguin Books Ltd., Registered Offices: 80 Strand, London WC2R 0RL, England

This is a work of fiction. Names, characters, places, and incidents either are the product of the author's imagination or are used fictitiously, and any resemblance to actual persons, living or dead, business establishments, events, or locales is entirely coincidental. The publisher does not have any control over and does not assume any responsibility for author or third-party websites or their content.

BONE BY BONE

A Berkley Book / published by arrangement with the author

PRINTING HISTORY
G. P. Putnam's Sons hardcover edition / December 2008
Berkley premium edition / November 2009

Copyright © 2008 by Carol O'Connell.
Cover photographs: *Trees* copyright © by Nick Daly/Getty Images. *Birds* copyright © by Mary-Ella
Keith/Alamy. Cover design copyright © 2008 by mjcdesign.com.

ISBN: 978-0-425-23105-0

BERKLEY®
Berkley Books are published by The Berkley Publishing Group,
a division of Penguin Group (USA) Inc.,
375 Hudson Street, New York, New York 10014.
BERKLEY® is a registered trademark of Penguin Group (USA) Inc.
The "B" design is a trademark of Penguin Group (USA) Inc.

PRINTED IN THE UNITED STATES OF AMERICA

10 9 8 7 6 5 4 3 2 1

This book is dedicated to men and women who stood in harm's way, to those who came home with the damage that shows and also the damage that no one sees and no one else can know.

Acknowledgments

Many thanks to those who helped me with my research, among them an entire army that operates from a five-sided building and prefers to go nameless on this page (something to do with not going through proper channels for an interview). And thank you, Mr. Hanlon of Hanlon's Razor.

One

A batty old man of the cloth had once described the Hobbs boy as a joke of God's: an archangel of the warrior cast and a beacon for women with carnal intentions.

An *angel*.

Would that he had wings.

Oren Hobbs, now a man full grown, opened his eyes in the dark and took deep breaths to quell the panic. Every time he dreamed, he died. Neither awake nor asleep, he was caught, for a second or two, between the nightmare of going home again and the solid world, where he had arrived—where a dog was barking in the yard.

He lay sprawled upon the old horsehair sofa. The upholstery smelled of tobacco and spilt whiskey, the best-loved vices of his father and the housekeeper. These stale odors were cut with a slice of cool, sweet air from the open porch window. He had forgotten to lower the sash after climbing inside, and now Oren recalled that the door to the house had been locked against him for the first time in memory. Still drowsing, his eyes were slow to pick out the surrounding shadows of furniture that took on familiar form but no detail.

What the hell?

One of the shadows scuttled across the carpet, agitated and flapping its wings like a gray moth—a moth that could skin its shin on the coffee table and whisper curse words.

Memory guided Oren's hand to a lamp, and he switched it on the better to see a woman wrapped in a purple robe with great floppy sleeves. "Hannah?"

Nearing sixty, the housekeeper was a small, slight figure beneath that oversized garment—the same old bathrobe. She might be as tall as a ten-year-old, but only if she stood on her toes. The long braid of black hair had gone to iron gray, and her smile lines had deepened, but she seemed otherwise unaltered by the past twenty years. Her heart-shaped face had no sag to it.

Pixies aged so well.

"Oh, damn it." Her wide-set hazel eyes blinked in the lamplight as she leaned down to rub her wounded shinbone.

He followed her lead of a whisper that would not wake the old man, who was near death. "Hannah, it's me—Oren. Sorry if I scared you." Rising from the couch, he stood barefoot in his sweatshirt and blue jeans. At thirty-seven years of age, he might be the one more changed by time. She looked him up and down, and shook her head, as if she could not reconcile him with the longhaired boy who had left this house when he was seventeen. His dark brown hair was shorter now, and a strand of it covered one blue eye.

He nodded toward the open window, the evidence of his housebreaking. "I got in late, and I didn't want to—"

"Hush." Hannah held a veined hand in the air, frozen there, and he fancied that her ears were attenuating, straining to hear something. Her attention was rewarded with the bark of a dog very close to the house—and then the sound of something dropped, an object clattering to the floorboards of the front porch.

The housekeeper jumped as if a cannon had sounded.

Oren walked toward the foyer, one hand outstretched to grab the doorknob.

"Don't go out there!" Hannah switched off the lamp in the front room.

He had a feeling that she had played out this little drama before. "What's going on?"

More barking came from the yard.

The front door would not open. In the dark of the foyer, he found a bolt by touch, but he could not undo the lock. Oren returned to the predawn gloom of the parlor. He found his duffel bag and pulled out a gun. This was reflex, and he thought better of it. Best not to shoot somebody's pet on his first day back in town. He put the weapon away and closed up the bag. Zip—gone. "It's okay, Hannah. Go back to bed. It's just a dog."

"That's not *our* dog," she whispered, creeping closer. "Horatio died ages ago."

As he moved toward the open porch window, Hannah reached out with both hands to catch him and snatch him back.

Too late.

Oren climbed outside. The sky was early-morning gray, and the tall trees had no colors yet. Smooth, worn boards were cool beneath his bare feet as he hunkered down before the gift that had been left at the edge of the porch—a lower jawbone, bare of flesh and laced with teeth.

Even without the evidence of a silver filling in one molar, he would have known that this bone belonged to the skeleton of a human being. He was well acquainted with human remains in every stage of decay.

TWO

As the sky brightened in the east, Oren could see that this was no innocent find of the barking dog. An animal would have left wet traces of saliva, but the jawbone was dry. It had been dropped on the porch by someone who walked on two legs.

He peered into the woods, looking for signs of trespass, trails in the air, left there by waving ferns and low branches. After delivering a present like this one, a pervert might linger awhile to watch the reaction—and the dog might betray its master with one more bark. Oren sat down on the porch steps to wait—and listen.

The smell of moist earth wafted up from a garden that ran the length of the porch. Nothing had blossomed yet, but it was certain that the old man had planted the bulbs of lilies, dahlias and gladiolas. Come a fine warm day in high summer, all of them would rise up in a riot of bright yellow blooms. On this early June morning, the bulbs were still hiding and biding their time. Oren's mother had been partial to yellow flowers, or so he had been told. There were no memories of her—only of this enduring ritual of gardening, the only sign that his father was a fool for love.

How much time had passed, he could not say. Behind him, he heard the door unlatch, then the creak of a floorboard, and now he caught the aroma of coffee. He looked up to see his tall, lanky father standing over him, holding two steaming mugs.

Not dead yet, old man?

Far from it. The retired judge appeared to be enjoying robust good health, though he was no longer impervious to cool mornings. Henry Hobbs wore a flannel shirt over his faded jeans. His feet were shod in replicas of the old sandals with crepe soles that had allowed him to sneak up on boys who were up to no good. For this reason alone, Oren and his little brother, Josh, had often wished that the judge would wear shoes and socks like other fathers. A long ponytail had also been the old man's trademark. Now his head was bald. As compensation, he had allowed his beard to grow long. The wispy white ends of it moved with a gentle current of air.

Bowing, almost courtly, Judge Hobbs handed one of the coffee mugs down to Oren, and then joined his son on the steps. The two men sat, side by side, in companionable silence, as if twenty years had been but an hour's separation—as if a human jawbone had not been left out in plain sight on the porch, resting there between them.

The sun was up, and the color of their surroundings had ripened into lush forest green. Yellow wildflowers peppered the meadow.

And the jawbone had a reddish cast.

A flock of crows rose up from a nearby tree, screeching. *Khaa! Khaa! Cowp-cowp-cowp!* His father watched their flight. "Damn birds. I never did need an alarm clock." With the same nonchalance, the old man said, "So you've come home."

"Well, yeah." Oren sipped his coffee. "I thought you were dying."

"What?" The judge turned to face his son. "Hannah told you that?"

"No, sir. She never spelled it out in her letters." Yet she had left him with the impression that a funeral was pending—just a crazy inference drawn from her line about shopping for coffins.

The judge waved one hand, dismissing this notion. "I'll outlive her. She drinks more than I do." He flicked a ladybug off the rim of his coffee mug, proof that he was not blind—except to the skeletal remains of a human being only inches from his elbow.

The door opened, and Hannah rushed out onto the porch in a racket of wooden clogs. Bending low, she covered her employer's shoulders with a woolen afghan.

"Stop fussing over me," said the judge, though he snuggled into the wool, grateful for the warmth. When his housekeeper had gone back inside and the door had banged shut behind her, he turned to his son. "Damn, she's in a state this morning."

Oren lightly tapped the fleshless body part that perched between them on the edge of the porch—just a hint that this might be the cause of Hannah's distress.

"Well," said the old man, oh so casually, "it's not like she hasn't seen that kind of thing before."

That much Oren had already surmised, but he would not take the bait and ask an obvious question. Lessons of boyhood had made him into a patient man. In a contest of sorts, he sipped the dregs of his coffee—*slowly*—then looked up to the sky and said, "I heard the dog died."

The judge nodded. "Horatio was lame and half blind when he chased down his last squirrel." He drained his coffee mug and set it down beside the jawbone. "Never heard a car pull up. How'd you get here, boy?"

"Planes and taxicabs." Even if he had waited another twenty years for this reunion, his name would still be *Boy*. "I got out of the cab on the highway and walked for a while." Last night, he had thought it best to sneak up on this place of profound pain and night terrors and the best times of his life. Oren smiled somewhat insincerely. "It was late. I thought the noise of a car might disturb a sick old man on his deathbed."

Judge Hobbs laughed. Approaching his seventy-fifth birthday, he could pass for ten years younger. There was no sign of illness in his rosy flesh, nor had age slowed his brain. He announced every thought with the flicker of bright blue eyes, quick to note everything, missing nothing, not even what went on behind his back, for now he turned to catch Hannah watching from the window.

Reaching down to a lower step, Oren plucked a small

clump of yellow hair from the splintered wood before the next breeze could take it. There was no need of a microscope, no doubt that this was fur recently shed by the barking dog.

"I thought you'd be wearing your uniform, boy."

Oren stuffed the fur ball into the watch pocket of his jeans. "I left the Army."

Finding human bones on the porch seemed to be an everyday thing with the judge, but this news from his son was clearly unsettling. "You quit? Not on *my* account."

"No, sir. It was time for a change." Years ago, he had ceased to define himself as a soldier. He was a man in search of a second act, and Hannah's most recent letters had pried him loose from the inertia of military life. The mail from his father had always been returned unopened, twenty years of letters, and yet the old man had remained a constant correspondent all that time. The silent war of father and son was a one-sided thing.

Oren, formerly Warrant Officer Hobbs of the U.S. Army's Criminal Investigations Division, picked up the jawbone and pondered the rust-colored stain. "So . . . this happens a lot?"

The door opened wide, and Hannah stood there, hands on hips, wearing a shapeless denim dress. Her hair was massed on top of her head and magically held in place by two wooden sticks. The new day had officially begun, and the balance of power shifted to her side of the porch. "*Oren,* I need you to carry that bag of yours upstairs. It's too heavy for me."

In times past, the housekeeper had used this voice of

authority only for special offenses, such as the grimy rings of a boy's life left on the porcelain sides of the bathtub. Smiling, he rose from the steps and followed her into the house. Closing the door behind him, he paused to stare at the dead bolts. Once, there had been a quaint keyhole lock—only one—and there had never been a key. Now there were three heavy-duty bolts, and each one required a key to unlock it from the *inside*.

The parlor of the old Victorian was flooded with sunlight, and Oren had his first look at what time had done to this room. It was disturbing. The shabbiness was not a symptom of apathy; it was worse—a conscientious thing. A broken vase of no value, sentimental or otherwise, had been glued back together so that it could remain a fixture of the mantelpiece. The rug was faded and near bald in places, evidence of scrubbing spills or maybe the accidents of an old dog in its dotage. And though Henry Hobbs had bags of money, the old man had kept the same furniture. Rips in the massive red sofa had been carefully mended, as had the cracks in the old brown-leather club chairs and the recliner. This was no act of preservation, but more like hard-core denial that two decades had passed since the loss of Josh.

An Irish setter lay on the floor near the fireplace. The dog was posed in sleep, but nothing could be so still as death. "Horatio?"

"Your father had him stuffed twelve years ago," said the housekeeper.

Not the brightest of animals, Horatio had never learned to do tricks or obey commands; he had only known how to slime his family with kisses and wet them down with drool. So happy was he to love and be loved, his tail had wagged in his sleep.

This stuffed—*thing*—was nothing like Horatio.

Hannah squinted, as if to see the lifeless carcass more clearly. "I suppose it *is* a bad joke on a dead dog." She gestured by hand signals that he should follow her upstairs, where they would not be overheard.

He picked up his duffel bag, his socks and cowboy boots, and then he climbed the steps behind her, noting the rut worn into the center of the staircase carpet—the same old carpet. Up to the second-floor landing and down the hall they went. The housekeeper led the way, and Oren spoke to her back. "So, Hannah, you mentioned a coffin in your last letter."

Surprised, she stopped midstride. "The judge didn't tell you?" She continued on her way down the hall, saying over one shoulder, "Your brother's been coming home—bone by bone."

Three

O ren dropped his bag and boots. Grabbing the housekeeper by the shoulders, he turned the tiny woman around to face him. "The judge thinks that jawbone belongs to *Josh?*"

"Well, yes. But that's not the crazy part." She rolled her eyes and sighed. "It never ends." By her tone, she might be describing a long parade of ants in the kitchen instead of his younger brother's strange homecoming, one bone at a time. Hannah turned solemn as she studied his face. She must have seen that he was stalled somehow. The wiry little woman scooped up his belongings from the floor, as if the heavy bag and boots weighed nothing, and she carried them to the bedroom at the end of the hall.

He was slow to follow her through that last door. Unlike the parlor downstairs, his old room showed no signs of time passing. Oren stared at the familiar blue bed-spread and its history of soap-resistant stains. It was un-wrinkled, not quite the way he had left it when he was a teenager who struggled with the concept of tucked-in sheets and smoothed-out blankets. The same photo-graphs hung on the walls. His old fountain pen lay on the writing desk alongside a book he had never finished read-ing. All that appeared to be missing was the knapsack taken with him on the day when the old man had sent him away.

Hannah settled his duffel bag on the bed and opened a bureau drawer. "You travel light."

"I shipped a trunk. It'll be along in a day or two."

"Good. That sounds more permanent." The house-keeper unzipped his bag and removed an old Colt .45 with two fingers and a look of surprise. "How on earth did you find it?"

"That's not Granddad's gun. I bought that one from a collector." He had seen it as a sweet reminder of early childhood, a day when the housekeeper had found him and Josh playing with an old revolver in the attic. They had just figured out how to load the bullets when Han-nah had snatched it away from them. Then she had hid-den the gun with only the clue that it was buried, and the two brothers had dug up large sections of the yard by flashlight and moonlight in a quest that had gone on for years.

Next, she pulled a heavy wad of T-shirts from the bag and unwrapped them to find a bottle of Jack Daniel's Tennessee whiskey buried inside.

"A present," he said.

She carried the bottle to the window and grinned at the label in this better light. "You remembered my brand. You good boy."

"We need to talk about the judge—and the bones."

"I know." Hannah set the bottle down on the desk and left the room. She returned a few moments later with two small paper cups from the bathroom dispenser. Three fingers of alcohol had been poured and drunk before she said, "You know it's possible for a man to be crazy *and* functional. Take the judge for instance."

"Right," he said dryly, "just hypothetically."

The housekeeper crumpled her paper cup into a ball—the only sign that she was vexed—and set it on the bureau. She turned her back on him to fold the T-shirts and place them in a drawer. "This business of stuffing the dog—turning the house into a damn museum." More clothes were pulled from the duffel bag. "It's like one little crazy spot in the middle of a real clear mind. That's called a fixation."

"Fixation?" Pain had ebbed away with the medicine from the whiskey bottle, and Oren smiled as he parroted the housekeeper's old mantra: "You've been reading books. You know that can't be good for you." Countless times, she had said this to him when he was a child spending too many daylight hours in the judge's library. It had been her mission then to save him from literacy and send him out of doors in search of a life.

He poured and downed another shot of whiskey as he

leaned back against the only patch of wall not cluttered with photos in white mats and black wooden frames.

"I've got a present for you, too." The housekeeper opened the top drawer of the desk. She pulled out a photograph framed in silver and handed it to him. "You were such beautiful kids."

He studied her gift, a portrait of two boys. Oren, pictured at the age of seventeen, stood half a head taller than his younger brother. He had never seen this shot, though he remembered when it was taken. No detail of that day could be forgotten. Josh had mounted his camera on a brand-new tripod and used a cable release to snap this picture from a distance. And so the two brothers were standing together—for the last time. The photograph was black-and-white, and Oren's blue eyes looked very dark. He seemed so subdued in that moment, and today he was not so changed after all, still brooding in his countenance, as if he had made a pact with Josh, for whom change was impossible.

He sank down on the bed beside Hannah.

She wrapped her arms around him in a hug. "It's good to have you home."

He had sorely missed this little woman, and she released her hold on him too soon. He bowed his head to look down at the picture in his hands. "So . . . about that jawbone?"

"Ah, the bones. They're always left on the porch late at night. You're the only one who knows—besides me and your father."

No, there was one other person who knew—the trespasser who traveled by night with a yellow dog. "I'm guessing this has been going on for months." He dated that guess by the housekeeper's letters and their cryptic allusions to something amiss. "If the old man doesn't call the sheriff, I'll have to do it myself."

She placed one hand on his knee and squeezed it with the gentle warning, "He won't like that, Oren."

"He was a judge. He knows the law."

"But you don't know the half of it—not yet." Hannah stood up, a little unsteady for the liquor. Late in life, she had evidently become a pansy drinker.

He followed her down the hall to Josh's old room, where the braided rug and the striped wallpaper were holding up well. But the bedspread had once been brilliant green, and now it was a muted shade. The closet was open, and Josh's favorite denim shirt hung by a hook on the back of the door along with the Sunday-best blue jeans. His brother had been wearing knock-around jeans the last time he was seen alive.

Hannah seemed lost in reverie and a whiskey buzz, perhaps forgetting why she had brought him in here. To refresh her memory, Oren slapped the top of the coffin that had pride of place in the center of Josh's bedroom. "This is new," he said.

Did that sound sarcastic? He hoped so.

The varnished rosewood was trimmed with shiny brass that spoke of a recent purchase. It was the wildly upscale model hawked by funeral directors whose souls were interchangeable with used-car salesmen. And this could only mean that one such undertaker must have seen enormous grief in the old man's eyes. And tears? Oh, yes. The expense of the coffin was proof. This obscene trick could only be worked on a fragile mourner deep in pain.

Hannah raised the lid and laid it back on its hinges. "The judge didn't want anybody to know about this until he had all the bones—till Josh was finished coming home. He made me swear not to tell."

The satin lining was green—Josh's favorite color—and the skeleton nestled there was the same red cast as the jawbone outside on the porch. The hands and feet were missing. Perhaps the judge's night visitor was an amateur at exhumation and had overlooked remains that might pass for sticks and stones. What destroyed Oren was the slight overlap of the skull's front teeth, the only physical imperfection of a fifteen-year-old boy.

Hello, Josh. Did you miss me?

Hannah stepped back from the coffin. "You wouldn't expect bones to smell."

By profession, Oren was accustomed to decomposition. He knew it was the confined space and the seal of the coffin that gave the bones the reek of an ossuary. And there was also an earthy smell. He leaned down, as if to kiss his brother's lipless face. "Hannah. Did the judge clean the skull? Did he do anything to it before it went into the coffin?"

"No, not a thing. The way Josh is now—that's the way he came home."

The bones of the body were dusted with soil, but the skull bore the circular marks of cloth-wiped dirt. No part of the skeleton showed signs of exposure to the elements, and there was no damage from the fangs of animal predators—only the stains of sheltering earth.

Raw burial could only be read as murder.

The torso and limbs were more lightly colored than the skull, a sign that they had been protected for a time by a layer of clothing. Oren took small comfort in the knowledge that his little brother had not been thrown naked into some hole.

Hannah tugged at his sleeve. "The judge won't want to give Josh up to the sheriff, but he might be willing to part with one or two bones."

Oren nodded, as if she had said something sensible. It had been easy enough for the judge to part with his first-born son. But it would be too hard on the old man to give up the other child, the dead one.

Hannah raised one finger to herald another thought. "Maybe we could just hold off on reporting Josh's skeleton—at least until it's finished." One hand went up to her mouth to stifle any more mad ideas. Her head tilted to one side, as if to shake out this contagion of an old man's insanity, and then she gripped Oren's arm. "Before you call the sheriff, you have to prepare the judge."

And how would he convince a crazy old man to surrender his dead son? Well, he would avoid any useless words like *closure*. Oren could not even bring himself to close the coffin. He wanted to crawl inside with the bones, to lie down with them and die.

Hannah stepped up to perform this small service for

him. She was lowering the lid when he said, "Wait!" and stayed her hands. "They don't match up."

"What?"

"Look at the thigh bones, Hannah."

She leaned over the coffin to stare at one and then the other. She looked up at him, quizzical—worried. "They're the same."

"Look again. The left one's off by an inch. Now look at the arms." He pointed to radials and femurs, not wanting to touch them. "These bones belong to two different skeletons . . . at *least* two."

Four

After returning the telephone's receiver to its antique cradle, Oren knew he could count on thirty minutes, maybe a solid hour, before a deputy was dispatched from the county seat. There would be no sirens screaming, no haste. The deputy from Saulburg might even stop for breakfast along the way. The County Sheriff's Office was long accustomed to similar reports from hikers in the woods, and the remains always turned out to be the bones of animals. Oren had made no mention of the skeleton in the coffin—only the jawbone, but not its dental filling.

He climbed the stairs and returned to his old bedroom, drawn there by the photograph in the silver frame, the shot taken on the day Josh had vanished. That was the only time that his little brother had used a tripod, the only instance of Josh appearing in one of his own pictures. Among the hundred examples of his brother's work on all the walls of the house, this posed composition was a rarity. The boy had favored a handheld camera for candid shots taken on the fly—hit and run. In this picture, there was more than a foot of distance between Oren and his brother, as if Josh were already leaving him in that moment.

Other photographs, more than a dozen, hung on the bedroom walls, and they chronicled five years of Josh's love affair with the camera. Oren stared at his favorite, one of himself and a girl who had only appeared in the summers of his boyhood. He colored her black-and-white image with a memory of long red hair and eyes the color of dark honey. As a boy, he had availed himself of furtive glances to count the freckles on her nose. At the age of twelve, this had been his life's work. In his early teens, he had progressed to a fascination with her red toenail polish.

He might have been thirteen years old when this shot was taken. Boy and girl were pictured walking away from one another, heading toward opposite ends of the frame. Between them yawned a great empty space—nothing but sky. His little brother had never taken a picture without the intention to tell a story or a joke, and this was both. Nothing had ever happened between Oren and the summer girl. They had not exchanged a single word. He had never heard the sound of her voice.

"Isabelle Winston."

"Hannah, don't *do* that."

She should know better. Creeping up behind people

had always been the judge's job. Oren turned around to see the housekeeper eyeing the same photograph. How long had she been standing there?

"Josh was good, wasn't he?" She moved closer to the wall. "A real artist."

Oren reached out to the bureau and picked up her homecoming gift, the picture of two brothers. "I know this shot came from Josh's last roll of film, the one he left behind that day. When was this developed? Was it before or *after* the judge sent me away?"

"You make it sound like he kicked you out of the house." She smiled, taking no offense at his tone of interrogation. "After Josh went missing, I found a roll of film stashed in his sock drawer. I left it there for a while. The judge didn't want anything disturbed in your brother's room. He had a real bug about that. I don't remember exactly when I took the roll down to the drugstore to get it developed." After a furtive glance at the door, she lowered her voice. "The judge doesn't need to know I did that. He'd pitch a fit." Hannah gave him her best conspirator's grin. "So don't you rat on me, okay?" She returned the photograph to the bureau. "It's a good picture, but I know Josh would've done a better job in his own darkroom."

"That's still in the attic?"

"Just the way he left it."

"Is that where you put the rest of the pictures from his last roll?"

Hannah turned to the window. "There's a car coming."

He did not doubt her, but a few moments passed before he also heard the sound of tires on the gravel driveway. At the hour of a shift change, there would be no deputies on duty in this area, and it was too soon for any official vehicle from Saulburg.

The owner of the pickup truck had streaks of blond hair the light shade of a towhead child's. If Hannah Rice had been in a more charitable mood, she might have credited those highlights to the sun instead of vanity. "The judge says you have to wait until that warrant shows up."

Dave Hardy was hunting for a shovel amid the pile of bags and gardening tools in the bed of his truck. "I give the orders, Hannah."

"Sure you do." She was not convinced that anyone in a rock-'n'-roll T-shirt and blue jeans could have any authority over her; though, even out of uniform, everything about this man announced him as an officer of the law.

His I-run-the-show attitude had begun to form at the age of eight when he got his first pair of dark glasses. Dave had worn them even in the rain, and some people who had watched him grow up could no longer recall the color of his eyes. When Hannah thought of this man as a child, she always embellished this picture of him with a tiny, fully loaded gun. Today he was not carrying a weapon, and, without his dark glasses, he looked nearly naked. Obviously feeling the need to bolster his credibility with her, he clipped his deputy's star to a belt loop, and then he resumed the chore of ransacking his pickup truck.

The retired judge sat on the porch steps beside Josh's jawbone. Hannah leaned down and lightly touched his arm, her prelude to every strong suggestion. "If you'd just tell Dave what's upstairs in that coffin, he might lose interest in that patch of dirt." She jabbed her thumb in the direction of freshly turned earth at the end of the garden, where the judge had planted his last batch of bulbs.

Henry Hobbs shook his head. No deal. He called out to the deputy, "For the last time—the bone didn't come from my garden!"

"We'll see." Triumphant, Dave Hardy raised a shovel high above his head. "Found it." He climbed down from the truck bed, turned toward the house—and turned to stone.

Hannah looked back over one shoulder to see what had stunned the deputy. Oren stood in the open doorway, only curious at the moment and relaxed in his stance.

The deputy could only stare at him, but everyone stared at Oren Hobbs. It was not merely the good looks of her blue-eyed boy that drew this kind of attention— more like attraction with the pull of gravity. Twenty years ago, in Hannah's estimation, Oren had been interrupted on the way to becoming somebody. She had never forecast the Army in his future. No, she had always seen him at the center of a stage. Indeed, this morning, it was almost like a performance, him standing there, hands in his pockets, wrapped in the aura of a rock star in an idle moment. His audience, Dave Hardy, was spellbound.

Spell undone, Dave rolled back his shoulders and

gripped the shovel in both hands. "Odd thing, Oren—that jawbone showing up the same time you do."

The judge rose from the porch steps and walked toward the deputy, eyes on the shovel. "You can't dig up my garden. Those bulbs will never bloom if you—"

"That's enough, old man." Dave freed up one hand to point at the porch. "Now go back and sit down. That's an *order!*"

The whites of Hannah's eyes got wider. One did not disrespect Judge Henry Hobbs—not in *this* town. The old man hesitated, and there was confusion in his face, silently asking how this could be happening to him. Hannah's hands went to her hips in a pose that conveyed to Dave Hardy, *Now look what you've done.*

Dave marched toward the far end of the flower bed and never saw his predictable demise in the eyes of Oren Hobbs, who descended the porch steps—slowly—angry and focused on the deputy.

Poor deputy.

Hannah Rice had always loomed large and mighty, even after Oren and Josh had grown taller than she was. The slightest pressure of the housekeeper's hand on any part of a boy that she could catch had been enough to restrain the two youngsters. And this influence of hers had lasted into their teenage years. It simply had never occurred to either of them that, once caught, they could ever get away from her.

And now he felt Hannah's small hand closing over his right fist, the one he favored for beating the crap out of Dave Hardy. Oren stood very still, powerless to go anywhere. He looked down to catch her brief smile, the equivalent of rolling up her sleeves in anticipation of doing some damage.

Hannah trained her eyes on the deputy and worked her old magic, hurling words across the length of the flower bed with the crack of lightning bolts. "Put that shovel down this *instant*!"

Dave looked up. The shovel hovered.

The housekeeper lowered her voice for the next salvo. "Don't you make me call your mother."

Run, Dave, run.

Apparently, the deputy's mother still held the office of town monster, a woman in the habit of publicly castrating her own son in ten words or less. Oren recalled that Mrs. Hardy had sometimes rhymed her lines, and, around town, she had been much admired as an obscene poet.

"I can have Mavis over here," said Hannah, snapping her fingers, "just like that."

Once, it had been rumored that Dave's mother was a vessel of demonic possession. More rational townspeople had argued that, in any arrangement of that sort, Mavis Hardy would be the *possessor* and not the *possessed*.

Dave dropped the shovel.

A jeep rounded a stand of trees by the driveway and parked in front of the house. The star of the County Sheriff's Office was painted on the vehicle's door, and Cable Babitt was behind the wheel. The sheriff cut the engine and climbed out. He was grayer now, but still shaped like a pear with a moustache. He wore an amiable smile while he slammed the jeep's door—the only warning of things to come. In his quiet, almost genteel, manner he lowered a hammer on the deputy without raising his voice. "You're late for work."

"No, sir." The deputy stood at attention, his back ramrod straight. "I picked up the call before I left the house this morning. I'm on the job."

"Out of uniform? I don't think so, Dave."

The younger lawman picked up his shovel, his proof of innocence. "I'll get changed right after I dig up this—"

"No, no, no!" the judge called out from the porch steps. He was more his old self again when he shook one fist at the deputy. "There're no bones buried in my garden!"

Cable Babitt strolled over to the porch and tipped his hat to the retired judge, a greeting of friends, both local boys grown into old men, though Henry Hobbs was senior by twelve years. "Morning, Henry. What've you got here?" The sheriff picked up the jawbone and turned it over in his hand. He held it up high as a lure to draw his deputy closer. "Well, Dave, you're half right. There's no sign of exposure—lots of staining. This bone was buried all right, but not around here. You see this reddish coloring? It comes from iron-rich soil. That puts the burial site to the north and straight up." He pointed to the high mountainside of deep woods tapering to bald rock. "There's a streak of iron ore up there."

Iron ore?

Oren wondered how the sheriff had come by that bit of arcane knowledge. Coventry had its roots in a small mill town. There had never been a mining operation within a hundred miles of here, nor even a hint of iron deposits in this northern neighborhood of California.

Sheriff Babitt jerked one thumb toward the deputy's pickup truck, and this was enough to send Dave Hardy on his way.

When the truck had disappeared around the stand of trees, Oren stood toe-to-toe with the sheriff. "Iron ore? You knew about that jawbone before I called it in." This was more than an accusation; it was bait. He studied the older man's face, looking there for signs of a lie in the making. "Maybe you already had one of Josh's bones. You'd need a sample to get a soil analysis for—"

"That's enough, Oren. I've got a few questions for *you*."

Showdown—or maybe not.

Hannah, an experienced wrangler of boys and men, worked her way between them. "Oren, I need you to run an errand in town." She pressed an empty pharmacy bottle into his hand, then faced the porch and shouted to the judge, as if he might be deaf, "I'm sending Oren into town for your pills—your *heart* medication!"

Henry Hobbs, who was not deaf, nodded with some puzzlement. "No idea where the car keys are."

"I do," said Hannah.

Oren followed her inside and down the hall to a room with Dutch-blue walls and white cabinets. Like the rest of the house, the kitchen was unchanged except for a new refrigerator of stainless steel and a matching dishwasher. Apparently, the judge was a failure at patching up worn appliances, and here he had fallen short of his insane mission to stop time.

"You might've guessed—it's the same old car in the garage." Hannah retrieved a stepladder from the broom closet. "But the judge keeps the engine in real good condition. If you ask me, I think it runs better than brand-new models." She kicked off her wooden clogs and mounted the metal steps to climb on top of the counter. "Even the poor white trash in this town drive those cars. They never die—they just get passed down and around." Bare feet firmly planted on the countertop, she opened a cupboard door. "I swear if Coventry had a town flag, the emblem would be a Mercedes hood ornament."

The tiny woman rose up on her toes to reach a high shelf. After moving a few canisters out of her way, she pulled out a tea tin, extracted the car keys and handed them down to him. "It's still a one-drugstore town. You know the way."

Startled, Oren wondered if Hannah did this each time she took the car out, but he only pocketed the keys, asking no questions.

It was that kind of a day.

In Coventry's insular idea of geography, the northwestern town perched on a cliff at world's end, where the earth fell away in a wicked drop to a rocky coastline. An elderly man posed close to the edge as a companion pho-

tographed him against blue California sky and the Pacific
Ocean; he leaned one shaky hand upon a metal rail installed to prevent witless tourists from falling to their
deaths. Across the street, a pastel row of small art galler-
ies and boutiques was waking up to the morning trade,
opening shutters and raising shades. These buildings were
dwarfed by the Straub Hotel with its four flights of windows capped by attic gables.

Every street was lined with the cars of weekend travel-
ers, and it was Oren's good luck to find a parking space.

On the hotel verandah, a stout gray-haired woman was
ensconced in a high-back wicker chair. Deep frown lines
gave her the air of one who took offense at all that she
surveyed, and her ample flesh hung in jowls and a double
chin. Imperious, she presided over the comings and goings
of hotel guests, giving each a curt nod, as if to say, *Okay,
I've acknowledged you. Now move on!* And they did.

He should know this senior citizen. She knew him.

Though the lady wore sunglasses, he sensed that her
eyes were tracking him when he left the car and stepped
onto the sidewalk. As he came closer, she graced him with
a smile and lowered the dark glasses. Her smile quickly
slipped away, and Oren knew that he had failed a test of
some kind. The woman raised one clenched fist and
slowly extended her middle finger as an invitation for him
to perform an unnatural act upon himself. And by this
hand gesture alone, he recognized her. He had been a
teenager the last time they met. Then, she had been a
woman in her forties with a lean body and long hair the
color of lions.

Then and *now* were different creatures.

He approached the hotel steps, calling up to her, "Hello, Mrs. Straub."

She leaned forward, causing the wicker to creak with the sudden shift of her bulk. Her voice had the husky quality of booze and cigarettes when she said, "Oren Hobbs, we've had sex in half the rooms of my hotel. I think it's time you called me Evelyn." Impervious to the peasants, a startled pair of guests, Evelyn Straub donned her sunglasses. She sat well back in her chair and turned her face away from him.

This audience was clearly over.

Thus dismissed, he gave her a wave, almost a salute, and continued down the sidewalk toward the drugstore. As always, the traffic moved slowly, not even close to the posted twenty-five miles per hour. By some mystical agreement of tourists and residents alike, all the drivers slowed down at the sign that welcomed them to town. Yet Oren was mindful of the slowest car, the one keeping pace with him. In sidelong vision, he noted only that it was black and low-slung, for his eyes were fixed on the pharmacy bottle in his hand.

This was not the judge's medication.

Another name was printed on the label. He recognized the drug, and he knew why it was prescribed. When had Hannah's days become so stressful? High anxiety and three strong locks on the front door—what else had changed during all the years of his exile?

The black car still crawled beside him. Now it put on a short burst of speed to capture a freshly vacated parking space up the street. Oren raised his eyes as the car door slammed—and he missed a step.

The summer girl always had that effect on him.

Isabelle Winston left her black sports car to face him down on the sidewalk half a block away. There was great purpose in her stride as she moved toward him. Though the morning was a cool one, a light, white cotton dress swirled above her knees, and he saw the flash of red toenails on sandaled feet. Her hair was shorter but still the color of raw carrots. Her freckles could not be seen at this distance; Oren took them on faith.

He slowly released all the breath in his lungs.

The first time he had come near her, she had smelled of horses and, in later summers, a succession of perfumes, a different scent each time they met. Now she was almost close enough to inhale. As the gap between them narrowed, he averted his eyes and edged closer to the storefront side of the pavement, unwilling to risk touching her in passing.

And so they fell into their old childhood dance, the look-away two-step.

He watched her reflection in a shop window as she came abreast of him. In the glass, he saw her pause just long enough for her left foot to lash out in his direction.

A direct hit to one shin!

His legs tangled, and he was tripping, falling. The ground flew up to meet him with the painful crack of his kneecap on the cement and the vision of stars that came with a bang to the head.

First contact.

Oren rolled onto his back and raised himself up on one elbow to watch the summer girl, now a woman in her thirties, as she moved on down the sidewalk. There was never a backward glance to gloat over the damage she had done to him, and he thought that spoke well of her character.

Five

The rear doors of the coroner's van hung open, waiting to receive his child's remains—to *rob* him.

Judge Henry Hobbs dangled his feet from the wide stump of an ancient tree. He had the meadow all to himself. His housekeeper had been so distracted by the events of the morning, she had allowed him to sit here in the sun without a baseball cap to shelter his bald head, and now she had deserted him for an interview with the sheriff. The judge could only watch his own front door from a distance, forbidden to enter it.

The old Mercedes rolled past the house and parked where the gravel driveway widened into a turnout. His son left the car and walked toward him, not hurrying any. Apparently, Oren had completed Hannah's odd errand, for he carried a small, white bag imprinted with the drugstore logo. The prescription for his heart medication only interested Henry Hobbs because he had no heart ailment and took no pills of any kind. The pharmacist would have apprised Oren of that fact, and now the boy would want to know what Hannah was playing at.

His son idly shifted the bag from one hand to the other as he sat down to share the generous expanse of the stump. Oren pretended interest in the clouds passing by overhead when he said, "I saw Mrs. Straub in town—just to say hello."

Well, how nice, but what's in that damn sack?

In the ensuing silence, the judge had to smile, for now they had a game. His son was enjoying the tension of a query that could not be voiced. Obvious questions were against the rules.

Heart medication indeed.

However, declaring his housekeeper to be a bold-faced liar would be rude, and bad manners were also against the rules of the game.

Oren set the pharmacy bag on the stump—and the mystery of its contents hovered in the air between them.

"Oh, Evelyn Straub," said the judge, keeping up his end. "I always wondered if she was the one who taught you to smoke cigarettes." He also suspected that woman of committing worse crimes against his son while the boy was underage.

Oren picked up the paper bag, opened it and looked inside. "And I saw Isabelle Winston, too. So she still comes back every summer?" He closed the bag and set it down on the stump.

"This time she came in April." The judge squinted and

strained his eyes to read the receipt stapled to the paper sack, but this only told him the price. "I think the Winston girl moved back to the lodge so she could look after her mother."

And the flimsy paper bag that did *not* contain the judge's heart medication was gaining more weight with every passing second. It had to be Hannah's own prescription. What ailed his housekeeper? Was it something serious?

"So Mrs. Winston's not well?"

"Sarah? Oh, she drinks a bit," said the judge. "When I was still on the bench, I had to revoke her driver's license."

Could the bag contain heart medication for Hannah?

Endgame.

The judge picked up the bag, ripped it open and stared at the label on a bottle of tiny white pills prescribed for his housekeeper. "Lorazepam?"

Oren smiled—no, call it gloating—as he dangled the car keys in one hand. "I wonder why Hannah keeps these in a tea tin at the top of the cupboard."

So that's where they were.

"Well, age takes a toll, and she's getting up in years," said the judge, who was fifteen years older than his housekeeper. "Did the pharmacist mention what these pills were for?"

"He didn't have to. I already knew."

Beaten again, the judge looked down at the mystifying label.

"It's for her anxiety," said Oren, a gracious and charitable winner.

Hannah anxious? Never.

Henry Hobbs regarded the pill bottle as if it might be filled with little white bombs. "That can't be right. She's so calm, she's downright sluggish. She goes to bed early, takes naps in the afternoon." He addressed the object in his hand. "There's got to be another use for this medication. You know, over the past six weeks or so, I think she's gotten a little paranoid. Hiding the car keys—that fits. And you've seen all the locks on the front door? Kitchen door, too. That's Hannah's doing."

"Well, sir, you've got human bones dropping on the front porch like clockwork. That might account for the locks."

The sash was raised on the window in Josh's bedroom, and both men looked up to see the sheriff leaning over the sill and calling out in a neighborly fashion, "Oren? A word?"

Hannah came down the stairs as Oren climbed upward.

"I plan to throw a quick lunch together. You fancy a chicken sandwich?"

"Yes, ma'am."

She paused on the step beside him. "I told Cable everything." In passing, she whispered, "I don't think he'll need to question the judge today."

"Good job."

Reaching the second-floor landing, he saw a stranger standing idle in the hallway. Printing on the back of his jacket identified him as the county coroner's man—still waiting for the bones. That was odd. Hannah's small store of information would have filled ten minutes at the outside. What had Cable Babitt been doing with all this time?

Oren hovered on the threshold of his brother's bedroom. He stared at the open closet, the rod packed tight with smashed-together clothes, a shelf piled high with junk—and he wondered if the sheriff had noticed the single anomaly in that chaos.

Henry Hobbs was surprised—and wary.

No revved-up Porsche had announced the arrival of Addison Winston, who so loved a noisy entrance. The lawyer came strolling across the meadow—quietly, and that alone was cause for suspicion. Though technically neighbors, the Winstons owned a great deal of acreage, and it was a good hike from the lodge—for an attorney in wildly expensive dress shoes. All decked out in a superbly tailored suit of gray silk, Addison hardly looked the part of a man in early retirement. But then, he had never fit that role by so much as a single strand of gray hair.

"Hello, Henry. I saw the sheriff's jeep in the driveway. Thought you might need a good lawyer." Ad Winston had a smile that could charm a suicide bomber—but not the judge.

The attorney's lean jawline was suspiciously well preserved. His hair was cut to a youthful shoulder length, and the Vandyke beard, no doubt dyed the same shade of brown, was trimmed to a sharp point. The judge was convinced that if he could only see the man's ears, they would be pointy, too. And so, in a Dorian Gray kind of way, Addison never seemed to age.

"I don't need a celebrity lawyer," said the judge.

"Well, Henry, if you're down to your last million, I could take you on as a charity case." The attorney sat on the tree stump and raised his face to the sun, as if he were not tanned enough.

The judge also looked up, but to the north where the Winston lodge perched on a foothill. All that could be seen above the tree line was the conical roof of the tower atop Addison's castle of logs. "You got a telescope up there?"

"Three of them," said Addison. "Tools of the trade for an ambulance chaser. Actually, I passed the coroner's van on the road. So, naturally, I assumed you were dead." His smile faded off as he turned toward the house. "Please tell me the coroner didn't come for Hannah."

"Hannah's just fine." Or was she? He was still speculating on the pharmacy bottle in his hand.

"Not dead. Glad to hear it. My daughter mentioned seeing Oren in town. So the boy's come home."

"Josh, too."

Ad Winston wore a look of stunned surprise. And the judge would have enjoyed that so much if he could only believe that it was genuine.

Oren stood at the center of Josh's bedroom and looked down at the coffin, where his brother's bones blended with those of a stranger.

"It's official now," said Sheriff Babitt. "Twenty years late, but we got ourselves a homicide investigation." He rolled up a cloth tape measure that looked like something borrowed from Hannah's sewing basket.

So this was where the time had gone. The sheriff had been measuring the bones of arms and legs.

As a CID agent, when Oren had no DNA samples or dental records, he had sometimes used these same markers to identify victims found in the mass graves of combat zones. And, on one occasion, all he had was the vertebrae of a baby mingled with bones of the mother. But Cable Babitt was probably more concerned with the body count in the coffin. This man would not care to wait on a pathologist's report to tell him how many people it had taken to make this one partial skeleton.

"A double homicide," said Oren. "Unless you think there might be three victims."

The sheriff smiled. "Nice catch, son. Hannah told me you figured on at least two people here. If I come up with a different number, you know I won't be sharing that with you."

"Yes, sir."

Cable Babitt glanced at his wristwatch. "Where the hell is Dave?" He called out to the coroner's man in the hallway. "Harry? No need to wait for my deputy. I guess we can just load the bones into a body bag."

"No," said Oren. "Don't bag them." He reverently lowered the heavy wooden lid. "Just load the casket into the van."

The sheriff nodded to the man in the hall. "Go get another pair of hands, Harry." When the other man's footsteps had died off down the hall, he said, "Good idea, son. It's best if your dad doesn't keep the coffin in the house. He might get to thinking that's a normal thing to do. Now, about these bones showing up on the porch. Hannah tells me this has been going on for a while . . . but you just got home last night."

Oren nodded, looking down through the open window as a jeep pulled up in front of the house. The door opened, and the driver dropped to the ground on the run. Only seconds later, the coroner's man entered the room, followed by Dave Hardy, who had changed into his uniform. They each grabbed a brass handle, then lifted the coffin and turned it toward the door with some haste on Dave's end.

"I made a call to the Army," said the sheriff. "Oren, you know how this works. I had to account for your time while the judge was collecting those bones."

The coroner's man and the deputy were in less of a hurry now. Though the coffin must be heavy, they lingered at the bedroom door.

If this annoyed the sheriff, it never showed on his face. "The boss of your old outfit vouched for all your duty hours. He told me you were the best CID agent he ever met. He thinks I'd be a fool not to make use of all that talent. But I guess you know why I can't do that."

"Yes, sir." Oren well understood the reason: One day, two brothers had walked into the woods, and only one had come back alive.

Six

The road was narrow, and new shoots of foliage reached out to touch the sheriff's jeep, just a kiss of leaves in passing. As Cable Babitt traveled toward the coast highway, the dense forest was left behind, and he had a broad vista of town and sea and sky. He turned to the silent man beside him to make one more attempt at an actual conversation.

"I hear the Army gave you a real fine education—a damn master's degree in forensic science. They must think a lot of you, son. I'm surprised they let you go without a fight." This was doubly surprising in wartime, when the military was strained and stretched thin, when National Guardsmen much older than Oren were pressed into active duty. "Your commanding officer didn't say why you quit. I had the feeling he didn't know."

A station wagon sped past. The name of a news program was printed on a sign anchored to its roof. Oren Hobbs turned in the passenger seat to watch this vehicle heading back toward the judge's house.

"Reporters," said the sheriff. "Those guys are from a local radio station, and the signal's pretty weak." He pointed to the sky and a low-flying helicopter with station call letters boldly printed on the bottom. "Now that's the outfit that worries me. They broadcast statewide."

"Turn around," said Oren. "Take me home."

"Bad idea, son. But don't worry. I'm the one who called Ad Winston. He'll look out for your dad and Hannah. Nobody handles reporters better than Ad does."

"The judge doesn't even like him."

"So what? Henry Hobbs is like royalty around here, and Ad would never miss a chance to do that old man a favor. It's better if you stay away from the media. You know that, right?"

"I know I'm the prime suspect."

"Son, you could confess right now, and I'd still put you to work."

Oren Hobbs was stunned and quiet for all the time it took to point the wheels of the jeep toward the county seat. In sidelong vision, Cable kept an eye on his passenger as the younger man struggled with the logic of this proposition—the absolute lack of legality, not to mention common sense.

"You know I can't help you," said Oren. "You laid it out yourself back at the house. You told me—"

"What I said back there—that was for my deputy's benefit."

High school grudges were long-lived, and Dave Hardy would never forgive Oren for beating him bloody and senseless in front of half the town.

Isabelle Winston, Ph.D., stood upon a wooden deck that encircled her mother's retreat, a tower room at the top of the lodge. The crisp, cool air was filled with spraying birdseed, loud caws, whistles and trills, and the rush of wings. Hungry birds landed at feeders hung all around the railing, and the sated ones took flight.

The ornithologist ignored them. Birds were not her passion today.

Her binoculars were trained on a helicopter landing in the Hobbs meadow. She could easily identify her father, Addison, as he crossed the tall grass, one hand extended to greet the reporters piling out of the aircraft. Overhead, a private jet was making a descent at the county airstrip. More media? Of course. First the local radio station had created a serial murder from the bones of one lost boy, and now the circus had come to town.

She moved around to the other side of the tower and set the binoculars on the railing, startling a cowbird into flight and a high whistle of *wee titi*. She looked through the eyepiece of a telescope, one of three that were permanent fixtures of the deck. This lens was focused on the town of Coventry. Her mother, a gifted amateur naturalist, did more than note the passage of birds.

Isabelle looked back at the sleeping woman on the other side of the glass wall. How many years ago had that bed been moved up here? When had the tower room become Sarah Winston's whole world?

Turning back to the telescope, Isabelle shifted it, and kept the sheriff's jeep in sight until it made the turn onto the coast highway, carrying Oren Hobbs away. Keeping track of Oren had once been the schoolgirl hobby of summer vacations. And now that he was out of sight, her interest in voyeurism faded. She opened the sliding glass door and stepped inside.

The tower room offered shade from the midday sun but no greater sense of privacy. The northern and southern exposures were floor-to-ceiling panes of glass, and there were no curtains. The walls, east and west, were made of plaster and covered with framed drawings from her mother's sketchbook. There were also photographs taken by the judge's youngest son, Joshua Hobbs. They pictured the early birthday balls, a time when her mother had looked forward to that annual event. By Addison's account, the festivities of later years had been stressful. On those nights, Sarah Winston had been allowed no alcohol until the last guest had departed, and then her own private parties would become drunken stupors lasting for days.

This morning's stress had been resolved not by the bottle but with sleeping pills.

Sleeping beauty.

In her middle fifties now, the woman lying on the bed

was greatly changed by time. But in repose, wrinkles smoothed, the good bones of a fabulous face could still be seen. Her eyes fluttered open, so blue, so wide. "Belle?"

"Yes, Mom, I'm here." Isabelle reached down to stroke her mother's hair. Once, the blond tresses had been natural, so silky. Now they felt coarse. "It's after one. You must be starved."

Her mother sat bolt upright on the bed. "Is it true? I wasn't seeing things?"

"You were right. Oren Hobbs came home. I ran into him in town this morning."

More accurately, she had chased him down with a very fast car and an old grudge.

Oren Hobbs stood by the window and looked out on the Saulburg street. This town seemed like a bustling metropolis compared to his lethargic Coventry, where a dog on crutches could outrun every car. Behind him, a fly buzzed round the room, and Sheriff Babitt's fingers drummed on his desk blotter.

"Pull up a chair, son."

Oren was more inclined to leave, but the judge had raised him to be well mannered, and so the gentleman in blue jeans and cowboy boots accepted the invitation to sit down. By his posture, no one would guess his military background, for he slouched low in the chair. By outward appearance, he had shaken off twenty years of soldiering, as if that part of his life had been lived by someone else. This might well be the day after Josh had gone missing, the last time he had sat down to a conversation in the sheriff's private office.

"So," said Cable Babitt, "we have a deal? This is an old cold case, and I don't—"

"It never was a case. You wrote my brother off as a runaway."

"The hell I did." The sheriff spun his chair around to unlock a drawer in his credenza. When the chair swiveled back again, the man held a stack of files in his hands, and he settled them on the desk. "There must've been a thousand people combing the woods for Josh. And I'll bet you not one of them ever saw that boy as a runaway."

To be fair, a search of the forest had gone on for a solid month, long after all hope of finding Josh alive was gone.

"It's always been an open case." The sheriff slapped one hand down on his pile of paperwork. "This is it, all the files. There are no copies. Now this is a one-way deal. I don't share anything with you. But everything you find, Oren—you bring that straight to me."

No copies? Active files should be in the hands of a case detective. The sheriff had at least five of them to cover a county this size. Why would this man shut out his own investigators?

"I'm a civilian now," said Oren, "*and* a suspect. What you're suggesting is against—"

"Son, this is between you and me. It's not like I'm gonna give you a deputy's star."

As if the sheriff might be only half bright, Oren carefully measured out the words, "I'm—the—*prime*—suspect."

"Oh, hell, I never thought you had anything to do with Josh's disappearance, and neither—"

"When I was seventeen, you asked me for an alibi."

"And your alibi's one thing that isn't in these files. It was a good one. I believed it . . . but I never put it down on paper." He tapped his temple. "It's all up here. So I guess you're working for me. Now that it's a homicide investigation, you might need that old alibi."

"I never—"

"No, Oren, you never said a word. Someone else came forward to account for your time that day. You wouldn't tell me a damn thing when you were a kid. But now you'll work this case for me."

A gang of ravens made an assault on the bird feeders surrounding the tower room, and the flight songs of smaller birds were fading in the distance. The ravens had no song. They croaked.

Cr-r-ruck and *pr-r-ruck*.

"I don't see Judge Hobbs. He must've gone inside." Sarah Winston handed the binoculars to her daughter and then bowed her head to look through the eyepiece of a telescope. "I see your father. He's in the middle of that crowd of reporters."

"The sheriff asked him to handle the media. That's his job today." *Father* was not Isabelle's preferred name for Addison, but all of the four-letter names disturbed her mother.

More reporters had joined the feeding frenzy below, where Hannah Rice was chasing a station wagon off the grass. When another helicopter descended to the meadow, the housekeeper threw up her hands and retreated to the porch.

"Oh, Christ," said Sarah, one eye to the telescope. "You see that yellow Rolls-Royce? That's Ferris Monty's car. You remember him, don't you?"

Yes, Isabelle had a vivid recollection of Monty, though he had only come to dinner once, never to be invited back. His yellow Rolls pulled into the judge's driveway. It was a beautifully restored vintage model. She loved the car, but the little man behind the wheel revolted her. She had never shaken off the first impression of him formed in her childhood. "Wasn't he a *real* writer once? I think I read something of his when I was in college."

Her mother nodded, never lifting her eyes from the telescope. "Thirty years ago, he was a literary star on the rise. But he turned out to be a one-trick pony."

This slur was charity. The man had de-evolved into a celebrity muckraker, a writer of gossip columns and ex-posés in the form of true-crime books. As a frequent guest on television, he was known to millions of viewers who had never read nor even heard of his one good piece of art.

"So he still keeps a house in Coventry?"

"Oh, yes," said her mother. "And he's still the only one in town who's never invited to my birthday ball."

Isabelle imagined that the gossip columnist left a trail of slime instead of footprints as he walked toward the

Hobbs house. The first reporter had spotted Ferris Monty, and now they all ran toward the slander man like children who have heard the calliope music of the ice cream truck. She focused on Monty's face. The pasty white blot in her lenses was capped with a thatch of black that might have been made of fur or feathers. "He still has the same bad toupee. He should give it a name and buy it a flea collar."

Monty was holding court with the crowd of reporters, and a war of egos was predictable. Her famous father would not enjoy sharing the spotlight with another celebrity.

The sheriff only listened for a few seconds and then said, "Thanks, Addison," and slammed the telephone receiver down on its cradle. "One more thing, Oren. Stay the hell away from Ferris Monty."

"Who is he?"

"He's famous," said the sheriff, as if this might help. It did not. "Well, maybe he only shows up on TV in California. Ferris's trade is gossip. If you see a chubby little jerk, white as bug larvae, that'll be him. You might remember his yellow Rolls-Royce."

Oren nodded. He never forgot a classic car. "It belonged to one of the summer people."

"And now he lives in Coventry year-round." Cable Babitt gathered up his file folders—all but one—and locked them away in his credenza. Then he picked up his car keys and sunglasses. "I'll be gone for a while."

When the door had closed on the sheriff, Oren glanced at the remaining folder that had been overlooked. It would be rude not to open it—since the sheriff had gone to some trouble, all but decorating this file with a neon arrow and then providing time and privacy to read it.

The name on the first page was not familiar, though, according to the sheriff's notes, this man had been a citizen of Coventry for years before Josh had vanished. William Swahn was identified as a former police officer from Los Angeles, wounded in the line of duty after barely one year on the job. Disabled, he had been pensioned off at the tender age of twenty-one. Today this ex-cop would be in his late forties.

Penned in the margins were the sheriff's updates, noting that the man was not licensed as a private investigator, though Swahn had conducted many interviews around town, all of them related to Josh's disappearance. Handwritten words at the top of one page described him as uncooperative, refusing to divulge the name of his client. A margin note listed the most likely client as Oren's father. This would make sense from Sheriff Babitt's point of view. The relatives of crime victims commonly hired private police when a case went cold.

Oren recognized the address on Paulson Lane, a house so well buried in the woods that lifelong residents of Coventry might be unaware of it. That property was well beyond the means of an ex-cop on a disability pension.

Was Swahn bleeding his client dry to make the mortgage payments?

No one looked up as Oren passed by the desks in the

outer room. Apparently the deputies and civilian staff had been told not to interfere with him. Once outside the building, he stepped into the street to flag down a ride. A woman stopped. Whenever he had occasion to hitch-hike, it was always a woman who stopped for him.

Ferris Monty led his flock of reporters through the town on foot. As a favor to Addison Winston, he had taken on the job of keeping his fellow jackals away from Judge Hobbs.

He was more than happy to do whatever Addison asked of him. For the first time in twenty-five years, he had hopes of receiving an invitation to Sarah Winston's birthday ball. It was a gala event that cost the moon and made the society pages, a night when the famous and the infamous danced with the local folk until dawn. Ferris Monty had the distinction of being the only Coventry resident ever to be *dis*invited. Each year, he received a formal card that bore the printed script of his *un*invitation, and it was always bordered in black like a funeral announcement.

The reporters gathered around him on the sidewalk, and he preened for the handheld cameras. "The dead boy's photographs can be seen in a number of places around town. We'll start here." He led them up the steps of the Coventry Bank, a modest two-story landmark that dated back to the mill-town days. In the small lobby, a triptych of photographs hung on the wall. Ferris pointed to an image of himself standing in line to make a deposit more than twenty years ago. "This is me when I was young and beautiful."

A reporter said, "So you knew Joshua Hobbs personally."

"Oh, yes. In fact, I liked these photographs so much I bought a set of prints from the boy."

"What was he like?"

"Very sensitive. An artist." He shrugged to say, *You know the type.*

The day he had purchased those custom prints, there had been no conversation. Joshua Hobbs had been edging back toward the door from the moment of his arrival. Without a word, the young photographer had handed over the pictures and held out his other hand for the check. Ferris had blinked but once, and the boy had vanished.

A few weeks later, following a second, more permanent vanishing, Ferris had begun his comeback book, the story of a tragedy in a small town. It had opened with descriptions of townspeople, haggard and tired, marching past him in the streets, homeward bound after another fruitless day of searching the woods for a lost child.

Outside on the street again, a reporter broke into Ferris's reverie and pointed toward the library. "Any pictures in there?"

"I couldn't say. No one in Coventry ever goes to the library." And, lest they find this fact too intriguing, he marched them down the sidewalk with a lie of something more interesting at the other end of the block. As they

He stood before an oak door with a small, square grille of ornate iron at its center. There was no outside furniture, no chairs that might invite a visitor to stay awhile. There had never been anything inviting about this place.

He remembered it well.

Twice a week, he had come here with Josh when they were still in elementary school. The judge had sent them to this address on Good Samaritan duty. In those days, an old woman had resided here, and the boys had been charged with the mission of verifying that she was still alive and well and possessed of all her faculties, neither raving nor starving.

Oren pressed the doorbell. The ringer was loud so that the former tenant could hear it from every corner of her house. He waited for the new owner and listened for sounds of movement within. The householder was certainly at home. A car was parked in the driveway, a Mercedes. What else? It was the unimaginative choice of Coventry, and the previous tenant had also owned one.

The Hobbs boys had never been allowed inside the house. Oren and Josh had always spoken to the elderly woman through the iron filigree at the center of the locked door, rather like an interview with a cloistered nun. They had never seen her face, only her backlit shadow in a frame of light that made a square halo about her wispy unkempt hair. One morning, she had not come to the door, and they had reported this to the judge. In the afternoon, the boys had been told that the old woman was dead.

The current owner must be stone-deaf. Oren pressed the bell again, and this time he leaned on it, listening to the shrill ring reverberating throughout the house. After one full minute of this, a small square panel opened in the center of the door, and a shadowy head was outlined there behind the iron grille. Seconds ticked by. Evidently, no hello was forthcoming.

"Good afternoon," said Oren. "Sorry to disturb you, sir."

"Apology accepted," said the shadow man, and the panel was closed.

Oren waited for the massive front door to open—and he waited. Two minutes passed before he pressed the bell one more time—and for a long time. When the panel opened, he said, "I need to talk to you, Mr. Swahn. It's about Josh Hobbs." The panel was closing, and he rushed his words. "Wait! Please! I'm not a reporter. I used to be a cop—like you."

"I hate cops." The square panel closed with a slam.

Seven

Oren Hobbs walked down the driveway, intending to hike the quarter mile home, but the sheriff's jeep was waiting for him by the side of the road. The passenger door hung open as an invitation to climb inside. When he had settled into the front seat, he stared at the windshield as he spoke to Cable Babitt. "I'm guessing you left something out of Swahn's file."

"Oh, the most interesting parts of my files are the things I leave out." The sheriff started up the engine. "He wouldn't talk to you, huh? Well, don't feel bad, son. I never had any better luck."

"You *knew* Swahn was a cop hater."

"Oh, yeah. Lord knows he's got reason." The sheriff pulled into the road and drove off at the leisurely pace of a man going nowhere. "Next time you talk to him, I'd leave cops out of the conversation." He made a right turn, and they traveled the back roads for a mile before he said, "One other thing I left out of that file—Swahn's no fool. He had two college degrees when most kids were still in high school. Then he picked up another one while he was waiting to turn twenty-one. That's when he joined the LAPD. All his life that genius kid only wanted to be a cop."

The sheriff turned to his passenger, no doubt waiting for the obvious question. But Oren was the judge's apprentice, and he knew better than to show any interest.

Another mile down another road, the sheriff wearied of the apathy. "It took me years to get the whole story. I went to a few police conventions down in Los Angeles. Had to get stinking drunk with cops before they'd talk to me. And I bought a lot of beer for Swahn's ex-partner, Jay Murray. The guy left the force—kicked out—so it took me a while to find him. Murray told me he called in sick the night his partner got ambushed on patrol. After another six-pack, he told me he wasn't sick at all. Interesting, huh?"

Oren could see where this story was going, but he said nothing to move it along. He only had to wait for the sheriff to fill the holes in his one-way conversation.

"This happened back in the eighties. The bad old days of the LAPD. You know—anything goes, cowboy cops. Lots of shoot-outs. They didn't wanna swap body fluids with a gay AIDS carrier. That was the rumor on William Swahn." Sheriff Babitt squinted into the light of the afternoon sun slanting through the trees.

"So Swahn's riding solo that night, and the dispatcher sends him out on a domestic dispute. Well, it's a bad area.

He calls in for backup—but nobody shows. The kid goes in alone." The sheriff shrugged. "A rookie mistake. The next time Swahn called for help that night, he was hurt bad. Officer down—that should've brought out every patrol car on the planet. Not one cop came to help him." He gave his passenger a sidelong glance, but got no payoff from the younger man, who showed more interest in the road rolling by his window. "Son, I know what you're thinking."

Oren doubted that. He was wondering if any part of this story was backed up with proof, anything in the way of physical evidence or facts.

"Back in the eighties," said the sheriff, "AIDS was a death sentence. And all these years later, Swahn seems healthy enough—except for a bad limp. According to the police report, he walked in on a drug deal in progress, and took a bullet in the leg. Hardly made a blip on the evening news. The department press release left out what was done to his face. And here's the kicker—I heard that drug dealer hacked off Swahn's balls."

Not likely.

Oren had interfaced with many police departments on joint investigations where the Army had an interest. In or out of the military, drug dealers had never been prone to starting cop wars in any era. Nothing about this story rang true. Too many rumors passed for fact, and way too many police officers were involved to keep any gory details out of the newspapers. "This isn't right."

"That's what I say," said the sheriff. "And it's the cover-up that proves the crime."

Oren shook his head, though the other man probably took this gesture for shock and awe instead of disbelief.

"Here's another thing you might find interesting," said Sheriff Babitt. "William Swahn sued the LAPD, and it was settled out of court for a pile of money. I know he paid cash for his house. And I got a niece in State Revenue— she tells me Swahn gets a real nice income from his investments. But you won't find the settlement in the public record. It was handled real quiet with nondisclosure agreements. That *proves* the cops were in on it."

No, it did not.

However, Oren had no plans to point out flaws in logic and reason. The man beside him had won his first election with the bare minimum of requirements for the job. Apparently, the sheriff's skill set had not improved any.

"I've got no idea who outed Swahn." Cable Babitt made another turn of the wheel. "Jay Murray said it wasn't him, and I believed that much. Never occurred to him that his partner was gay. First time Murray heard that rumor was during his interview with Internal Affairs."

Finally—a fact that could be documented. "Murray was interrogated right after the ambush?"

"Oh, yeah. He said the sun was just coming up through the window of the interrogation room when the detectives lit into him. That's when they told him his partner was a gay man with the plague. Well, Swahn never mentioned a girlfriend in the year they'd been riding together, but Jay Murray thought the kid was just inept with the ladies."

"What about the dispatcher who sent him out on that bogus call?"

"Oh, she disappeared. The woman never made it home from work that night. Now I figure that's just cops being tidy. But Swahn still won his settlement. I suppose it helped that Ad Winston was his lawyer. And those two stayed tight. I know it was Ad who put him onto this house."

They had come full circle. The jeep rolled to a stop beside William Swahn's mailbox on Paulson Lane. The sheriff leaned across Oren to open the passenger door. "Go back in there, son. Get what you can. Kiss him on the mouth if that's what it takes. Just bring me something useful."

Oren kept his seat, disinclined to follow any orders from this man. "You think Swahn's a likely suspect in my brother's murder. Why?"

"You know how this works. I can't—"

"You can't even tell your own people, can you? That's why there are no copies of the files. You've got what— five, six detectives countywide? One of them should be interrogating William Swahn. But you want *me* to break your suspect."

The sheriff had bungled something badly, or he had stepped outside the law; one of these two things must be true. Cable Babitt needed an outsider who would not mind working in the dark, someone with something to lose—a good soldier who would ask no questions.

But Oren was not in the Army anymore.

And now he planned to finish this man off, to knock

him down with a civil tone. "Oh, and that old alibi of mine—the one you're holding over my head? Screw that."

A few seconds passed before the older man appeared to understand that he was not in charge here—he never had been—and there was cause for worry.

"I need leverage." Oren climbed out of the jeep and issued his first order to the sheriff. "Find out when Swahn's ex-partner left the force. And I need to know if Jay Murray got any part of his pension. Don't call the LAPD. I don't want rumors. Use your niece in State Revenue. She can get that off Murray's tax records." Walking away without turning back, he barked his final order. "Call me here as soon as you've got *facts*!"

Oren pressed William Swahn's doorbell, but there was no sound. Evidently the loud ringer had been disconnected for the sake of peace. He knocked and then banged on the door with his fist.

The small square panel opened behind the grille. This time, the householder was the first to speak. "You've got ten seconds of my time."

"Josh Hobbs was my brother."

"I already knew that. You look like him." The panel closed. The ten seconds were gone.

Oren shouted, "My brother's bones were found today!"

He heard the click of a lock being undone, a bolt

drawn. The front door opened wide, and Oren was ushered inside with the wave of a silver-handled cane.

This sunlit house was far from the cavelike hermitage he had once imagined for the old woman who had died here when he was a boy. At the far end of the vast foyer, a marble staircase tapered up to the second-floor landing, where a large window framed blue sky and treetops. On the parlor floor, the rooms had pairs of ornate wooden doors built to the scale of giants.

Oren saw only the back of William Swahn's denim shirt and jeans as his host led the way in stocking feet. The man was tall with a slender build, the iron gray hair of middle age—and that cane was no prop. He leaned heavily on it and walked with a gait slightly out of control, as if his house pitched and tossed upon a roiling sea. This stirred an old memory in Oren, but he could not connect that signature limp to a face. Perhaps this man was someone he had, once or twice, seen around town and then only from a distance.

They entered a corner room, large and airy, filled with light from tall, arched windows, and it housed more books than could be found in the town library. The built-in shelves lined every bit of wall space. More volumes lay open on an antique writing desk, and others were stacked up on the floor.

William Swahn turned to his guest and used his cane to point to an armchair. "Sit down, Mr. Hobbs."

Oren remained standing, staring, unable to look away.

Eight

Oren had come face-to-face with the subject of his brother's finest photographs. This was the Letter Man. The scar was not gruesome, but faint, and just as Josh had described it—a jagged *A* carved into the left cheek. The scar had not been visible in pictures taken of the man's profile, for Josh had captured the ordinary side of William Swahn. None of his brother's work had ever been titled, and so it had been the boy's secret pun to sell the Letter Man portraits to the postmaster.

"What fascinates you, Mr. Hobbs? Could it be my mutilation?" Swahn's dark eyebrows arched with anticipation, probably awaiting the guilty shift of feet or the blush of a gawker caught in the act.

"No, sir. I recognized you from the photographs in the post office." Oren wondered if that trio of pictures was still hanging there after all these years. "My brother never knew your name, and neither did I—until just now."

Swahn settled into an armchair and laid the cane across his legs. "I understand you're with the Army's Criminal Investigations Division." This was said with contempt, a virtual announcement that the two of them would never be close friends, for a cop was a cop, and this man's hatred of police was old and very precious to him.

"No, sir. I left the Army." Oren stared at the cane, the symbol of a life derailed—all that they had in common.

"I'm told that CID agents wear street clothes during an investigation, and they don't have to salute superior officers. That must've given you quite a sense of power."

"Mostly, I just liked the idea of wearing my cowboy boots on duty." And now the pleasantries were officially over. "I know you investigated my brother's disappearance. The sheriff thinks my father hired you."

"Judge Hobbs?" A puff of air escaped Swahn's lips in a mild show of incredulity. "How much sense would that make?"

"None at all. He would've hired a first-rate agency before he'd use an ex-cop with only one year on the job. For all I know, my father did hire somebody, but it wasn't you."

Swahn's nod was almost imperceptible, the small acknowledgment of a glove thrown down, a contest begun. "Judge Hobbs never hired an investigator. I would've noticed that kind of activity in a small town. And he never asked for help from the state Justice Department—even though he had the political pull to call them in." The man addressed the handle of his cane. "Don't you find that odd?" He raised his eyes to Oren's. "By that, I mean your father's lack of interest."

"Josh was a missing person. There was no evidence of foul play."

"Of course there was." Swahn's tone said, *Liar.* "Everyone knew that boy didn't run away. Your brother had a bank account, but he left his cash behind. He didn't take any clothes, either. And we both know he wasn't lost. This town has a wonderful reputation for finding people who lose their way in the woods. They always found you, didn't they?"

Oren ignored the question, knowing better than to fall into this old trap of turnabout, the interrogation of the interrogator. He had to wonder about Swahn's inside information; no newspaper account would have mentioned an abandoned bank account. And how would this man know that Josh had not packed any clothing? His brother's knapsack had never been found.

"Now," said Swahn, "if I wanted to *bury* an investigation, I'd do what your father did. I'd leave it in the hands of the County Sheriff's Office. That department is a joke, and I'm sure that made it easier to whisk you out of town—out of the sheriff's jurisdiction." He raised his cane to point it toward Oren's chest, his heart. "When Judge Hobbs sent you away that summer, did he suspect you of killing your brother?" The tip of the cane settled to the floor, and Swahn rested both hands on the silver handle as he leaned forward. "Or do you think that venerable old man murdered his own child?"

The next shot belonged to Oren. He sat down in an armchair and leaned back into the plush upholstery. Outwardly, he was unrattled, a man in repose and almost drowsing. "Hard to believe you were a cop." He let that settle in as a blunt insult and then added, "You don't talk like one." His adversary's accent made him a transplant from the world of upscale Bostonians, possibly uprooted in childhood, for the geographical marker was faint. This and the advanced college degrees would have been enough to alienate William Swahn from his brother officers; he was so obviously not cut from the same blue cloth. "You sound more like a college professor."

"I'm a guest lecturer at Berkeley. My area is criminology, but I'm sure the sheriff told you that."

What else had Cable Babitt failed to mention about this man?

"How well did you know my brother?"

"I never met him."

This could be true despite the evidence of the Letter Man photographs in the post office, three shots taken at close quarters. His little brother had been a thief of sorts, stealing people's images and running off with them. Sometimes a subject would hear the click of the camera and turn to see an empty space where a boy had been standing.

Oren rose to his feet and turned to the shelves, pretending interest in the titles on the book spines, while he considered the source of Swahn's inside information. "Let's talk about your client."

"I told the sheriff—several times—no one paid me to—"

"I didn't ask who paid you." Oren faced Swahn, wanting to see the man's eyes when he said, "Hannah Rice was the client." Satisfied with the reaction, he pressed on. "Hannah couldn't afford the day rate of a PI, but then— you're not a licensed investigator." He turned back to the shelves and trailed one finger from book to book, as if this matter meant very little to him. "And you don't need money, do you? That's why she picked you." He glanced back over one shoulder. "Oh, I'm sorry. Maybe you thought she came here because you were so smart?"

Swahn's eyebrows rose in a subtle touché, and the man almost smiled with approval—almost. "I don't pretend to know how Miss Rice's mind works. She's the only walking enigma I've ever met. And there's something about her speech. She's not from this part of the country, is she? Sometimes, when she's tired, I think I hear the ghost of a southern accent."

That touch of the Southland in Hannah's voice had begun to die off in the early years of Oren's childhood, along with idioms and odd words. He shrugged and splayed his hands and said, "As far as I know, Hannah's always lived in Coventry."

This evidently passed as truth, for the older man seemed disappointed.

When billeted in the state of Tennessee for the duration of a manhunt, CID Agent Oren Hobbs had gotten a taste of the food and the regional dialect. He had realized then that Hannah Rice must have hailed from there, and this had led to another revelation: He knew every vital statistic in the life of the runaway soldier he hunted;

he knew nothing about the woman who had raised him.

As a boy, he had been comfortable with the notion that the housekeeper had sprung to life on the day his mother was buried. At the age of three, Oren had been too young to remember Hannah's arrival in Coventry, but he knew the story told a hundred times: The judge had laid his dead wife to rest in the family plot and returned to his house in the company of neighbors, whose extra arms were needed to carry casseroles and baby Joshua. Oren had played the little man that day and walked everywhere on his own two toddler's legs, bumping into everything, "—blinded by tears, and batting away every hand that offered comfort." Those were his father's words.

Judge Henry Hobbs had always told the tale in the same way, word for word. "So we come back from the cemetery, and there's young Hannah—a stranger and a *trespasser*—standing on my front porch like she *owns* the place." The story had been repeated until the children's eyes had glazed over, and this segment of oral history was burned into their little brains. "Real brassy for a runt housebreaker," the judge would always say.

The young stranger, Hannah Rice, had greeted the funeral party and served them a feast made from scratch materials found in the pantry. Her bite-size bits of finger food—with three flavors apiece—lingered for years in the memories of all those present on that long-ago afternoon, but the fine coffee had been enough to ensure Hannah's legend in the neighborhood.

Her suitcase had been unpacked in the upstairs guest

room hours before her future employer had even known of her existence, and the judge still had no idea who she was at the close of the funeral supper. That evening, while she cleaned up after the mourners, the judge had thought to ask for her name. Days later, they had come to terms on a salary, but he had never pried into her past.

That would have been rude.

Apart from a core of third- and fourth-generation lifers, there had always been a coming and going of residents. Some were attracted by the raw beauty of the coastline; others sought the privacy of in-country woodlands. One abiding charm of the place was the whole town's lack of curiosity about the outside world—as if a citizen's life had not begun until they set foot in Coventry. A fair number of outsiders had come here to hide themselves away until they could reinvent their lives or rest up from a chase. After a month or a decade, some of these people would decamp with no word of goodbye or forwarding address, but others stayed long enough to be buried in local ground. After thirty-four years, Hannah appeared to have staying power.

Oren had become curious about her past, but he loved that little woman dearly, and he would never ask for her story, nor would he betray the fact that she had surely been a fugitive.

Henry Hobbs spoke to his housekeeper's back as she pulled down two coffee mugs from the cupboard. "Why did you do it, Hannah? I know you convinced the boy to come home. Why now of all times?"

"You have to stop calling him *boy*." It was her custom to deflect every rebuke with one of her own. "I know how you hate change—oh, don't I know it—but boys *will* grow into men." She set the mugs on the table and turned to the window that looked out on the meadow. "At least the reporters are gone." She sighed. "That's one small mercy. They're all following Ferris Monty. He took them on a walking tour of Coventry."

"My idea." Addison Winston's voice preceded him down the hall, and now he materialized in the doorway. A puff of smoke and a whiff of sulfur would not have surprised Hannah.

"Don't worry about Oren," said the grinning attorney. "After all this time, there can't be much of a case against him."

The judge rose from his chair, knocking it over in his rush to make a stand. "There's *no* case—period!" He pounded the table to bring this point home. "There *never* was a case against Oren." The old man stomped out of the kitchen, though the effect of this angry exit was somewhat blunted by the crepe soles of his sandals.

Addison Winston's professional smile never faltered. He stared at the old-fashioned coffeepot percolating on the stove, and then he turned to Hannah, willing her to offer him a cup of her wonderful brew. Hands on hips, her eyes narrowed to tell him that this was not going to happen.

He handed her a business card. "You never know when you might need a lawyer. The pressure's on. The sheriff will have to arrest *somebody*."

She never glanced at his card, but let it hang there in the air. "How many years have I known you, Addison? I've *got* your number." She had taken this man's measure long ago. "And I *know* what you do." Nothing good.

Far from taking umbrage with her tone and a double entendre or two, his eyes lit up, and he was laughing when he left her.

"So the sheriff found Josh's body." Swahn tapped his cane on the floor for punctuation. "Of course, it's murder. If there were any possibility of an accident, you wouldn't be here, Mr. Hobbs. So there was an obvious cause of death. A bullet wound? A blow to the head?"

Oren shrugged, allowing the other man to believe that he had not yet seen his brother's body. "The coroner hasn't made a finding yet."

"That should be interesting. Our new county coroner used to be a dentist."

"I'd like to see all your interviews with the locals," said Oren. "The sheriff won't let me read his."

"Perfectly understandable. You're his prime suspect."

"And yours, too?"

Swahn was deaf to this question, or maybe he thought a countering jab just too easy. He reached out for the telephone by his chair and placed a call. The person at the other end of the line must know the sound of his voice, for all he said was, "The judge's son is here." After listening for a moment he said, "If you wish." He hung up the phone and rose from his chair with a grimace of pain. "I'll get my files."

No need to ask who had given the instruction to play nicely with Oren.

Thank you, Hannah.

The older man limped across the room, opened a narrow door and stepped into the cage of a small elevator. The gears clicked and whirred and carried him upward. The ironwork of the cage dated it back to an era long before Swahn's purchase of the house. This conveyance on the premises must have been a great selling point. Climbing stairs would pose a problem for a man who winced as he walked. But an elevator could also be a technology trap for a hermit.

When the former owner was alive, she had two small boys to keep track of her. Who was looking after Swahn?

Oren had his answer when he ran one finger over a tabletop. Not a day's worth of dust had collected there, and the wood floor around the area rug had the shine of fresh waxing. Swahn's wealth and his handicap were two more indications of a full-time cleaning lady on the payroll, and that woman might be worth an interview.

The passing minutes were spent reading book titles in earnest this time. Many were familiar. Most of them related to the field of criminology, an interesting choice for a man whose natural enemy was the police. The sound of gears signaled the return of the elevator. It slowly settled to the floor. The man in the iron cage stood beside a carton piled high with file folders and envelopes. Oren was quick to cross the floor and help with the unloading.

"I hope you plan to stay awhile," said Swahn. "None of this material leaves my house."

"Fair enough." Oren lifted the box and carried it to the center of the room.

With both hands gripping the cane, Swahn lowered himself to the floor and sat down in an awkward pose, one leg drawn in and the twisted one sticking out, unable to bend at the knee. The two men emptied the contents of the carton to cover the surrounding carpet with manila folders, large envelopes and banded bundles of paper.

Oren leafed through a stack of typed interviews. Each one was clipped to a photograph. "My brother took these pictures." Some of these same compositions were framed on the walls of the judge's house. "But Josh didn't make any of these prints."

They lacked the crisp perfection that Josh had achieved by manipulating his negatives. The boy's attic darkroom had been a place with a language of its own, words like *dodging* and *burning* to play down bright lights and coax lost details from areas of gray. Other things came back to Oren, a memory of that room bathed in red light and the array of bottles, some of them intensifying chemicals. And there were special grades of paper and filters to push the contrast of every picture into the darkest shadows, the brightest highlights.

Almost magic.

He looked down at the print in his hand. This was—ordinary.

"It's a bad job, I know," said Swahn. "Miss Rice loaned me the negatives, and I ordered these prints from the drugstore in town. No comparison to Josh's work. He was gifted in a dying art form. I don't think he would've cared for the age of digital cameras."

Oren picked up a photograph of a birthday ball. In this shot, the stout hotelier, Evelyn Straub, was in her thirties, still lean and fine, her short skirt showing the endless long legs of a former Las Vegas showgirl.

Swahn leaned over to glance at it. "Your brother was probably ten when he took that one, and I'm not just guessing by Mrs. Straub's age. It's the perspective of a child looking upward. That angle changes subtly as he gets taller." He looked down at the other pictures spread out on the rug. "Even though Josh doesn't appear in any of these pictures, it's like watching the boy grow up."

Oren noticed that only his brother was referred to by his given name. Even Hannah, a longtime acquaintance, was always called, more formally, Miss Rice. Was Swahn only comfortable with the dead, or had he lied about never meeting Josh?

"I think your brother knew his killer."

The photograph fell from Oren's hand.

"According to your housekeeper, the boy was carrying a camera the last time she saw him."

"He always took one of his cameras when he left the house."

"But this one wasn't his pocket camera," said Swahn. "It was the old Canon FTB, the heavy one. Why would he carry that dead weight on a hike in the woods? The boy wasn't a nature photographer. Look at these images—only people. That was his subject. Did he take pictures of you that day?"

"No." Oren saw no need to mention the picture Josh had taken before they left the house, the portrait of two brothers that Hannah had framed in silver.

"Miss Rice said she packed a lunch in Josh's knapsack . . . but nothing for you." Swahn waited a moment for the explanation. It never came. "I understand that you and your brother went your separate ways after a while. So Josh had his own plans for the day. And he obviously intended to take pictures in the woods—but the boy only photographed people." Swahn allowed the import to settle in for a moment, and then he said, "Beer?" Without waiting for a reply, he slowly rose to his feet, using the cane as a climbing pole, and limped out of the room.

Oren emptied a bulky envelope containing pictures that had not been married up with interviews. Nowhere in this lot was a standard print of the photograph that Hannah had enlarged for his homecoming present. Every detail pictured in that silver frame was fixed in memory, and it brought to mind the interview with Cable Babitt shortly after Josh had gone missing.

"Talk to me, son," the sheriff had said to him then. "I need to account for your time." The judge had answered for Oren, saying, "Cable, you can't expect the boy to know where he was at *this* hour or *that* hour. What teenager wears a watch on a Saturday?"

In the silver-framed portrait of two brothers, Josh had been wearing a wristwatch.

Swahn returned with two bottles. He leaned down and handed one to his guest. Oren accepted the cold beer, but hesitated to pop the cap and drink with the man—given his errand in this house. He stared at the telephone, as if this would make it ring.

"Expecting a call, Mr. Hobbs? Oh, shot in the dark, a call from Sheriff Babitt?"

One casual wave of Oren's hand took in the surrounding paper storm. "Did you share all of this with the sheriff?"

Swahn set his own bottle on a table by a chair, but he remained standing. "I gave him everything that might help with the investigation."

"But not everything, right? You held out on him."

"Is that what Babitt told you? I suppose this means I'm on his short list."

"I'm sure you are." Oren glanced at the phone. How long did it take the sheriff to make a simple call? He chose his next words carefully, aiming to rattle and topple a cripple. He studied the man's face, hoping for giveaway tics and other tells when he said, "A cane makes a good weapon."

Swahn never blinked, nor did he miss a beat. "That it does." He leaned his walking stick against a small table and made an effort to stand up straight, though it caused him pain, and he could not quite achieve it. One shoulder was lower than the other because of one leg twisted inward. The hand that had held his cane was empty but still frozen in a curl. Beginning with the scarred face, all the damage ran down the left side of Swahn, a man broken by half. "You thought I might do a lot of hiking in the woods?"

"If my brother's grave is near a road—you'll make *my* short list."

The man retrieved his cane. "So Josh was buried . . . and Sheriff Babitt said more than you let on." The atmosphere of the room had changed; the air was charged. "He also passed along some old rumors, didn't he?" The tip of the cane rose in a warning. "Please don't deny it. I'm aware that he's been digging into my past. So now you think you know all about me." Swahn lightly touched his scar, the jagged *A*, a show-and-tell exhibit for AIDS. "And you've just got to know—in addition to my other crimes—rampantly fucking men and spreading disease—was I also in the habit of diddling young boys in the woods?"

"Were you?"

The telephone rang, and Swahn ignored it, though it sat on a small table only inches from his hand. "I believe it's for you."

On the third ring, Oren rose from the floor and approached the phone, skirting the man. He picked up the receiver and said, "Hobbs." After listening to the sheriff for less than a minute, he answered the only question. "No, that's not a case of cops being tidy."

Hanging up on Cable Babitt, he turned to his host. "About those old rumors. It surprised the hell out of

your ex-partner when he found out you were gay. Jay
Murray heard that rumor during his interrogation by Internal Affairs—*after* you were attacked. So tell me if I've
got this right. You believe a whole precinct full of cops
conspired against you for being a gay man with AIDS."
Oren splayed his hands. "But your own partner never
heard that rumor? How is that possible?"

"I can't discuss this with you."

"Of course not. You signed a nondisclosure agreement
with the LAPD. Lots of money at stake if you talk." Oren
sat down on the couch and stretched out his legs. "You
and Jay Murray rode together for a year. All that time,
and it never occurred to him that you were gay. He just
took you for an overeducated geek, an awkward kid who
had no shot with women. You don't believe that? You
were a rookie. So your first partner would've been an
older guy, a mentor. I bet Murray gave you more advice
about women than police work. Am I right?"

He *was* right. He could see the first fault line in Swahn's
composure. Gears were shifting behind the man's eyes as
he considered this one true thing.

"You *were* set up that night." Oren raised his beer
bottle and took a swig. "You were just wrong about everything else." He pointed at the scar on Swahn's face.
"Cops had nothing to do with that."

Ah, this was heresy. Was the man gripping his cane a
little tighter with that damaged hand? Yes. But Swahn
said nothing. Continued silence was worth millions, and
Oren was counting on that. He could bang away at his
leisure and never have to dodge a counterpoint.

"Your ex-partner made some cash for calling in sick that night. I'll tell you how I know. According to Murray's tax records, he left the force without a pension. He was terminated right after you were ambushed. That's what the sheriff called to tell me. So there was no time for a formal department hearing. That's how I know Jay Murray lost his pension in a plea bargain. He was looking at jail time for taking a bribe, and there had to be solid evidence. Detectives probably tossed his place and found the payoff money. You think Murray knew what was going to happen to you that night? Give me a break. Calling in sick was like painting a target on his own chest. So what's left? The dispatcher, who conveniently disappears before she can make a sworn statement—a *civilian* dispatcher. And that's how I know—when you called in for help that night—you got the same woman who sent you into that ambush."

Oren knew that he had guessed right when the man's eyes flickered with new interest.

"Swahn, you can't believe that cops passed the hat around the station house for the dispatcher's go-away money. Maybe you think they *killed* her?" Could he be more sarcastic? No. "Cops are not that stupid." He stared at the scar on Swahn's face. "And whoever did that to you is smarter than you are. That's one case that'll never be investigated."

He saw confusion in Swahn's eyes, fleeting—gone now.

"The dispatcher never relayed your call for help. Those cops you hate so much, they never knew you were in trouble. If they had, they would've turned out for you that night. And they would've turned L.A. upside down to find the guy who hurt you. But you closed the case yourself—the day you took the settlement, the *hush money*."

The older man's stance was weighted to one side, and it seemed that the breath of one more word might knock him down. But no.

Resurrection time.

"Old business," said William Swahn, too cavalierly dismissing a quarter-century of hatred for every cop ever born. His lips pressed together in a line of new resolve—fresh anger. Oren would not be allowed to get away with attacking this very personal mythology. That much was in the man's face.

Payback was coming.

"Let's return to the case at hand . . . your dead brother. Poor Joshua." Swahn settled into the nearby chair and stared at his cane, hefting its weight in one hand and paying special attention to the heavy silver handle. "You're right. This *is* a good weapon. And, since you favor the idea of death by bludgeoning, that tells me there were no bullet holes in Josh's remains. Too bad. You see . . . the seclusion factor always troubled me. Privacy for a murder can be had in any enclosed space. Why would the killer pick a meeting place in the deep woods? Obviously, he wasn't worried about the sound of gunfire. No gun. Maybe he didn't want anyone to hear the screams. Some murders, the cruelest, the most perverted kind, require *more* privacy—more *time*. I was hoping it was a quick death. Apparently . . . it wasn't."

First blood from a master of retaliation.

Oren settled to the floor and sat there—very still. His own scream was an interior noise that only he could hear.

And Swahn was not done with him yet.

The man was leaning toward Oren and into that range for exchanging ugly little secrets, almost whispering when he asked, "Did your brother seem apprehensive that day? Josh asked you to come with him, didn't he?"

No. In fact, it had been Oren's idea to go along on that hike.

"So you started out together that morning," said Swahn. "And then you left your little brother. You left him there all alone in the deep woods. I always wondered why."

Oren closed his eyes. He was not remembering it; he was reliving it. From the moment they entered the woods, Josh only wanted to get away from his older brother.

"Miss Rice wouldn't allow me to question you when you were a teenager." Swahn leaned closer to his guest, too close. "You were in very bad shape in those days. After Josh disappeared, you were always running off into the woods. Sometimes it took days for the townspeople to find you. What drove you, Mr. Hobbs? Was it guilt? Didn't you just want to die?"

That part was true—still true.

A second pot of coffee had been delivered to the tower room by the maid, Hilda.

Sarah Winston eyed it with chagrin. She opened the drawer in her bedside table and pulled out an empty bottle. Turning to the open door, she called out to her daughter. "This was full when I went to bed last night. You poured it out, didn't you, Belle?"

Isabelle Winston stood outside on the deck with a telephone in hand, its long cord trailing a few feet beyond the doorway. She barely paid attention to her mother. The phone's receiver was pressed to one ear, and she could not listen to both of her parents at once—not with the other distractions of hummingbirds hanging in the air, dive-bomber starlings and the piping whistles of orioles. She ended the call when her mother joined her outside.

A bird came to light on the older woman's shoulder, a common enough occurrence, but her daughter always marveled at it. Sarah turned her face to the lark and mimicked its short song of flutelike notes. The bird sang back to her and took flight. Isabelle was the one with an ornithologist's credentials, but her mother was so well acquainted with these wild things that they bid one another hello and goodbye.

"They never come to *me*." Isabelle stretched out one hand to a nearby feeder. Wings unfurled and flapping madly, the birds flew off to the next seed holder farther down the railing. "They never light on me."

"And they never will," said Sarah Winston, as if they had not held this conversation many times. Endlessly patient, she said to her only child, "But this is a *good* thing,

Belle. You're so animated, so alive. No bird would ever mistake you for a tree limb or a post—a lifeless thing." Never spoken were the final words, *like me.*

Yet Isabelle always heard them.

"Did your father tell you who was taken away in that coffin?"

And now Isabelle realized that her mother knew nothing about the bones. There was no radio in the tower. There never had been. Her mother only listened to the birds. "The coroner's van came for Josh. They found his remains."

"At the judge's house?"

"Yes. Someone's been leaving the bones on the old man's porch late at night."

The coffee cup crashed to the deck. Birds flew off in alarm, screaming. And her mother screamed.

Nine

I found out what they want." Dave Hardy stood at the door to the sheriff's private office. He raised his voice to be heard above the noise from the street-side window. "That maggot, Ferris Monty—he told them you arrested Oren Hobbs."

Traffic in Saulburg was snarling, horns honking. The parking lot was full, and latecomers double-parked in front of the building. One reporter brazenly pulled up onto the sidewalk. Cable Babitt stood at the window, frowning. "I suppose it would be wrong to shoot them." He glanced back at his deputy. "Son? Just make them all go away."

"How?"

Cable joined him at the door and pointed to another deputy in the outer room. "Take John with you. Go out there and ticket the crap out of all those cars and vans.

Then you can just let it slip that Oren's gone somewhere else—anyplace that's not Saulburg."

Outside on the street, while writing tickets and slapping them on windshields, the new recruit, Deputy Faulks, flirted with the pretty woman who tagged after him, microphone in hand. When they were within earshot of two other reporters, he answered her twice repeated question. "My guess? Hobbs is probably hiding out in the Coventry Library."

The newswoman tilted her head to one side. "You're kidding, right? Why would he go there?"

Her colleagues were turning their heads, staring at the deputy, and he called out to them, "It's the perfect hideout! Nobody in Coventry ever goes to the library!"

Three reporters raced for their cars. Others in the pack picked up the scent and followed. But one camera was still filming when Deputy Faulks turned around to receive a bloody nose from Dave Hardy's fist.

"Cop fight!" yelled the cameraman.

The radio was tuned to a local jazz station. The delivery boy had come and gone. And civility was provisionally restored at William Swahn's house.

Oren sat on the floor, eating a slice of hot pizza and drinking a second cold beer with his host. He had not given up any details of the sheriff's case, not a word about finding the bones of a second victim. For now, the prospect of a multiple homicide was only a rumor on the radio during the newsbreak.

Swahn appeared to give the idea no weight. "Next, they'll be saying there's a serial killer in the neighborhood."

"Not likely." Oren drained his beer bottle. "There might be thirty serials at large in a country of six million square miles."

"Right. What are the odds of one finding his way to Coventry? Although," said Swahn, in the tone of an afterthought, "Josh could've been killed to conceal another murder."

The man was left to make what he could of the silence. Oren had not come to this house to collaborate with a suspect. After reading the last interview, he laid it down among the others scattered on the floor all around him. "I don't pull motives out of thin air. I like facts."

"Anyone with a secret could have a motive for murder." Swahn opened another envelope and pulled out a thin stack of photographs. "Take your secrets for instance." One by one, he laid out the glossy prints like cards dealt from a deck.

Oren looked down at pictures of himself at the ages of fifteen and sixteen. In one print, his hair had only covered his ears. In the next, it grazed his shoulders. Each one showed him walking down one street or another, oblivious to the stares of middle-aged women turning his way.

"Now I'd say those ladies looked a bit hungry." Swahn laid out more pictures in a march across the carpet.

Oren's hair grew longer as he turned seventeen. This

succession of snapshots had been taken inside the Water Street Café. The pictures were ganged together to represent ten seconds of time passing frame by frame. In the first image, Oren saw his younger self walking near a table of matrons. The next shot focused on one of them, a pretty woman in her forties. Evelyn Straub had just raised her head to look up at him. In the last photo, teenage Oren turned her way for only the click of a camera, and this photograph had captured a clandestine passage, something said in a glance that went unnoticed by the other women at the table. Only lovers had these conversations of the eyes. Only Josh had seen it.

And William Swahn.

"I'm sure Mrs. Straub thought she was being discreet," said Swahn. "Have I made my point? Maybe Josh stumbled on a bigger secret and sold the negatives with the prints. How do you see your little brother as a blackmailer meeting a mark in the woods?"

"No way. He was a decent kid."

"I agree. According to your housekeeper, Josh didn't care anything for money. The boy was only a passionate collector of small dramas."

Oren looked down at the carpet and its covering of Swahn's old interviews with the people of Coventry. There were interesting omissions. "You never questioned Addison Winston. He's a criminal defense attorney—a man with lots of secrets. And what about his wife? Mrs. Winston was a bird-watcher. She was always out in the woods with a pair of binoculars. But you never talked to either of them."

"Everyone's a critic." Swahn, unfazed, ate the last slice from the pizza box and chased it down with beer. "So, tell me, Mr. Hobbs, how did you know about Mrs. Winston's bird-watching forays? Did you ever meet her in the woods? Did her husband know?"

Isabelle screamed at him. Yet Addison Winston still had no regrets about formally adopting his wife's only child, though he sometimes wished the girl had come with a volume control.

"*Do* something!" Isabelle yelled.

His wife flew about the room, hands waving, tears running down her face, and Sarah's daughter followed after her as the self-appointed handmaiden to a drunk with delirium tremens.

"There's a doctor coming from Saulburg," said Addison.

"She needs help *now!* She's terrified!"

"Of course she is. Your mother's seeing things that aren't there."

The empty bottle of Scotch was odd. He knew that his wife's secret stash had been restocked. Contrary to what his daughter believed, he did pay attention to Sarah's drinking. By doubling the large tips that the maid received from her mistress, he kept track of the daily consumption of alcohol. However, there was no liquor on Sarah's breath to account for the empty bottle. "You cut off your mother's booze again, didn't you, Belle? That was naughty."

She glared at him with hate, but he had grown accustomed to that. It killed him to see it, and he laughed each time she did it.

"Weaning your mother is a gradual process." He set the bottle down. Hands in his pockets, smiling broadly, he sauntered up to Sarah, who had found the only corner in a circular room, that place where the deep armoire met the wall. She swatted the sleeves of her robe and then raked her fingers through her hair, looking there for bugs that only she could see.

Addison studied his wife as he spoke to her daughter. "I usually start tapering off the liquor supply a few days before the birthday ball. That way she can get through an entire evening cold sober—and no hallucinated creepy crawlies." The lawyer looked down at his watch. "Doctors. They like to make you wait, even when you're paying cash—no taxes." He winked, and Isabelle seemed to find that obscene. So he did it again.

On the deck outside, hungry rats with wings were feeding at the many seed holders fastened to the railing. In her early schoolgirl days, Isabelle had created a pet name for this avian sanctuary at the top of the house, and the child had always regarded him as an intruder here, the bogeyman of Birdland. He caught his reflection in one wall of glass and smoothed back his hair, finding himself rather handsome for a monster.

"She needs help now! Get an ambulance!"

"You wouldn't like that, Isabelle." He knew his wide smile was wholly inappropriate, a display of entirely too many teeth. "They'll put your mother in restraints, and then she won't be able to brush the spiders away. Think of her terror when she's tied down—and the bugs are crawling into her eyes. Is that what you want?" In the ensuing silence, he watched her face turn pale. "No? I didn't think so. Now the good doctor just gives her a shot and knocks her out cold. No fear, no pain."

His expression sobered as he looked in on his wife's invisible world, watching as Sarah brushed small bugs from her nightgown. Ah, and now she batted her hands at a particularly large one. He could always gauge the size of the imagined spiders by the wideness of her eyes. She lapsed into one of her brief intermissions from the horror show in her head. Exhausted, she sank to the floor and covered her face with both hands.

Smiling again, Addison turned to the younger woman, so like Sarah at the same age, though not a stunning beauty—merely pretty. "After the doctor gives her a shot, your mother will sleep for the rest of the day. Tonight, when she wakes up for dinner, she'll drink as much as she likes. You won't even count her shots. Is that clear?"

Isabelle seemed a bit less ruthless now, and he knew that the reason was guilt. She was beginning to under-stand her own folly, her fault in this—damage. He strolled through the open doors to the outside deck, and she trailed after him.

Addison bent down to look through the eyepiece of a telescope. "Dangerous toy." There was no need to focus the lens. "And powerful. Do you know where this thing is pointing, Belle?" She was Belle to him again, now that she was contrite and more manageable. "This morning, your mother had a perfect view of that jawbone sitting on the judge's porch." Smile in place, he looked up at his daughter. "On a typical day, the most startling thing in Sarah's world is a confused bird migrating in the wrong direction."

All along the curving deck, wings flapped, and pointy beaks sprayed seed in all directions—greedy feeders. He had learned to hate birds.

"Mom didn't even know about the bones until I—"

"No matter. Any change in her routine would stress her out. Even the sight of Oren Hobbs would've been a shock after all these years. But you know that didn't cause your mother's hallucinations." And now, to drive the point home, he said, "In fact, a drink might have helped. Too bad you poured out her bottle. And then you gave her those sleeping pills on the nightstand. Where did those pills come from, Belle? Is that *your* prescription? You wanted your mother to rest, to sleep—while you went into town . . . so you drugged her. What a good girl."

He walked back into the room and looked at more damning evidence, the carafe of coffee, the second one today, so said the maid, his spy in Birdland. "Cold turkey withdrawal—always a mistake—then sedatives and caffeine. What were you thinking, Belle? Your doctorate is in ornithology—not *medicine*, not *chemistry*."

Sarah screamed and ran across the room, as if she could outrun her small tormentors, hands fluttering in a panic, eyes full of fear. Left to her own devices, his wife would have gotten through this day with a pleasant buzz. As usual, she would've passed out after dinner. That was why Sarah was such an early riser. She awoke with the light and the songs of filthy, winged vermin come to feed outside her glass walls—and a good-morning drink to kill the pain.

Addison Winston dropped his smile. "Leave your mother's care to me."

"You're not helping her."

"I'm not the one who did this to her." Well, that shut her up. And now, verbal spanking done, he left Isabelle alone with her handiwork, her weeping, frightened mother.

Only three people remained on the Coventry street outside the library. The rest of the reporters and their news crews had departed after failing to construct a jailbreak from Deputy Faulks's offhand comment.

"This is a waste of time," said the young segment producer, and she was not referring to the useless phone as she folded it into the back pocket of her jeans. There was no cell-phone tower within twenty miles of this backward town. She stared at the foothills, perhaps looking there for dinosaurs—something, *anything,* to film. She turned back to face the middle-aged reporter and attempted to reason with him one last time. "The sheriff told you Oren Hobbs was never under arrest."

"And that's what we lead with," said Reggie Mason.

"A hot denial." He closed the door of what might be the last telephone booth in America. It even had a rotary dial—a charming artifact from his youth.

The producer banged on the booth's glass wall.

What the hell was the girl's name?

All of his segment producers were interchangeable, and none of them looked a day over thirteen years of age. This one—deluded child—truly believed that she was in charge of production.

"We're leaving!" she yelled. "Right *now!*" Turning her back on the phone booth, she climbed into the van and closed the sliding door behind her.

The cameraman would have followed the girl, but Reggie grabbed his arm. "Hold on. The operator's back." He had been placed on hold by a 9-1-1 operator, and now the woman resumed their telephone conversation. "Yes, ma'am. . . . That's right. . . . Yes, it smells."

Reggie cupped the phone's receiver with one hand when the cameraman leaned into the booth and asked, "Is she laughing?"

From the window of the van, the sullen child producer yelled, "Hey, it's time to pack it in!"

The cameraman stared at the small brick building. "Did you read the hours posted on the door? There's nobody in there."

"But the *smell*." Inspired now, Reggie reopened his dialogue with the laughing 9-1-1 operator. "I think there's a dead body in the library. . . . Well, it *smells* like death. . . . So you'll send the sheriff?" After a few seconds, he placed the receiver back on its cradle. "She hung up on me."

The cameraman unstrapped his equipment and laid it down, final notice that his workday was done. "Do you know what a dead body smells like? I don't. You can't make something out of nothing."

Oh, contraire.

Reggie pointed at the library. "Did you see that?"

"What?"

"Something moved in that window."

"Reggie, are you making this up?"

"Where's that lame producer when I need her?" He banged his fist on the side of the van. "Hey, sweetheart. The wind's blowing our way again. I want you to smell something."

"I know Ad Winston was your lawyer," said Oren. "All that settlement money. You must've been a grateful client. Is that why you never interviewed him or his wife?"

After calmly wiping his hands on a napkin, Swahn finished his beer. "He was your lawyer, too, Mr. Hobbs."

What?

"You didn't know?" Swahn wore a satisfied smile. "Judge Hobbs retained him for you right after Josh disappeared. Wise move. You wouldn't give a reason for leaving your little brother alone in the woods. And you wouldn't tell anyone where you were all day and half that night. Your father was probably holding his breath, waiting for the sheriff to turn up at the door every second of every day. He wanted to be ready if it came to a trial. So he hired the best lawyer in the state. That's why I didn't interview either of the Winstons. They *couldn't* talk to me."

One old mystery was solved for Oren. This explained why he had been left alone after one brief and fruitless interrogation by the sheriff—after time had been allowed for the scratches on his face to heal.

Swahn picked up a sheet of paper attached to a photograph of Evelyn Straub. "You probably noticed—this interview's very short. I'm sure you wondered why. When did this woman ever censor a thought in her head? Absolutely fearless. It took me an hour to find her soft spots and break her."

Evelyn? Oren suppressed a smile. He wanted to laugh at this man, this amateur. Interrogation was not a criminologist's game, and he would pit Evelyn Straub against the best of the best in his own trade. The lady was made of unbreakable stuff. He waved off the proffered piece of paper. "I read it. Seems light."

"Most of her conversation was never typed up for my files." Swahn pulled out a small notebook. "However, I do have a more complete version. It concerns your lack of an alibi for the day your brother disappeared." He fanned the pages to show the handwritten lines—so many.

Oren was backing up in his mind, bracing.

Swahn glanced at the first page of his notes. "I had the feeling that Mrs. Straub knew *all* your secrets." He looked up and paused for a beat. "And she probably knew about the other women you were sleeping with."

Oren sipped his beer, appearing only mildly curious and keeping to a boyhood habit of never confirming or denying those rumors.

Leaning back against the side of a chair, Swahn dragged out this lull. "Mrs. Straub was very attractive in those days. These past twenty years, she hasn't aged well. And that's odd. You know she has the money to stay young forever."

Absently turning a page in his notebook, the man never took his eyes off Oren. "Your housekeeper asked me to find you an alibi witness. *That* was my job. She had no inside information about your affairs, but she had eyes. Miss Rice knew the effect you had on females. When she first came to me, her focus was on your refusal to say anything in your own defense. It was her theory that you might keep silent to protect a married woman. So I didn't just single out Mrs. Straub. I talked to all the women posed with you in Josh's photographs. Unfortunately, my efforts backfired. *Two* women came forward. The two alibis should've cancelled each other out. But the sheriff believed one of those stories. Hers." Swahn tapped the photograph of Evelyn Straub.

"You had good taste, Mr. Hobbs. She was a pretty woman in those days. I liked her. Very jaded—very hip. I figured she was only in it for the sex. A teenage boy never runs out of juice. No real emotion in play. That's why I thought the sheriff believed her when she told him you spent the whole day in her bed. But I was wrong. Later, I discovered she had a prenuptial agreement. If she was caught cheating on her husband, she'd get nothing in a divorce settlement. Mr. Straub was an old man—good as dead. His wife only had to bide her time for another year. But she put everything on the line for you."

Swahn flipped another page, though he never looked down at the lines written there. "I never told Mrs. Straub how I found out about her affair with you. I suppose she assumed that you betrayed her. For all I know, she still believes that. But after I talked to her, she went to the sheriff anyway. You were only seventeen—probably younger the first time she took you to bed—the underage son of a judge. That woman risked a lot more than money." He leaned forward, the better to study the younger man's face when he asked, "Did she tell the truth? Or did she risk everything to *lie* for you? . . . Did she love you, Mr. Hobbs?"

Oren looked at his watch. "Time to go." He brushed pizza crumbs from his jeans as he stood up. Extending a hand down to his host, he helped the man to rise from the floor.

Swahn seemed deeply disappointed. He had dug his hole, his trap of words, and covered it over with twigs and branches, but Oren had not fallen in.

"That wasn't an idle question." Swahn's limp worsened as he followed his guest into the foyer. "It doesn't matter if Mrs. Straub lied or not. Just consider what she stood to lose."

Oren opened the front door.

"Mr. Hobbs, either this woman loved you—or she needed an alibi as much as you did."

"Thanks for the beer and pizza." Oren stepped outside, escaping. He was walking down the driveway when he glanced back.

Swahn had followed to the edge of the portico and now called out to him, "When you report back to the sheriff, ask him about Mrs. Straub's séances in the woods. The judge and Miss Rice go out there to commune with your dead brother."

Oren stumbled and then moved on.

Ten

The phantom spiders had been vanquished by the doctor from Saulburg.

While Sarah Winston slept off a sedative in the tower room, her husband and daughter stood outside on the deck. Isabelle focused a telescope on the winding fire road. In the twilight hour, the running lights of vehicles made them visible through the scrub pines of the foothills. These were the witchboard people.

"Yes, it still goes on." Addison Winston swirled the whiskey in his glass. "Since when do you care what happens in Coventry? When was the last time you paid us a visit, Belle? I can't seem to remember the decade."

This failed to make her angry, but he liked a challenge.

She looked up from the telescope. "Those people didn't used to meet in the woods."

"Well, they have for the past fifteen years. And you'd know that if you'd bothered to come home more often. However, your mother so enjoyed the crummy little postcards you sent her from Europe." Addison held the binoculars up to his eyes and wondered why the spook-fest in the woods should interest Isabelle. "They're heading up to Evelyn Straub's old cabin. You were just a little girl when she built that place."

As he recalled, Evelyn's last name had been Kominsky back in those days. Well into her thirties then, she had aged out of her showgirl career and snagged an elderly millionaire for a husband. And these days? Well, the woman had gone to hell from the hips up, and her long legs were not on display anymore, but they tended to linger in a man's memory. Evelyn's best quality was the heart of a pirate, and this alone was enough to make her worthy of his admiration.

"Did you ever go to one of the séances?"

"Yes, I took your mother once. Everyone in Coventry went to at least one of them. Some people go back again and again." The witchboard group was an old one, but hardly exclusive. He drained his glass and rattled the ice cubes. "Any other town in America would've formed a bowling league."

The parade of vehicles had almost cleared the pygmy forest of scrub pines. He lifted his wife's binoculars and trained the lenses on one straggler. "You see that jeep following them from a distance? That's the sheriff. Evelyn's place is the only cabin on that fire road. If she catches Cable, he's toast. Legally, he shouldn't be within a half mile of that séance." Addison's grin spread wide. "I smell a lawsuit."

The jeep disappeared under a canopy of tall trees as it climbed the mountain into denser foliage. The show was over, and Isabelle abandoned the telescope to lean back against the railing. "How did Mrs. Straub get involved with séances? She doesn't seem the type."

"She's not. However, the lady does have an eye for opportunity, and her pet psychic is worth a fortune."

"How much does she charge?"

"Not one dime," said Addison. "The séances have always been free."

The Coventry Pub was a quiet place. A television set was bolted to the wall over the bar and always tuned to a local news station. By custom of long standing, the bartender never turned on the volume until the sports coverage was nearing airtime. So five steady patrons, sports fans all, were watching an anchorman moving his mouth in silence. They liked their news delivered this way—so restful.

And now they were startled by the image on the screen.

"That looks just like our library," said the bartender, stepping up to the set for a closer look. "Can't be."

A customer squinted and then donned his spectacles. "Sure it is. Hey, Fred, turn on the sound."

The bartender turned the volume up high, and an anchorman's voice boomed out of the box to tell them that this was indeed film coverage of the local library. It was also the scene of a standoff with a fugitive from justice. Unconfirmed was the rumor that the escapee was armed.

One of the men stepped outside for a look at the library two doors down and across the street. He called back to his fellow patrons, "Just a van parked out front and a couple of guys standing around the phone booth, smoking cigarettes." He walked back inside, looked up at the screen and scratched his head.

The picture of the library was replaced with coverage of a California race for the senate, and the volume was turned off again. Fresh beers were served up and down the bar, and reality was restored to the Coventry Pub.

"I'd never take my own car up here." The sheriff steered the jeep through a turnout to avoid a large cavity in the dirt road. He gave his passenger a wary glance. "I understand how you feel, son. If I'd known that Hannah and the judge were sucked in, I would've kept tabs on the séances. But I still say Alice Friday's harmless."

"Psychics are never harmless." Oren Hobbs had already made it clear that psychics were the precursors to blowflies lighting on a fresh corpse, and their favorite prey was the parent of a murdered child.

"This one's different. I learned a lot about the psychic trade when your brother disappeared. All the pros turned out. I must've talked to twenty con artists. Alice was the only one with a Ouija board. Now that's one way to separate hustlers from amateurs. Pros won't use 'em. There's no money in a board game that anybody can play at home."

"What about Evelyn Straub's connection?"

"When Alice Friday moved into the Straub Hotel, the other guests really liked the nightly Ouija board sessions on the verandah. So Evelyn cut a deal with the woman— free room and board and some walking-around money." The closer Cable got to the cabin, the thicker the trees and ferns—almost there. "It's just a gimmick to fill the hotel off-season. Now some people got hooked on the séances, but there was no charge. As long as nobody got fleeced, I never saw the harm." He had never foreseen a day when rock-solid people like Hannah and the judge would go looking for Josh in a witchboard.

As the jeep approached the cabin, Cable began a pre-amble to his worst fears. "It's been quite a while since I was up here," he lied. "The land changes as years go by. You think you know a place, and then you find out you don't. I wouldn't want to be up here when it gets dark. There'll be a full moon, but you can't count on it—not tonight." He leaned forward to look up through the windshield. "The clouds are already rolling in."

Searching the woods for a teenage Oren Hobbs had once been the pastime of an entire town. After a while, they had ceased to hunt for Josh, giving him up for dead, but young Oren had spent all his days in the forest, hunting for his brother. No matter how many times the boy lost his way, townsfolk would stop what they were doing, shops would close, and people would walk into the deep woods to find Judge Hobbs's only surviving child and bring him home again—and *again*. They never failed that good old man or the boy. Too often, Oren was found dehydrated and disoriented. So many times the boy could have died, but Coventry would not allow it.

Oren Hobbs nodded his understanding that he should not get lost one more time. "Why did Evelyn Straub move her psychic from the hotel to the woods?"

"That was actually pretty smart. Evelyn gets a tax write-off by using the cabin for business purposes." The sheriff turned onto a private road of hard-packed dirt, slowing to a roll when the roof of the log house came into view. While he still had trees for partial cover, he stopped his vehicle, cut the lights and let the engine idle. "I'm not supposed to be here. Evelyn's got an injunction to keep me off her property. She says police harassment ruins the *ambiance*. So I've got to get this jeep out of here real fast."

Yet his passenger remained in his seat, patiently waiting for more, and of course more was owed to him.

"Swahn was right," said Cable. "Evelyn's the one who gave you that alibi. She told me you spent the day in the cabin with her. She said Josh went deeper into the woods by himself."

"Who was the other one? Swahn said *two* women came forward."

"Well, what does it matter now? And son?—just how many women were you sleeping with? You weren't too talkative as a teenager."

Silent then, and silent now, Oren opened the passenger door and stepped out.

"Hold on." The sheriff rummaged through his glove compartment and pulled out a flashlight. "Can't remember the last time I changed the batteries. Use it sparingly. If you're smart, you'll start out for home while it's still light."

Oren reached through the open window and took the proffered flashlight. "Thanks."

"If you get caught spying on these people, don't tell Evelyn I was here. That's all I ask."

"I won't get caught."

"One more thing, Oren. On your way out, stay clear of traffic on the road. Evelyn drives the hotel's shuttle van." Cable leaned toward the passenger window. His voice was in the low warning notes. "Son? I know you found your way home from this place more than once, but don't go taking any shortcuts through the woods."

He was talking to the air. Oren Hobbs was gone.

The sedatives had worn off, and Sarah Winston reached for the whiskey bottle held just beyond her outstretched hand.

"Dinner's ready." Using the liquor as bait, Addison coaxed her out of bed and down the tower's narrow flight of steps. As they walked along the second-floor landing to descend the grand staircase, he placed one arm around her shoulders, forgetting for the moment that his wife was merely tired, no longer drunk and in danger of falling.

Well, soon enough.

They entered the dining room, arm in arm, and a drink—a reward—was poured for her.

Isabelle was already seated at the table, head lowered, but not in prayer. She had no religious faith. However, she did believe in walking evil.

"Hello, Daddy."

Long ago, she had called him that to please her mother. These days, the sarcastic tone of this salutation could only be read as *Drop dead*.

Throughout the evening meal, Isabelle watched her mother toy with food and drink her dinner. The older woman was in a stupor by the time dessert was served. Her husband and daughter talked around her body while she remained upright. When Sarah laid her head on the table and closed her eyes, they conversed over her bowed back. Their argument was an old one.

"I take care of your mother," said Addison.

"You're more like her jailor," said Isabelle. "You killed off every plan she ever had for getting back out in the world."

"Your mother didn't need another college degree. She's beautiful, and beauty is power. I gave her whatever she asked for . . . just for the pleasure of looking at her." He stared at his wife's sleeping face, her open mouth, the bit of spittle on her lips.

Sarah was awakened for the postprandial brandy, another lure. Steadied by Addison's arm, she was led to a couch in the cavernous front room, where a window spanned thirty feet to a pitched roof and offered a view of darkening woods.

When an hour had passed, and his wife was at the point of passing out, Addison gently lowered her head to the pillow of his lap. "Tomorrow the weaning begins," he whispered in her ear. "Only a little booze for breakfast and lunch, none for dinner."

When her eyes had closed in sleep, he smoothed the hair back from her brow. He looked up to see Isabelle glaring at him, hating him, and so, of course, he smiled: "One year, I cut her off on the day of the ball. Huge mistake. That was the first visit from the spiders. Three days is about right."

Isabelle's hands curled into fists, a good sign that she was paying attention.

"By the time your mother's birthday rolls around, she'll be able to go all night without a drink. Do you think Oren Hobbs will come to the ball this year?"

"Why should he? He hasn't been here since he was twelve."

Addison doubted that she would be disappointed if Oren never came to another birthday ball. Though Isabelle liked to nurse her grudges, even she could not carry this old obsession for so many years. However, it was worth a dig. "There's a rumor that Oren always had a thing for older women, *married* women." He looked down at his sleeping wife.

"And you think he slept with Mom?" Isabelle was incredulous.

Or was she jealous?

"Well, I know he didn't sleep with *you*." He saw heat

rising in her face to color it with a flush. "I know what you did, Belle—all those years ago. It's going to come back and bite you."

Isabelle rose from the couch and stood over her sleeping mother. "I don't know why Mom stayed with you. But I know why she drinks. The alcohol dulls your sharp little teeth when you nip at her ankles."

What a roundabout way of calling him a son of a bitch. Isabelle was normally so direct. He looked down at his wife, the woman who shared his house if not his bed. In a stage whisper, he said, "Oh, look. She wakes."

Sarah Winston lifted her head in the manner of a timid animal peering out of a burrow and finding the world unsafe. Her head dropped. Her eyes closed.

Isabelle sank to her knees and stroked her mother's hair. "This is torture. Why do you let her go on like this?"

"Oh, I don't know." He leaned forward with a smile, something between a tease and a leer. "Because I love her madly?"

Rising to her feet, Isabelle crossed the room with long strides and no wave or word of good night.

Addison caressed his wife's sleeping face. He loved her madly.

Deputies Dave Hardy and John Faulks had done a poor job of removing bloodstains from their uniforms. The pink blotches were not the only evidence of a fight. They had been caught on film. Waiting for the fallout from their skirmish on the streets of Saulburg, they stood before the window of an appliance store and watched the images of ten television sets tuned to different channels.

"We're screwed," said Dave Hardy. "If that fight makes it to the evening news, we'll get suspended."

John Faulks was equally worried, and this carried in his voice, but he was also a man in denial. "That guy was just a cameraman, not a reporter." He turned his eyes from screen to screen. "I wish I could remember the name of the news show. I know the station call letters were printed on that camera."

Dave pointed to a TV set at the top of the display. "What the hell is that?"

The screen showed them the still image of a window set in a brick wall. A banner of type ran across the bottom of the screen, telling them what they already knew: the bones of a lost boy had been found in Coventry. And now something different: the hunt for a fugitive was under way.

"I wish we had sound," said Deputy Faulks.

The camera pulled back to show more of the building.

"It's the library in Coventry," said Dave. "Those stupid reporters believed you. They went to the library."

"I'm sorry," said the man beside him. "It was just a joke. How was I supposed to know they'd actually go there. Nobody in Coventry ever goes to the libra—"

"Don't ever say that again." Dave Hardy's fist was raised and promising more than a nosebleed this time.

Evelyn's cabin had once been her shelter from a hateful old man. Millard Straub had punished his wife every day of their marriage—because he was dying and she was not.

Tonight, Oren studied the ruins. Nature was reclaiming the structure, sending tree shoots through broken windowpanes. There were cracks in the foundation, and the porch roof sagged under the weight of a fallen branch. He could smell wood rot from the yard.

There was one improvement. The turnout for the driveway had been expanded into a parking lot. The van belonged to the Straub Hotel, and the sedans would be owned by local people. He judged some of the cars to be twenty years old and older, with cracked dashboards, dents and bald tires. Others were brand-new luxury models. The theme of wealth parked next to poverty played out all over Coventry, where a millionaire might build his mansion next to an acre parcel with a mobile home—or an old knock-down cabin like this one.

The land sloped downward as he moved toward the rear of the property, and the cabin's foundation had been built to accommodate this incline. He remembered concrete footings six feet high at the back end and a large opening used for storing yard tools. Even better, there was a trapdoor that would give him a view of the goings-on in the rooms above. As he rounded the cabin, he discovered that the opening had been enclosed. Behind the wooden steps leading up to the kitchen, he found a metal door set into the new wall of cement, and it was padlocked.

A pity. The old crawl space would have made a perfect spy hole. Now he would have to risk being seen. Oren walked up the back stairs and looked through a cracked windowpane. There was no one in the kitchen. He opened the door and entered the room, stepping light and slow. A rough interior wall was pocked with light leaking through the crumbled mortar between the logs. It offered him a selection of peepholes large and small. He moved silently from one to the other until he found a good view of the gathering in the next room.

No money had been wasted on props for the séance. Spiderwebs hung from the ceiling in ghosty gray curtains, very theatrical, but all too real. Six people sat on metal folding chairs gathered around a flimsy card table. They were encircled by the light of candles on cracked plates that sat on the floor. Other people were seated in shadow on the far side of the room. Evelyn Straub occupied a love seat, and no one dared keep her company.

Oren remembered that small sofa. Once, he had thought the plush velvet upholstery and gilt frame were too grand for this rustic setting. Now the old love seat seemed tired and sad in the lean and the sag of it, and the woman who sat upon it had also gone this route, less recognizable now than her furniture. Even by the kindness of candlelight, he could not find Evelyn Straub in this older woman's face.

Inside the circle of candles, all but one of the people

rose up in a body and yielded their chairs. As players from the sidelines took their seats, Oren had a clear view of the table and an uncommon Ouija board. This was nothing bought in a store. The numerals and the alphabet appeared to be handmade. He recognized the small object at the center of the board. Made of rough carved wood, the three-legged heart had a hole at its center to display single characters from the painted lines of letters and numbers.

The sheriff had been right about one thing: the Ouija board was an anomaly. None of the grifters that Oren had encountered ever used one. And tonight he did not draw on his experience as a CID agent. This was a game from his childhood, played in secret places, dark cellars and deep woods. His little brother had loved the game—at first—calling it by its older name, *witchboard*.

A stick-thin woman, who had kept her chair, now gave instructions to the second shift of players. "Place your fingers on the planchette," she said, and, by fingertips, the other five people touched the heart-shaped piece of wood. "No pressure, mind you. It moves by other forces."

This could only be Alice Friday. Her face had a gaunt, starved look, and her eyes were sunken and heavy-lidded. The woman's voice had a nasal twang of the Midwest and a no-nonsense tone. She might well be giving a lecture on aluminum siding when she said, "Now we'll ask my spirit guide to answer your questions." She raised her head and raised her voice, calling out, "Joshua Hobbs! Are you here with us tonight?"

So Alice Friday used his dead brother to earn her living. Oren would not lay any blame upon Evelyn Straub. It had always been her nature to make money off of everything that moved and everything that did not. Why not the dead?

The planchette jumped on the board, startling people who must be new to the Ouija board. The more seasoned players only smiled. The psychic dryly chanted above the noise of crickets and the sounds of small animal paws scurrying across the ceiling. Six people leaned into the center of the table, and their heads bowed over the board each time the planchette stopped over a letter, and together they spelled out a chant, *"I-A-M-N-E—"*

Starlight could be seen through the mortar chinks in the upper walls, but Oren stared at another light, small as a star and electric green, and this one was in the floor. A cable fed out of one baseboard and traveled up a wall. He looked up to the ceiling, but it was too dark to find a camera lens in the rafters.

"A-R-S-O-D-A-R-K."

Evelyn Straub rose from the love seat and walked toward the kitchen, moving with the limber grace of a woman who had not grown old and stout. This vestige of her younger days fascinated him. It took a moment to collect his wits, to back out through the open door and softly pull it shut behind him.

Good night, pretty woman.

Mercifully, he was gone before the chanters spelled out, *"O-R-E-N-H-E-L-P-M-E."*

Eleven

High up where the roof joined walls of glass and walls of plaster, a circular bookshelf ran around the tower room, and Isabelle Winston climbed a ladder on wheels to reach it. Since returning home, it had become her nightly custom to covertly replace a borrowed bird-watcher's log and pull down another one. She shifted the remaining volumes on the shelf to fill in the space so that the absence of a single book would not be noticed.

What was the point of worrying over this?

Her mother had drunk herself into oblivion, and, on the rare occasions when Addison visited here, he probably never looked past his own reflection in the glass. The man would have no interest in records of bird sightings, though these were not the typical birder's journals. And, even if he should peruse a book or two, he would never crack the code.

Crafty Mom.

After kissing her sleeping mother, Isabelle carried the purloined journal downstairs to her bedroom, hiding it in the folds of her robe, knowing all the while that her parents would care nothing about her reading habits.

When had she become so paranoid?

An hour later, propped up by pillows, the ornithologist was still reading by the light of a bedside lamp, utterly engrossed in a book that had little to do with birds, though feathered characters were drawn on every page.

Once upon a time, with a child's egocentric view of the universe, Isabelle had believed that these volumes were created for her. The fanciful illustrations better lent themselves to children's books than a birder's journals. And there were story lines and lines of dialogue in song. Before learning her ABCs, Isabelle had learned the human phrases used to identify a hundred birds, words that mimicked rhythm and the rise and fall of notes. As a little girl, her favorite song belonged to the pewee, and she had sung it all day long, "Ah di dee, pee a wee, ah di dee, pee oh," because it had driven Addison crazy.

Her mother's logbooks made departures from traditional notations, though the songs could still be recognized. Upon returning to Coventry, Isabelle had read many of the old volumes again with a new understanding: Some of the birds drawn here did not appear in northwestern climes—nor anywhere outside of her mother's fragile mind—and these were not fairy tales.

It had taken six weeks to work through the early years of life in Coventry. With the exception of the birthday balls, Addison had discouraged his wife from mixing with the residents. Isabelle, always away at boarding school, had felt abandoned and resentful in those days, but now she realized how lonely her mother had been. Yet Sarah Winston appeared to know a great deal about the town and its people, secret things gleaned by three telescopes and a pair of binoculars.

Hannah Rice had been the Rosetta stone, pictured here as an elf owl in constant company with a tall thin bird that had lost its crown of long feathers over the years—the balding Judge Hobbs. And, thanks to this morning's sighting of Ferris Monty, Isabelle now knew the identity of the black-capped chickadee. The man's bad toupee resembled the bird's cap, and the yellow feathers of the breast matched the color of his Rolls-Royce. The gossip columnist did not sing, "Chicka dee dee dee." He sang, "Look at me, me, me," to the lark, who paid him no attention. And everywhere the lark went, the black-capped chickadee was sure to follow. Sometimes the lark would follow another bird, and they made a procession of three through the streets, the chickadee always at the rear, singing his hopeless song.

Her mother seemed to like Evelyn Straub, who was portrayed in colored pencil as an exotic pink heron with a graceful wingspan, long legs—and two nests, one in the town and one in the woods. In this volume, the lovely heron's mate was still alive. Isabelle could not mistake the gray and shriveled starling for anyone but Millard Straub. He rode on the heron's back.

Throughout the state of California, television viewers were annoyed by interruptions in their prime-time viewing hours. The late-breaking news was always the same image of the Coventry Library bathed in bright electric lights. The story was periodically updated by a manic anchorman's message that the sheriff had *still* not responded to the emergency of a strange smell emanating from the premises.

Patrons of the Coventry Pub considered walking down the street to view the unfolding events of the sheriff *not* responding to a 9-1-1 call. However, upon being told that they would not be allowed to take their beers with them, they elected to stay and watch a picture of the library on television.

The camera angle swung around to show the approach of a jeep. The lawman emerging from the vehicle was identified as the county sheriff. The reporter approached him, microphone extended, excitement mounting. "Are you here to investigate the smell?"

"No," said the sheriff. "I understand you've been fooling with a nine-one-one operator." He handed a folded sheet of paper to the reporter. "That's a summons to appear in court tomorrow morning. Then you can explain why a smelly library constitutes an emergency."

"There could be a dead body in there! Aren't you going to investigate?"

"Well, no," said the sheriff. "The library's closed."

"What about the *smell*?" The reporter pointed to the brick building, as if it might be hard to find. "You have to get closer to—"

"No, son, I can smell it just fine, thanks. Are we on live television?"

"You bet."

Sheriff Babitt turned his smile on the camera and tipped his hat. "It smells like a pair of really ripe socks." He stepped back to look down at the reporter's feet.

And so ended the statewide coverage of the Coventry Library.

When the lawman and the news crew had departed, lights came on inside the library, and they burned late into the night. A figure could be seen pacing across the window shades, but this was such a common sight, no one passing by took any notice.

The moon was on the rise and guiding Oren's steps down the mountain road that would lead him home. He spared the flashlight battery for pitch-black moments when clouds blocked the moon.

A pair of headlights came up behind him, rounding a hairpin turn in the road. Minding Cable Babitt's request that he not be caught near the cabin, Oren dove into the woods as the hotel van sped by. More cars came around the curve, their headlights aimed straight at him. He was back-stepping deeper into the cover of tall ferns, moving quickly, when his boots clipped a tree root behind him, and he fell to the ground, but not to a hard landing. He rolled down a steep incline. Reflex kicked in. He covered his face, only scratching his hands on shoots and deadwood, rolling, rolling, and finally coming to rest flat on his back.

Fool.

He lay at the center of a depression shaped like the hollow of a giant hand. Above the rise of encircling land, he could see a glow from the parade of cars in the distance. Seduced by lack of sleep, he meant to close his eyes for only a moment. When he opened them again, all the light had been sucked out of the world. There was no demarcation line between sky and earth, no sense of up and down. Blackness only. Where was his compass, the moon?

Killed by clouds.

Where was the flashlight? Crawling sightless, he searched the ground by fingertips, touching brush and dirt until his hand finally closed on the metal casing.

Click.

No light. The batteries were dead.

On all fours, he climbed up the slope of the hollow and crawled toward the road. He crawled forever. The road was gone. He had gotten turned around in the fall and traveled the wrong way. For how long? How far? By touch, he found the root and rough-bark column of a tree and sat down to lean his back against it.

So tired.

He clicked the useless flashlight in his hand, desperate for a miracle, just a few seconds of light. Darkness was another dimension, where natural law did not apply. Separated from every visual clue to the solid world, he hugged himself for reassurance that mind and body had not gone their separate ways, but he could not lose that sensation of being suspended in a void.

The road could not be far. He listened for the sound of cars.

Useless.

There was only one cabin on the fire road, and the séance was long over. All the players had gone home by now. He rose to his feet and walked two steps into an alien land, hands outstretched to fend off low-hanging branches that might reach out for his blind eyes.

Which way?

He might be on a parallel route, only twenty feet from the road—or twenty yards. How long had he crawled in the wrong direction? Space and time had no meaning here.

This is not the first time you've been lost in the woods in the dead of night. Sit down and wait. At sunup, you'll see the road, the way out.

Whenever he listened to that inner voice of reason, it always sounded a lot like Hannah. She would be worried, and so would the judge. How long would they wait before the alarm was sounded? He remembered other nights in these woods and the sight of waving yellow stalks of light, hundreds of voices calling his name. Every woodland creature had been awakened to flee on the wing or on the run, frightened by an army of searchers, their shoes and boots shaking earth and bough.

Not again—not one more time.

Even when he was a teenager, he would have known better than to move on tonight. And yet he did. Every soldier's survival skill was forgotten as he felt his way from tree to tree. All that he could count on was the natural circle of one who was lost. His feet might bring him back to the beginning—and just as likely carry him away again.

High in the invisible canopy of tall trees, an owl called out. *Hoo! Huh-hu-hu. Hoo! Hoo!*

Another night bird answered with hollow whistles in the rhythm of a bouncing ball or footfalls losing their momentum, slowing, slowing.

All stop.

Wits lost.

Oren screamed his brother's name.

All around him, he could hear things moving in the dark, small animals alarmed and stirring in the underbrush, creeping, running. He felt their panic, the same old fear, a coldness stealing up his throat. Shivering, he hugged himself for warmth. And what of Josh? His brother had left his jacket behind.

Josh is dead. You've seen his bones.

How many days had he gone without food or water?

No hunger, no thirst. Today you had a chicken sandwich in the kitchen with Cable Babitt.

Oren turned toward the sound of a car engine in the distance, and he heard it die—suddenly—switched off.

He sucked in his breath and held it.

A small ball of light floated on the air, appearing and disappearing behind the trunks of trees. Was he dreaming this? Every time he dreamed, he died.

Twelve

Hannah Rice was the resurrection and the light.

Oren fell to his knees on the dirt road. "How did you find me?"

She brushed the hair away from his eyes. "I got a tele-phone call to ask if you made it home from the séance." Hannah gently coaxed him to stand up. Then she took him by the hand and led him to the car, treating him as a handicapped person—and he was one tonight. "Evelyn Straub saw you dive off the road when her van came around a curve. Everybody knows you have a penchant for getting lost in the woods."

After settling him into the passenger seat, she leaned across his body to fasten the safety belt. And here, all concept of road safety ended. The little woman provided him with the medicine of comic relief as she turned the car toward home. She strained to see over the steering wheel, sometimes using the wheel as leverage to raise her body up. Raising the seat was not an option, not if she wanted to reach the foot pedals. Yet Hannah loved to drive. She *lived* to drive.

"Odd—this sudden interest of yours." She leaned toward him—big smile. "Séances, Oren?"

"I heard you and the judge were big fans of Alice Friday," he said—big smile.

"Oh, everybody went up to that cabin at least once or twice." Hannah looked at the dashboard clock and then put on some speed. "Dave Hardy called tonight. He wants to buy you a beer sometime."

"I didn't expect to see him this morning. Most kids leave the day they come of age." His brother had been the rare boy who never dreamed of escaping from his small coastal town. Josh had loved Coventry—and he had loved his life.

"But Dave Hardy *did* leave," said Hannah. "That boy made it all the way to Chicago. And now you're wondering why he came back."

"He forgot to shoot his mother on the way out of town?"

"Dave heard she was dying—a tumor in her stomach. Well, in this world of real estate gone nuts, his mother's five-acre parcel is worth quite a bit. But I don't think he came back just for Mavis's money."

"Maybe he wanted to watch her die? Around here, you could sell tickets to a thing like that."

Hannah shot him a look of disapproval. "You don't want to say things like that when the judge is around.

He won't tolerate anybody making fun of that poor woman."

Oren recalled that Mrs. Hardy's other champion was Hannah. He had never heard the housekeeper say one word against Dave's mother—not in earnest, not in fun. And now he grabbed the dashboard as she made a sharp turn onto the road that would lead them home.

"Dave came back to town about eight years ago," said Hannah. "Now here's the odd part. Mavis didn't die. Her tumor keeps growing, but she just won't die."

Oren wondered if Mrs. Hardy was toxic to tumors as well as people.

Hannah shushed him, and this should have spooked him, for he had not voiced that idea aloud. But Oren remembered all of the housekeeper's parlor tricks, and this had been one of her best: divining impure thoughts from a smirk or guilty downcast eyes and the antsy feet of boys.

She looked from the dashboard clock to her wristwatch, double-checking the hour. This might be the first time he had ever seen her wearing a timepiece, and this thought chained back to his brother. "That photograph of me and Josh—he was wearing a watch that last morning. Don't you think that's odd? Josh never cared about the time of day before."

"You mean, not so you noticed." She reached out to pat his hand. "When you were a kid, you missed a lot of things. Take Isabelle Winston. I remember the first birthday ball, the first time you kids set eyes on one another. You were only twelve years old, but I saw your whole life all laid out in front of you that night. I could see all the way into a generation of your grandchildren. But something went wrong, and that was long before Josh disappeared. The life you've been leading isn't the one you were meant to have."

Isabelle Winston focused her lenses on the distant glow of a porch light, and she watched Hannah and Oren enter the judge's house.

She lowered the binoculars and carried them inside, where her mother lay on the bed in a drunk's blackout sleep. No dreams. Was that the reason for her mother's drinking? Was there no peace for her, waking or sleeping? Sarah Winston lay with arms outstretched, her wrists exposed, and her daughter stared at the old razor scars running across the veins. Though these suicide attempts were old events, years in the past, Isabelle had first learned of them only months ago when she had come home for a short visit.

And now she could not—*would not*—leave.

She climbed the ladder to replace the bird log borrowed earlier and to take another one down from the shelf. At the end of the last journal, the beautiful long-legged heron was pursuing a bird much younger than her gray starling husband. The young hawk and the heron soared together, describing circles around one another in the sky. However, Isabelle's mission tonight had nothing to do with Evelyn Straub's extramarital love affairs.

This time, she did not take a journal and steal away

with it, for she had remembered something learned at her parents' dinner table. One of the guests had been a well-known politician. "Kid, if you're gonna do something wrong," the man had said to her then, "do it right out in plain sight. It's the hidden things that attract attention."

She sat down in the chair by her mother's bed and switched on the lamp to decipher the code of drawings and birdsong. A letter fell from the pages, and she recognized the quirky handwriting on the envelope, though she had not seen a sample of it in decades. The lines of longhand were small and lightly penned, all but begging to go unnoticed.

Crazy Mavis.

In the old days, her mother and Mrs. Hardy had gone bird-watching in the woods. In the summers of childhood, Isabelle had sometimes accompanied them, and she had loved the conspiracy of keeping these outings a secret. Addison would never have approved of his wife befriending the town monster.

The opened letter in her hand was filled with descriptions of flight, the colors of feather and sky, and the music of the deep woods. Almost poetry. Apparently Mrs. Hardy had depths unknown and qualities that were not monstrous.

Oren paused by the closed door at the bottom of the staircase. He leaned down to the housekeeper and whispered, "I heard something."

"I'm sure you did." Hannah consulted her wristwatch.

"It's about that time." She turned to the judge's door. "Did you know that used to be the sewing room? That's why it's too small for anything but a twin bed. A few days after your mother's funeral, your father moved all of his things out of their old bedroom. He said he wanted to sleep down here so he could catch you boys if you tried to sneak out late at night. Well, you were only three years old, and Josh was still in diapers. Personally, I think his marriage bed just got too wide for him." She tapped the crystal on her watch, as if that would make the hands move faster. "Any minute now. I got this down to a science."

The judge's voice could be heard inside the small room, but the words were unintelligible. Oren cracked the door and looked inside, asking, "Did you need something, sir?"

"He's sleeping." Hannah lightly tugged on Oren's arm to pull him back.

"He sleeps with his eyes open?"

"Just wait." After closing the bedroom door, the housekeeper produced a string of cowbells from a drawer in the glove table and hung them on the knob. She walked down the hall saying, "You'll see."

Oren followed her into the kitchen, where the table was laid out with a whiskey bottle, two empty shot glasses and an ashtray—evidence that Hannah and the judge continued to enjoy their postprandial drinks and cigars. She set out two clean glasses and Oren's gift, the bottle of Jack Daniel's. Next, she laid down a stack of paper with printed text.

Oren pulled out a chair for her, a habit learned in childhood. He turned his own chair around and straddled it, folding his arms across the wooden back—another habit, one learned in his years as a CID agent. This was his preferred interrogation posture. "So the old man sleeps with his eyes open—and he walks in his sleep? That's why you hang bells on his doorknob?"

"You just wait—and watch."

"And that's why you installed all those dead bolts—so he can't leave the house at night without a key."

Hannah picked up a sheet of paper from the pile in front of her. "This report's from a sleep clinic in San Francisco. They claim you can't predict an episode of somnambulism. But I've got a computer printout from another outfit in L.A., and that one tells you how to make it happen. So much for expert opinions."

"*Printouts*? You're surfing the Internet, Hannah? I thought you'd be the last person on earth to get a computer."

"Oh, the judge wouldn't have one of those damned things in the house. I use the computer at the library."

"But no one in Coventry ever goes to the library."

Down the hall, the cowbells were ringing.

"You have to see this for yourself," said Hannah. "That's why I stopped his medication when I knew you were coming home."

"You mean *your* medication—the prescription I filled at the drugstore, right?" Oren got up from his chair and left the kitchen. As he walked down the hall, Hannah was close behind him.

"He won't go to a doctor," she said. "So I go. It doesn't matter much if the doctor sees him or me." She spat out the word, *"Doctors*. They can't agree on anything. One tells you it's not psychological—and another one says it's all in your head. And your father believes it's all in *my* head."

The judge stood before the front door, pulling on the knob, then jerking it. His eyes were vacant and so at odds with his urgency to get out of the house.

Hannah looked up at Oren. "This morning I changed his decaf for regular coffee, real strong and lots of it. Caffeine is one of the triggers that brings it on, and the medication keeps it turned off. It's like working a pharmaceutical light switch."

The old man twisted the knob with one hand and banged on the door with the other. Oren took his cue from the housekeeper, who showed no sign of alarm. This was something witnessed many times.

"Your father doesn't see the locks. The door he's looking at doesn't have any yet. I got locks on the windows, too, but he's never tried to get out that way. I don't know why. Only doors."

"The window wasn't locked when I came home last night."

"No need. I was waiting up for you. Must've fallen asleep in my chair."

Her second job as the sleepwalker's watcher would explain why the judge thought she seemed sluggish at times, and this must be why she took naps in the afternoon.

His father began to cry, and Oren came undone. He

had never seen the old man in tears before, not even after Josh went missing.

"He wants to get out of here so bad," said Hannah. "He's got the night terrors."

"How long does this go on?"

"You don't have to whisper," she said. "It's real hard to wake him. This can last a few minutes or half an hour, sometimes longer."

The judge gave up on the door. Oren and Hannah followed him down the hall and into the kitchen. The housekeeper motioned for Oren to take a seat as she poured their whiskey. She pushed one of the shot glasses to his side of the table. "You'll need that."

So spake Hannah the Oracle, and he knocked back the whiskey with unconditional faith.

His father had found the back door and struggled to open it. His obstacles were three strong bolts, but he never tried to undo them, not that he could—not without a key.

Hannah watched, almost bored by this. "It began after Josh went missing, but it only happened a few times. You were never around in those days—always out in the woods, looking for your brother. Then the night terrors started up again when the judge sent you away at the end of that summer. The sleepwalking went on for a long time, but then it finally stopped. Years and years went by."

"And then the bones started turning up on the front porch."

"Anxiety." Hannah rewarded him with a smile. "That's the key."

Oren looked up to see the judge staring at him. "Sir?"

"Don't get fooled," said Hannah. "He's looking your way, but you don't know who he sees in your chair."

"You should've told me this was going on. You didn't have to go through this alone."

"I promised your father I wouldn't worry you with this silly notion of mine—that he walks in his sleep."

The desperate need for escape was forgotten. The judge opened the refrigerator, perused its contents and pulled out a jar of pickles. Next he raided the breadbox, and then he stood at the counter, using a fork to smear one slice with the juice from the jar.

"He thinks that's mayonnaise," said the housekeeper, shaking her head. "There's as many theories about what's going on here as there are experts who think they know what they're talking about."

"He's acting out a dream?"

"Some say yes." She riffled the papers in the stack on the table. "Others say he can't be dreaming. Sleepwalking happens in non-REM sleep." She laid one of the printed sheets in front of him. "But according to *this* doctor, he *can* sleepwalk in a dream state. When you deal with more than one medical opinion, it's always a crapshoot."

The judge sat down with them. An invisible object was cradled in one arm, and now, with great care, he set it down on the table. After lifting a latch that only he could see, he stared at the contents of a box that was not there.

"I've seen that before." Hannah shook her head. "I mean to say—"

"I know." Oren also stared at the nonexistent box. "Any idea what it is?"

"Wish I knew. It drives me nuts. No sense in asking him. His answers don't always work with the questions. Watch this." She leaned toward her employer and raised her voice. "What's in the box?"

The judge turned to her without expression and said, "The soup was burning on the stove."

"Nothing to do with my question." Hannah sat back in her chair and turned to Oren. "But you heard his answer clear as can be."

He nodded. His father might be reliving a night months after Josh had vanished. Oren had come home from the woods, dirty and exhausted. The judge and the housekeeper had waited up for him long past the dinner hour. Distracted and frazzled, Hannah had allowed the soup to bubble over in its pot and burn. Now Oren could see it, and he could smell it, too. A trace of that same broth lingered in the air tonight, mingled with the stale odor of lamb cooked for dinner. He had a collection of scents that triggered strong emotions. In combat zones, the stench of burning flesh called up the adrenaline rush of a man standing out on a ledge. The smell of Hannah's soup conjured the helplessness of a teenage boy in free-fall.

The housekeeper held up a sheaf of papers clipped together. "This doctor says a sleepwalker's speech is *incomprehensible* gibberish. That's how I know the fool phoned in his research. He for damn sure never talked to anybody who lives with a sleepwalker." She crumpled these sheets into a ball and tossed them over one shoulder as she pushed the rest of the stack to Oren's side of the table. "It's not like any of these idiots talk to each other, either."

Oren touched his father's arm, asking, "What's in the box?"

"Our child is lost," said the judge. "I need another miracle."

"Well," said Hannah, "now we know he's talking to your dead mother."

"*Another* miracle. What does that mean?"

"The stuff of dreams," she said. "Nothing more. You know your father doesn't hold with miracles when he's awake." She pulled the pharmacy bottle from her pocket and set it on the table. "He sleeps through the night when I slip Lorazepam into his whiskey. It won't cure him. Nothing will—and that's the only thing the experts agree on. But the drug keeps him out of mischief, and I can get some rest."

Oren watched the old man close the lid of the dreamed box. "This is why you hide the car keys in a tea tin."

She nodded. "One night, I found him behind the wheel. He was almost to the end of the driveway when he woke up. He can do lots of things when he's sleeping. My big fear is that he'll get out of the house one night and go for a walk in the woods."

"Answer the phone," said the judge, though the telephone was not ringing.

Hannah leaned toward him, saying loudly, "It's not

my call! It's for *you!*" She turned to Oren. "Sometimes he can understand me—so long as it works with what's going on in his head."

The judge rose from his chair and walked to the telephone mounted on the kitchen wall. He picked up the receiver and held it to his ear. After a few seconds, it dropped from his hand and swung from its cord. There was surprise in the old man's eyes, as if he were seeing his surroundings for the first time. He looked down at his bare feet, not wanting to meet the eyes of his son and the housekeeper. Shyly, he slipped out of the kitchen and padded off down the hall. They heard the cowbells ring as the bedroom door closed behind him.

"Your father gets embarrassed when he wakes up that way." The housekeeper retrieved the dangling receiver and set it back on the wall cradle. "But he won't remember any of this in the morning." Hannah returned to the table to pluck another paper from her stack. "This expert says it's dangerous to wake a sleepwalker." She laid it down and covered it with another. "And this one says it isn't dangerous at all." She crumpled both of them. "You see why I get frustrated?"

"What do *you* think, Hannah? What's going on with him?"

"Well, what's in a nightmare? It's the intolerable thing. You remember your dreams, don't you? He never does. I think he's struggling with something that can't be said out loud. This unspeakable thing, it's something he can't deal with in a wide-awake brain. Sleepwalking is like his safety valve. His worst thoughts come out at night, and he never has to remember them when he wakes up." She sat back in her chair, downed her shot glass in one gulp, and then she poured another. "That's why I used to take him to the séances. Things slip out there. Sometimes things bypass your brain and just pop out on the witch-board."

"It's a scam." Oren filled his glass again.

Hannah smiled. "I remember a time when you thought different. How old were you when Mrs. Underwood died? You know who I mean—the old lady who used to live down on Paulson Lane."

"Our Good Samaritan duty."

"Right. I guess you were eleven and Josh was nine. That woman was very old, close to ninety. The judge was real surprised when you boys took her death so hard—all those nightmares." Hannah's grin spread slow and wide. "But you and I both know what caused those scary dreams. It was the witchboard you hid behind the washing machine. Did you boys really believe that I *never* cleaned behind the washing machine?"

Oren smiled. With the destruction of that old Ouija board, Hannah had ended the midnight conversations between two children and a dead woman in the dark of a cellar. Most of Mrs. Underwood's communication from the grave had been simple yes or no responses, but whole words had also been spelled out. Cold drafts of air had sometimes blown out their only candle, causing the boys to stifle screams of fear and delight. And all through that winter, Josh and Oren had believed in magic.

"Kid stuff." He shook his head. "This is different.

Alice Friday is a con artist. That Ouija board of hers is just a cheap trick."

"It is, and it isn't," said Hannah. "Nothing magical or supernatural about it, but it does work in a way. You used to have an open mind." She laid one small hand atop his. "And then you grew up." This was said with a small measure of pity.

Oren poured himself another shot. "I've dealt with lots of psychics in homicide cases. They turn up at the funerals so they can meet the grieving relatives—and fleece them. Bloodsuckers."

"But there's no charge, Oren. The séances are free. So where's the crime?"

"It's fraud." He made no distinctions between the fakes who charged and the ones who did it for attention. In his experience, they all did real damage to the families of victims.

Hannah sipped from her shot glass. "A witchboard can only tell you what you already know. That's my take on it. Most of the time, the board spells out nonsense words. You have to work at it to force out a meaning. More like therapy than magic, but it's way more interesting than that. And you'd be surprised at who turns up out there in the woods."

"Like the judge? That surprised me."

"At first he went on my account. I told him I was scared to go alone."

"And he believed that? You're not afraid of anything. He *knows* how you drive a car."

Ignoring this, Hannah continued. "So your father, always a gentleman, escorted me out there one night. He only watched for a while. The little wooden thing—a heart with a hole in it? Well, none of the players could believe they were moving it around the board."

"Somebody moves it, and it isn't my dead brother."

"Oh, Josh, the spirit guide." She nodded and smiled. "Now that part's fake. When Alice asks if his spirit is there, the wooden heart just settles over the letter Y for yes. The witchboard never spelled his name. But one night, the board spelled out the words *red comb*. It helps if you know that the judge took Josh in for a haircut the day before he disappeared, and the barber gave the boy a red plastic comb."

"Oh, *please*."

Hannah leaned toward him. "Don't you roll your eyes like that. The barber always gave every customer a *black* comb. That red one was a fluke. It just turned up in the box with the barbershop's regular order of solid black. Josh was the only boy in town with a red one."

"And Alice Friday probably heard that from one of her victims. Don't tell me the judge was fooled by—"

"Your father is no fool—and Alice Friday never touches the witchboard. Half the men at that séance were tourists—and the others were regulars at the town barbershop. I'm sure they all heard about the red comb. So, for a while, the judge sat down to play on a regular basis—and the sleepwalking stopped. All that's left of Josh is little snatches of memories, and lots of people have them. When they sit around that witchboard, all those little bits of the boy come out to play. You might say your father was collecting pieces of Josh long before the bones started coming home."

Oren leaned back in the chair and stared at the ceiling. "And *that's* why he never asked for more help—never called in state cops or the feds? The old man was waiting for somebody to drop a clue in a damn séance?"

Did he believe that? Did she? No, and no.

He refilled his shot glass and hers. "You weren't quite that patient, Hannah. Right after Josh went missing, *you* asked for help. You got William Swahn to find me an alibi." He lifted his glass and drained it. "I always knew who really ran this house—our lives. Was it your idea to send me away that summer?"

"No, I was against it." The shot glass seemed almost too heavy for her as she lifted it to take a sip. "I told your father to send *Josh* away. He didn't listen to me then. After the boy disappeared, the judge probably thought about that all the time. I wish I'd never said a word."

Now all her words were spent, and so was she. Her eyes were closed by half. Her day was done.

Oren switched on the bedside light and then rose to pull on his jeans. Though he was tired, sleep would not come, and he was grateful. He lacked his father's gift of forgetting every dream. Sometimes acts of nightmare violence broke into his wide-awake mind, but it was worse when he lay helpless, wrapped in sheets, eyes closed in the dark. And some nights he would wake up screaming the soldier's song, *Makeitstopmakeitstopmakeitstop!*

He sat down at his old desk and wrote a letter to Evelyn Straub. Then he put out the lamp and padded down the stairs in his stocking feet so as not to wake the house. Having no keys to the bolts on the front door, he climbed through the porch window, pulled on his boots and struck out for Coventry on foot.

No need for a flashlight. The moon was back, and it was bright. Oren walked down the road, undisturbed by any traffic. His only company was a dead boy and a dead dog. Josh had walked this same route with him on many a summer morning, and Horatio had trotted along between the brothers. Occasionally, one boy or the other would reach down to ruffle the dog's fur, reassuring their pet that he was still part of the family, though Josh never wanted the dog to come along on trips into town. Horatio had been shameless about kissing strangers and drooling on them, and he had been banned from every store where customers preferred to do their shopping dry and unloved.

One standout day, Josh had locked the poor beast in the kitchen, using his let's-be-reasonable voice to say, "No, you can't come today." That had set off the barking tantrum, followed by whining that was almost human. The dog had cried, as if in fear that he would never see his boys again.

Oren remembered his own words. "I know why you don't want Horatio along. He gives you away. This has to stop. It's creepy."

Josh had ducked his head under the weight of that comment. *Creepy* was a word that could turn a boy's high school life into a living hell of derision. Oren had released Horatio from the kitchen, and the dog had jumped his brother, paws on shoulders, kissing and slobbering. All was forgiven. This was followed by the old familiar line, screamed at the top of Josh's lungs, "Get *off* me! I'm gonna *puke*!"

Horatio had done his mad little dance on hind legs, barking to say, *Let's go! Let's go!* The boys could have set fire to him, and the dog, who was love incarnate, would have assumed that they were only having a difficult day—and promptly forgiven them.

Tonight, Oren resolved to get rid of the stuffed carcass on the living room rug, that bad joke on a good old dog.

The lights of town were up ahead, and he pulled the letter from his back pocket. He planned to leave it with the night-shift clerk so that Evelyn could read it first thing in the morning. As he approached the Straub Hotel, it was a surprise to see her sitting on the verandah at this late hour.

Oren walked up the steps and sat down beside her. She never acknowledged him, not even by a nod in his direction. By unspoken agreement, they sat in peaceful silence for a while. The beach could not be seen from this view, only the straight lines of the road, its railing and the broader stripes of sea and sky.

He studied her profile by moonlight, looking there for signs of Evelyn trapped inside that aging stranger's body. Her lean jawline and high cheekbones had disappeared into loose folds of flesh. Her breasts sagged above a thickened waist and protruding belly. Yet he persisted in his search for a clue to her, as if she might be only hiding from him—though that was hardly her nature.

In the younger days of her forties, she had been the aggressor, taking him down with her strong tanned arms, sinking with him deep into a feather bed, her long legs wrapped around him—no escape—and never was it enough, not for him, not for her. And there had been feeling between them, as much as Evelyn had allowed. As a boy, he would never have betrayed her—even if it had meant jail. He would've lied for her, died for her. And was he still tied to her?

Yes. The strings were still there. He could feel a tug in the dark when she said, "Good evening, Oren."

"Hello, Evelyn." He said this as if he had just discovered her—and he had.

"Glad to see you made it out of the woods tonight."

When she spoke, it was easier to recognize her. He only had to close his eyes, and there she was. "Hannah told me you called the house tonight."

"I can guess why you're here," she said. "When you see Cable Babitt, you tell that old bastard I *know* the sound of his jeep. It's a piece of crap with a skippy motor. I know it like I know the sound of his voice." The wicker chair creaked as she turned to face him. "I could put Cable's ass in a legal sling for taking you out to the cabin tonight. But I won't mess with him—not *this* time. Satisfied?"

"That's not why I'm here." He gently laid his letter in her lap. "After Josh disappeared, you must have won-

dered why Swahn came to see you—how he *knew*. I swear
to you, I never told anyone about us."

"I know that, Oren."

"When you went to the sheriff . . . to give me an
alibi . . . why did you lie for me?"

"Get off my verandah, Oren."

Upstairs in her bedroom, locked in the safe among her
jewels, Evelyn Straub kept a yellowed envelope. Inside it
was a photograph that Oren Hobbs had sent to her from
a boarding school in New Mexico. The image was a cold
nightscape of barren rock formations and vast tracts of
sand—so different from the forestlands where he had
grown up. Scrawled upon the back of the picture, a brief
note had voiced the only complaint of a teenage boy in
an alien world far from home: "The judge has sent me to
live on the moon."

Alone again, Evelyn resumed her vigilance over that
cold ball of light hanging in the sky. She had never read
a human face into its surface features, but always saw it
for what it was, a sterile and distant chunk of rock. And
now, because she refused to recognize the grown man
who had come to sit with her tonight, she fell back into
her old ritual of the lunar cycles. Her eyes turned upward
as she spoke softly, bidding good night to the boy on the
moon.

Thirteen

Though he was off to a late start this morning, Ferris Monty drove his yellow Rolls-Royce into town at the leisurely pace of a longtime Coventry resident. He had sacrificed a night's sleep to review his abandoned notes and false starts, reams of words written many years ago. Fortunately, all the landmarks and most of the people were right where he had left them on the pages of his unfinished opus.

He parked at the curb in front of the public library, a one-room brick building made ludicrous by grand marble pillars and a lintel that overshot the roof. A hundred years ago, when Coventry's only employer had been the sawmill, this building had been the lofty donation—call it a joke—of the town founder, a man who believed that only a handful of his workers could read or have need of more than a few books.

Ferris stepped out of the car, and a small woman with mouse-brown hair caught his eye. She stood on the sidewalk and gaped at him as he turned onto the flagstone path that led to the door. Her hands flew up, fingers fluttering a warning. Ah, but now her eyes turned toward a front window, perhaps in fear of a watcher, for she thought better of reminding him that no one in Coventry ever goes to the library. He envisioned twitching whiskers when she scurried away, as mice will do when they are in the neighborhood of a cat—or worse.

Oh, definitely worse.

The library door opened onto a room filled with rows of bookshelves, and he walked into a wall of stink. Although the librarian was nowhere to be seen, he knew she was here. The smelly epicenter could only be Mavis Hardy. Her body odor was formidable, even mythic; it was said to have permeated the pages of every book. However, he could hardly neglect to interview a town icon as important as a murderess at large.

He rounded the first bookcase, getting closer—the stink was stronger now—and he resisted the urge to cover his nostrils with a handkerchief. According to legend, Mrs. Hardy took her annual bath on the eve of the birthday ball, but she had not attended one for twenty years. Apparently, the attendant bathing had been allowed to slide.

Ferris Monty still had hopes of going to this year's ball, though the gala's gatekeeper might pose a problem. Well, certainly there would be some fancy tap-dancing around his most recent bad behavior. Addison Winston might wonder why his chosen envoy to the media had sicked reporters on Oren Hobbs—a clear conflict with the lawyer's intentions. But betrayal was mere technicality to an author turned zealot, a born-again writer of real literature. Ferris saw himself as an aging come-back kid and a ruthless Cinderella; he would find a way to go to the ball.

Turning down a narrow aisle of books, he walked slowly, creeping actually, following the sound of heavy breathing. The aisle ended at the center of the room, an open area of tables, chairs and a hulk of flesh wearing a cotton housedress. Ah, there she was in all her smelly unwashed glory, graying brown hair hanging to her shoulders in oily strings. She grunted and glistened with sweat.

What a prize.

He had been told that, though she went barefoot winter and summer, she had always been properly shod for the early birthday balls. It was doubtful that she had worn anything as delicate as high heels. Her well-muscled legs had the girth of tree trunks.

Oh, and now she was turning his way.

His visit to the library—perhaps any visitor at all— must come as a shock. One clue was the woman's slackening jaw. He had never been so close to her, and now he was near enough to count the missing teeth by the gaps in her open mouth—but he had to look up to do it. Mavis Hardy's size was impressive, more muscle than fat, as evidenced by the barbells tightly gripped in her hands.

There were other items of bodybuilding equipment on the floor behind her. This argued against the rumor that she was dying, and it gave credence to a theory, oft repeated by the locals, that she could not be killed except by supernatural means.

"Mrs. Hardy, I wonder if I could speak to you?"

"You just did." She held the barbells high above her head.

Did she have it in mind to smash him out of existence? Legs gone to limp noodles, he felt the sudden need for support and sat down at the reader's table. "My name is Ferris Monty."

"I know who you are." The librarian remained standing, lowering and lifting her weights as she counted aloud. "*Sixteen.* You don't look like the author photos on your book jackets—that true-crime trash. *Seventeen.* I know they airbrushed those droopy eyes of yours. *Eighteen.* But damned if I can figure out how they made you look smarter."

He pulled out his bifocals and donned them. "Is that better?"

"*Nineteen.* Somewhat." On the count of twenty, she set the weights on the floor, then pulled out a chair and sat down next to him, edging closer until he could smell the rot from her mouth of broken and lost teeth.

"I'd like to ask you about Oren Hobbs and his brother, Joshua." On best behavior today—and fearful—Ferris smiled, as if he were dealing with a normal person, a sane person.

The extreme order of military life had been discarded in a single day. The bedroom floor was strewn with cast-off clothes and cowboy boots. Oren's habit of early rising had also been lost. When he stepped out of the shower, it was almost noon—if he could believe the windup alarm clock on his bedside table—the same old clock.

He glanced at Hannah's homecoming gift, the eight-by-ten portrait of two boys in a silver frame, fruit of the purloined roll of film that had been hidden away in his brother's sock drawer. Even if Hannah had not mentioned taking that last roll to the drugstore for development, he would have known that Josh had not printed this picture. Missing was the magic that his brother performed in the attic darkroom. The quality of this print was no match for the ones on the wall.

And where were the other photographs from that last roll of film?

Dressed in the bathrobe he had worn as a teenager, Oren padded barefoot down the hall and entered his brother's bedroom. The last time he was in here, the coffin had been a distraction. Now that it was gone, the room had a timeless quality, and he was in danger of falling into the judge's state of mind—a scary place where old dogs and young boys never died.

The tripod leaned against the wall where Josh had left it on the last day of his life. A pair of sneakers lay on the floor, so casually arranged, as if the boy had just changed into his hiking boots for a walk in the woods. Oren picked up a jacket that had been draped on the back of a chair twenty years ago. He held it to his breast as he lay down upon his brother's bed and lost an hour there, staring at the ceiling.

When he remembered his purpose for coming here—the one odd feature in the bedroom of a teenage boy—he rose from the bed and opened Josh's closet to a familiar mess. The clothes on hangers were jammed together, and the shelf above was packed with magazines, a broken bicycle pump and stacks of cigar boxes favored for catching the smaller items of junk. The jumble seemed about to fall on Oren's head at any second. But the floor of that chaotic space had always been sparsely covered, so orderly. As a teenager, he had never found that odd—and now he did.

He knelt down before the closet and took out two pairs of shoes to expose tool marks on the floorboards. He reached up to pull down a coat hanger and used the stiff wire as a pry bar. The boards did not lift easily. It was a few minutes' work to remove them. He reached into Josh's hidey-hole and brought out a thick photograph album.

Private pictures. People's secrets?

Flipping through the pages, he scanned the images and then stopped to linger over one. In this picture, Oren saw himself as a sixteen-year-old boy out walking with the judge on a winter day. Cowboy boots had given him an inch of height, but he had not yet reached the old man's stature. Here, he had been caught in the act of dropping back a step to check out his father's long ponytail, probably measuring it. Though Oren's hair was a good six inches shorter, the judge's hairline had begun to recede in those days, and a bald spot was visible at the back of his head. Oren was smiling in this picture, assured that this was one contest he could not lose.

Come the summer he turned seventeen, Oren was sent away, and his hair was cut off with a razor.

He closed the album.

Why had Josh hidden a roll of film in a sock drawer? Why not stash it with this secret cache in the closet?

Not enough time.

Josh had worn a watch that day; he had been in a hurry to start out for the woods.

The photographs from that last roll were now of greater interest than any film that might be recovered with the rest of his brother's bones.

He lowered the album back into the hole. The boards were replaced, and the closet floor was restored to the way he had found it. Oren returned to his own room to find a clean change of clothes laid out on the bed. Just like old times.

Thank you, Hannah.

But where were the blue jeans he had worn yesterday? He ransacked all the drawers, knowing all the while that this was futile. By now, his dirty clothes had certainly made their way to the laundry room in the basement. Hopping on one foot, then the other, he pulled on the clean pair of jeans as he moved down the hallway. Pants zipped up, he descended the stairs three at a time, calling out, "Hannah!"

"Down here," said a distant voice.

He opened the cellar door and rushed down the cold cement steps to find the housekeeper pulling a load of wash from the dryer.

No, no, no!

He bent over her wicker basket and found his jeans still warm from the dryer. He searched the watch pocket for the fur of a yellow dog, his only tie to the grave robber who had left the jawbone on the porch. And, of course, it was gone.

He sat down on the floor and covered his eyes with one hand. Of all the screwups he had ever—

"You should have more faith." The housekeeper squatted down beside him. She looked around at the cluttered shelves, an old trunk and storage boxes that had not yet found their way to the attic. "Oh, the memories in this cellar. Do you recall that little tree frog you crammed into your pocket when you were six years old?" She pointed to the small window in the door of the washing machine. "I'll never forget him—plastered to the glass, spinning round and round. That frog looked *so* surprised." She patted Oren's hand. "I guess that was the only time I didn't go through your jeans before I washed them." She reached into a deep dress pocket and produced some loose change, a few ticket stubs from his travels—and the fur of a yellow dog.

"You're a goddess." He took the ball of fur from her hand and held it up to the light of a basement window. "Do you know anybody who owns a dog this color? I found this on the porch steps right after the—"

"That dog doesn't belong to anybody." She returned to the dryer to load in a fresh batch of wet laundry. "He's a stray. At night, I leave him scraps down by the garden shed."

Now he made sense of the barking on the night when the jawbone was left on the porch. "That stray is your burglar alarm?"

She nodded. "Beats wiring up the house. The judge would never let me do that."

"I'm sure there won't be any more late-night bone deliveries. So I guess you can stop feeding the stray."

"Oh, the dog has other uses. One day the judge will invite that mutt into the house. And I'll be dragging Horatio's stuffed carcass out the back door for a proper burial."

"Good plan." Oren stared at the useless ball of fur in his hand. "I love the photograph you gave me. Did I thank you for it?"

This made her smile.

He carried her laundry basket to the folding table. "I remember the morning Josh took that shot." He watched for signs that Hannah knew it was the day that Josh went missing, but there was nothing in her manner to give this away. "When you had the film developed, the drugstore gave you a pack of standard-size prints, right? Where are they now?"

"Oh, who knows? That was a long time ago. It's not like you're asking me what I did with the morning news-paper."

And now he knew she was hiding something, for Hannah's memory was flawless, archiving even the stunned face of a frog drowned in a washing machine over thirty years ago. "Could those pictures be in the attic?"

"In Josh's darkroom? No, too risky. The judge is always up there looking through old pictures. He would've pitched a fit if he knew I had that last roll developed. I told you he didn't want Josh's things disturbed."

And it was unlike Hannah to repeat herself. She was stalling for time. He could almost see the bright work going on behind her eyes as she hunted for the right response.

And now she had it.

"I remember this much," she said. "I looked over the pictures before I left the drugstore. That shot of you two boys was the only one I cared about. I ordered the enlargement right then and there. So I would've left the negatives with the druggist. Maybe I left the whole envelope, negatives and prints, too. It's possible I never got them back."

"Do you remember anything about the other pictures?"

She shook her head. "Sorry, Oren. It was so long ago."

"Then you didn't see anything worth showing to William Swahn?"

She jerked her head to one side, her eyes wary and searching the stairs. Satisfied that they were alone, she turned back to him. Her voice was low, almost a whisper. "The judge doesn't need to know about my business with Mr. Swahn."

"You've known this guy for a long time, but you call him '*mister*'? That's not like you. And Swahn calls you Miss Rice. He might be the only one in town to use your last name since I was three."

"So what else did he—"

"I know you gave Swahn all of Josh's negatives when you asked him to find me an alibi witness."

"And he did."

"He overdid it." Oren held up two fingers.

"*Two* witnesses?" Here she paused, sensing that he was not buying her pretense of surprise. She stuffed her hands into the pockets of her housedress, Hannah's version of a pout. "I think Mr. Swahn might have mentioned that."

"And he told you their names."

"No, he only told me that two women went to the sheriff with two different stories. Well, I could see where that might be worse than no alibi at all. Then Mr. Swahn called me one day and said everything worked out all right. One of those alibis held up."

"Was Swahn still working on my alibi when you developed Josh's last roll?"

"Oren Hobbs." Her tone carried the threat of no dessert and no television tonight. "Let it be." And now she must have remembered that she could not even stop his allowance anymore. Both hands flew up in surrender, but then she turned her face to the cellar window. "The judge is home."

After a few moments, he heard the sound of tires on the gravel driveway.

Hannah walked to the foot of the stairs, looking up,

listening for the front door. She turned to him, silently asking if they could end this now.

No, not quite yet.

The librarian's madness appeared to have an off-switch.

The barbells sat on the floor, and Mavis Hardy sat in a chair, her hands folded in a ladylike fashion, as she answered a question for Ferris Monty. "Both of the Hobbs boys were readers, but the judge had a bigger library than this one. I think they came here because their father had better taste in literature—no science fiction or horror genre."

Ferris noticed that her hands were clenched tightly, as if holding on to something precious, or merely holding on. After scribbling a line of shorthand in his notebook, he lowered his reading glasses. "Did the boys get along well?"

"They did. Oren had a few years on his brother, but that didn't matter. In some ways, Josh was a hundred years older. That little boy *listened* to people like he really cared about what was going on in their lives. I miss that child. I didn't see much of him after he turned ten—except from a distance . . . the way I see everyone now."

And this must be the marker for the year when life had soured for the librarian.

There was no need to consult his old notes. By the time Joshua Hobbs turned ten years old, Mavis Hardy had evolved into the monster of the public library. Ferris remembered that year very clearly. The librarian was the one who had drawn him to Coventry in hopes of covering a sensational murder trial. Her homicide case had ended too soon and too softly, a few words spoken in open court for the public record and a quiet dismissal of charges.

And five years later, she had not figured as a suspect when a young boy disappeared.

Now that Ferris had become accustomed to her body odor, he could at least endure it, and he leaned toward her in the manner of inviting a confidence. "When Josh first disappeared, did you think he was a runaway—or did you suspect foul play?"

As if she were a perfectly rational person who had never done a murder of her own, Mavis Hardy paused to give this some thought. "Well, that's what kids do in this town. They run off as soon as they're able—usually older kids right out of high school. They just can't leave Coventry fast enough. My own son ran off. But Josh Hobbs was barely fifteen—way too young. No, I don't suppose I ever saw him as a runaway."

"So other teenagers have disappeared?"

"A few, but it's not like they dropped off the face of the earth. They packed bags. Josh didn't. And most kids drift back to town after a while, like my son, Dave—he came back."

"I heard a rumor that there was more than one set of bones found yesterday. Can you think of anyone else who might have gone missing around the same time?"

"Mr. Monty, you've lived here for a good long while." She pointed to the window with a view of the foothills.

"You *know* what we've got out there in the woods—people nobody wants to keep track of. I imagine they disappear all the time, and who'd ever know?"

"You think one of those people could've murdered Josh? Maybe someone with a criminal background?"

"Not likely," she said. "Not one of *our* criminals. In my experience, outlaws make the best citizens. They pay their bills on time—in cash—and they never get speeding tickets."

Her eyes took on a crafty look as she rose from her chair. Ferris feared that the interlude of sanity might be drawing to a close.

She loomed over him. "You think I've got an inside track? I know what they say about me around town. Parents tell their children to behave or they'll be sent to the library, and I bet those kids don't sleep well at night. Do I figure into your nightmares, too, Mr. Monty?" She leaned down and placed both hands flat on the table. "If you've got a question to ask—*ask*."

"You haven't attended a birthday ball since the Hobbs boy disappeared." He looked up at her with expectation.

The librarian coughed up a mouthful of mucus and let it fly. So good was her aim that she hit one lens of Ferris's spectacles on the first try. He rose from his chair and fled the library.

Oren stood beside Hannah at the laundry table in the cellar. He rolled a pair of socks and added them to the pile, having already amazed her with his skill in smoothly folding T-shirts. "So you still go to the library."

"At least once a week. Mavis taught me how to work the computer, and sometimes she special-orders books from other libraries."

"Then you weren't kidding yesterday—when you told Dave you could get his mother over here to ream him out."

"Oh, I wouldn't have done that. I just wanted Dave to drop that damn shovel. You know how the judge feels about his flower garden."

"So nothing's changed. Mrs. Hardy still—"

"Everything has changed," said the judge from the top of the basement staircase. He walked briskly down the steps and joined them at the folding table. One hand ran back over his bald scalp in a loving memory of a time when he had hair.

Back in the days of the old man's long ponytail, most people would have taken him for an aging hippie. But Oren knew the judge's favorite poet was Ferlinghetti, and there was more evidence to date his father back to the Beatnik generation—medals of the Korean War stored in the pacifist's attic. The judge must sometimes wonder if joining the Army had been Oren's idea of teenage revolt—or revenge. The question would never be asked by this quintessential gentleman.

The judge picked through a pile of unmatched socks. "So what's this about Mavis Hardy? You think the press is going to dredge up that old business again?"

Oren rolled another pair. "You mean her *murder* case?"

The judge did not rise to this old bait. He placidly hunted the sock pile for a match to the one he held in his hand.

"*Premeditated* murder." Oren smiled.

And the judge countered with, "Justifiable homicide."

Murder.

Oren leaned closer to his father. "How long do you think it took Mrs. Hardy to lay her plans? I'd say a year at least."

The judge turned his full attention on a hole found in the toe of one sock. "I came down here to tell you that your trunk arrived. I had the deliveryman haul it up to your room. Did you pack a good suit in there?"

"Yes, sir. I packed everything I own."

"Good. Sarah Winston's birthday ball is only a few days away."

"I'm not going," said Oren. And this should have ended the conversation by the old man's own rules of debate. His father would never resort to the obvious question. It would diminish the twin arts of conversation and manners to ask, *Why not?*

"Why not?" Hannah stepped between them as the judge's foil. "What is it with you and Isabelle Winston? The pharmacist told me that girl kicked you all the way down the sidewalk yesterday. Now why would she do that?"

Oren shrugged to tell her that he didn't know and "she didn't say."

Why ruin a perfectly good rumor by trimming it back to a single act of minor violence? In the next telling of this story, it was predictable that Isabelle would have shot him once and stabbed him twice.

Collecting gossip was sometimes a trial of endurance. Ferris Monty pretended to take notes on the postmaster's lecture, which—if there was a God in heaven—was winding to a close.

"I bought these three pictures from Josh and framed them with my own money—not one dime from the taxpayers' pockets," said Jim Web. "I intend to leave them behind when I retire next year. My gift to the town."

Ferris nodded absently as he studied Joshua Hobbs's triptych. The boy had taken shots of postal patrons in a waiting line. The people appeared to move as the viewer's eye made the jump from one frame to the next. He stepped closer, the better to study the primary subject, the one at the center who posed with a silver-handled cane. Though Ferris had seen this person around town, he had only registered the scar and a peculiar limp in memory. But Joshua had focused upon the undamaged, unmemorable side of the man, and that was curious. A view of the wrack-and-ruin side would have been a more worthy angle.

Pointing to this image, he said, "I don't recall this

man's name. He's lived in Coventry for a long time, hasn't he?"

"Yeah, but not as long as I have. I started as a clerk thirty-five years ago," said the postmaster in the mistaken belief that his interviewer might care. "That's Mr. Swahn. I can't say I actually *know* him. He's a hermit. Hasn't been in here since we started rural delivery, but he does show up for all the birthday balls. Will I see you at the Winston lodge this year?"

"I think you might."

The author followed the postmaster into a small office, where he endured Web's version of high tea: a fig bar and a cup of Earl Grey dosed with honey. The man looked out a window that faced the narrow street and watched cars crawl by. Ferris imagined this as the prime activity of Jim Web's day—watching. "So you knew Oren Hobbs as a boy."

"Oh, yeah. And by nine o'clock yesterday morning I knew he'd come back to town. That's a perk of the job. I get the gossip earlier than most."

Ah, gold.

"I understand that Oren Hobbs had a thing for older women—married women."

"Is that what you heard?" Postmaster Web pretended to find a spot of dirt on one lens of his perfectly clean eyeglasses, and he polished it with a tissue. For the first time in the past half hour, the man seemed oddly reticent to gossip. Spectacles restored to the bridge of his nose, he smiled at his visitor. "If there's any truth to that rumor, I'd have to say it was the other way around. Older women had a thing for Oren. Understandable. You've seen him?"

"Yes, a very handsome young man."

"When he was a teenager, my wife described him as beautiful—and inadvertently charming. Or did she say *accidentally*? Something about his smile. No, I'm wrong. She said it was his eyes. When my wife spoke to Oren, he made her feel like the center of the universe. She said I didn't come off well by comparison."

"So it wouldn't surprise your wife . . . those rumors of an accidentally charming boy *accidentally* falling into strange beds when school was out—but the husbands were still at work."

"I can't say what's true or not." Jim Web turned to the window. "All I ever saw with my own eyes was a bad case of twisted puppy love."

Ferris leaned forward. "You mean the Winston girl?" This was another bit of Coventry lore that he had collected two decades ago, just the snatch of a story that had no beginning and no end.

The postmaster removed his bifocals and turned to the window, his watery eyes in soft focus, looking at some middle ground of memory. "Isabelle and Oren, they made me feel young again at least three times a week. You see, the judge's boys used to switch off on picking up the mail. This was before we had rural delivery. Back then, I knew the faces of everyone in this town, even the ones that lived out in the woods. Everybody picked up their mail at the post office—except for Mrs. Underwood, the old lady who used to live in Mr. Swahn's house. The boys would pick up her mail, too—not that there was much.

"Anyway, it's not like Josh and Oren had a schedule. I never knew which boy it would be or when he'd show up. But little Belle Winston always knew, and she always beat Oren Hobbs into town. Now this only happened in the summer. The rest of the year she went to a boarding school in the East. Belle was about eleven, I'd say. On fine summer days, she'd come flying into town, little legs churning up dust, long hair flying. She'd run in the door and ask for her mail like it was a matter of life or death—and couldn't my clerk understand that speed was everything to her? And then she'd just stand by the lobby window, watching the street. Sometimes ten, fifteen minutes would go by. Such a patient little girl."

"She was waiting for Oren Hobbs."

The postmaster nodded, never taking his eyes from the window. "The minute she saw him coming, she'd *slowly* open the front door like she had all the time in the world." Smiling, he tapped the window glass, as though he might be watching this story play out. "She'd saunter down the stairs and pass him on the sidewalk out there—like she didn't notice that boy was alive."

"Did Oren notice her?"

"You bet. The second he saw Belle, the boy's eyes were glued to the sidewalk, or sometimes he'd find something fascinating to look at on the other side of the street—until she passed him by. The boy always took a deep breath before he turned around to watch her walk away. This went on all summer long for years and years. It was the greatest little love affair that almost happened."

Done with old memories, the postmaster donned his glasses again, prepared to see the world as it was today. "You can hear rumors anywhere—and from people who tell them better than me." He jerked one thumb back at the windowpane. "But that's the only secret Oren Hobbs ever had that I ever knew about—me and the rest of the town."

When Ferris Monty turned to the window, it was easy enough to pick out the distinctive copper shingles of the tower atop the Winston lodge. No doubt young Isabelle Winston had used that high ground to keep track of the boy she fancied. He wondered if that habit had lasted into her teenage years. Had she been spying on Oren Hobbs the last time the boy walked into the woods with his little brother?

If Sarah Winston had not been a devoted follower of the birder's life, she might have had a career as an artist; this was the opinion of ornithologist Isabelle Winston. The renderings in her mother's journals were beautiful. Exotic birds with brilliant plumage did not exist in this part of the world, and yet there they were, singing and dancing with common sparrows and crows. These were the guests of the annual birthday ball.

It was a temptation to hurry through these books, but something important might be missed. Invisible spiders had not crept up on her mother in a single day. That kind of damage took years, but Isabelle examined every page with the hope of finding a signal event. She looked up from her reading to glance at the deck beyond the glass wall and the telescopes positioned to see the world from here, if the world be Coventry. Her mother's journals never hinted at life elsewhere.

"Let's see," she whispered to her sleeping mother, who had passed out after a midday binge. "When did it all start to go wrong?"

She climbed the tall ladder on wheels and, by one hand, rolled it along the high circular shelf. The dates on the book spines told her she was approaching the largest event in her own reckoning, the vanishing of Joshua Hobbs. She scanned the labels of months and years, then pulled down a volume out of order, a sneak preview of things to come, and she opened it to leaf through the pages. This journal only depicted birds of prey. One stood out from the rest. Isabelle's first thought was borrowed from an old fairy tale—and twisted a bit.

What strange, crazy eyes you have—what long teeth.

On these pages, Coventry had lost its charm and become a nightmare state where monsters roamed, walking birds with fangs and curled knives for talons.

Fourteen

"That was Ad Winston on the phone." Hannah's wooden clogs clattered down the cellar stairs. "He says the reporters won't be bothering us today. They're all joining up with the sheriff's search party."

Approaching the table, she seemed pleased to find her last batch of laundry folded and neatly stacked by Oren and the judge. Smiling, she inspected their work. "From the kitchen window, I could see bits and pieces of a long line of trucks and cars moving uphill through the trees."

The housekeeper frowned at three stray socks with no mates, and Oren waited for the old magic that had made him Hannah's laundry slave when he was six years old. As she rolled the orphan socks, each one became a pair, and he never caught her pulling the mates from her pockets.

"I wonder what Cable uses for brains." She glanced at

the cellar window. "He should've waited till morning. Not enough daylight left to search a whole mountain."

No problem. Oren knew it would be a short outing for all concerned, no bivouac, no campfires under the stars. The searchers would stumble upon the rest of his brother's bones long before dark.

William Swahn gripped his cane tighter. Some days, any weight on his twisted leg would cause him pain, and he had pills for that, but medication fogged his mind. He limped across the wide foyer, cursing his mistake in re-connecting the doorbell. Upon opening the center panel, he saw Sarah's redheaded daughter standing on the other side of the iron grille.

"Belle." What a happy and awkward surprise. How would he explain why he had not paid her a visit since her return to Coventry?

"Hello, William."

The door opened wide, and the pretty woman in blue jeans entered the foyer, lifting her face to receive a hello kiss. At their last meeting, she had been sixteen years old and had to stand on her toes to kiss him goodbye.

Stepping back a pace, she said, "So you remembered my name."

Isabelle's rebukes had never been understated.

He led the way into the library. "I remember every woman who ever proposed to me." And now he could see that this occasion had slipped her mind. "You were shorter then, only four years old."

"Olden days." Isabelle settled into an armchair. "Mom's school days. You were the youngest Latin scholar at UCLA."

"No, I majored in criminal justice." He sank down on the couch and laid his cane to one side. "But I did tutor your mother in Latin. That's how we met."

"You were her friend. How could you let her marry Addison?"

He laughed for the first time in ages. "I had nothing to say about it. I was a kid—only ten years older than you were."

"But you were so smart—a damn genius IQ. Mom *listened* to you."

"I was just a geeky little boy—an oddity on a college campus." And Sarah had not listened to him; it had been quite the other way around. She had been his mentor, passing on to him all of her wisdom on the survival of freaks—that woman of freakish beauty. Sarah had been the salvation of a lonely pimple-faced child with a mon-ster-size brain. "Memories can be treacherous, Belle. I think I like yours better than mine."

"You *loved* my mother."

He had worshipped her.

"You moved to Coventry so you could be close to her."

"No," said William. "That was Addison's idea. He told me this was a good place to hide from the world, a place to lick wounds." However, in fairness to Isabelle's reckoning, he had looked forward to the reunion with Sarah and her little girl, the two people he loved best in all the world. And he had begun to heal in the early years—while Sarah was still at home to him when he came knocking on her door, while she continued to mentor him on the subject of their mutual freakdom. And what an odd pair they had made in those days, Beauty and the limping Beast.

Isabelle's smile was unsettling. "You used to come to the lodge once a week. You were the only friend of Mom's who ever came to dinner. Anything wrong with *that* memory? I know you stopped coming after Josh Hobbs disappeared."

She sat on the edge of the chair cushion, though not perched there, nothing like a bird but something rather more dangerous. How contrary was this quiet bomb exploding slowly. She continued to smile at him, but she did not breathe—she seethed.

Behind him a clock was ticking, ticking.

Isabelle bolted from the chair and yelled, "How *could* you abandon my mother! I *counted* on you!"

The slope owed its gentle incline to an outcrop of bald rock on the south face of the mountain. There might be two hundred people gathered here—if Oren did not count reporters as people. More volunteers were climbing out of vans and trucks parked along the fire road.

Deputies handed out maps while a young forest ranger addressed the crowd. The bullhorn was unnecessary, but the ranger was new to this part of the world so high in the air, where sound could carry from one mountaintop to another. He explained the process of a grid search, and the citizens of Coventry listened politely, as if they had not done this before and done it well, finding every lost soul—except for Joshua Hobbs. That boy had been their only failure, though this was not their fault, for he had been hiding from them, dead and buried underground. But today they had returned for him—the rest of him, the bones that had not yet been found. Their mission, said the ranger, was to locate a grave. The nameless stranger buried with the hometown boy was only a rumor to these people.

When the bullhorn was laid down, the crowd split into small groups and followed their section leaders off to different compass points. No search party had ever combed this part of the mountain so close to bald rock, reasoning that no one could be lost in an area between a fire road and a well-worn hiking trail, a high place with a view of the town below.

Cable Babitt nodded to a pair of late arrivals with cameras and microphones, and he handed each of them a map. "Stay with your group, boys. Don't wander off. We haven't got all day to go looking for strays."

Oren Hobbs pointed these two stragglers toward one of the search parties. When they were out of sight, he said to the man beside him, "Waste of manpower, isn't it, Sheriff?"

"You shouldn't be here, son. This place is crawling with reporters, and they all want a piece of you."

"Well, that's disturbing. If reporters can't find me while I'm standing right in front of them, how will they find a hole in the ground?" Oren looked down at his own copy of the map and made a pretense of studying it. "Damn. You forgot to mark the gravesite for them."

The sheriff's smile was strained but game as he let this pass for a joke.

Oren spread the map on the hood of his father's car. This copy still bore the stamp of a university geology department. The perimeter lines for the grid search were drawn in odd shapes and restricted to areas where the soil was rich in iron. "Lucky you just happened to know about these ore deposits."

"The coroner sent the—"

"You knew where to look *before* I reported the bones. I was there—standing in my front yard, when you pointed this site out to Dave." Oren folded his map. "I'll make sure you get credit for that."

The sheriff's smile faltered and died. He walked away, trailing behind a group of volunteers. There were no reporters assigned to this party, only townspeople spread out in a long line and walking abreast, eyes to the ground, looking for signs of disturbance in the earth.

Oren caught up to Cable Babitt. For twenty yards of silence, he watched the older man's face for signs of fear. "Sheriff, I hope you picked the search party that's headed straight for my brother's grave."

"It shouldn't take long to find," said Cable, ignoring the innuendo. "The iron ore is all narrow streaks, real short runs."

The fire road ran parallel to the path of the searchers marching ahead of him, downhill and deeper into the forest. And this was more evidence against the sheriff. In Oren's experience, even the best-concealed graves of murder victims had been found in close proximity to a road. The volunteers walked at arm's length from one another, some crab-walking sideways to avoid fallen trees and boulders.

As if opining on the weather, Oren said, "I know you're the one who left the bones on the judge's porch." And when the sheriff stumbled, then stopped—dead still—Oren added, "You figured that would bring me home—back to your jurisdiction."

"I never suspected you." Cable Babitt looked up at the sky, as if he gave a damn about the gathering clouds. "But your father was always at the top of my list. A few months ago, I found Josh's skull in my garage. It was sitting on the hood of my jeep. I thought the judge might've left it there. Guilt maybe. Who knows?"

"You knew right away it was Josh's skull?"

"Oh, yeah." The sheriff was silent until the last volunteer was no longer visible through the dense foliage. "I could tell by the overlap of the front teeth and a chip in one back molar. I've had the boy's dental records in my files for twenty years. And that skull was in real good shape, no predator marks. Between that and the soil stains—well, the boy didn't bury himself. You know the parents are always at the top of the suspect list. I had to rule out your father—or make a case against him."

"So you took a soil sample from the skull, but you

didn't send it to a state lab." Oren held up the map with its telltale stamp of origin. "You had it analyzed by a university geologist."

The sheriff nodded. "Then I went looking for the rest of the bones on my own time. It took me a while to locate the grave—just a hole in the ground, not very big. And I dug up the—"

"Why would the judge kill Josh?"

"Oren, you know damn well I don't need a motive. Who knows what goes on inside of that old man's head? The day you got home, you must've realized your dad had a few screws loose. The way he keeps that house. My God, he even stuffed Horatio." Cable hurried his steps to catch up to his own group of searchers. He glanced back over one shoulder to see Oren dogging him. "Son, you don't want to be here when they find that hole."

True enough.

In U.S. Army terminology, he had *exploited* too many such holes from Bosnia to Baghdad, gathering evidence of mass murders so cruel that some had encompassed whole villages, and bullets had not been wasted on babies to spare them the slow death of live burial. The graves had always yielded clues to the manner of murder, and he had no desire to be here when his brother's grave was found.

"You want me to go? Fine," said Oren. "Give me the keys to your office and that file cabinet."

Too late.

They ran toward the sound of the scream.

The elderly owner of the dry-goods store, Mrs. Mooney, had found the burial site by falling into it. After treading on a canvas tarp, camouflaged by windblown leaves and dry brush, she had fallen into the narrow trench beneath it. The canvas now covered the old woman as well, almost like a shroud, and possibly that had also been her own thought when she screamed. Her gnarly white hands reached out of the grave to be saved.

Oren dragged out the tarp, then climbed into the hole and gently lifted the old woman up and into the waiting hands of volunteers.

The last time he had stood on the floor of a grave, there had been so many bodies, fifty or more, and a plethora of clues to the cause of death: bullet holes and blindfolds still tied around the skulls, hands bound behind the backs of men and women. Some of the evidence collected for identification had been small toys taken from the skeletal hands of children.

This more barren grave was a greater assault on his mind. He was not ready for this. He stood frozen, looking down at a familiar belt buckle, a shred of his brother's rotted blue jeans and a freshly exposed shard of bone.

Part of a yellow plastic garment jutted out from the loose dirt, and this must belong to the stranger whose remains had been mixed with Josh's in the coffin. Oren and his brother had owned yellow slickers that same color, but both of them were back at the house, still hanging side by side near the kitchen door—exhibits in his father's museum.

The sheriff, to his credit, pretended no surprise at this find, and he called out to one of the deputies, "Get that body bag out of the trunk!"

"Not so fast." Oren kept his voice low as he climbed out of the hole. "You have to call the Justice Department. They'll find you a team for the excavation—specialists."

"No time for that, son." The sheriff slowly turned his head to stare in disbelief. A female volunteer, a tourist in an out-of-state T-shirt, stepped up to the edge of the grave to snap a picture of her summer vacation.

"That's enough of that!" Cable Babitt snatched the disposable-box camera, and a deputy led the souvenir hunter away. "Oren, the reporters must've heard that scream. They'll be here any second. Anyway, there's nothing in that hole but rags and bones."

"And evidence of a grave robber." Oren took the camera from the sheriff's hands and snapped a picture of the hole. He raised his voice for an approaching deputy to hear. "See the ridges on the sides? The shovel had a nick in it. Almost as good as a fingerprint." He snapped another picture of that shallow wall of dirt, and then he heard the sound of running feet. The reporters were coming through the woods, and they were legion.

Almost here.

"You don't want to lose this evidence, do you?" Oren pushed the film forward and snapped a photo of Cable

Babitt. There was no flash, but the sheriff blinked in surprise.

Unwilling to trust this man to follow any protocols, Oren barked orders, military style, to the nearest deputy. This woman never even glanced at Cable for confirmation, but ran to her jeep to radio a request for an evidence officer on the scene. Oren issued another order to fence off the site with crime-scene tape. "And get these people out of here! *Now!* No reporters within thirty feet of the hole!"

He turned his back on his brother's grave and walked uphill toward the turnout where he had parked the judge's car.

"Son? Wait up!"

"I'm in a hurry, Sheriff." Oren kept walking, making the older man run to catch up. "Lots of work to do. I have to check out toolsheds for a nicked shovel. Maybe just *one* shed—yours."

"You're not a cop anymore! You've got no authority to—"

"I think we're past that little technicality." Without breaking stride, Oren glanced over one shoulder to see deputies pushing the reporters back and others stringing yellow tape from tree to tree—all on the authority of a man who was not a cop anymore.

"Son, you only think you know what's going on."

"Well, you tell me when I get something wrong." Whirling around, he faced the startled sheriff. "You tampered with a crime scene." As Oren walked toward him, Cable Babitt stepped backward. "You hand-delivered evidence to the judge, a suspect at the top of your list. You spent six weeks playing ugly little games with my brother's bones. I bet you even know the day when my father bought Josh's coffin . . . and then you left him *more* bones. You son of a bitch."

The sheriff had his back against a tree. "I was working this case. I knew I wouldn't have much time before all hell broke loose."

"When you found Josh's skull in your garage, was it in a bag or a box?"

"A plain old cardboard box. No prints on it. I still got the box. I'll show it to you."

"You'll need to voucher it as evidence."

"Oren, you *know* I can't do that. It's gone too far. What with the search party and all those reporters—"

"Right. And how could you explain leaving all those bones for a grieving old man to find in the dead of night? Why couldn't you work this case the right way?"

"It was a favor to your father." The sheriff almost whined this line, and then he flinched, as if afraid that the younger man was going to strike him.

Oren only folded his arms and kept his silence—waiting.

"I wanted to see what the judge would do when I left that skull on his porch. It was like a test."

Oren saw it as an act of cowardice. The sheriff, a political animal, had not wanted to risk the wrath of an influential man by asking an honest question. "So you stayed to watch. Did my father cry?"

"No, he just sat there on the porch for the longest

time. I hoped he'd call me, but he never did. He didn't do anything. A week went by."

"And you left him more of his son's bones. Did you think he wouldn't *feel* anything?"

"When Josh went missing, your father was a sitting judge, and he had a lot of clout, but he never pushed for results, never once asked me for an update. Not one damn call to my office." The sheriff lifted both hands to stay Oren's next words. "I know he got help from William Swahn. But I figure that man's job ended when he found you an alibi."

"The soil analysis led you to an open grave." Oren rolled one hand, motioning for the older man to continue that thought.

"Yeah. Like I said, the hole was a small one. No sign of digging anywhere near it. Whoever left me that skull knew right where to look and found it on the first try. I had to widen it some to dig up more bones."

"Did you put that sheet of canvas over the grave?"

"Well, yeah. I had to protect my evidence."

Ironical was not the word that Oren was looking for. *Clown* would fit the sheriff better.

"Son, if you *don't* happen to find a nicked shovel at my place, I can hold on to this case and see it through."

"Don't call me *son*." And now—a little payback, a little fear. "You sent my brother home one piece at a time. For six weeks, you drove the judge crazy with those bones. Why should I help you?"

"Because I need more time to clear your father. Just something to think about, Oren. If I lose this case to the state, they'll tear into that old man. He'll be at the top of somebody else's list. You *have* to help me."

"While I'm thinking that over, I need the name of the woman who gave you my second alibi." He watched the sheriff's eyes as the man weighed a nicked shovel against this old bit of evidence.

Cable Babitt shrugged. And now it was obvious that it had never occurred to this man that one of the false alibis could have been made by a witness to a murder—or a killer.

"I suppose it hardly matters now," said the sheriff. "Nobody in this town would've believed her. I wish she'd never come in. I had Evelyn's story to clear you. But two alibis, well, that just—"

"Alibis you said you never wrote down, statements never signed. You've got *nothing*. Now you can explain that *and* the shovel to the reporters . . . or you can give me a name. Who was my second alibi?"

After being turned away from the gravesite, Ferris Monty was outraged. His bile spilleth over with indignation, and he poured it into the telephone. The California Bureau of Investigation was remarkably nonchalant about homicides north of Sacramento. However, they did have a CBI agent billeted in Saulburg on special assignment.

Ferris drove to the county seat, where he marched into the local headquarters of the Highway Patrol and demanded to speak with Special Agent Polk.

Following a wait of thirty minutes—another outrage—he laid out his case in the office temporarily assigned to the CBI agent. "Oren Hobbs was giving the orders," said Ferris. "I *heard* him. You *know* this isn't right. He's a civilian for God's sake. Why would the sheriff let him take charge like that? And another thing—if that grave is on state land, it's *your* jurisdiction."

Sally—call me Sally—Polk was years younger than Ferris, and yet this investigator reminded him of his mother, though he could not say why. Perhaps it was the rounded maternal shape, the gray in her hair—the plate of warm cookies on the desk.

"Sweetheart, is your tea too hot?" she wanted to know.

It was peppermint tea. Every article ever written about him had mentioned his love of this variety. He would swear this was even his brand.

How preposterous.

He had imagined this scene in advance of his arrival, and nowhere in that scenario did a cop call him sweetheart like she really meant it, and there was no damned tea or cookies. Adding to his disappointment, the atmosphere of Polk's office was all wrong, and it hardly seemed like a temporary accommodation for the visiting CBI agent. Cheery potted plants abounded in this sunlit room. The photographs of relatives were not discreetly placed on the desk. Oh, no. Her devotion to family was advertised on every wall. He had envisioned this meeting with a savvy, hardened detective, a man who would hang on every word of Ferris's theory. Reality was a dumpy hausfrau in a flowered sack that passed for a dress, a woman with a limited attention span, so easily distracted by any small plant that needed watering.

He raised his voice. "Why was Oren running that crime scene when he was always the prime suspect—the *only* suspect?"

The woman clearly did not care. Her back was turned to him as she stood before the window with a view of the parking lot. "So that's the famous yellow Rolls-Royce. Was it really owned by Al Capone?"

It was all too apparent that he would have to lead this fool woman by the hand. "Oren was the last one to see Joshua alive. I know that for a fact. I've interviewed a lot of people in Coventry. Of course that was twenty years ago."

"When you were writing a book? Isn't that what you said?" She left the window to stand by his chair. "A book about murder in a small town, I suppose." Not waiting for a response, she pressed on. "Well, how prescient. Until recently, Joshua Hobbs was only a missing person. But all those years ago, you decided that he'd been murdered." She placed one soft hand on his shoulder. "That's odd. I mean the boy might just as well have died in a fall out in the woods."

Now he had her attention.

"I never said my book was about murder. I said it was about a tragedy in a small town. The effect it had on the—"

"But that's not your style, is it, dear? You write the gossip behind the headline news, and I think you're damned good at it. I make a point of reading your column. Call me a fan."

"Thank you, but I wasn't always a gossip columnist. I began my writing career as a serious novelist. Now here's another point to consider. Oren's father was an active judge in those days. And he came from an old California family—lots of money. He could've used his influence to get Oren out of town and beyond the reach of the sheriff."

This information about Henry Hobbs seemed to make no impression on her. She gave him a kindly smile as she sat down behind her desk. "A novelist? You don't say. Well, I thought all your books were nonfiction—true crime. What sort of novels did you write? Murder mysteries?"

Oh, God. He imagined that crime genre must be her idea of literature.

"I only published one novel," he said, teeth on edge. *Stupid* woman. "And it didn't have a single murder." And now he intended to lead her back to the matter at hand, the stuff of his *current* book. "I think it's obvious that Cable Babitt cooperated—no, he *conspired* to send Oren away."

Sally Polk pushed the plate of cookies across the desk. "Joshua Hobbs was only fifteen years old." Her eyes gleamed with genuine interest. "Were there lots of young boys in that old novel of yours?"

Apparently, the sheriff had called ahead to warn his people off. No one took notice of Oren when he entered the private office alone and locked the door behind him. He pulled Cable Babitt's keys from his pocket and opened the credenza to plunder the man's files.

The pile of old case folders made less than an hour's read—a waste of time, mostly rumor and hearsay. William Swahn had done a more thorough job of interviewing the people of Coventry. Oren had already formed an opinion of the sheriff's incompetence, but there must be more evidence than this. Turning back to the credenza, he opened the lower drawer to thumb through unrelated files, looking for something out of place, and he found an unmarked red folder.

Revelation.

The sheriff had lied to him about never committing the old alibi statements to paper.

There had been no formal interview with young Isabelle Winston, perhaps because Cable Babitt was, at core, a kind man. The teenager had submitted her four-page story in longhand, a schoolgirl script of curlicues and rampant sex in the deep woods with Oren Hobbs. Its content was the stuff of romance novels and bad movies. The wording described nothing more than a young girl's lack of experience, and it inadvertently exposed her as a virgin. Twenty years ago, the sheriff had probably slipped this statement into a drawer and smiled as he let her go unpunished for lying.

Oren moved on to alibi number two, a more official document. Evelyn Straub's statement had been transcribed from a taped interview, only one page of words neatly typed. He recognized her signature below the final line.

EVELYN STRAUB: Usually, I screwed the boy at the hotel. There's always an empty room to use. There was only one time at the cabin. I never took anyone there for sex. It was special. But that day, I made an exception.

SHERIFF BABITT: Why? I need something I can believe in, Evelyn.

EVELYN STRAUB: Too many birthdays, Cable. I'd just broken every mirror in that cabin. And then I looked through a back window and saw Oren out there on the trail. I needed him. I just needed him.

SHERIFF BABITT: And what about Josh?

EVELYN STRAUB: He went on ahead. He took that old hiking trail that runs past the cabin.

SHERIFF BABITT: So Josh goes up the trail by himself—believing God knows what—and Oren was fine with that?

EVELYN STRAUB: I think Oren stayed with me that day because I was crying. And my feet were bleeding.

She went on to describe the details of her crime: the carnal knowledge of a boy.

To make her lie more credible, Evelyn had told the truth. Except for the mention of Josh, she had perfectly described a memorable day. He recalled those broken mirrors—her fear—the bloody cost of vanity. He had carried her up the stairs to the bedroom so that the broken shards could not cut her soles anymore. After laying her down on the bed, he had washed her bleeding feet and bound the wounds with strips of old sheets. At the end

of a day in that bed, their names were still Hey Boy and
Mrs. Straub. They had seen the moon sail past the bedroom window, and the light of the sun had awakened
them in the morning. But he had been sixteen years old
on that day, not seventeen. And she had described their
first time together—not the last.

A full year would pass before Josh was lost and Oren
was banished. On long nights in far-off New Mexico, he
had sometimes lain awake and wondered if the mirrors
had gone after her again and left her bleeding.

The next page was another interview. Though the
sheriff had led him to believe otherwise, apparently William Swahn—another man without an alibi—had made a
formal statement.

All of the previous coroners had been funeral directors.
Dr. Martingale, DDS, was the first dentist ever elected to
that county office. At the burial site in the woods, the
new coroner posed for a photo opportunity with the
press, and he smiled broadly, knowing that fame was only
as far away as the dinner hour and the evening news.

The sheriff's evidence officer had no need of a dentist's skills in the excavation of bones, but the reporters
had used Dr. Martingale as a human shield when they
broke through the line of yellow crime-scene tape.

And now, at the request of a cameraman, the coroner
obligingly jumped into the grave. "More bones," he said,
holding one high for the camera.

An angry deputy yelled, "Get the fuck out of there!"

The press corps salivated. Though the obscenity would be bleeped for the television audience, four-letter words were the finest kind. Cameras whirred and still photographs were snapped as the humiliated Dr. Martingale climbed out of the hole.

State troopers arrived en masse to herd reporters back behind the enemy line of the fallen crime-scene tape. The next people to cross the line carried screens and trowels, soft brushes and other tools for unearthing the dead. Reporters identified them as university students and their archaeology professor. The group's official escort was a gray-haired middle-aged woman in a shapeless flowered dress. "Call me Sally," said the agent from the California Bureau of Investigation.

A reporter yelled, "I thought this case belonged to the County Sheriff's Office! Is this a turf war?"

"Oh my, no," said Special Agent Polk in a folksy tone of *Perish the thought*. "We're just here to lend a hand."

The county sheriff was not available for comment. According to his deputies, he had left the scene on a matter of urgent business elsewhere.

Cable Babitt was hard at work in his own backyard. He squatted before the open door of his toolshed, swinging a hammer and bringing it down on the edge of his shovel—*clang*—obliterating a distinctive nick, the mark of a grave robber.

When he was done with this chore, he entered the shed and unlocked a tin cabinet. He stood there for a while, eyes adjusting to the poor light, and then he opened the small metal door to expose a most precious object. It had been protected by dusty plastic and darkness these past twenty years. He unwrapped the knapsack. Marred by only a few spots of old dried blood, it was still as green and bright as the day Josh Hobbs had dropped it in the woods.

Where would he hide it now?

Fifteen

This time, there was no need to knock. The door was opened before Oren reached the top step of the portico. And now the two men stood face-to-face.

"Good afternoon," said William Swahn, a day late in remembering his manners.

In lieu of a greeting, Oren handed him a twenty-year-old statement made to the sheriff. "I don't want to hear any crap about being railroaded by cops, okay? Your interview was typed from a recording." He held up a dusty cassette from that era.

The householder sat down on the marble steps and leaned his cane against a pillar. He held up the sheet of yellowed paper and read the lines:

WILLIAM SWAHN: I can't prove I was home alone that
   day, can I? I can only tell you that I never had any
   interaction with Josh.

SHERIFF BABITT: There's three photographs of you hanging in the Coventry Post Office. The boy took those pictures a year ago.

WILLIAM SWAHN: They're candid shots. I didn't pose for them. I wasn't even aware of those pictures until the postmaster hung them up in the lobby.

SHERIFF BABITT: Then maybe you met Josh at one of Sarah Winston's birthday balls. I know you attended all of them.

WILLIAM SWAHN: And I usually left early.

SHERIFF BABITT: Josh went to all of them, too. Sarah made him her official ball photographer when he was just ten years old. That kid made a nice piece of change selling pictures to the guests. If you bought one of his prints, I'm sure you'd remember a good-looking kid like that.

WILLIAM SWAHN: You mean pedophile candy, don't you? At least a hundred children show up at the lodge every year. As far as I know, Josh never took a picture of me at any of the balls.

SHERIFF BABITT: And that's odd, isn't it? I searched the boy's darkroom. I looked at five years of photographs, all the ones he took at the Winston lodge. There's not one single picture of you at the ball—everyone else in town—but not you. Now I call that strange. You'd think he would've caught you in one of those group shots just by accident. So, naturally, I assumed that you bought those pictures from the boy—maybe the negatives, too. You see why I can't let go of the idea that you met him, talked to him, maybe did a little business with him?

Oren leaned down to point at the margin note in Cable Babitt's handwriting: *I thought the man was going to wet his pants.*

Swahn smiled as he read this line. "I believe that was wishful thinking on the sheriff's part. As I recall, I declined to answer any more questions without my attorney present."

The elevator descended to the parlor floor with its passenger and a storage carton.

"I couldn't defend myself to the sheriff—not without giving up Miss Rice as my client." Swahn opened the cage door and nudged the box out with one foot. "That's all of them. Your housekeeper gave me the contact sheets so I wouldn't have to develop all the negatives. That's why the sheriff never saw them. Babitt only saw the pictures that were made into full-size prints." He rummaged through a drawer and pulled out a magnifying glass. "You'll need this."

Oren opened the cardboard carton and pulled out stacks of glossy paper, each one filled with miniature photographs the size of postage stamps. He had watched his brother make these sheets by laying strips of negatives on the paper, side by side, and then exposing the lot with a burst of light. Circles of a red wax pencil highlighted images chosen for the labor-intensive process of making eight-by-ten prints. "Josh never wanted anyone to see these. Ninety percent of his shots were rejects. I thought he destroyed all the contact sheets."

Swahn sat on the floor beside the box and picked up a sheet of twenty small images. "This one has shots from a birthday ball." He turned it over to show Oren a list of names in Josh's handwriting. "And these are the guests who ordered prints from your brother. You'll find me in some of these group shots, but none of my pictures are circled in red. Josh never made them into full-size prints, and why would he? I never ordered one. For the last time, Mr. Hobbs—until the day he disappeared, I didn't even know your brother was alive."

Oren knew that some of the uncircled shots *had* been printed. But Swahn had not been the customer, though the man figured prominently in a picture marked by the indent of Sarah Winston's fingernail. This was how the lady had chosen the photographs she wanted to buy, and then she and Josh would always argue over her selections.

Once, Oren had accompanied his brother to the frame shop where Mrs. Winston was waiting. Josh had wanted moral support for a fight he could never win. That day could have gone worse. Fortunately, the shop's owner had been in the back room when Josh dived between Horatio and Mrs. Winston, waving his arms, dancing and dodging to block the dog's every avenue of assault on her by drool or tongue licking.

"Hey! Settle down!"

In a happy accident of timing, the dog had chosen that moment to lie down on the floor.

Mrs. Winston was Josh's patron. He would have killed Horatio to save her from a slobbering. On that long-ago morning, Josh had handed her the chosen print, saying, "You know it's not the best one."

"Yes, dear, I know that. But it's the one I want."

That time, Josh had a plan to defeat her. He pulled another envelope from his knapsack and gave it to her.

This second photograph delighted her. "Oh, this is beautiful. Really first-rate."

"It's the best work I've ever done."

"Well, I want this one, too. I'll buy it from you right now."

"No, it's free," he said. "Just give me back the other one."

In the end, Mrs. Winston had beaten him in her very charming way. She had so gracefully worn the boy down and won both photographs—and crushed him. Josh had been forced to bear many compliments on the second picture, the good one, and he was made to accept a check for an outrageous amount, the most he had ever earned for one print. But Josh cared so little for money. He had only wanted to get back the bad photograph—so that he could destroy it.

When the two brothers and the dog left the shop that day, even Horatio had been subdued, sensing Josh's loss.

Oren wished that he had paid more attention to that

transaction in the frame shop. But now he had a second chance. He went through all of the contact sheets for the birthday balls and looked for the indents of Mrs. Winston's fingernails beneath the small images.

He found five, one for each ball, and all of them pictured William Swahn's face in the crowd. One other guest was featured in each of these shots, and now he understood what had eluded his brother for years: These two faces in one photograph were key to the lady's selections.

"Swahn? How well do you know Mavis Hardy?"

It was a rare day when the sheriff visited the County Coroner's Office, a small building between an electronics store and a coffee shop. In a quiet county with a low crime rate, there were few occasions that might call him here. This late afternoon, he had arrived before the appointed hour.

After a long talk with a title company, he knew jurisdiction was dicey. The gravesite was on private land, but Evelyn Straub had suckered the state into a lease of mineral rights that had not panned out. And now he was in a contest for the bones.

His adversary, the CBI agent, drove her black Taurus into the parking space next to his jeep. It was said that a man could be judged by the caliber of his opponents. If this was true, then Cable Babitt was insulted. Special Agent Sally Polk stepped out of her car, and the wind whipped up the hem of a flowery dress. It was the sort of thing she might wear to a meeting of the garden club. Also, he had to wonder what kind of woman was too lazy to dye the gray out of her hair.

And the answer?

He decided that, unlike himself, she was not at all anxious about holding on to her job in the California culture of youth. And that stupid dress was another sign that she must be good. This woman didn't care one whit about her public image. Sally Polk slipped a purse strap over one shoulder and headed for the entrance, indistinguishable from any matronly civilian who had business with the coroner.

The race was on.

Cable was first to the door, but he did not pause to hold it open for her. Hell no. Chivalry was dead, dead, dead. He let the door swing shut behind him to slow her down a pace. He smiled, as if scoring a point that might help him hold on to his double homicide. And he had another game point in his pocket. The county coroner was nothing so grand as a pathologist, and whatever Dr. Martingale imparted to the CBI agent would be useless.

Down the hall they went, the sheriff in his footrace with the state's investigator. The woman, unhurried, lagged farther behind. Cable slowed his steps, aiming to effect a mosey when he entered the refrigerated back room.

A stainless steel table was laid out with two incomplete skeletons, but all the major bones had been accounted for between the mountain grave and Joshua Hobbs's coffin.

An overhanging lamp bathed the remains in light so bright that the stains from the earth were washed away. These people might have been flayed of flesh only this morning.

The CBI agent had caught up to him. Sally Polk stood by his side, offering him a hello nod and a smile. And now the unthinkable happened. Dr. Martingale stood back from the table and introduced him to a celebrity anthropologist from San Francisco, a white-haired man, tall and thin—who needed no introduction to the CBI agent. They seemed to know each other quite well.

Cable recognized the anthropologist from his book covers, having devoured every one, bestsellers all. Dr. Brasco's other name was the Bone Man, a preeminent authority on skeletal remains.

Dr. Martingale gave the sheriff a sheepish smile. "Investigator Polk invited him."

All hope was gone. Cable's case was surely lost. He had not even been consulted about bringing in this expert.

The CBI agent was, at least, not smug when she turned to Dr. Brasco—*her* Dr. Brasco. "I know you've got more bones to recover, tests to run and all that, but what can you tell us up front?"

Us? Her nod included Cable in this company. The sheriff now recalled that a pissing contest was a man's game. The lady was only here to work the case—*her* case, all face-saving gestures of inclusion aside.

Dr. Brasco bent over the table, calling their attention to

one of the skeletons. "This is an adolescent male, approximately five feet seven inches tall. The skull is delicate. It could be taken for a glacial male or a robust female."

The county coroner raised his hand like a schoolboy to catch the CBI agent's eye. "I used to be a dentist. The teeth match up with the Hobbs boy's old X-rays."

The anthropologist nodded in agreement with his colleague. His pointing finger moved on to the second skull. "But you can see the same combination of traits in this woman's skull."

Sally Polk pulled a small notebook from her purse. "That one's definitely female?"

"Yes," said Dr. Brasco, "I sexed the skeletons by the pelvic structure." He moved to the center of the table and looked down at the woman's remains. "This pelvis is wider and rounder—more shallow." He lightly touched the bumpy edges of winglike bones that defined the skeletal hips. "As you can see, the anterior ilia spines are more widely separated."

"Fine." The sheriff raised one hand in the manner of swearing an oath. "I *believe* you. How old was she? How tall?"

"Judging by the fusion of bones, I'd say she was at least twenty-five years old, but she could've been forty at the outside. She was tall for a woman, five-ten. The bones of her face are consistent with Caucasians. I won't rule out mixed race, but I see no obvious markers." Dr. Brasco moved to the head of the table and picked up the woman's lower jawbone. "No wear on the teeth from grinding—not a stressful life. Whatever she did for a living, it was light work, no heavy lifting. That would've shown up in the arms, places where muscle separates from bone with manual labor." He tilted his head to one side and smiled. "Her teeth are just too perfect." He fitted the lower jawbone back into position with the skull. "Excellent alignment. You'll find an orthodontist in her childhood, and I'm sure she had regular cleanings as an adult." He stepped back and regarded the skeleton as a whole. "As for the rest—no signs of malnutrition, no visible markers for disease. She wasn't poor—not a homeless person."

"Good to know." The CBI agent scrawled a line in her notebook. "Nobody notices when the homeless drop out of sight, but there's bound to be a missing-person report on this lady. Can you tell us how these people died?"

"I can't be precise with the Hobbs boy," said the thin man. "Not yet. I'd like some time to differentiate the pre-mortem fractures of a fleshed-out body and the post-mortem cracks of drying bones. Burial does its own damage. In the boy's case, no single trauma stands out as the fatal injury."

Now that the bones had been properly matched up, Cable could see that it must have been the woman's torso resting in Josh's coffin. The boy's rib cage was now properly matched up with the rest of him. Most of the ribs were broken, and so were two of the arm bones.

"The woman's cause of death is more obvious." Dr. Brasco turned her skull in his hands to show them the back, where cracked bits of bone bent inward, and lines of breakage spread out from this indent. "One massive trauma with a blunt instrument. It could've been a rock. That's my best guess. I'd rule out any man-made object with a smooth surface. The woman died quickly. And the boy—not so fast. Some of his fractures are consistent with defensive wounds."

"Well, here's one way to look at it." Sally Polk's pen hovered over a page in her notebook. "I see it as a classic bop-and-drop rape. The perp comes up behind the woman and drops her with the rock. But he goes too far, hits too hard. She's dead. And then . . ." Her eyes turned to the skeleton of the boy. "And then, he turns around—oh, damn—a witness. The boy saw him coming and fought back. That would explain the defensive wounds and all the time it took to kill him."

Dr. Brasco nodded in approval. "Yes, excellent, Sally— if not for the boy's broken fingers." He retrieved a box from the countertop near the table and opened it to show them what appeared to be small reddish sticks caked with dirt. "The excavation team hasn't recovered all of them yet, but I have enough for a working theory." As he laid out the skeletal fingers of Joshua Hobbs, he described a different scene with Josh as the primary target, and the killer as someone with reason to hurt the boy—to drag out his death for hours.

William Swahn shrugged off any connection between himself and Mavis Hardy. "I know her on sight. Everyone does. But we've never spoken." He held the magnifying glass over the small image of the librarian on the contact sheet. "I wouldn't have recognized her in that gown. She cleans up nicely."

"You know the kind of people who go to the ball," said Oren.

"Everybody in town."

"And a lot of Ad Winston's clients—criminals."

"*Celebrity* criminals." Swahn pointed to another small print. "Here's one of you. I'd say you were twelve the year this shot was taken." He handed Oren the magnifying glass and the contact sheet. "It appears that you only had eyes for one little girl that night."

"Isabelle Winston. You knew she was my second alibi. You gave me Evelyn's name, but not hers. Why?"

"I didn't know. . . . My source told me there were two witnesses. Mrs. Straub was the only one I could verify."

"I've only got your word on that."

"Why would I lie?"

"Maybe you thought the Winston family was tied into a homicide."

"Her father was your lawyer, Mr. Hobbs. That's probably how Belle knew you needed an alibi." Swahn held up the contact sheet with tiny images of a boy and a girl at the birthday ball. "Obviously, she had a crush on you."

"She was only eleven years old in that picture." And, evidently, Ad Winston's daughter was close to this man—as close as Josh—on a first-name basis. "When she was sixteen, she had no reason to lie for me."

"Oh, really?" Swahn groped around in a carton he had

brought down yesterday. He plucked out the photograph of two teenagers passing each other by on the sidewalk, each looking the other way. "You and Belle were professional strangers in those days. How old was she when this one was taken? Fourteen? Fifteen?"

Oren opened the red folder and pulled out Isabelle Winston's false statement to the sheriff.

Swahn read it, bemused. "You can't just ask her why she did this, can you? No, you'll never even tell her you read it. What a gentleman." He studied Oren's face, no doubt looking there for signs of hits and misses, and he seemed vaguely disappointed. "I don't think you need to know what happened to Josh."

Encouraged by a flicker of surprise in Oren's eyes, Swahn continued. "It's my impression that this investigation was forced on you. I don't see the passion of a man on a mission. You're in mourning, and it shows. You know what else I see? Guilt. I understand you held the rank of warrant officer. That's not like a job you can apply for, is it? You were hand-selected, the best of the best. It's interesting that you had all this talent in police work, so much experience—and twenty years went by before you investigated your brother's case."

Without a military interest, CID agents were forbidden to participate in civilian investigations, but Oren had a better counterpunch, and now he let it fly. "What about your own case? I know you never saw one shred of evidence against the cops in your old precinct. You just sicked a lawyer on them and grabbed the money."

Swahn only inclined his head a bare inch to acknowledge the truth of this. "Perhaps no one should investigate a case with a personal involvement. No objectivity. Hard, isn't it? Being Josh's avenger *and* his brother."

"He's always Josh to you. You've known Hannah for years, and you call her Miss Rice. The sheriff is a mediocre cop, but I'm sure he picked up on that. He probably thinks you were on a first-name basis with my brother *before* he disappeared."

"Before he *died*," said Swahn, correcting him. "Your housekeeper calls you and Judge Hobbs the *kinderlost*. Did you know that? It's a word she made up for the ones who get left behind when a child dies. She said the widows and orphans get titles of sympathy, but there was nothing like that for you and your father. So she coined a word to fill that awful void."

"Hannah spent a lot of time here, didn't she?"

"Yes, she used to be able to drink me under the table. These days, her tolerance for alcohol is diminishing. Now, when she stops by, it's less embarrassing."

"She's your friend."

"Yes. And now I think you believe that I didn't kill your brother. Like me, you trust Miss Rice's instincts."

"I need to see the last batch of photographs she gave you, the ones she had developed after Josh went missing."

William Swahn's surprise appeared to be genuine. He splayed his empty hands to say that he did not have any such pictures.

———

It was late in the day when the CBI agent entered Cable Babitt's office and introduced him to her pet forensic technician, a small man with a pug nose that made him appear ten years old at first glance. "I want this to be a joint investigation," said Sally—he must call her Sally. "So I'm here to share what we've got so far."

Did he believe this? No. At least she had not come to arrest him for tampering with evidence, but that might well be in his future.

She rested one hand on the shoulder of her companion. "This young man has a few details you might find interesting."

Her *young man* seemed a bit on the sullen side, maybe thinking it was pointless to update him on a crime that no longer belonged to the County Sheriff's Office. If that had not yet been spelled out, the youngster's attitude made it plain enough.

Cable gestured toward the two chairs in front of his desk, and his visitors sat down.

The woman reached out to the forensics man and lightly thumped the back of his head in the way of prompting an unruly child. On this cue, the technician pulled out his notebook and read from the pages with no inflection, clearly bored by this chore. "A yellow raincoat was found in the grave."

"I was there—I *saw* it," said Cable. "Just get on with it, son."

"Some of the woman's arm bones were found in the

sleeves. That might fix the time of death. According to the weather bureau, there was only one shower that day."

"And it didn't last long," said Cable, "only fifteen or twenty minutes."

With another thump from Sally Polk, the younger man ceased to slouch in his chair, and his voice was more respectful when he said, "Yes, sir. *Thank* you. The yellow raincoat was manufactured in New Jersey, but it's not traceable by stores. They were sold all over the country."

"*I* traced it," said Cable, with a satisfied smile, and the younger man looked up from his notes. "Son, we call it a slicker, and so does the company that makes it. I'm sure you've got their name in your little notebook. They *did* sell them all around the country—for a while. A few years after the sales dried up, the stock was sold to a liquidator. That was the year Josh Hobbs disappeared. And the liquidator's best customer for those slickers—more than half the stock—was Mrs. Mooney. She owns the dry-goods store in Coventry. She sells lots of stuff like that to visitors who believe it never rains in California. The victim probably bought it locally, but her description won't fit any missing-person report filed in this county. So I guess we got a dead tourist."

This bit of detection had been a cakewalk, for he had stopped by the dry-goods store where his own yellow slicker had been purchased that same year. And all of his information had come from a five-minute chat with the proprietor. However, the crime-scene tech was clearly impressed.

Sally Polk seemed amused, even pleased, by the sheriff's little victory.

He would never understand women.

"Well, there goes half your problem," she said. "If the female victim's not county, then the state's obliged to track down her identification. Oh, and the tourist angle—good catch. That locks her into a new tourism mandate for the CBI. The governor's just death on anything that might discourage the tourist trade."

Cable closed his eyes. All hope of contesting jurisdiction was shot to hell. He had just handed it to her. She must see him as the kind of fool who should not be allowed to tie his own shoelaces for fear of accidentally hanging himself. He turned his attention back to the technician. "Son, what else you got?"

"The hiking boots suggest that the female victim went into the woods of her own accord. Very good boots—held up real well. They were bought for function not style. No personal effects were found on or near her remains. That could indicate that she knew her assailant. The perpetrator might've disposed of her identification because he knew he'd be the prime suspect."

Cable nodded, though the same could be said for Josh Hobbs. This was padded-out information, probably scripted by Sally Polk. And now he knew that she was not planning to share *everything*—just the obvious things. "What about Josh's camera? I know he had one with him that day."

"Nothing like that was found," said the younger man. "We did a perimeter search and came up dry. But there's still excavation work going on at the gravesite. It might turn up." Once again, he bent over his notebook. "Judging by what's left of the woman's clothing, she was slender. We agree with Dr. Brasco's estimate of five-ten."

"Tall women do stand out in a small town," said Sally Polk. "Does that sound like anyone local?"

"Yes," said Cable, "but not a dead local. And you already know that woman wasn't from around here. So you're working on a theory of mistaken identity, right? Now why is that?"

"No particular reason, Sheriff. Let's say I'm open-minded. Is there anything else I can do for you today? Any more questions?"

Cable shook his head. "No, that does it, thanks."

"You asked about the camera," said Sally Polk, "but not the boy's knapsack. I looked up your old missing-person report, and there it was. Josh Hobbs was carrying a bright green knapsack the last time he was seen alive." She smiled.

If a spider could smile—

Cable flirted with the idea that she had already found Josh's knapsack in its new hiding place behind his garage.

No, that was paranoid.

Before he could recover from this little ambush, she raised one fluttery hand to wave away any necessity for a response. "Who remembers details after twenty years?" Preparing to leave him now, she slipped her purse strap over one shoulder and dropped one more bomb. "How come you never arrested Oren Hobbs?"

"Oren had an alibi for his time that day. A witness puts Josh on a hiking trail by himself."

"I need a copy of that witness statement." Sally Polk said this so sweetly. She might be a neighbor lady come to borrow a cup of flour.

He spun his chair around and reached for the key that Oren had left in the lock of the credenza, but it dangled from the lock of the *lower* drawer—not the one that held the labeled case files. After a full minute of searching, he realized that the unmarked red folder was gone.

"Lose something, Sheriff?" asked the woman behind him—*right* behind him—standing over his bowed back.

He opened the upper drawer and thumbed through the other folders, but the red one was not among them. "Damn reporters." Cable slammed the drawer. "One of them must've taken a file. It was bright red, so that'd be the one to catch his eye." Always best to mix truth with the lies. "Those bastards were all over this place yesterday."

"Reporters." She mulled this over, as if taking him seriously. "I suppose that's . . . possible. I understand Oren Hobbs was in here yesterday. Local boy—I think he'd have a better chance of getting past your people out there in the squad room."

So she had interviewed his deputies and discovered Oren's unescorted office visit. And now Cable called himself six kinds of a fool. He had never seen this moment coming.

Sally Polk was holding her notebook, idly leafing through the pages. "Ferris Monty seems to think that

Oren Hobbs is working this case with you." She looked up from her reading, to smile at him. "I'm sure that must be wrong. You'd never give a civilian—a *suspect*—access to evidence. Let's say Mr. Hobbs gave one of your deputies a story about being told to wait for you in your office. I think that story works well for everybody concerned about covering their tails. Don't you agree? Did you say this was a *red* folder?"

Sixteen

Oren Hobbs was seated at a table for two in the Water Street Café, where he waited for the sheriff and watched boys shooting hoops in the playground across the road.

The large plate-glass window looked out on the schoolhouse. Though built to resemble a hundred-year-old landmark, that building had replaced the abandoned mill-town school when he was in kindergarten. The large gymnasium was underground, a concession to the Coventry Landmark Society, defunct with the demise of its only member, Millard Straub, who could not bear the idea of his hotel being dwarfed by any larger structure.

The wealthier citizens had made it possible for every child in town to obtain a fine education, though teams for football and basketball had to draw their players from a smaller-than-average pool of students, and contests with other towns had always been a countywide joke.

Oren's last day of high school had been capped by a night game with an unexpected twist. The bleachers had rocked with stomping feet, applause and wild cheers from the crowd, though not a single point was scored. No player ever touched a basketball.

Visitors and townspeople had witnessed the spectacle of schoolboys bursting through the locker-room door, Dave Hardy half flying and Oren following on the run. The two had rolled, boy over boy, to the center of the gymnasium. None of the spectators had complained about the fight—they *loved* it—though the blood gushing from Dave's nose had made the damage look more exciting than it was.

When it was over, and the fight fans had gone home happy, the principal's office smelled of blood and sweaty boys. Oren's knuckles were raw that night, and so was Dave Hardy's face. They sat with Josh in chairs lined up before the desk. Without being told, the adults queued up like schoolchildren to stand with their backs to the office wall—all except Hannah, who stood behind Josh's chair.

Oren had a clear memory of Hannah fussing with a bandage that covered his little brother's wound. Josh had looked up at her, eyes pleading, silently begging, *Don't baby me, not here, not now.* With a slow wink of understanding, she had turned away from him to join the judge and Mrs. Hardy at the back of the room, where they kept company with a worried Coach White.

Principal Mars made eye contact with each of his three students in turn. "I don't suppose you kids want to tell me who started the fight." After a few seconds of boy-squirming silence, the man said, "No, of course not. Much too easy. What was I thinking?"

Heavy footsteps clumped forward from the back of the room. Without turning his head, Oren knew it was Mrs. Hardy. He could smell her.

"I bet it's got something to do with Josh's camera." There was a sneer in her voice when she said, "Maybe Josh took a shot of my boy's little pecker."

"That's enough, Mavis." The principal's tone was not angry. He seemed only bone-weary of his dealings with Dave's mother. This was hardly her first visit to his office. He focused his attention on Josh. "You're not on the basketball team. What were you doing in the locker room with a camera?"

"I was taking pictures for the school yearbook. No pecker shots . . . sir." Josh gave the principal his widest, goofiest grin, and this was the boy's best trick, for the man had to smile; he was helpless to do otherwise. Josh was that charming.

"It was my idea," Coach White called out from the back wall. "I brought the boy into the locker room to get a few pregame shots."

The principal beamed at the coach. "So you were there when the fight started. Well, now we're getting somewhere." He pointed to Josh. "This boy was hit from behind. Is that right, Coach?"

"No!" Coach White stepped forward to lay both hands

flat on the desk, insulted and on the offensive. "None of my kids would ever do a thing like that."

"Really? I couldn't help but notice—the bandage is on the *back* of the boy's head."

In a more offhand tone, the coach said, "Josh cut his head on a locker with a broken handle. . . . Dave could've pushed him. . . . It might've been an accident."

The heat of a blush rose in Josh's face. The scalp wound had been his only battle scar—ever—and now all his hopes of shared glory were gone.

Oren had seen his own error in that moment. He had been too quick to go after Dave, never giving Josh a chance to strike one blow for himself. That night, his little brother would have given anything to be the boy standing under the bright lights of the gym with blood on his hands.

"David?" The principal rapped the desk, calling for Dave Hardy's attention. "Is that right? You bounced Josh off a locker, and then his big brother went after you? Now why would you do a thing like that to a smaller boy? What set you off?"

All three maintained their schoolboy's honor code: *Thou shalt not rat on thine enemies.*

Once again, crazy Mrs. Hardy advanced her theory on the camera shot of an undersized penis. "Not very good porno in my estimation."

The departing group of boys and adults were gathered in the corridor, all but Dave's mother, when they heard the principal yell, "Mavis, sit your ass down in that chair!" And the office door was slammed shut.

The judge herded his two boys toward the stairwell, and Oren turned back to see their housekeeper reach out to the enemy and lightly squeeze Dave Hardy's arm. He suspected that she was offering comfort. Whatever she said to him was too low to be heard from any distance.

Outside in the parking lot, his father was heading toward the car, keys jingling in his hand. Oren hung back to wait for Hannah. When she appeared on the schoolhouse steps, he faced her down, arms folded in quiet resolve. "I'm done with Dave Hardy. I don't care what the judge says."

Josh tried vain hand signals to tell his brother that the judge was coming up behind him on cat's feet. Both boys hated those crepe-soled sandals, though they had agreed that the old man's long ponytail was kind of cool.

"It's over," Oren said to Hannah, oblivious to his brother's sign language. "I'm not asking Dave home to dinner one more time."

"Yes, you will." The judge smiled, so pleased to see his firstborn spin around so quick. *Gotcha*. With the waving arms of a goose tender, he shooed his family into the waiting Mercedes.

Purchased that very day, its interior had the wonderful new-car smell of rich leather. Oren opened the rear door and inhaled deeply. And then he was told that, because of the fight, he would not be allowed to drive it for one solid month. Oren slumped low in the backseat, and Josh slumped in sympathy.

They rode in silence for a mile of dark road before

pulling into the driveway. Horatio came bounding toward them, barking and slobbering, his jaw hanging open in a dog's idea of hysterical laughter. Up on his hind legs, dancing in the headlights, he was so excited to see them—so eager to get at them. He had never grasped the fact that the car could not bring his family all the way home until he got out of the way. Fortunately, the dog was easily distracted. Hannah fished about in her purse for a plastic bag where she kept one of Horatio's soggy, smelly toys. Tossing a toy into the woods sometimes worked, sometimes not.

The dog was deliberating.

The judge used the time to reiterate that Oren certainly *would* invite David Hardy home to dinner on the following night. "That boy has gone to live in hell, and it's no fault of his. No wonder he acts out from time to time. So, once a week, we *will* reach into the pit and pull David out for a good meal in a sane house. That boy is your good deed."

"You mean like the old lady on Paulson Lane," said Oren, reminding the judge of another good deed done under duress. "She *died*."

"Nonetheless," said the judge. "This is how we care for one another."

That night, Oren had wondered what the old man's next project would be—after Dave Hardy died.

Days later, Josh was gone. And for months of mornings after that, Oren had awakened in shock, as if he had suddenly discovered that he was missing an arm or a leg.

Twenty years later, almost to the day, Sheriff Babitt walked into the Water Street Café. The man had an anxious look about him when he sat down at the table. His eyes were fixed upon the red folder resting on the checkered cloth alongside an untouched ham sandwich.

Oren pulled the folder back a few inches to make it clear that this was no longer the property of the County Sheriff's Office. He opened it to remove a single sheet of paper and handed it across the table.

The sheriff read his own interview with Mavis Hardy and her teenage son, Dave, a statement made back in the days when an entire town was searching the woods for a lost boy:

SHERIFF BABITT: I know you had an argument with Josh Hobbs a few days ago. I understand you bounced that boy off a gym locker. What was that about?

DAVID HARDY: I pushed him.

SHERIFF BABITT: Some push. The way I heard it, the kid was bleeding. But I didn't ask what you did. I asked you why you did it.

DAVID HARDY: Josh was in my way that night. So I moved him.

MAVIS HARDY: You know how I can always tell when my boy's lying? His little pecker just shrivels up like it's trying to crawl back inside of him. Makes

him look kind of girlish. If you like, we can unzip
him and—

SHERIFF BABITT: Mavis, shut the hell up. Dave, go
home. I need a word with your mother.

Cable looked up from his reading. "This might've
been the shortest interview I ever conducted."

"That was the *only* interview with Dave. You felt sorry
for him, didn't you? His crazy mother and all."

"Son, I misspoke. Your old interview was even shorter
than this one."

"Dave Hardy was the only one who ever hurt my
brother. I was there. He didn't *push* Josh. He picked him
up and threw him into a wall of lockers. Dave should've
made your short list."

The sheriff shrugged. "It was just a matter of time
before he got around to Josh. Dave had fights with every
boy in school."

"I know the second victim you found in Josh's grave
was a woman."

A worry line cut down the middle of the sheriff's fore-
head and deepened. "I have to wonder how you know
that, Oren."

"You just told me. And that's another strike against
Dave. His mother probably taught him to hate all
women."

"No, that was his father's job," said the sheriff. "That
bastard used to beat on Mavis all the time."

"And what *about* crazy Mavis Hardy?"

"Not so crazy. I think Mavis was real smart about getting sympathy for Dave. *I* sure felt sorry for him. The kid never did anything that his mother couldn't top. Every parent-teacher night was a crawling horror show. One time, Principal Mars found a teacher hiding under her desk, crying real soft so Mavis wouldn't find her. Everybody felt damn sorry for Dave. No matter what kind of trouble that boy got into, he never got thrown out of school."

"And you never suspected him? You couldn't see Dave beating Josh to death?"

"I thought about it. I even thought it couldn't hurt to keep the boy close. So, when he came back to town, I made him my deputy. Satisfied, Oren?"

Seventeen

Only days ago, Henry Hobbs had been crazed by Dave Hardy's threat to dig up the flower garden, and now Hannah was surprised by the old man's calm demeanor. While five state troopers opened every drawer in the living room and dumped them out on the floor, the judge was content to sit and read a search warrant by the light of the bay window.

Special Agent Sally—damned if Hannah would call her Sally—Polk stood by the judge's chair. The woman had a down-home country way about her—miles too friendly, and every word out of her mouth was suspect, even to saying hello at the front door.

"I'm *so* sorry about this mess," said the CBI agent, as if this carnage had come about by accident.

"Sorry? No," said the judge, "I don't think you are—

not yet. But just wait half a minute." He read a few more lines. "Your work is a bit sloppy, Miss Polk."

"*Agent* Polk," she said to sweetly remind him that she was in charge.

He raised his eyes from the warrant to watch another drawer crash to the floor. "And, by sloppy, I don't mean the ham-handed way these boys conduct a search. Now that mess, as you put it, is all for show—pure intimidation. And I can make that charge stick." He held up the warrant. "This doesn't cover the common areas of the house. The way I read it—the way any judge would, retired or not—you're restricted to Oren's residence, and that's his bedroom. He doesn't own this place. *I* do. And the only item you can seize—from *Oren's* room—is a red folder that holds standard-size documents."

He pointed to one of the young men in uniform. "So that boy shouldn't be searching anything as small as that ceramic candy box. Incidentally, the box belonged to my late wife. Trust me on this—you really don't want the trooper to drop it, not until you find out just how many ways I can hang you out to dry. So tell him to put it down right now."

The young trooper never even glanced at his boss. He was looking at Hannah's angry upturned face and finding the tiny housekeeper more formidable. Very gently, he set the ceramic box back in its place on the mantelpiece.

"So this," and *this,* by the wave of the judge's hand, included everything in sight, "this is illegal and damned incompetent."

The telephone rang, and Hannah retreated down the

hall to the kitchen to answer it in privacy. When she returned to the front room, the search had ended. "Not good enough," she said to the troopers. "I wasn't born to clean up after you boys."

Two of these young men had known the housekeeper all their lives, and now they gathered up the spilled contents of drawers. They treaded lightly around Horatio, who lay on the rug, doing his only trick—pretending to sleep while dead.

Hannah stood at the center of the room and raised her voice for all to hear as she spoke to the judge. "That was the sheriff returning your call. He wants you to know that he found that red folder behind his credenza."

Heads lifted all around the room.

"And he's real sorry that Miss Polk went off half-cocked the way she did. But she just wouldn't wait till he had time to do a proper search of his office." Hannah glared at the CBI agent. Why was that woman still smiling?

Another state trooper entered the house. The first person he saw was Hannah with her arms folded—waiting. And now the young man backed up a step to make his courtesy knock on the front door. He removed his hat and nodded hello to the housekeeper, who knew his parents and their parents all too well. The trooper drew Sally Polk into the dining room, wanting a word with her alone. Their voices were so low that even Hannah could not make out the conversation, though it was rumored that she could hear birds fluffing their feathers in the next county.

"You arrested my son?"

The trooper and Sally Polk whirled around to see Henry Hobbs standing behind them. Hannah grinned as she looked down at the judge's sandals, the old man's creepers.

"Well, that's another warrant I'd like to see," said the judge. "And all of your paperwork should be in order. Now what are the odds of that?"

Agent Polk's folksy veneer was still holding. "I'll be more careful from now on." Her voice was butter-smooth when she asked, "Have you always been in collusion with the sheriff—or is that a recent thing?"

A plate of brownies had pride of place on the desk. The fresh-baked aroma was tantalizing and unexpected at the local headquarters of the California Highway Patrol.

"Oh, is that light too bright? Well, of course it is." Sally Polk drew the blinds in her office. "There, that's better." Smoothing back her gray hair, she smiled benignly as she faced her prisoner, Oren Hobbs. "I can't see Cable Babitt just *giving* you that red folder." She paused a beat, most likely waiting for a signal that she was on the right track—and that the county sheriff was dead meat. Apparently, she did not believe the fairy tale of a critical piece of evidence getting lost behind Cable's credenza.

Disappointed by Oren's tell-nothing face, she moved on. "So let's say you borrowed that old folder without permission. But wouldn't the sheriff's credenza be locked? I'm so sure I remember a set of keys hanging from a lock on the bottom drawer." Her smile broadened as she waited out the silence of a few seconds. "All right then. We'll just forget those pesky charges of stealing official documents. And—no promises, mind you—but maybe the sheriff can keep his badge."

She turned her back on him to water a potted geranium on a stand in the corner. Smaller plants, pansies and African violets, sat on the windowsills, and personal photographs lined the walls. The whole room was a study in domesticity—and it did not have the look of an office on short-term loan to the lady from Sacramento.

Special Agent Polk sat down at her desk and straightened a stack of papers, then picked up loose pens and pencils and returned them to their glass container—just tidying up in a housewifey way. She pushed the plate of brownies toward him and raised her eyebrows to ask if he would like one.

As he was reaching out to the plate, she said, "Sweetheart, in a manner of speaking, I've got you by the balls." She raised one hand and slowly curled her fingers into a fist, smiling all the while. "Please don't make me squeeze 'em until they split open and spatter the wall. That's gotta hurt something awful." Her voice was so friendly. She was almost motherly, if one discounted her intentions toward his testicles.

But the brownies were good.

He chewed slowly as he stretched out his legs, preparing to spend a few hours in this interrogation. Behind him, the office door opened and—*bang!*—closed.

Addison Winston appeared, briefcase in hand and

wearing the body armor of a silk tie, a suit with a lustrous sheen and diamond cuff links. His eyes were fever-bright. The man was shining inside and out. Smiling, he moved around the desk to hover over the state's investigator. This sort of smile might be the last thing a mouse would see before a cat ripped its head off. "Hello, Sally, old girl. How've you been?"

Agent Polk countered with strained goodwill. "Well, Ad, I can't complain."

"I can," said Winston. "I know Judge Hobbs informed you that Oren was represented by counsel. But here you are—interrogating my client. Oh, Sally, Sally . . . The judge will be *so* pissed off." He shook his head in mock sadness. "As if you aren't in enough trouble."

"What *interrogation*? Me and your client were only passing the time, just waiting around for you to show up."

This was news to Oren, who had no idea that an attorney was coming.

Ad Winston resumed his smile, merely evil this time. He settled into the chair next to Oren's and stared at the plate of brownies. "She buys them at a bakery down the street. And she gets that fresh-from-the-oven smell by running them through the microwave in the lunchroom. Sally's idea of torturing prisoners. . . . It's scary how often that works."

Sally Polk sat back in her chair with a smile for Oren. "At my regional office down in Sacramento, when we find out Ad's in town, we just run out and arrest whoever he's representing. Then, later on, we come up with the charges. They're always guilty of something."

The lawyer winked at his client. "She's good." He turned his attention back to the CBI agent. "Oren's better. When he was an Army cop, he closed out all of his cases. He was one determined soldier, and his evidence always stood up in court. I won't even bother to dazzle you with the conviction rate, but it was stunning."

"Of course," said Agent Polk, "that was *military* court, and guilt was always a foregone conclusion—even before the judges sat down." She turned to Oren and spoke to him in the way that women talked down to small children. "Nothing personal, sweetheart. I'm sure you did a *very* good job. Have another brownie."

"Nonetheless," said Addison, "I'd stack up my client against any cop in this state. He didn't just work domestic disputes on some military base out in the sticks. No, they sent him all around the world. My boy brought in terrorists and killers, smugglers and mad-bomber types. He put a goddamn *general* in Leavenworth."

Untrue. The highest-ranking officer Oren had ever bagged was a lieutenant colonel, and he had yet to meet any *live* mad bombers. Only pieces of them could be found on the streets of Baghdad. If asked for his job description as a military detective, he would have explained his special knack for ripping a human being's mind inside out—without damaging the flesh. He would have said, *"I break people."* But he allowed the lawyer's lies to slide.

"You should be begging for Oren's help, not harassing him." Ad Winston continued to smile at the CBI agent as he spoke an aside to his client. "That startled look in her eyes? Obviously, the lady never bothered to check out your military record, nothing past your serial number and rank. To quote your father—a *very* sloppy job."

Sally Polk leaned toward the lawyer. "Well now, Ad, I have to admit that's an eye-opener. You see, I was gonna let your client off easy—no charge of obstructing an investigation. But with a record like that one . . . I think he should've known better."

"She's bluffing, Oren. That's Sally's trademark. We met in Sacramento when a major case of hers fell apart in court—a case of hot air."

"The way I remember it, you suborned one of my witnesses."

Addison rested an avuncular hand on Oren's shoulder. "They always send the screwup agents to the hinterlands. But she's the first one ever to be condemned to the Highway Patrol."

"Oh, this is just a temporary assignment, Addison. I won't be here long—just long enough to gut your client. Have another brownie, Oren."

Eighteen

Hannah! Stop that! I can't hear!"

The housekeeper switched off the vacuum cleaner.

After a brief telephone conversation, the judge hung up on his caller. "That was the sheriff. He says Oren's on TV." Not a believer in remote-control contraptions, Henry Hobbs leaned down to turn on the television set. "Oh, my God." He stared at the glowing screen and a scene of reporters mobbing a parking lot. His son stood at the center of this frenzy, and the backdrop was a brick building, headquarters for the Highway Patrol in Saulburg. The shouts of the mob were unintelligible. Addison Winston climbed up on the hood of a trooper's cruiser, and, with a bit of coaxing, Oren joined him there.

"This is Ad's idea of handling things quietly?" The

judge raked one clawed hand over his bald scalp. "It's a circus."

More than that—this was Hannah's old premonition come true. She had always pictured the judge's son taking center stage, surrounded by people and bright lights, a screaming public. "The camera loves him."

The cameras could not get enough of Oren Hobbs. When the afternoon sky grew dark with overcast, lights on poles bore down on him, and strobe lights popped in smaller cameras as photographers edged closer.

"Oren and his damned cowboy boots," said the judge. "He's going to dent the hood of that car."

On screen, Addison Winston stepped in front of his photogenic client, though not to shield him. The grinning lawyer had the look of an elegant sideshow barker with tickets to sell. "Sorry you were called out on a false alarm. I'm afraid Sally Polk has a rich fantasy life."

Hannah turned to the judge and reached out to nudge his arm. "You see? It wasn't Ad's fault. That Polk woman must've called the reporters."

"It was Addison," said the judge. "He's addicted to this kind of attention."

The picture had changed to a close-up of the building in the background, where Sally Polk stood in the open doorway, clearly unhappy with this event. And then the camera turned back to Oren, the one it loved best.

"Did you see that?" Hannah edged her chair closer to the screen. "That was Evelyn Straub standing not two feet away from that door."

"Oh, *fine*." Henry Hobbs covered his eyes with one hand. "Let's just drag out all the sordid details."

"There she is again." Hannah pulled down the judge's hand. "Look. You see that bright pink thing in her hand? That's the color of Evelyn's checkbook. I bet she planned to bail Oren out of jail."

As if in response to this, Ad Winston's voice boomed from the television set, "Bail? No, there was never an issue of bail. My client came in as a courtesy."

A reporter shouted, "Your guy was wearing handcuffs!"

Addison raised both hands in a crucifixion pose. "Another screwup. It seems there was a breakdown in communications between Sally Polk and the storm troopers."

"Well, that's not right," said the judge, indignant. "And it wasn't necessary. That man has no respect for law enforcement."

"As I recall," said Hannah, "you told Addison to grind up Sally Polk for dog meat."

Still following those instructions, the lawyer yelled, "It gets better! Judge Montrose—the man who signed the warrant—he was under the impression that there was probable cause. There wasn't. Let me tell you, that's one pissed-off judge."

"Now that last part's true enough." Henry Hobbs nodded at the screen. "Judge Montrose and I had a little talk. Good man. Seems Miss Polk likes to stretch the truth a bit. But so does Addison. He's talking about the search warrant. There never was a warrant for Oren's arrest. He must've been brought in for questioning. That means there's no evidence against him."

"But you always knew that."

"That I did."

They turned back to the television set as a reporter asked, "Oren? Will you be offering any assistance on this case?"

"Absolutely," said Ad Winston, answering for his client before Oren had a chance to open his mouth and say something true. "He's a decorated CID agent. That's the Army's Criminal Investigations Division. He has quite a track record for solving homicides. Incidentally, my client was the one who found the first evidence of his brother's murder. So you might say he's been on the case for a while now."

Oren seemed about to disagree with this, and the lawyer pushed him, forcing him to jump off the hood of the car before he could fall. Ad Winston also jumped to the ground and propelled his client through the crowd to a waiting limousine. The reporters regrouped and followed them across the parking lot. All that was missing was the music of a marching band.

In the distance, Evelyn Straub could be seen standing alone as the parade passed her by. To the camera's undiscerning eye, she was a stout, drab figure who blended into the background and faded away.

Oren rode in the backseat of the stretch limousine hired for this special occasion of a carnival press conference. It was equipped with a stereo, television, a coffeemaker and a full bar. All that seemed to be missing was a hot tub. He turned to his lawyer. "Did my father really hire you?"

"Who else? You thought Isabelle might've asked me to defend you?" Ad Winston depressed a button on the console to raise a glass privacy barrier behind the chauffeur's seat. "And now, may I ask, what goes on between you and my daughter?"

"Sir, I've never even spoken to her."

"And yet, reliable witnesses tell me she recently decked you, flattened you out on a town sidewalk. That could pass for rough sex in the third world."

"I tripped."

"Of course you did."

"I'll pay for this myself," said Oren. "What do I owe you?"

"Not one dime. I never earned out the retainer your father paid me twenty years ago. And I won't make much of a dent in what's left. It looks like you're going to walk away from a double homicide."

"You think I murdered my brother and that woman?"

The attorney stared at him with keen interest. "The other set of bones belonged to a woman? Interesting. Don't ever tell me how you knew that. It'll make my job easier if I have to put you on the witness stand." He lifted his briefcase from the floor and settled it on his lap. "But I'm not anticipating a trial. Sally Polk's about to get a direct order to stay out of the sheriff's way. And Cable Babitt doesn't have the talent to catch a shoplifter."

"When Josh disappeared, was it your idea not to bring in the feds and the CBI? Or was that the judge's call?"

"Your father and I discussed the matter. I thought it was in your best interest if there was only one police agency to deal with—the mediocre one. I call it damage control."

"You told him to send me away?"

"No, that was the judge's decision. I was against it. At least he waited a few months before he shipped you out of state, but it was still a bad move. I gather you had some kind of alibi. The sheriff isn't a complete idiot." The lawyer's fingers did a little dance on the top of his briefcase while he awaited a response.

Oren had no plans to share the details of two bogus alibis. Evelyn Straub's old statement was folded in his wallet, and there it would stay. He had set fire to Isabelle's statement in full view of the sheriff and the patrons at the Water Street Café.

Ad Winston opened his briefcase and perused the paperwork inside. The top sheet was a list of military commendations and decorations, ribbons from combat zones, medals for Oren's valor and medals for his wounds.

"Stunning record," said the lawyer. "I was relieved to discover that you were honorably discharged. And that's all the information Sally Polk is likely to get from the Army. She probably doesn't know as many five-star generals as I do. When my general looked into the matter, what he found was very jarring." The lawyer consulted a sheet of handwritten notes. "I know you left Coventry when you were seventeen years old, but you didn't join the Army until your eighteenth birthday—legal age. When you quit, you were nine months shy of qualifying for a twenty-year pension. You walked away from that— every dime, every benefit."

Winston paused for a moment. "No comment?"

The lawyer turned back to his notes. "Well, with no prompting from me, the general investigated." He pointed to a paragraph. "This lists all the perks you were offered. In the general's own words, the Army offered you the moon if you would only stay. He tells me you never had to quit. They would have given you a leave of absence—all the time you needed. You could've claimed a family emergency, but you didn't. And your father insists you knew nothing about Josh's bones being found— not before you came home."

"My father never lies."

"Henry's better at arithmetic than I am. He knows what you lost when you walked away. He never asked why?"

They rode the rest of the way in silence.

The sun had come out again, and the light from the immense window was brilliant. Beyond the glass were the muffled sounds of hammers and the sight of workmen building a large wooden platform on the grass behind the Winston lodge. Truckers unloaded tables and chairs for the guests who soon would fill the house to overflowing.

Oren had not set foot in this place since the age of

twelve. Today the front room was an empty cavern of cedar paneling and glass. All the furnishings had been removed to accommodate a night of dancing beneath a ceiling that soared more than thirty feet, and the floor space had the dimensions of a grand ballroom.

Walking alongside his lawyer, he was told that the lodge had been built with the annual festivities in mind. Oren could only see it as a needy display of wealth, a stage for a man who was always performing, always smiling. He wondered what Ad Winston was like when there was no one around to play the audience. He pictured the lawyer sitting in a darkened room, insanely grinning for no reason at all.

No difference.

"You must come to the ball this year," said Winston, leading the way across the wide expanse.

"Maybe I will." Oren delivered this line in a manner close to a threat.

The lawyer paused and turned, eyes flickering, uncomprehending, and then he walked around a screen of potted fruit trees, motioning for his guest to follow him. On the other side of the foliage was a small mahogany bar, ornately carved. A cabinet full of bottles had been built into the wall, and its shelves were enclosed by glass doors with a sturdy lock. A single key lay beside a glass of melting ice cubes. The keeper of the key, a woman in a maid's uniform, was capping a whiskey bottle.

"Hello, Hilda," said the lawyer as he joined her behind the bar. He looked down at the abandoned glass. "No refills, right?"

"She's only had the one—"

"That's enough. You can go, Hilda. I'll do the honors. Young man, pull up a bar stool."

Oren was distracted by his view of a small private terrace beyond a pair of French doors. Outside in the sunlight, Isabelle Winston's red hair was fire bright. A taller woman with long pale hair stood beside her. This champagne blonde could only be Sarah Winston, and she was slowly turning toward him, but he never saw her face. The lady was led away like a passive invalid.

Ad Winston set out two glasses. "What'll you have?"

"Jack Daniel's straight up if you've got it."

"I have everything, my boy." The lawyer uncapped a whiskey bottle and poured him two generous shots. "We should talk strategy."

Oren looked down at his glass and idly ran one finger around the rim. "You're fired."

The older man leaned across the bar, for surely he could not have heard this right. "You're firing *me?*" He laughed at this great joke.

"I know you're the best," said Oren. "But I know how you work. . . . I know what you did to William Swahn."

Perhaps for the first time ever, the lawyer had lost his sense of humor, and he was slow to pour his own drink. "I never discuss my clients with anyone. So any aspect of Swahn's old case is—"

"Nondisclosure agreements. You talk—your client loses money. I got that." Oren drained his glass and slammed it down on the bar—but not in anger. He simply wanted to make Ad Winston jump—and he did. "It only took me six minutes to figure out the scam. Swahn was just a rookie cop in those days. . . . I'm the real deal."

Oren poured himself another shot from the bottle and sipped his glass slowly, enjoying the wary look in the lawyer's eyes. "You were at the hospital the night Swahn was ambushed. You were waiting in his room when he got out of surgery."

There was an unspoken—unspeakable—question in Ad Winston's eyes.

It was Oren's turn to smile. "No, your client didn't tell me. He never said a word. But I knew his partner took a bribe to call in sick the night of the ambush. I'm sure the civilian dispatcher got paid off, too. But that woman was smart enough to disappear before detectives came knocking on her door. Jay Murray stayed. That proves he had no idea why he'd been bribed. And that should've led the investigation away from a cop conspiracy. They would've been looking at civilians."

"The LAPD was liable. There's no disputing that. The dispatcher was employed by—"

"But the lawsuit would've dragged on for years." Oren picked up the bottle and poured himself another shot. "So you blackmailed the LAPD into a fast settlement, a big one. You fabricated evidence of a police conspiracy against a gay man with AIDS. And you had to work fast. When a cop goes down on duty, nobody goes home. Detectives work around the clock. It was probably still dark when you accused Swahn's precinct of ambushing your poor *diseased* client. The next morning, during an interrogation—that was the first time Swahn's partner heard the rumor. Now that's only odd if you know that cops gossip like little old ladies with guns. So that rumor—your rumor—was started *after* the ambush and before the sun came up on Jay Murray. And that's how I know you were in Swahn's hospital room when he got out of surgery."

"Interesting theory, Oren. Pure conjecture, of course, but—"

"It's a *fact*. The only thing I don't know is whether or not Swahn was lucid when you signed him up as a client. I used to think he was in on this con game. Now I'm not so sure."

"None of this would hold up in court."

"That doesn't matter," said Oren. "I can still do a world of damage. Every reporter in the state wants to talk to me—thanks to your little performance today."

"You've got no proof."

"Don't need it. Rumors make the best headlines."

Winston's smile was back. "You can't revive any interest in Swahn's case. It's ancient history."

"The reporters will want to know why I fired you, the great Addison Winston. Now that's *news*. I can tell them it's because you smeared a precinct of innocent cops— and scammed them for money."

"Oh, I've always had lots of money, Oren, more than I can spend. What I do, I do for fun." The lawyer reached for the bottle and poured himself a triple shot of whiskey, the only sign of defeat. "What do you want?"

"Information."

"**Millard Straub.** Now there's another man with a motive to kill a woman." Addison Winston volunteered this tidbit, this breach of client-attorney confidence, as he parked his Porsche in front of the judge's house.

The bulb over the front door must have burned out. Hannah usually turned it on in the twilight hour.

The lawyer was still talking nonstop and very fast. A sign of frayed nerves?

"Old Millard was fixated on the idea that Evelyn was cheating on him. But he never asked me to cut her out of his will. Maybe he didn't want the paper trail of a poisoned relationship—a motive to kill his wife. He makes a fine suspect, but you seem skeptical, Oren. Quite understandable. It's hard to picture that old codger dragging his oxygen tank into the woods. However, this theory works rather well with the latest gossip about Evelyn. It seems she was a bit indiscreet yesterday when you came calling. It's all around town—the rumor of your old affair. What if the woman who died with Josh was the target of a hired assassin? Could be a case of mistaken identity. Suppose Millard Straub hired someone to kill his wife—because she was sleeping with you? Assuming Josh was an innocent witness—then you'd be responsible for your brother's death."

Oren stepped out of the car, and the lawyer was laughing as he drove away.

Behind him, he heard the squeaking hinges of the screen door.

"Don't let him poison you." Hannah stepped out on the porch. "It's real convenient, blaming murder on a dead man. I could make the same case for Addison. His wife drinks a lot. I think she cries a lot." The housekeeper— eavesdropper—stood at the railing and raised her eyes to the Winston lodge. "Makes you wonder what goes on up there."

Oren climbed the porch steps and reached up to twist the dark bulb in its socket—and there was light. He sat down in the wooden armchair next to Hannah's old rocker. "Tell me about Evelyn Straub's husband. I don't remember him very well."

"Millard? I'm not surprised." The housekeeper leaned back against the porch railing. "He hardly ever traveled farther than the verandah of his hotel. He was mean, but too old and too sick to lift a hand against Evelyn. He found other ways to be cruel."

"Why did she stay with him? Did he have something on her?"

"You mean something besides an affair with an under-age boy? If he'd known about that—never mind what Addison thinks—Millard would've divorced Evelyn and kicked her to the curb without a penny. He'd sooner do that than part with money to hire a killer. Cheap old bastard."

"You knew about the prenuptial agreement?"

"Evelyn and me, we talk from time to time. In any case, you're not to blame for your brother's death, and you know that, Oren." The housekeeper sat down in her rocking chair. Josh had always called it Hannah's lowrider because of the seat built close to the ground. It was the only piece of furniture that allowed both her feet to sit flat on the floorboards instead of dangling in the air.

"Well, here comes my burglar alarm." She pointed toward a yellow dog of dubious pedigree, floppy ears and the big round eyes of a spaniel with a collie's long coat. The animal approached the porch, and then hesitated, one paw resting on the bottom step. He had a sad, wounded look about him as he stared at the housekeeper.

Oren noticed an empty bowl on the floorboards near the door. The dog was no longer eating his dinner of scraps down by the garden shed. "I guess you forgot to feed him."

"I fed him hours ago." She nodded to the dog, as if in answer to a question, and the yellow stray bounded up the stairs. With better manners than Horatio ever had, the animal politely sat down in front of her rocking chair and cocked his head to one side—waiting. "This time he came for love." She gently stroked the dog's fur.

"Does the judge like that mutt as much as you do?"

"This afternoon, he was out here tossing sticks for the dog to fetch. It won't be long now."

Oren smiled. He approved of her plan to end old Horatio's days as a stuffed decoration of the parlor. He reached out to cover her hand with his. "You were going to tell me about the séances in the woods."

"Was I?"

"You and the judge go out to Evelyn's old cabin and—"

"No," said Hannah. "We used to go to the séances, but not anymore, not for years and years. But sometimes we watch the videotapes." Rising from the rocker, she kept hold of his hand and pulled him toward the porch steps. "We should go now while there's still some light."

The tiny woman peered over the steering wheel, sometimes rising off the seat to get a better view of the hairpin turns on this mountain road. It was scary and dangerous and great fun. Oren sensed that a legal driver's license might take some of the joy out of Hannah's rides.

They were the first to arrive at the old cabin. Though parking spaces out front were plentiful, she drove down and around to the back and stopped by the door to the crawl space. Hannah cut the ignition and searched the ring of keys until she found the one she wanted. "Let's go."

"How do you happen to have a key?"

"This one belongs to the judge." She fitted it into the lock and opened the door to the sound of an exhaust fan.

"Do people know they're being videotaped?"

"Of course. Evelyn sells copies to hotel guests, the ones who come for the séances."

"And what about the local people?"

Hannah hesitated too long. "Oh, I'm sure they know." She reached into the darkness and flipped a wall switch to flood the small room with light. From a nest of cables, lines trailed upward and disappeared into the low ceiling. He recognized the wicker armchairs as worn castoffs from the verandah of the Straub Hotel. Outdated recording equipment sat on a table alongside a pair of old television sets that would only accept videocassettes.

"It's a little old-fashioned. Evelyn wants to change over to DVDs and computer monitors, but you know your father. He doesn't take well to change." Hannah slipped a cassette into a slot at the base of one of the TV sets.

"Never mind the tourists," said Oren. "Are you sure the locals know they're being filmed?"

"Once a cop, always a cop." She plucked a sheet of paper from a stack on the table. "This is the consent form. Everybody signs one. You can't say they don't get a sporting chance. It starts out by holding Evelyn harmless for heart attacks and hauntings, strokes and madness, hair turning white from fright. Lots of nonsense like that. And then, toward the bottom of the page, the consent for the taping is buried somewhere in all that legalese. But that comes long after people get tired of reading the damn thing. Usually, they just sign it." She fed another cassette into the second television. "There's two cameras. One shows the whole room, but this one's my favorite view."

Oren stared at the screen with the overhead camera angle. It looked down at the card table and the tops of the players' heads all leaning toward the Ouija board.

"That's a homemade witchboard," said Hannah. "Nothing like the one you and Josh used to play with. As I recall, that one glowed in the dark."

"And you burned it."

On the videotape, the players' fingers were touching the small wooden heart as it moved in wide circles around the board, faster and faster. Then it stopped. Alice Friday led the chant as they all looked through the hole in the heart and called out the letter *S*. The planchette moved again to settle over another letter.

"They're always talking to your brother—the spirit guide, always asking him how he died. It was like that from the beginning. No one ever asked if he ran away." Hannah pointed to shelves of cassettes lining the back wall of the crawl space. "There's lots of tapes with nothing but gibberish. Some nights the board spells out real words and whole sentences. Depends on who's playing."

Oren focused on one of the players. All he could see from this camera angle was the pale crown of blond hair. He turned to the second screen and identified her in this ground-level shot of the table. "Is Mrs. Winston a regular?"

Hannah nodded. "She's on quite a few tapes."

The wall of shelves held a daunting array of cassettes. How long would it take to view all of them? "Just tell me the highlights. Give me the—"

"Maybe this was a mistake," she said. "My interference always comes to a bad end, and I should know that by now."

He could hear the muffled sound of engines and car doors closing outside. And now, overhead, feet were walking on the cabin floor. "We stayed too long."

"The hell you say. We're going to the séance tonight."

"I don't think Mrs. Straub would like that."

"No one's ever turned away—except Cable Babitt. Evelyn never minded when he'd send a deputy out here now and then—so long as it wasn't somebody in uniform. But then, Cable started driving his jeep up the fire road every damn night. Well, that road only leads to this cabin."

And, farther on, a hole full of bones.

"So Evelyn figured he was spying on her full-time. These days he can't legally come within two hundred yards of this place." Hannah rose from her chair. "Stay here if you like. I'm going to the séance."

He followed her outside and up the back stairs to the kitchen door. "I'll just watch."

"You should play," said Hannah. "It's only scary for true believers." She looked up at him and smiled—a clear invitation to a dare.

They passed through the kitchen and walked into the small front room. The chairs around the card table were filled, and other people waited their turn in the dark. Hannah spoke in whispers. "You remember why I took that old witchboard away from you and Josh? I bet you still remember your nightmares."

He did. And he also remembered Josh's bad dreams, the screaming in the night that had always followed visits from their good-deed lady, the old woman who once lived on Paulson Lane. The dead Mrs. Underwood had spelled out vile curses on a witchboard that two small boys had purchased at the dry-goods store.

"Will Mrs. Winston be here tonight?"

"Maybe," said Hannah. "It's catch as catch can with

her. Addison likes to think that he knows where his wife is every minute of the day and night. He also thinks Sarah stopped driving when she lost her license. But, I'll tell you, the lady gets around."

"You think Josh could've photographed a secret of hers?"

"I don't see her killing the boy, if that's what you're asking." She lightly poked him in the ribs with her elbow. "Watch the game. Listen."

The small piece of wood moved around the board, making a slow circle over the characters of the alphabet, and then it picked up speed. Each time it stopped, the players called out the letter framed in the planchette's circle.

Hannah whispered, "I tried to explain this when you were a boy, but I don't think you were listening—not then. The players don't decide to make the planchette stop and start. There's no decisions being made. The hands have brains of their own. And the mind of a true believer calls it magic."

"Or somebody's cheating."

"No one cheats," she said. "And it's not magical."

Ferris Monty, who believed in nothing, sat with his back to the shadow side of the room. Oh, the things he did for his art.

He drank in the details of candlelight and a magic act, making mental notes about the abundance of spiderwebs and a tree limb growing through a broken window. This was his first séance, and he had been unprepared for the movement of the planchette. Though it was in contact with so many hands, he would swear the small wooden heart moved around the board of its own volition. This was no manipulation by the psychic. Her hands never touched it. According to his research among the citizens of Coventry, Alice Friday was the only constant presence; the others were replaced with new players for every session. And so he could also rule out a confederate in this mix of townspeople and tourists.

The planchette circled the Ouija board, moving faster and faster, and he felt inexplicable exhilaration. He looked up at the psychic. Her eyes were closed, and she trembled—and so did the heart-shaped piece of wood beneath the tips of his fingers.

A player asked, "Does it ever go in a straight line?"

And then it did—back and forth across the board.

A voice to his right complained, "When will it ever stop?"

It stopped over the letter Y that stood for *yes*. Yes, the dead boy was among them tonight. A man on the other side of the table asked the next question. "Do bears shit in the woods?"

Alice Friday's eyes snapped open. "Goddamn tourists!" With a dramatic wave of her hand in the direction of the door, the offended psychic dismissed the man from the table.

She was backed up by another woman, probably the wife, who yelled, "Harry, you idiot! Go wait outside in the hotel van!" And he did.

And now they were five.

Ferris leaned toward Alice Friday. "Could you ask if the boy has a message for one of us?"

She nodded and closed her eyes once more as she posed this question for her spirit guide, Joshua Hobbs.

Ferris was grinning, hoping that this would be a good quote for his book—a dead child speaking from beyond the grave. The wooden planchette shot across the board to stop over the first letter, and then the second, shooting, stopping, and all around him players chanted the letters in unison.

"D-O-Υ—"

He sensed that the wooden heart had come alive to emanate its own energy, a palpable beat.

No, that's insane.

"O-U-S-T-I—"

The planchette jumped like a spider from letter to letter.

"L-L-L-O—"

Logic and sanity flew out the window. Ferris was a passenger on a runaway train, helpless, waiting for the rest, hanging on each letter, and only hanging by fingertips to the speeding piece of wood.

"V-E-M-E—"

He drew back his hands, as if the planchette had wounded him. He sat very still—still as death, no blinking. He held his breath—digesting the message from a murdered boy.

Alice Friday opened her eyes and looked beyond him to the people gathered at the back of the room. "Won't you join us? There's an empty chair." Heads were turning all around the table in the manner of a celebrity sighting.

Ferris looked back to see Oren Hobbs walk out of the shadows and into the circle of candlelight. An adrenaline chill filled his veins as he imagined that the older brother was accusing him with Joshua's eyes—the same blue eyes.

But no, Hobbs only showed interest in the retired pharmacist, who sat in the next chair. He and the elderly Mr. McCaully exchanged "Sir, you're looking well" for "About time you came home, young man." After a few more pleasantries, the old man invited the younger one to his house for a nightcap after the séance.

Hobbs sat down and joined the others in placing his fingertips on the planchette.

Alice Friday closed her eyes, and her head rolled back. "Does anyone have a question for Joshua?"

A voice from the back of the room called out, "Why did Oren leave you all alone in the woods to die?"

The planchette flew off the table and shot across the room, lost in the shadows. The cabin door had closed on Oren Hobbs before one of the players found the small wooden heart in the darkest corner of the room. And the question was never answered, though other people posed it again and again.

Nineteen

The final days of Joshua Hobbs were shaping up on the glowing screen of a computer monitor. Ferris Monty left it to his future readers to ponder how he came by this information. He had done it the old-fashioned way, on foot—stalking a child. And an exhibitionist quality led him to parade his fixation across the pages of his book.

He lovingly described Joshua's face washed in bright sunlight as the boy stood by the safety rail across the street from the Straub Hotel.

Even with his camera hanging by a strap around his neck, Joshua did not blend in with out-of-towners, tourists taking pictures of one another against the backdrop of the sea. The posers changed. Their poses did not. All the smiles and compositions were identi-

cal. These amateurs only amused the boy for a few minutes. He turned his own long lens on the hotel. Evelyn Straub stood on the verandah. She hardly looked her age, fortyish in those days. She was so much more than just another pretty woman. The former showgirl went everywhere wrapped in a full-metal jacket of steely personality, invulnerable—and maybe inhuman.

He would not mention here that she had always intimidated him.

The tourists identified Joshua as an alien in their midst because he was facing the wrong direction, away from the boring vista of sea and sky. A few of them moved close to the boy, taking an interest in the complexity of his manual camera, a standout among their own idiot-proof equipment. Once they recognized him as a source of expertise, Joshua graciously answered questions about film speeds, and then he explained the concept of F-stops, useless data for people with point-and-shoot cameras. This child had exquisite good manners and great patience.

If this scene had been illustrated with pictures instead of words, Ferris Monty would have been detected near the boy. Hiding behind dark glasses and the wide brim of a straw hat, he had stood within touching distance of Joshua Hobbs. He remembered his hand reaching out to touch the boy's hair, hesitating in the air, then quickly drawing back.

When the young photographer parted company with the tourists, he had walked away at a rapid pace, his camera focused on the street ahead. Had the boy been following someone that day? Ferris would never know, for his own surveillance had come to an end when the boy suddenly turned around and snapped a picture of his stalker.

After dinner, Hannah had surrendered the car keys, and now Oren set out for Mr. McCaully's house, aiming his headlights at signs posted along the back roads.

Offered the option of streetlights, the outlying citizens of Coventry had turned down these modern conveniences, arguing that they would pale the starlight. Ever backward-thinking, the town had also voted against cell towers, for who would want to carry a telephone in their pocket? It was annoying enough to have one in the house.

Amen.

Oren did not miss the trappings of a world that ended where the town began. Tonight he was counting on the old-fashioned methods of the man who once ran the local drugstore. Mr. McCaully's recordkeeping would have bypassed the age of computers in favor of hard copy. And that old man never threw anything away.

The wood-frame house was in sight, and the windows of the parlor floor were lit. The sound of the Mercedes' ancient engine had preceded him, and the elderly house-holder was waiting on the porch when Oren turned off the ignition.

"Hello again." The retired pharmacist gave him a sweet smile of false teeth and extended a frail hand lined with blue veins and freckled with liver spots. "So, you came for that nightcap. Well, good."

When the judge's regards had been passed along and condolences offered on the death of Mrs. McCaully a decade ago, Oren explained his errand to the delight of his host. The old man put a fresh bottle of beer in the hand of his guest, then led him outside and across the backyard toward a long wooden structure of plain walls and boarded-up windows.

As they walked, the older man recounted the story of his family drugstore. "My father was a historian of sorts. He built that shed in 1932 to warehouse the records my grandfather collected. Did you know that Coventry's first druggist was the town barber?" Mr. McCaully opened the door to the low hum of a motor, and he flipped on a wall switch. Long fluorescent tubes spanned the ceiling and illuminated row upon row of boxes sitting on metal shelves as high as walls. "My son installed the climate control years ago. That's why we boarded up the win-dows. He says paper lasts longer this way. Some of it dates back to the eighteen hundreds."

Oren followed his host to the last narrow alley of ar-chives, and they walked through more recent history. "So you kept everything? Inventories, too?"

"Oh, it's much more than just a collection of receipts and inventories. It's the heart of the town, a history of what ailed Coventry for more than a hundred years. Prescriptions from 1887 will tell you that the town's first mayor didn't sleep well at night, and that might be the sign of a guilty conscience. And there were potions and poultices for bullet wounds, too."

He paused to give Oren a sly wink. "Outlaw days. There's some who'll tell you that period never ended. And then there were nerve tonics for the lunatics and stimulants for depression. Outlaws and mental cases have always been a big part of our customer base. You could lose your mind in Coventry, and that was nobody's business but your own. The same held true if you robbed a bank—as long as you did it in some other town."

The old man stopped by a shelf for the 1980s and donned his bifocals to run one finger over the dates on box labels, drawing closer to the end of the decade and the year when Josh disappeared. At last, he came to the right boxes. He pulled them off the shelves, frowning when help was offered. "I can manage." One by one, he settled four cardboard cartons on the floor. "History, that's what it is."

Oren hunkered down beside the boxes and lifted one lid to turn back folders and loose papers. "I'm not sure about the exact date. It was an order for black-and-white photographs. Does that help?"

"Oh, yeah. That would've been rare even twenty years ago." Mr. McCaully opened one of the other cartons and perused the contents. "I remember Mr. Swahn bringing in a slew of negatives and contact sheets. It was a *big* order."

"That's not it," said Oren. "I already know about that one. I'm interested in a single roll of film. Hannah brought it in to have it developed. She ordered an enlargement, too."

With no hesitation at all, Mr. McCaully opened another box, and his hand went straight to one folder. He opened it and skimmed through the papers, plucked one out and smiled. "This is it. A receipt for the development of twenty prints, all standard-size." He pulled out another sheet. "And here's another one of Hannah's orders. This one's for an eight-by-ten enlargement."

Oren took the folder from the old man's hand. It contained only paperwork—no forgotten photographs. "I know she had to leave negatives with you to get that enlargement made. Any chance she left the pictures, too? Maybe she forgot to pick them up when the enlargement came in?"

The retired druggist smiled. "Over the years, a few tourists have forgotten to pick up their orders, and all of those photographs are stored in these boxes. But you won't find the pictures from Hannah's roll. I'm eighty-seven, Oren, and I'm not senile *yet*. I saw Hannah at least once a week. Don't you think I would've remembered to give her the other prints?"

Oren was distracted by the date on the paperwork. The housekeeper had led him to believe that years might have passed by before she developed Josh's last roll of film. And now he understood how Mr. McCaully had found this record so quickly—why the date would stand out in the old man's mind.

"Sir, does the drugstore still close at six o'clock?"

"Always has, always will."

On this date, the days were long. At six o'clock in the evening, the sun still shone. Oren remembered that it was dark when he returned home—without his brother. The townspeople had gone into the woods with flashlights blazing to search for a lost boy.

Long before the alarm was sounded, Hannah had brought Josh's last roll of film to the drugstore.

While Oren searched for the housekeeper in the back rooms of the house, calling her name, Hannah was out front, starting up the Mercedes with the spare keys. At the sound of the engine, he came barreling through the porch door on the run. And then he stopped.

She smiled and waved and rode away.

One mile later, Hannah nosed the car onto the old fire road and headed uphill. When the Mercedes pulled into the cabin's parking lot, the yellow Rolls-Royce was no longer there, but most of the witchboard people had stayed to play, and that was strange at this late hour. She rolled through the lot and then down to the rear of the cabin, where Evelyn Straub was waiting with a worried look about her—not her nature.

Trouble?

"Thanks for coming back." Evelyn fumbled with her

key in the padlock of the crawl-space door. "We need some privacy."

Hannah followed her into the small room in the cabin's foundation. She sat down in one of the wicker chairs and then looked up to the ceiling, listening to the faint chanting of letters.

"*D-O-Y*—"

"I've never known them to stay so late."

"They won't go home," said Evelyn, "and there's never a shotgun around when you need one. I'm sorry to drag you out here again, but I didn't want the judge around when I talked to you, and I don't think this can wait till morning."

"What can I do for you?"

"I'm in a tight spot." Evelyn settled into the chair next to Hannah's, her eyes turned toward the ceiling, listening.

"*O-U-S-T*—"

"I heard they found a woman's bones in Josh's grave."

Hannah leaned toward her. "A woman, you say? How do you know that?"

Evelyn pointed to the ceiling and the room above. "They all know. They heard it from the witchboard half an hour ago."

"Well, then it must be true," said Hannah, leaning heavy on the sarcasm. "And when did you become a believer in psychic nonsense?"

"*I-L-L-L*—"

"I knew about the woman's bones this afternoon. I

heard it from one of Cable's deputies. Dave Hardy always stops by my hotel bar when he's in town. I give him free liquor, and he talks up a storm. He'll tell me anything, but there was one thing I couldn't ask. I know Oren went out with the search party today. He was there when they found the grave. Did he mention seeing anything odd in that hole? Maybe some clothes?"

"Shopping for anything in particular?"

"A yellow rain slicker. Plastic would hold up for twenty years in the ground. The damn things are indestructible."

"O-V-E-M—"

Upstairs the witchboard people were stamping their feet to the rhythm of the chant.

"That's new," said Hannah, looking upward. "So tell me more about this yellow slicker that can't wait till morning."

"E-O-R—"

"It ties back to a statement I gave the sheriff twenty years ago. I told him that Oren spent the whole day with me. I said Josh went on alone, heading uphill on the hikers' trail. Cable asked if anybody else came by, and I said no. How can I go back on that now? How can I tell Cable I made a cup of tea for a strange woman that same morning and sat with her for half an hour? Next he'll think I made up the whole thing, and he'll toss out Oren's alibi."

"E-N-I—"

"I see," said Hannah. "What do you know about this woman?"

"She was a day-tripper. I only remember that because she checked her watch against a bus schedule. She didn't want to miss the last ride home. Before she left, she pulled a yellow slicker from her knapsack. There was a shower that day. Didn't last long, but it was raining when she finished her tea."

"M-H-E—"

Evelyn looked upward, irritated now. "I might have to set this place on fire to get rid of those idiots." She turned her eyes back to Hannah. "I made that woman a map of the old hiking trail that runs past my cabin and all the paths that connect it to the fire road. I let her out the back door and watched till she was out of sight . . . heading uphill."

"Where the bones were found." Hannah nodded. "What did this woman look like?"

"R-E-O—"

"Her hair was blond, a real light shade. I only remember that because it looked natural. And she was tall. Everything else was ordinary—her face, her clothes. I couldn't tell you what she was wearing that day—apart from that yellow slicker." Evelyn opened her purse. "I can show you. I've been carrying a picture around. I was hoping to catch you alone tonight."

"You have her photograph?"

"No, of course not."

"R-E-N-H—"

Evelyn pulled out a picture postcard of a Coventry street in a different season. "I got this off the rack in the hotel lobby." She pointed to a figure in a hooded yellow raincoat. "This slicker looks exactly like the one that woman was wearing." There were other specimens of the same garb in the background.

"Well, everybody in town had one of those," said Hannah. "I remember when they went on sale at the dry-goods store." And the price had been ridiculously low. Back at the house, Josh and Oren's slickers still hung on hooks by the kitchen door.

"E-L-P-M—"

"I think the stranger must've bought hers in town that morning," said Evelyn. "She probably couldn't resist a big sale like that one."

"No woman could," said Hannah, in full agreement.

"There's no other reason she'd have that slicker tucked in her knapsack. That was a freak rainstorm—nothing about it in the weather forecast. Surprised the hell out of me, a downpour like that one. I remember that morning began with a clear blue sky. So everybody in town might've owned a slicker just like hers—but how many people would've been carting one around that day?"

"Only a woman with an eye for good sale prices."

"E-O-R-E-N—"

"You think this might help the sheriff find Josh's killer?"

"I doubt it," said Hannah. "It's not like you can tell him anything useful. Maybe that other set of bones in Josh's grave belonged to your visitor—maybe not. I don't see that it matters. I wouldn't be surprised if the sheriff already knew her name and address by now." Hannah rose from the chair. "Oh, and we never had this little conversation. Understood?"

Evelyn nodded, mildly distracted by the voices overhead. "How do you suppose those people knew about the woman's bones?"

"Same way you did. One of them probably bought a drink for Dave Hardy today."

Upstairs, the witchboard people had ceased to spell out letters. They stamped their feet and chanted, *"Oren, help me, Oren, help me, Oren—"*

Twenty

The county sheriff's workday had just begun when Special Agent Polk walked into his office unannounced.

The man leaned back in his chair. He was trying not to smile and failing badly. "I guess you heard the news."

"You mean this?" She slapped a copy of a recent e-mail on his desk. It bore the letterhead of a high-ranking politician, who instructed her to step away from the double homicide. She damned the luck that made this an election year for the office of State Attorney General. The top dog of the Justice Department had based his campaign on strong local authority.

Power to the people, my ass.

"I won't ask how you pulled that off," she said. "I don't think you did. Now who's behind it?"

"Your own outfit, the California Bureau of Investigation. They made the final call on jurisdiction."

"The grave is on state land."

"Not anymore. Evelyn Straub just granted a petition of relief on that hundred-year lease. I guess she felt bad about ripping off the taxpayers. Those mineral rights weren't worth a nickel when she sold them to the state."

"No," said Sally. "I don't think that's *quite* it. Years would go by before that petition worked its way through ten layers of bureaucrats. So I'm guessing Mrs. Straub just filed an *intention* to quit the lease. Good try, though."

She dragged a chair to the other side of the desk and sat down next to Cable Babitt. "Well, now," she said in the friendly tone of sharing gossip over a wash line, "I heard you made some headway on identifying that dead tourist, the woman who died with the Hobbs boy. That's the rumor at the CBI down in Sacramento. Is that what you told them? And some solid citizen gave the Justice Department the funny idea that I might be hampering the investigation. Oh, you know—covering the same ground twice, getting in the way and such."

"Nothing personal, Sally, but there might be some truth to that. If you like, I'll get back to you when we have a name for that poor lady tourist."

"I already identified her."

Well, that wiped the smile off his face. The man shook his head in disbelief.

"It's true," she said, as if he had been unable to find the words to accuse her of lying. "I got the woman's name and address from a missing-person report on file with the SFPD. Took me an hour."

"No, I ran all of those reports," said the sheriff. "I checked them myself."

"I'm sure you did." She knew he was lying, but tact forbade laughing out loud. It was certain that this man had never bothered with anything beyond a cursory search. "I guess that poor woman didn't have any friends. It took a long time for someone to notice that she was missing."

Sally pulled the missing-person report from her purse and laid it on the desk in front of him. "It's dated three and a half months after Josh Hobbs disappeared." She gave the incompetent bastard her warmest smile. "Our lady tourist didn't have a day job. New in town, they tell me. And she'd never spoken to the neighbors. They say she only talked to the plants on her balcony. She liked plants a lot. People—not so much. So it took the landlord a few overdue rent checks before he reported her missing. And he only did that so he could legally sell her stuff to cover what she owed him. I backtracked the rental application to her last address and found her dentist. His X-rays matched up with our victim."

"*My* victim," said Cable Babitt. "But thanks for all your help, Sally."

"Oh, I'm not done." Her neighborly grin spread wide. "I plan to go *on* helping you."

"This is my case." He used a tone more properly reserved for a child's sandbox brawl. "The State Attorney

General said so." And this was a variation of *I'm telling Mom.*

"But you can't complain, can you, Sheriff? You don't even know the area code for the Attorney General's phone number."

The small lounge in the Straub Hotel was best described as a toy bar, only room for three stools, and two of them were occupied this morning. The waitress, who doubled as bartender, was busy with guests in the dining area.

Dave Hardy sipped his beer from a coffee cup. Oren drank actual coffee as he gathered slow details of the days before his brother disappeared. His drinking companion was inadvertently accounting for his time.

"God, I hated that old bastard," said Dave.

"I barely remember Millard Straub." Oren kept his eyes on the mirror behind the small bar, lest the Widow Evelyn should wander into the conversation.

"Well, I had to look at his ugly face every day."

"Right, I forgot." Oren had forgotten nothing. "You used to do chores here after school. So how did those two get along, him and his wife?"

"Mrs. Straub was the only one who ever liked Millard well enough to call him Honey. But she got past that. Then the two of them settled into pet names like Filthy Whore and Dickhead Bastard." Dave lifted his beer. "And those were their good days."

"You think that old man might've wanted his wife dead?"

Dave's cup hovered in midair for a moment as he considered this. "I'd say it was the other way around. He used to pay me extra to taste his food. I had to come by real early every morning to check his breakfast. And he wouldn't eat one bite of lunch till I got out of school."

"He thought Mrs. Straub was trying to poison him?"

"I wouldn't have ratted her out if she had. But old Millard died of a heart attack. That's what I heard. I was long gone by the time he croaked. I couldn't wait to get out of this town."

"But you came back."

"Yeah, I got a letter from the sheriff. He wrote to tell me my mother was dying. That was eight years ago. I'm still waiting."

Oren set his coffee cup down on the bar. "I haven't seen your mother since the last time we were sent to the principal's office. Remember that?"

"After the fight in the gym. Yeah, Mom was in good form that night. Did you know she's got a tumor as big as a basketball?" He finished his beer. "Maybe bigger— maybe she's just one big ol' walking, talking tumor. Bitch. But your dad and Hannah, they were aces. I still remember Hannah's cooking."

"I don't think you had another meal at our house after that fight." And now, back on point, Oren continued the pretense of catching up with an old classmate. "You never did say why you slammed my brother into that gym locker."

"Oh, hell. I didn't know the coach sent Josh in there

to take pictures for the yearbook. I thought the kid was just being a creep. Sorry, man. No offense."

Oren's hands tightened around his coffee cup. "Before that night . . . did Josh ever follow you around? I know he did that sometimes—following people with his camera."

Dave mulled over the question between slow sips of beer. "No, I don't think so. But I noticed him watching me in the locker room when I was changing my clothes. I wondered if Josh was queer or something. I guess that's what creeped me out. So, that night when he took my picture—I just snapped."

Oren's eyes were on the wide mirror behind the bar when Evelyn Straub walked into the lounge.

She seemed unhappy to see him sitting here with Dave Hardy. This had been a mistake. He should have run the deputy down in someone else's bar, for now she must realize that Hannah had given up Dave as the source of leaks from the County Sheriff's Office. The housekeeper had thrown him this bone as a consolation prize. On the subject of missing photographs and dates, she had pleaded amnesia.

Evelyn Straub sat down on the third bar stool. "Hello, boys."

The deputy lifted his beer in salute.

"Oren," she said, "give Hannah my regards." The light note of sarcasm was an instruction to also convey that she was pissed off. "Are you going to the birthday ball this year?"

"I never go," said Oren.

"You went to the first one," she said. "Not your finest hour."

"I remember that," said Dave. "Shit, we were still in elementary school that year." With great goodwill inspired by beer before breakfast, he slapped Oren's back. "I heard the Winston girl beat the crap out of you the other day."

"I saw the whole thing," said Evelyn, never taking her eyes off of Oren. "Payback's a bitch."

"Call me Sally."

William Swahn could think of other things that he might call this woman, and some were vaguely criminal. The CBI agent and her goons had crossed a line today.

Sally Polk sipped her tea and nodded toward his untouched cup. "Is that too hot?"

He could place her country-western accent in Bakersfield, a unique part of California where some migrant families had kept their transplant drawls from other states and passed them down through the generations. "Am I under arrest?"

"No, dear. But thank you for coming in."

"It was hard to refuse the state troopers. They took my cane when they opened the rear door of the car."

"Oh, those boys." With a light wave, she brushed off this bad behavior of children with guns. "You're a guest. You're also the only criminologist for miles around. Do your friends call you Will or William?"

"The Highway Patrol doesn't need a criminologist. In

this area, a speeding ticket might be the high point of a trooper's day."

"I'm with a different agency."

"The CBI. I know. And I also know the Coventry homicides were taken away from you."

"Oh, my, doesn't news travel fast? I only found out myself an hour ago. So I'm guessing you have some idea who pulled the strings to change jurisdiction. You and Oren have the same lawyer. Isn't that right? Was it Addison's plan? Or does Judge Hobbs still have that kind of influence?"

Swahn pushed his teacup away. "I can only repeat what my cleaning lady said. Most of her gossip is very reliable."

Smiling sweetly, so motherly, the agent held up a color portrait of young Joshua Hobbs. The boy was posed against the ersatz blue-sky backdrop used by school photographers. "He was a fine-looking boy, wasn't he? Maybe a bit on the delicate side. No interest in sports, I hear— not *quite* like the other boys."

"The *real* boys? Your bias is showing, Agent Polk."

"Call me Sally, just plain old gay-basher Sally."

He almost smiled. He *almost* liked her. "For a year after Josh Hobbs went missing, there were three teenage girls haunting the sheriff's office like widows. You still need a criminologist's point of view? *Fine*. The boy was rampantly heterosexual."

"But you're not. You can't claim to be straight at this late date. If you did, you might have to give back all that lovely settlement money. The police down in Los Angeles might say it was paid out under false pretenses. As an agent of the Justice Department, I might have to look into that."

"Apparently, the LAPD is holding to the terms of our nondisclosure agreement. Clearly, you've never been privy to any details. So you're blowing smoke. Is this your interrogation style? You just throw out a few lines of garbage and see what sticks?"

"I wonder which client Addison worries about the most—you or Oren Hobbs. I know the sheriff took a real hard look at you when Josh disappeared. Now why is that? You'd have to run naked in the streets to get Cable Babitt's attention. And then there's Ad Winston. If he's your attorney, I *know* you did something wrong."

William leaned on his cane, preparing to rise. There was no acrimony in his voice when he said, "You'll have to excuse me now."

"So you don't want this case solved, either. That doesn't speak well for innocence."

"I don't care."

"You will." This was no threat. She was worried.

He followed the track of her eyes to the window on the parking lot, where people were gathering with cameras and microphones. "I see you called out the media."

She shook her head. "That's your lawyer's style, not mine." She left her desk and walked to the window. More vans and cars pulled into the parking lot to disgorge reporters and film crews. "God, how Addison loves the cameras. That's why I had the troopers pick you up—so he wouldn't find out you were here. Believe it or not, I did that as a favor to you, Mr. Swahn."

William limped to the window to stand beside her. "Well, you know I didn't call my lawyer. This isn't his doing."

"Maybe not," she said. "Sometimes—when there's blood in the water—they just show up."

Twenty-one

Twenty years ago, Ferris Monty had begun his book on a typewriter, and now he was nearly done copying the old manuscript onto a computer. The screen glowed, and so did he.

Fat fingers typed out Joshua's dark brown hair and high cheekbones. Line by line, he animated the dead boy and made him walk the streets of Coventry with a camera strap slung around his long white neck. And sometimes, on one page or another, the boy was followed by a loopy Irish setter that seemed vaguely retarded.

What was the stupid beast's name?

He paused to page through an old notebook. Ah, right. The boy had called his dog Horatio, as in, "Get off me, Horatio!"

Ferris was revisiting a long-ago day when he had blended in with the tourists at a street fair. For an hour or more, he had kept watch on the boy and the dog, and then he had lost sight of them in the crowd, but found them again when a woman yelled, "Josh, you get this mutt off me! Now!" Once more, in keeping with the theme of ducks in a row, Ferris had followed behind the dog that followed the boy.

A woman had appeared to be the unwitting leader of this parade for a time—or perhaps not. According to his notes for that day, he had never been entirely certain, for the dog had suddenly jumped another victim in the street and slathered her with kisses until she also screamed. An old line in Ferris's notebook lamented: *How could the boy hope to shadow anyone with a dog like that in tow?*

On other pages, other days when the dog was not around, the objects of Joshua's curiosity had been clear. The boy had a gift for capturing the telling moments, snapping rants or confusion, a binge eater at the point of throwing up in a local diner, and—

And now Ferris recalled his own portraits—hung on public display for decades.

He had ordered prints from Josh after the originals had appeared in the lobby of the local bank. Ferris's private collection hung on the wall above the computer monitor, placed there so that he could daily see himself in a kinder light than his mirror could afford. He had so loved these portraits of younger days when he had black eyebrows to match his toupee. And Joshua's work was superior to every other artist's previous attempt at capturing Ferris's true essence.

Understatement.

Today these three photographs stunned him anew.

He saw his younger self standing in line at the bank all those years ago. In the first frame, he had noticed the boy taking his picture. Ferris's face was turned to the camera's lens with a look of happy surprise—and more. As the line moved forward in the second shot, he looked back over his shoulder in sweet flirtation. But his expression was most vivid in the final shot. He had been caught in the act of falling in love with the young photographer.

However, the boy had been repulsed by him. Ferris had discovered this on the day when Joshua had come by the house to drop off these prints and collect his money. Why, then, had the boy not turned away after snapping the first shot? Why stay to take two more? And why hang this trio of pictures out in public?

Slowly Ferris came to an understanding that increased his respect for the young artist.

It was all about the telling moments. Joshua had captured a rare thing, the instant of love at first sight. The boy may have been repelled by his subject, but he had surely taken great pride in this amazing thing he had done.

Over the years, thousands of customers had passed through the bank lobby and stared at these pictures while standing in line. Had any of them truly understood what they were seeing? His smile of superiority faded off.

Horror set in.

And it would keep Ferris company all through the day.

The only cab company in Saulburg had no cars to spare; most had been commandeered by television networks and newspapers. Against Agent Polk's advice, William Swahn had declined to allow the state troopers to drive him home. No thank you. He had also waived the offer of uniformed escorts to guide him through the crowd of reporters in the parking lot.

The media rabble had swelled in size, more rowdies with cameras and microphones.

William waited alone behind the glass doors, and he glanced at his watch. Enough time had elapsed for his ride to show up. She had promised to come with all possible speed. To the residents of Coventry, that might mean fifteen miles per hour instead of ten.

He could see nothing of the parking lot. Reporters and photographers blocked his view. After a few more minutes, he stepped out into the light of day, the hollered questions and the press of flesh all around him. He made his way through the lot, limping ungainly past the patrol cars and passing civilian sedans he did not recognize. All the yelling blended into a single roar, and the sound surrounded him. Here and there, a phrase was clear as one reporter called out, "Wait a minute!" and another one said, "Hey, man, slow down!"

A foot flashed out in front of him, and he was indeed slowing down. He was falling. Where was his cane? One of the bastards had taken his cane! He landed on his bad leg, and the pain made him scream. They stood over him, grinning, some filming the motion of his writhing and others snapping still shots of agony that was slow to subside. For one lost minute, William gave up, and one of them yelled, "Is he dead?"

He lay on his back, sliding into shock and motionless, forgetting to breathe or blink.

And now it was one of his assailants who screamed, and then another one cried out. William turned his head to see a camera fall as a photographer doubled over in pain, both hands protecting his crotch. A tiny figure was battling her way through the crowd, one pair of testicles by another, and then she snatched up his cane from the ground to do some damage to kneecaps.

Mighty Hannah Rice had come to take him home.

Oren entered the bank with the intention to empty a savings account that he had begun at the age of ten. He stopped just inside the vestibule and opened a small blue passbook to check his memory against the balance. It was the wrong one, though he had found it in his old writing desk. This was Josh's old bankbook. He read the total of three thousand dollars, a fabulous sum for his fifteen-year-old brother, and this did not include the interest earned over two decades. He had never realized that the sales of Josh's photographs had been so lucrative.

And might his own passbook be found in his brother's desk? How had they gotten switched—and when? Perhaps he put too much stock in every odd thing these days, as if he could divine signs and omens that way. His next thought was that he might not be paying close enough attention.

Without the right passbook, he had no business with the bank today. On his way out the door, he saw the yellow Rolls-Royce parked out front. The driver's bad hairpiece and pale skin completed the sheriff's description of Ferris Monty. Oren recognized this man as one of the players at the séance, but he had a less distinct memory of him from somewhere else and long ago—just a face in a photograph.

Monty was waddling up the walkway to the bank when their eyes met and the little man stumbled. Was he frightened? Affecting nonchalance in a pirouette, Monty spun around and hurried back to the Rolls-Royce.

And what was that about?

Only in Coventry was it possible to follow a car on foot. The Rolls turned a corner, and Oren strolled after it. He was only half a block behind when the yellow car parked in front of the post office. He gave Ferris Monty a minute of lead time before stepping up to the window. The little man stood in the lobby, studying Josh's three portraits of William Swahn, moving closer and squinting to see the details. Oren rapped on the windowpane and waved. Startled, Monty back-stepped onto another customer's shoes. Then he shot out the door and ran for his car.

Oren made no move to prevent this escape. He planned to allow Monty time for a little sweat, time to wait for the inevitable knock on the door. At the moment, he was more interested in his brother's old photographs of the Letter Man and why they so fascinated a gossip columnist. As Oren entered the small lobby, he remembered where he had seen Ferris Monty before. Josh's series of triptychs only pictured people waiting in lines. One such group of photographs had been sold to the town's only bank.

He stared at his brother's work on the post-office wall, eyes moving from one picture to the next.

Josh, tell me a story.

He had always believed that the subject was William Swahn. He had forgotten that the insane librarian was also pictured here. She stood in line in front of the man with the cane, and there was no backward glance to show that she knew him. This picture might support Swahn's claim that they had never spoken.

No, the Letter Man had lied to him.

As this pair moved forward in the sequence of three photographs, a bulky envelope disappeared from a group of letters in Swahn's hand to reappear jutting out of Mavis Hardy's shopping bag.

The next stop on Dave Hardy's patrol route was a small roadside bar two towns over from the county seat. It was nearly time for a liquid lunch. He liked to spread out his drinking across the day. His beer was always served in a coffee cup, and he was never asked to pay a tab—a courtesy to law enforcement.

He loved his job. Even after hours and out of uniform, he could drink for free.

The deputy slid onto his favorite bar stool, the one closest to the window, to keep an eye on the parking lot. He was always on the lookout for out-of-state plates, such easy targets for tickets, but all of these patrons were local people. He turned to watch the TV set behind the bar. It was early for a news show. The banner scrolling below the picture told him that this was a breaking story. On screen, only a few blocks away from the sheriff's office in Saulburg, the parking lot for the Highway Patrol was a mob scene.

He recognized the limping man as a recluse from Coventry. William Swahn was surrounded by reporters and swallowed up whole. The television camera cut to a shot of Sally Polk amid cameras and microphones. She was answering questions on the old Hobbs case—a case that was no longer hers. This woman did not know when to let go.

Dave broke with his tradition of one beer per bar and ordered another. Sally Polk reminded him of his mother, who could smile while she stabbed him with words in all the soft places.

Oren phoned home from the bank. While he listened to the rings at the other end of the line, he stared at Ferris Monty's three portraits on the wall.

His father answered the telephone, and Oren learned that Hannah had taken the car. And so, said the judge, he was out of luck if he needed a ride. However, the old man knew the address he wanted, adding, "It's not much of a hike, maybe a mile or so from town."

Walking along the narrow back roads, Oren called up a memory of Josh returning from Ferris Monty's house after dropping off an order of prints. Though this had been a big commission, the boy had not wanted to talk about it.

After studying the original photographs in the bank, Oren understood his brother's uneasiness, and now he considered the worst scenario for Josh's death. As a CID agent, he had dealt with predator soldiers, arresting more than a few in his career. He was so well versed in this crime that he could even name the freaks who specialized in the capture and rape of adolescents.

Something about a fifteen-year-old boy had called out to the strange little man with the black toupee. That much would have registered with Josh, and it would have placed the whole subject beyond the confidence of his older brother. In those days, Oren had an ugly word for Josh's stalking activities. Consequently, his little brother would never have mentioned any incident that involved Ferris Monty, the personification of *creepy*.

Oren wished that he had been more understanding then. Understanding *now* broke his heart.

Sarah Winston mimicked bright birdcalls as she filled the feeders all along the rail of the outside deck. A few steps away, her daughter adjusted a pair of binoculars to focus on the judge's old Mercedes as it turned into William Swahn's driveway and disappeared behind thick trees.

Isabelle circled around the deck for a better view, and the car was recaptured in her lenses when it reappeared in the small clearing in front of the house down on Paulson Lane. She anticipated Oren Hobbs, but it was Hannah who emerged from the driver's side to help William up the steps to the front door. His limp was worse today.

She wondered if he knew what they were saying about him on the news.

Sarah Winston was ignorant of the latest rumors. Isabelle had not wanted to spoil a day of rare good spirits. Her mother seemed so happy in her whistled conversations with the birds flocking to the feeders.

Leaning back against the rail, Isabelle watched wild things grow tame in the older woman's presence. After passing a few minutes this way, she noticed that one of the stationary telescopes was aimed downward. She looked through the eyepiece. It was already focused to give the clear view of a window framing a desk and chair. This was no accident. Every tension screw had been tightened to fix the position and keep the lens from straying off target. She was startled when William appeared in the window.

Which one of her parents was spying on him?

Twenty-two

The door was open to the noise of preparation for a birthday party, hammering and hollering, swearing and sawing wood.

Outside on the deck, a man in coveralls folded his ladder, having finished the chore of nailing strings of lights around the roof of the tower room.

Inside, Addison Winston stood by the bed, looking down at the face of his unconscious wife. "It's amazing that she could sleep through that racket." Though he should not call it sleep, this drunken stupor. He turned to Isabelle. "Well, now you know why she's been so cheerful today." He got down on his knees to drag an empty bottle out from under the armoire. "Where is she getting it from?"

"The maid?"

He shook his head. "Hilda gives her one drink for

breakfast and one for lunch. That girl knows better than to cross me."

The workman carried his ladder down the tower stairs, and Isabelle closed the door behind him. "Addison, it's long past time to put Mom in rehab."

"Worst possible timing." The lawyer walked out onto the deck. In the yard below, the workmen were breaking for lunch. Ah, peace. He was no longer troubled by the cawing and flapping of birds. They had learned not to come near him.

Isabelle joined him at the rail. "Why did you marry my mother? Was it because she was so beautiful?"

"She's *still* beautiful," he said, insistent on this. "But no, that wasn't it. Back in your mother's college days, do you remember how she supported you?"

"I think she had lots of different jobs."

"Well, you were only four years old. Belle, she literally sang for your supper. Such brave songs—brave because your mother couldn't sing very well. And she didn't play that guitar worth a damn. The first time I ever saw her, I was a visiting lecturer at UCLA. She was standing barefoot on the grass, and you were curled up in a little ball, fast asleep in a patch of afternoon sun. Students were coming and going all around you.

"The young can be very savage, but they never ridiculed Sarah—even though she played all the wrong chords and sang every damn note off-key. A truly awful performance, but the students dropped their loose change into her open guitar case. They weren't pity donations—more like showing respect. Sarah was so daring, hanging herself out on public display—and she even knew that she didn't have one shred of talent. I emptied my wallet into her guitar case, and that was the first time we said hello."

Addison leaned over the rail and pointed down at a long silver vehicle as it parked by the paddock near the old stable. "Keep your eye on that one."

The driver opened a door at the rear of the narrow trailer and lowered a plank. Led by a rope halter, a silver stallion emerged, tossing his head and shying at every loud sound around him as his handler guided him into the paddock and released him.

"Remind you of anyone we used to know?"

"He looks a lot like old Nickel." Isabelle picked up the binoculars for a closer look. "*Exactly* like Nickel." Her old horse had died the year after her mother had packed her off to a boarding school in Europe.

More trucks arrived in the yard below to disgorge lumber, long tables and round ones, linens and folding chairs. The stallion ran round the paddock, mad to escape.

"It took me a long time to find a horse with that same odd coloring," he said. "Call it a reward because you stayed for more than half a day this time. Your mother won't need you for a while, but that poor beast down there could use some company."

The day he had bought her the first stallion, she had instantly fallen in love with the horse. And Addison had believed that ten-year-old Belle had finally come to love him, too—for a day.

When she had flown down the tower stairs, leaving

him alone on the deck, Addison resumed his puzzle of
Sarah's most recent stupor and her secret stash of booze.
Where did she keep it? He had looked everywhere. And
now he searched the lay of his land. The garage was far
enough away that the start-up of automobiles would not
disturb the lightest of sleepers. The expensive engines
purred so softly in motion; they could covertly sail past
the lodge and down the drive.

Perhaps he should not be looking for secret bottles
but a secret set of car keys.

He turned back to the open door of the tower room
and raised his eyes to the high shelf of journals—an excellent hiding place.

Isabelle entered the stable's tack room to find her old
saddle waiting for her on a sawhorse. And the leather
saddlebags were right where she had left them after her
last time out with old Nickel. She filled both bags with
her mother's journals. Once upon another summer, they
had been packed with her own birder logs and lunches
for treks along the forest paths.

Years ago, Oren Hobbs had hiked those same trails.
Aided by one of her mother's telescopes, she had caught
glimpses of him from the deck at the top of the house.
And she had risked encounters with that beautiful boy—
risky because sometimes wishes came true, and, a time or
two, she had thought of running him down with her
horse and pounding him into the ground.

Saddlebags slung over one shoulder and bridle in

hand, she carried her saddle out to the paddock to make the acquaintance of the second Nickel. If birds would not come to her, horses had always liked her well enough, and this one trotted toward her with some urgency. The sight of the saddle must have given him hope that she would take him away from this place.

"I know just how you feel." She held out one flat palm to offer him the solace of a sugar lump grabbed from the kitchen. His breath on her hand was a warm memory of better days.

While Isabelle saddled the horse, intending to rescue them both for some quiet time in a calmer place, a yellow Rolls-Royce was heading toward her. Most visitors parked in the circular driveway at the front of the lodge. Ferris Monty had probably assumed that no one would be at home to him, and he was right. The car stopped by the paddock, and the driver waved to her. He stepped out, leaving the door hanging open, perchance to make a fast retreat. With all his money, she wondered why he did not buy a better hairpiece that would blend more gracefully with his thick gray eyebrows.

"Hi there." He hesitated at a distance, lifting off the balls of his feet, saying on tiptoe, "I was hoping to have a word with your mother."

Isabelle, having nowhere to hide, resented being cornered this way, but she recalled a lesson in journalism learned at Addison's knee: *Always toss a bone to the dogs of the Fourth Estate. If you make them work for their supper, they'll turn on you and eat you alive.* And so, because her mother was too fragile to be chased down for an interview, Isabelle bestowed a smile on the worm-white little man. "Mom's kind of busy right now." She gestured toward workmen on ladders, nailing up lights to frame every window. "It's quite a production. Will I do?"

"Oh, *yes*." He rushed forward, grinning.

And she took one step back.

His cologne was repulsive, though she recognized the brand as a wildly expensive one. No doubt Monty had bought it for status only. Certainly he had never realized that personal body chemistry added something to the mix of every wearer. In his case, the blend of his natural odor worked an unfortunate effect: riding just below the signature scent was a faint smell of piss, as if he had recently wet himself.

The little man pulled a notebook and pen from the inside pocket of his blazer, and his eyes slowly narrowed with a catlike smile. Later in the day, she would remember him with restrained claws and faint purring.

"It's about the birthday ball," he said. "I was so looking forward to attending this year. Assuming I'm welcome. Your father was—"

"Of course you're welcome. Everyone in Coventry has an open invitation." She smiled, as if she had no idea that Monty was the only exception. Addison despised this man, and Isabelle's only joy in life was thwarting her father. "I'll tell the caterer to seat you in the ballroom, unless you'd rather have an outside table." She borrowed his notebook and scribbled a personal invitation that would get him past a gorilla doorman hired for the event.

"Oh, this is wonderful," he said, insanely pleased.

While answering his interview questions, she slowly steered him back to his car, hoping to see him off before her mother awoke to appear on the deck. "Sorry," she said in response to his last inquiry. "I don't remember the year Addison started building this place." She looked up, shading her eyes to see the high tower. "It seems like we've always lived in the castle."

The mangling of this famous line of American gothic was not wasted on Monty. His eyes flickered, and his face brightened as he committed her words to paper, maybe embellishing on innuendo to create something worse than the truth about her family life.

Fat chance.

"As I recall," he said, "you left town a few days after Joshua Hobbs disappeared."

"Well, there was nothing odd about that." And now she thought of another lie. "It was time to go back to school. I had summer sessions that year." She neglected to mention that she had been sent farther away than her eastern boarding school. Her plane had landed in Paris, where she had learned to speak French and miss her mother.

"But you never came back." His pen described small circles above the page of his notebook, a subtle prompt.

"Oh, you mean for the *summer*. No, you're right. This is my first summer back in Coventry. In my college years, I did internships during school vacations, and I picked up my graduate degrees in London. That's where I work

now. So my visits home were short ones, holidays mostly."
And they had indeed been short stays, years apart and
never lasting for an entire day.

Isabelle and Ferris Monty smiled at each other, and
there was no protest or insinuation. They had mutually
and silently agreed that he would have to make do with
this stew of truth and lies.

"Oh, one more thing." He held up his index finger,
as if to test the wind. "Shortly after you left, your mother
also went away for a while."

And that would have been the time, recently recounted
by Addison, when her mother had been committed to a
hospital for wealthy people with eccentricities, patients
who eccentrically acquired the angry red tattoos of razor
scars on their wrists. On another occasion, her mother
had downed sleeping pills like handfuls of candy.

Bet you can't eat just one, Mom.

"My parents used to take separate vacations," said Isabelle.

And so they had. Her father had gone off to the circus
of his high-profile law practice down in L.A., and her
mother had gone insane.

The red cedar house in the woods had the steeply pitched
roof and filigree of a Swiss chalet. Oren Hobbs was sitting
on the doorstep when Ferris Monty came home.

The little man seemed resigned to his fate. His feet
were dragging as he left his Rolls-Royce and crossed the

yard to face his visitor. Without the exchange of a single word, the two of them entered the house.

The dust and debris of the large front room was the giveaway of a long malaise, but Oren could chart the past few days of recovery by inroads made in the mess and by the garbage bags lined up at the door. These signs of a brighter mood would not square with the anxiety of a murderer whose crime had recently come to light with the bones. He sank down in an armchair, and Ferris Monty stood before him, eyes cast downward, like an aged schoolboy awaiting punishment.

"I took a long look at those three pictures of you in the bank."

"I guessed as much." Monty slowly raised his eyes. "But tell me, what did you think of the *other* triptych?" His smile was strained. "The photographs in the *post office*?"

Oren's voice was calm. His eyes were cold. "I noticed the way you were looking at my brother when he took those shots—the ones in the *bank*."

"But the postmaster's pictures are miles more interesting. They give up a secret relationship. Your brother was very good at capturing secrets."

Oren nodded. "There's a word for what you are."

"A phebophile," said Monty. "One who preys on adolescent boys. That's the word you want. It doesn't describe me. I'm hardly a virgin, but I can assure you that all of my lovers have been consenting adults. I never touched that boy. I'd never set myself up for that kind of rejection."

Monty removed his toupee to reveal sparse strands of gray on a wrinkled scalp. He seemed even less normal without the fake hair—more insectile. The sheriff had correctly likened him to bug larvae.

The little man looked down at the black hairpiece in his hands. "A beautiful boy like that would run from the likes of me." His eyes wandered to Oren's boots. "And your brother could run very fast. He needed speed . . . considering what he was doing, shadowing people, following them around for hours—days. I think that's why he always wore sneakers. He imitated everything else about you, Mr. Hobbs—your walk, the way you combed your hair, clothes—everything but your cowboy boots."

"You just admitted to stalking my brother."

"I always kept my distance." Monty backed away as Oren rose from the chair. "I can help you, Mr. Hobbs." He tripped on one of his garbage bags and fell backward to land on his tailbone. "Today I *led* you into the post office." There was a trace of whimper in his voice. "I all but led you there by the hand and pointed out the pictures on the wall. I know you've seen them a hundred times . . . but today you actually studied them, didn't you?"

Oren moved toward him.

By hands and feet, Monty scuttled backward, eyes wide and frightened as he dragged his rump across the rug, and backed up to the wall. "You saw the pictures of Swahn secretly passing a letter to the town lunatic." His eyes were begging now, hands rising to ward off anticipated violence.

Seconds ticked by—half a minute.

Oren was motionless, arms at his sides. He knew how to wait.

Monty slowly lowered his hands. "You're disgusted by the idea that I could love Joshua. But I think you'll take my help. I know something about Swahn's letter."

Sarah Winston hardly paid attention to her husband. Addison had become accustomed to her hundred-mile stare, and so it raised no interest in him when her gaze went over his head to the high bookshelf that ran around the wall of the tower room.

A group of birder logs was missing.

Which ones?

Could Addison have taken them? No, her husband had nothing but contempt for this side of her life. Isabelle must have borrowed those Birdland chronicles.

If he should look up and see that empty space on the shelf, he might wonder where the books had gone; and then he might take an interest and open the others. What then? Would he commit her to another hospital?

He was talking in the lecture mode that followed her every binge. She nodded absently, lowering her gaze to meet his eyes. And now husband and wife were connected. She could still hold him this way. At core, Addison was a romantic man, blind to the changes of her aging and alcoholism. His smile was a constant thing, even in moments of anger, but she knew all of the subtle nuances.

She wished he would stop it, drop it—yell if he liked—but stop smiling.

Isabelle and Nickel Number Two had followed a well-worn trail past Evelyn Straub's old cabin. After a while, it should have led her to a landmark in one of her mother's journals, but she had been lulled by the slow rhythm of the horse and the warmth of the summer sun. Intoxicated by lush green forest and birdsong, trills that ran up- and downhill—distracted by the novelty of happiness—she had overshot the clearing.

She found another trail leading out of the woods and onto the fire road. Following a memory, she counted sharp twists and wide curves, and then she saw the turn-out up ahead, the place where her mother had always left the car. As the horse clopped toward that old parking space, Isabelle passed another turnout closer to a favorite place in the forest, and there stood an empty van. In the dirt, there were signs of other vehicles recently stopping here.

She dismounted and guided the horse through the trees where there was no clear path. High in the branches, warbling songsters were drowned out by a magpie's whining, quizzical song.

Maag? Aag-aag?

And then came a rapid fire of notes.

Wah-wah-wah-wah?

Sections of yellow tape were visible between tree trunks.

And now she heard human voices. Drawing closer, Isabelle could see that the tape cordoned off an opening in the ground. Two teenagers, wearing T-shirts with university logos, knelt beside the hole, sifting dirt through screens. A third student used a soft brush to dust away the dirt from an object in her hand.

A bone?

So this was the grave of Josh Hobbs and a nameless stranger—*here* in the place her mother loved best among the million acres of forestland.

Isabelle tightened her hold on the reins, and the horse shied in sympathetic anxiety.

Oren stared at the photographs on the wall of Ferris Monty's study. He stood close behind the gossip columnist, who was scrolling through a file on his computer.

"You see?" Monty ran one finger down a list on the screen and paused at mentions of individual students. "They were all at UCLA that same year. Here's William Swahn—something of a prodigy, barely fourteen when he got his first college degree. Here's the librarian. She was in her twenties then. And Sarah Winston was twenty-four." One finger tapped the screen on this line. "This is her maiden name."

"That's it? You've got nothing on Ad Winston." Oren's eyes traveled back to the damning pictures on the wall.

Ferris Monty rose from his chair and removed these

prints of the bank photographs to stack them facedown on his desk. "Concentrate on the photos at the *post office*. Before William Swahn was mutilated, I believe he had a relationship with Sarah Winston."

"When they were at UCLA? He was a little boy." Oren folded his arms and watched Monty's frustration grow with this little piece of bait. "I don't see Mrs. Winston as a pedophile."

"Not *then*." Monty paused to purse his lips and perhaps to censor his next words. "*Later*. When the child grew *up*—that's when they had the affair."

"The *alleged* affair," said Oren. Apparently Swahn's nondisclosure agreement had teeth and staying power. Ferris Monty's research had never turned up a rumor that the man was gay.

"All right," said Monty. "It's speculation. But what if it's true? What if that relationship continued after Swahn moved to Coventry? What if Addison found out about Mavis passing Swahn's love letters to his wife? I know a woman's bones were found with Joshua. Suppose Addison meant to kill Sarah . . . and he murdered a stranger by mistake? And let's say your brother was following her that—"

"You think any man could mistake a stranger for his own wife?"

"He could've hired one of his criminal clients to kill her—someone who didn't know her." Monty was like a dog vainly watching Oren's face for signs of approval.

Civilians and their damn theories, their television ideas of murder. First Millard Straub was hiring an assassin to murder Evelyn, and now Ad Winston was the one voted most likely to put out a contract on his wife.

"I know the dead woman was hit from behind." Monty waited for payback on this offering. Getting none, he made another. "And she's been identified. That's how I know she had light blond hair . . . like Sarah Winston's. I have a very reliable source."

"Someone in the sheriff's office? Maybe a deputy?"

Monty puffed out his chest in a small show of courage. "I would never give up a source."

"You bought your information from Dave Hardy." Oren knew he was right. Ferris Monty's eyes popped a bit too wide; he probably knew the penalty for bribing an officer of the law, and he would not fare well in prison. This little man was having a very bad day.

After a short canter down the fire road, Isabelle found an old picnic spot, a favored stop on the solitary horseback rides of childhood. She tethered Nickel to a tree and spread a blanket on the ground. Seven birder logs were laid out in chronological order. Upon opening the first one, she labored over the code of pictures and birdcalls. At the time of this entry, her mother was still happy to be alive.

The insanity began later, after Isabelle had worked her way through the pages of winter and spring. A day in early June had begun with a delicate bird that had no song. The blue-eyed lark lay on the ground, broken wings spread at odd angles. Its eyes were closed.

In death?

There was blood on the young bird's face just below one eye. The sun was shining.

Isabelle's mind turned toward the trio of student grave diggers in her mother's favorite clearing. The year on the book spine was right, and the page was dated to that fatal Saturday. How could the lark be anyone but Josh Hobbs?

What could her mother know of Josh's death on that afternoon? The town had not gone looking for the boy before nightfall. And what of the blood? This journal entry had been written two decades before the disappearance had been called an act of violence.

Nowhere on this page or the next was there any sign of the stranger buried with Josh. The omission of a second victim argued for her mother's innocence. Isabelle rationalized the journal entry as a story come by secondhand.

On all of the following pages, Coventry was grotesquely altered. It was always night, a nightmare town of birds with animal claws instead of talons. Their beaks were filled with long teeth.

And her mother had lost her mind.

It might be best to replace the birder logs on the tower bookshelf, to hide them there in plain sight. But what if the investigation should lead to an interrogation of her fragile mother and a search of the house?

She could destroy these books, but that might also damn her mother in the cover-up of a crime. At some later date, this evidence might be needed to prove innocence—or madness. Isabelle's mind continued to work along criminal lines as she decided to hide the journals in the care of an honest man.

Taking a shortcut through the woods, Oren neatly side-stepped a recent deposit of horseshit. And so it was natural to be thinking of Isabelle Winston, the only one who had ever used the hiking trails as bridle paths. In summers past, he and Josh had sometimes encountered her on horseback. The girl had always waved hello to his brother. Oren, of course, had been beneath her notice.

A path forked off the trail and led him out to the fire road. He was headed downhill and homeward when he heard the sound of a horse's hooves. Oren was hopeful as he turned around.

And there she was.

He saw her red hair on a distant rise—and the same silver horse.

Impossible.

That stallion had been old when the rider was a teen-ager.

Well, it was a day for ghosts, human or equine. And it was long past time to have a few words with Isabelle Winston. He stood in the middle of the dirt road and waved her down as she came trotting toward him, not slowing any, but riding faster, cantering, then galloping, *galloping*.

That horse was huge.

Oh, shit!

He dove into the woods, lost his footing in a tangle of deadwood and landed hard, all the wind knocked out of his chest as horse and rider sped by him. A near miss. And the lady never looked back.

Oren lay there for a while, idly ruminating. Isabelle was definitely escalating the violence. How would she top this?

He picked himself up and brushed the leaves and dirt from his clothes. It was a slow walk home. There was much to think about. His mind wandered back to a valentine from his childhood, the one mailed to him in an envelope with an eastern postmark but no return address and no signature. As a twelve-year-old boy, he had opened that heart-shaped card to read the words *I hate you!* writ large and bold. It had smelled of horse. He had kept it for years.

More than an hour had passed before he reached home. At the end of the driveway, it was a surprise to see the silver stallion tied by reins to a tree in the yard. Isabelle Winston pushed the screen door open. Eyes fixed on her horse, she failed to see the man with the foolish grin on his face, standing below her on the porch steps. She passed him by. After untying the horse's reins, she swung up into the saddle in one graceful motion and rode away across the meadow.

When Oren entered the house, Hannah was standing over a pair of saddlebags on the living room carpet. She crooked one finger, and he followed her down the hall to the kitchen, where the judge was seated at the table. Three cups had been laid out and emptied.

So Isabelle had stayed long enough for coffee.

Small leather-bound books were piled at the center of the tablecloth. The judge held one open and offered his son a glimpse of drawings and lines of writing. "These are Sarah Winston's birder logs. Her daughter thought we should keep them for a while. I don't think the girl has much faith in Cable Babitt."

"That's not exactly what Belle said." Hannah set out a clean cup for Oren. "She said Cable's a fool, and he shouldn't get near these books."

"In any case," said the judge, "I gave her my word that her mother's journals would be handled with care and in confidence." His fixed stare made it clear that his son was also bound by this oral contract.

Hannah turned her attention to a fresh pot of coffee percolating on the stove. "Those journals were written around the time Josh went missing. Belle Winston wants you to know that this is all you get from her. And there's no point in trying to question her mother. If you show up at the lodge, Belle won't even open the door. She'll just shoot you right through the wood—right where you stand."

The judge lowered his reading glasses, something he did in serious moments, though he was smiling. "The girl was very clear about that, Oren. She *will* shoot you."

"I believe it. She tried to run me down with her horse."

Hannah poured coffee into his cup. "I wish you two would get married and take the fight indoors."

Oren opened one of the small books and read the neat

script of Sarah Winston's notes on the songs and movements of—a dodo with a pipe? He looked up at his father to silently ask, *What?*

Judge Hobbs adjusted his bifocals, the better to study this drawing. "I believe that's Cable. He gave up his pipe a few years ago." The old man looked down to resume his perusal of the journal in his hands, and he idly turned the pages. "Belle Winston is an ornithologist, and she thinks there's something here." He held up the open book to show his son a graceful pink heron with long slender limbs of human form. "If I had to guess, I'd say this is Evelyn Straub in her prime. Longest legs in town." He pointed to the companion page filled with handwriting. "Sarah's notes are less clear. There's lots of shorthand for one thing and another, terms I've never heard before. It might make more sense to another bird-watcher."

"We can go see Mavis Hardy at the library," said Hannah.

"Nobody in Coventry goes to the—"

"Oren." The judge held up one finger as a warning. "Don't."

Hannah nodded in agreement as she opened one of the journals. "I hate it when people say that, even if it's true." She looked up at Oren. "So you'll talk to Mavis? She used to go birding all the time back in the days when she was still on the thin side."

"You mean before she started planning to murder her husband?"

Hannah closed the book and slammed it on the table. "Mavis can help you. Nobody in this county knows more about birds than she does. And, incidentally, that poor woman did *not* do murder."

"What? She spent a long time getting ready for it." Oren remembered a summer day when he and Josh had come upon Mrs. Hardy working out with weights in the library, building muscles, adding bulk. And the following summer, she had been arrested on a charge of murder. "Name one thing on her side."

"Mavis looked out for her son," said Hannah.

Oren folded his arms, telegraphing disbelief. "She made Dave's life a living hell. She castrated that kid all over town."

"She probably saved his life." Hannah's voice was getting testy.

Judge Hobbs, the peacemaker, lightly touched his son's arm. "Remember when Dave broke his leg? You were in the third grade that year. Well, that didn't happen falling off a bike. It wasn't enough fun beating his wife. Colin Hardy had to go after that little boy."

Oren had better recall of a later event, the day the coroner carried the corpse of Dave's father out of the house. The librarian's hands were raw, her face swollen and her eyes triumphant. "She spent a year planning it. That makes it a premeditated murder."

"Says who!" Hannah's tone did not imply a question. As punctuation, she banged one fist on the table, and a spoon bounced to the floor. "Half the town—the half that's male—they'll never forgive her. Mavis scared them that day. That was her real crime. *Men,*" she said, using this word to sum up the ills of the world. "Mavis didn't

sneak up on that bastard while he was sleeping, did she? No, she did not. Her husband was fully dressed for work. And I don't want to hear the lie that Colin Hardy was falling-down drunk and helpless. It was eight o'clock in the damn morning. So don't you call it murder. That woman went into a knockdown fight with a man—a fair fight. She matched him pound for pound—and with her bare fists, she beat him to death."

The housekeeper rose from the table and turned her back on him to fuss with a pot on the stove. Her voice dropped into the guttural range of Pay-attention-or-else. "You *will* show respect when you visit the library—no matter what Mavis does or what she says. She's been fighting this town all alone for so long, she just doesn't know how to stop. I don't care if Mavis beats the crap out of you, Oren. You *will* be a gentleman."

After Hannah had said her piece, the silence was loaded. There was nowhere to fit in a contradiction, and only a fool would try. The judge would not meet his eyes. Oren was on his own. This canny little woman had reached deep inside him, made certain adjustments to his spine and caused him to sit up a bit straighter.

The workday was done, and Dave Hardy had changed into his T-shirt and jeans. He was straddling a bar stool in Coventry, the first watering hole of his evening. The other patrons were watching the evening news with the sound turned off, as usual.

Odd old ducks.

None of them called for the volume to be turned on, not even when they recognized the limping figure of a cripple pursued by screaming reporters. The regulars of the Coventry Pub sat in silence, drunkenly, blissfully unaware of worse things being done to William Swahn— what the pictures alone could not tell them.

This was the same film the deputy had seen earlier in the day at another bar, and he was the only one in this room who knew the words that went with the broadcast. The phrase—*a person of interest*—had been repeated three times, though Sally Polk had only said it once. And, by snatches of film, Swahn was made to limp across that parking lot with each repetition.

In the earlier version of this news broadcast, it had been clear that the CBI agent had waded into the fray to draw the reporters away from their victim, William Swahn. In this new job of film editing, she seemed to be orchestrating the whole event, even stirring up the crowd to chase down the man with the cane.

It was a clear case of slander against both of these people, but Dave Hardy did not care. He had no sympathy for Swahn, and he hated that Polk woman.

A million other viewers could only rely on the pack of lies their eyes were telling them.

Twenty-three

I t was that gloomy hour when house lights were burning bright, but drivers were still debating the need for
headlights. Daredevil Hannah would be the last to
turn hers on.

Oren watched the streets crawl by his passenger
window.

Before the library had become a town joke, Josh had
often walked this same route with him, and they had
made better time on foot. In Coventry, time and distance
were not quantified or qualified in terms of *as the crow
flies*, but by the saying *If only snails had wings*. Oren
would rather have spent this evening reading Sarah Winston's cryptic journals in privacy, but he was on a mission
to mollify the little woman behind the wheel.

The old Mercedes rolled past the church, and Hannah

sighed. "I miss the Reverend Pursey's sermons. You haven't forgotten that crazy old fool, have you?"

"I remember him." Oren was not likely to forget Amos Pursey—ever. The minister had worn his Sunday robes seven days a week to fly around town, waving his arms and ranting about the end of days. "He must be the black bat in Mrs. Winston's drawings." Oren had been a month shy of seventeen when that old madman had accosted him on the street and proclaimed him to be an archangel appointed by God to smite the town.

It was a revelation that Hannah had heard any of the minister's sermons. "*You* went to church?"

"I used to—now and then."

"But why? You're an atheist. No—wait. You told me and Josh that *God* was an atheist."

"*No,* I said a real *smart* god would be an atheist. Who needs the pressure of being perfect? I favor the kind of Creator who drinks beer now and then, someone you can *talk* to. Now the Reverend Pursey—crazy old bastard—he fancied a miracle worker with a hit-man angel."

"Hannah, why does this place attract so many loonies?"

"Tolerance. It's Coventry's finest quality. So, despite what Amos Pursey thought, no god would ever smite a town that sheltered that nutcase preacher." Hannah brought the car to a stop in front of the library. "My other theory is that we all take turns being the lunatic."

"It's after hours," said Oren. "No lights in the windows."

"She's there." Hannah glanced at her wristwatch. "Mavis is always there, day and night. Has been for years. Nobody knew about it for the longest time."

Oren dared not speak the reason: *Because no one in Coventry ever goes to the library*. But Hannah hushed him anyway.

"Dave lives in his mother's house." Hannah nodded at the library. "And Mavis lives in there."

"That's insane," said Oren. "Why didn't Dave do something?"

"He tried. He wanted to get her locked up in a state mental ward, where they drug people senseless and stack 'em up like cordwood. The judge stopped him. Your father doesn't believe in God, but he's got the concept of hell down pat. He thinks she's better off in the library, and so do I." Hannah rolled up the right sleeve of her sweater, and then, with a wave of her hand, she said, "Let there be light."

And there was. The bulb over the door clicked on, and every window shade turned bright yellow.

The last time Hannah had done this trick, Josh was only six years old, and his eyes had popped. The little boy had been disappointed to learn that Mrs. Hardy was simply a creature of habit. With no regard for the seasonal position of the sun—or the moon—the library lights came on at the same time every evening.

How could he have forgotten that?

Hannah patted his hand. "You'll be glad you came. Mavis knows all the best stories, and she knows birds."

The housekeeper picked up the small stack of journals and tucked them under one arm. "She knows Sarah Winston, too. They go way back. You might learn something without getting shot by Isabelle."

"You held out on me? You *knew* Mrs. Hardy went to school with—"

He was talking to himself. Hannah was out of the car and moving up the flagstone walkway. The librarian opened the door wide to greet her. Oren had no memories of Mavis Hardy ever smiling this way. Even in her saner days, long before killing her husband, she had always been the saddest woman in town.

In the course of his travels from bar to bar, Dave Hardy drove his pickup truck past the library to check for lights, a sure indication that his mother was not yet dead. The judge's Mercedes was parked out front, not an unusual sight, but Hannah Rice wasn't the only visitor. The third silhouette on the window shade had to be Oren Hobbs.

Dave's hands tightened around the steering wheel as he sped up to a record of twenty miles per hour while still inside the town limits. Out on the coast highway, he drove at real-world speeds. He was on the way to an anonymous saloon on the outskirts of a distant town, a small biker bar, where no one was ever friendly enough or sober enough to ask his name. It was a place where he could hunker down and do some serious drinking—drink after drink after drink.

———

Tonight, the library did not smell. That was different.

All the windows had been opened prior to the visit. Mrs. Hardy had even washed her hair for this occasion, and it was still damp when the three of them sat down at the reader's table. They were twenty minutes into the visit, and the woman had yet to utter any profanity. She looked so tired. And Oren noted other signs that this semblance of sanity was wearing on her—the grinding teeth and rigid body.

The librarian handed a few sheets of paper to Hannah. "I printed this up from that file you started the other day." She turned to Oren. "Hannah's been doing research on the Internet."

"So I heard." In these familiar surroundings, it was easier for him to remember Mrs. Hardy in pre-monster-hood days, stripped of bulk and muscle, a time when a thin, fragile woman had guided the Hobbs boys through their changing phases of westerns and science fiction, steering them into the better writers of each genre that took their fancy. Tonight, he recognized the effort she made only to smile at him and make simple small talk.

Hannah was absorbed in her computer printout. "I just *love* hard science." She folded the papers into the pocket of her dress and winked at Oren. "It'll come in handy later on—when you tell me I'm wrong about how the witchboard works."

"Poor Sarah." Mrs. Hardy resumed her perusal of the birder logs. "I've never seen these books before, but that's her handwriting." And now she answered an earlier question of Oren's. "We both went to UCLA. But I can't say I really knew her then. In my younger, skinnier days, I almost wasn't there. I swear I could walk between raindrops. A good-looking boy like you never would've noticed me—and neither would someone like Sarah.

"We met at the university library. That was my workstudy job when I was in school. Sarah wanted books on ornithology. Well, that was my hobby. I told her about some rare sightings in Coventry, birds that hadn't been seen in fifty years. So she came to my dormitory for a look at my notes. It was like visiting royalty—the way people stared at that beautiful girl when she came in the door. That day we talked for hours and hours. I never spoke to her again, not on campus. . . . My fault. I was shy. But Sarah always waved every time she saw me. I wasn't invisible anymore. At the end of that semester, I heard she got married and left school."

"What about William Swahn? He went to UCLA."

"I never met him, but I knew who he was. Always saw him walking around with Sarah and little Belle. He tended to stand out even on a campus the size of a city. He was thirteen, maybe fourteen years old, and he looked younger. Geeky little kid. Big feet, big brain."

"Mrs. Winston was in her twenties then," said Oren. "Why would she hang out with a little boy?"

"I thought I just explained that. Sarah was very kind to freaks. Like him. Like me." Mavis Hardy's voice held no rebuke. "And years later, when that little boy was all grown up, I'm sure it was kindness on Sarah's part to have Addison represent him. That was a nasty business with those cops down in L.A."

Hannah was right. Mrs. Hardy knew all the best stories. It had taken Cable Babitt years to learn this much. "So Mrs. Winston stayed in touch with Swahn after she left school? Maybe they exchanged letters?"

This gentle trap brought out no response. The woman only shook her head and shrugged to say she didn't know. Even with the evidence of the post office photographs, he could not be certain that she was lying.

"After I graduated, years went by before I ran into Sarah again." The librarian looked down at the open journal in her hands. The drawings in this early one had a light and fanciful touch. "I've got the hang of it now." She pointed to a sketch. "That grouse hen must be me. It's a bird that puffs itself up when it's frightened." She turned a few more pages. "And this one seems to be frightened all the time—silly old thing." With a half smile, she gently closed the journal and opened another. Mrs. Hardy did not look up from the pages when she said, "Here I am again—in the woods with my binoculars. And this pale yellow songbird must be Sarah. The clue is the fledgling redbird. Who could that be but little Belle? So Sarah told you about our field trips. I never told anyone."

Field trips? Hannah's surprise was more obvious, and Oren signaled her to keep still. He waited for the librarian to fill the silence.

"Sarah used to visit Coventry years before Addison built the lodge. This area is birder heaven. She'd drive up on the weekends and stay at the Straub Hotel. I wasn't so much changed in those days, still skinny as a rail, and she recognized me on the street. I took her into the deep woods where the trails don't go and showed her some nests I'd found. She kept coming back all the time after that, longer visits. Sometimes she brought Belle along. Then Addison built her that log mansion."

"And all you two ever talked about was birds?"

"Oren, what else would we have in common?" She spread her arms as an invitation for him to look at her life, to see her as she was in those days—and these days.

"You said that Swahn and Mrs. Winston were friends in college. I thought his name might've come up in conversation."

The librarian shook her head. "I think I was the first one to mention William Swahn. That was a long while ago, more than twenty-five years. I saw his name on a list in a newspaper article. I told Sarah that he was graduating from the police academy. That made her happy. She said it was always his big dream to become a policeman. A year later, William moved to Coventry, and he wasn't a policeman anymore. That's when Sarah told me he'd been wounded down in Los Angeles."

"So she saw a lot of him after he moved here?"

"Well, he used to have dinner at the lodge once a week. That stopped after maybe five years. I never knew why. Around that same time, Sarah gave up our field trips in the woods. I lost interest in birds after that." Mrs. Hardy shook her head as she looked down at a drawing of monsters. "I guess Sarah stopped bird-watching, too.

I don't see a single creature here that matches up to an actual species."

Oren was hardly paying attention anymore. He was doing the math on Mrs. Winston's long-ago estrangements from Swahn and the librarian.

Mrs. Hardy flipped backward through the pages, then stopped and stabbed the heart of a drawing with one finger. "Here," she said. "The dead lark seems to mark the beginning of the change in Sarah."

When Dave Hardy entered Peck's Roadhouse, a cluster of patrons was gathered at one end of the bar and watching another repeat of the news. The volume was loud. One more time, he saw the film of Sally Polk and the reporters. This version was cut to make it look like a formal press conference—more like Polk's own idea instead of a media ambush.

The voice of a studio guest rode over the action on film, and this celebrity author profiled a child killer for the viewing audience. The bones of the female victim were never mentioned. Dave supposed a young boy made a more sensational story.

The camera cut to a photograph of Josh Hobbs as he was in life, that silly grin. The guest author was also smiling. "As you can see," he said to the anchorman, "Joshua was delicate—almost pretty, if you get my meaning. I believe he attracted a predator who couldn't handle a boy with more muscle."

The anchorman was professionally livid. "So we can't

rule out a pedophile who might be handicapped in some way."

And the next shot was predictable, the old clip of Swahn, branded by innuendo and editing, limping past Highway Patrol cars in the Saulburg parking lot. Sally Polk's voice could be heard riding over the film, saying, "—a person of interest." This was followed by the rerun of reporters in a frenzy as they surrounded the man, and Sally Polk's voice was once again clipped off to say, "—a person of interest."

Dave Hardy had grown to loathe that woman.

The volume of the TV set was turned up, the better to hear the questions shouted out from the crowd of reporters. "Does Swahn have a criminal record? Does he like little boys? He's a homosexual, isn't he?" But the only sound bite from Sally Polk was, "No, he didn't take a lie detector test." Cut from this new version was her statement that Swahn had never been *asked* to take a polygraph exam.

The current image was a studio shot that Dave had not seen in the earlier viewing. A psychiatrist was pointing out that the overwhelming number of pedophiles were heterosexual. And furthermore—

No one in the bar could hear the rest. Riding over the voice of reason, a chorus of voices shouted obscenities. A beer bottle hit the television screen.

The bartender, a man of many tattoos and a short temper, reached under the bar and pulled out a shotgun, yelling words to the effect that the unruly patrons should take their business down the road—or die.

In keeping with the judge's instructions, Mrs. Winston's birder journals had been left behind on the library shelves, where they would be safe from Sally Polk's warrants.

Hannah started up the car. "If you give Mavis some time with those books, she might be able to tell you more about this town than you wanted to know."

"I'd like to know why she kept her relationship with Mrs. Winston a secret." The librarian had not been willing or able to tell him. "Swahn went to dinner at the Winston lodge—but not Mrs. Hardy."

"Oren, I think you can figure that one out. You've spent enough time with Addison." She steered the car away from the curb. "Maybe Sarah and Mavis had something in common besides birds."

"You think Ad Winston beats his wife?"

"No, that's not it." Hannah craned her neck to see over the wheel. "You should come to the birthday ball this year. You'll never see a man more in love with his wife. But he's a controlling bastard, isn't he? I'm guessing Sarah's only contact with Mr. Swahn was at the dinner table—with Addison. He might not want her to have a friend that she could talk to alone." She turned a wide smile on her passenger. "Do you still shoot pool like a hustler?"

"I do," he said. "And do you still hustle the tourists?"

"I get my fun where I can." When they reached the edge of town, she decided on the mountain route, arguing that the coast highway was too tame. "And away we go."

The old Mercedes was not an automobile to Hannah; it was an amusement ride. Up and down they went, around and around, and at one point he believed that she could make it fly. Oren averted his eyes from the speedometer, though he knew the needle would never reach forty miles an hour. This road was treacherous at thirty, and every curve that blinded them to oncoming cars was an opportunity to crash and die.

After passing through two towns, then traveling awhile on a stretch of unpaved road with no helpful signs, they pulled into the crowded parking lot of the Endless Bar, a saloon that could not be found unless one knew the way.

Inside the establishment, nothing had changed. The music was loud and country, and this same song might have played on the jukebox when Oren was too young to legally walk through the door. Most of the patrons were corralled inside a revolving circular bar. It was rumored that some of the regulars never left; blind drunk, they could not find the hinge to the outer rim, where a patron could lift up a plank and escape. When people went missing for days and days, this was the first place their loved ones looked for them. The unloved were remembered on the hall-of-fame plaque for those who had died on their bar stools. It was positioned well above the line of sight to avoid the problem of a cautionary tale for paying customers.

Oren and Hannah walked past the bar, heading for the

pool tables in the back. The little woman nodded and waved to acknowledge hellos from large, hairy bruisers, who no doubt belonged to the gang of motorcycles in the parking lot. How they smiled to see her coming. It was easy enough to read those wide grins, the shake of heads, saying, *No, not this time, old lady. You ain't gettin' my money—not another dollar.*

Every table had been booked. Not a problem. Two men gave up their game so that Hannah could play, and they nodded to Oren with something approaching condolence, taking him for one of her patsies.

The tiny woman was on her toes and grinning when she leaned over the table to rack up the balls in triangular formation. "Let's make this interesting." She aimed the tip of her stick at the white ball and sent it slamming into the tight cluster. Balls of stripes and solid colors spread out on the green felt, slow-rolling along in their separate directions. "Loser buys the first round."

"Deal." Oren was a happy man. The last ball had come to a stop, and Hannah had failed to sink any of them into the pockets. He owned a spread of easy shots.

"One condition," she said. "We're not playing eight ball. You have to run the whole table in one turn with one hand behind your back."

"Nothing easier." He would not even need a brace to steady his stick. Every shot was a gimme, and a half-bright child could not lose. It reminded him of his very first pool game. It was almost as though she had set up the table this way. Later, this thought would cross his mind again. But now, with no suspicion at all, he lined up the first shot and took aim.

Before he could follow through, Hannah leaned in and touched his arm, saying, "The stick will shake."

"Yeah, *right*," he said. "Nice try." Smile widening, he completed his shot—and—he—*missed*—it.

"In case you're wondering," said Hannah, nonchalantly chalking up her pool cue in preparation for clearing the table. "That shaky stick? That trick's got a real fancy name. It's called the ideomotor effect."

Click. A striped ball dropped into a corner pocket.

"I wasn't talking to you when I made your stick shake," she said. "I bypassed your brain."

Click, click. Two balls in the corner pocket.

"I was talking to your arm."

"Sure you were." When Oren looked up from the last shot, Hannah was unfolding the sheets of paper given to her by the librarian.

"Here." She slapped the pages down on the rim of the table. "I've got science on my side. Read it."

Click, click, click.

Oren read the article's long title, "The Influence of Suggestion in Directing Muscular Action Independent of Volition." This was followed by lengthy text in small type. "Maybe you could just—"

Click.

"You want me to give you the gist of it?" She lined up her next shot. "Your brain's got what's called an executive module. That's what you use to do this." *Click*. She sank a ball. "But you've got other modules, independent ones, and they bypass the thinking process. I made a *suggestion,* and they moved your muscles to blow that easy shot. That's how I talked to your arm. And now you know how Alice Friday's witchboard works. A question might suggest an answer, and then all those hands move that little wooden heart to spell out a word on the board. Or maybe, when the players call out a letter, that one suggests the next one. But there's no connection between their fingertips and their brains. I told you—nobody cheats."

"That psychic runs the board," said Oren. "She's a con artist."

"No, she's an idiot."

Click, click, click, click.

When Hannah had sunk the last ball on the table, she straightened up to her full height of four feet nine inches and faced him down. "Only idiots believe in two-way conversations with the dead, and that woman is a true believer."

"The judge has conversations with my dead mother."

"When he's sleepwalking. That doesn't count."

"And the judge believes in miracles. He even asked my mother for another one."

"When your father's wide-awake, he's no believer in miracles. His perfect god died with your mother when she crashed her car on a rainy night. The judge believes in logical explanations. And you can believe in me when I tell you that Alice Friday has no idea how that board game works."

Oren had ceased to hear her. He was recalling the message spelled out at the séance: *Do you still love me?* "I'm betting that woman knows how to manipulate the Ouija board *and* the players. Like my missed shot—that was just one of your parlor tricks."

"Of course it was. And I've always explained my tricks." Two by two, she pulled balls out of the slot inside the table and set them back on the felt surface. "I didn't raise you to believe in magic."

True enough. When he was a child, she had always shown him the works and the wires behind her illusions. And, after taking a Ouija board away from two terrified little boys, she had tried to explain the trick to them in terms of expectations and the power of belief in horror movies. She had assured Josh and Oren that the old woman from Paulson Lane, crazy as she was in life, would never curse children from her grave. The dead spoke to no one.

Oren had not believed her then.

Hannah racked up the balls inside the wooden triangle, no doubt sensing that he did not believe her now, either. Her hazel eyes looked up to question him, and then she damned him with, "Oh, never mind." She took back her pages of science and crumpled them into a tight ball. "I can see it was a waste of time explaining the witchboard." Hannah bent over the table once more, poised for the first shot of a new game. "For my next trick, I'll show you how life works."

Twenty-four

The outcasts of Peck's Roadhouse had formed a loose union of drunks in the parking lot. And two more bars down the road, they had become an ugly crew as tight as family.

Dave Hardy followed their weaving line of cars, trucks and vans. If he had been in uniform tonight—and sober—this would have been an easy twelve tickets for driving under the influence. The parade swelled in numbers with every little Podunk bar these yahoos had been thrown out of, and he was keeping count on the vehicles.

The deputy reached down to the six-pack on the seat beside him, and then pulled back his empty hand. Maybe he should also be counting his drinks tonight. With a glance at the rifle rack above the windshield of his truck, he opened the glove compartment and pulled out a box of shotgun shells.

When the caravan of drunks pulled into the next bar, he waited awhile in the lot, loading his gun. After replacing it on the rack, he followed them inside, where the men were slowly gravitating toward the light of a television set that seemed to draw them by remote control. On screen was the same old film: Sally Polk was answering the same questions, and William Swahn was still limping. Long after day had turned into night, the sun was still shining in reruns.

The drunks talked back to Sally Polk and saluted her TV image with raised glasses of beer.

Dave wanted to put his fist through the screen.

In another bar on the other side of the county, Hannah was saying, "I can't help but win this game."

Oren agreed. At least no beers had been bet on this round. It would take Hannah another hour to finish nursing her first one.

When all but a few balls had been sunk into pockets, the only ones remaining in play were the white cue ball, the black eight ball and a solid red. Sending that red ball into the corner pocket would be the easiest shot by far. It was so close to the edge, it might drop in of its own accord. And perhaps that was what Hannah waited for as she held her stick an inch from the cue ball. Seconds ticked by. "I can't lose."

"I believe you," he said. "So *sink* it."

"Now that's not fortune-telling." She lifted her stick and waved it in small circles. "And it certainly wouldn't take any skill." She leaned down once more to line up the white and the red. "You can see the outcome of this game. It's in the way the balls are laid out. But even God Almighty can blow a simple shot now and then."

Apparently, so could Hannah.

The cue ball wandered far from the mark and connected with the black eight ball, nudging it toward the corner pocket where the red ball was hanging. In Hannah's parlance, the sneeze of a housefly could sink it.

"Well, that's life," she said. "Hits and misses. There's a reason for everything, but you don't need to know all the answers. So the next time you hear the judge asking your dead mother for another miracle, just let the old man slide."

"You're throwing the game?"

In answer, she stepped back from the table and lifted her glass for a swig of beer.

His turn.

Damn. No, she had *not* thrown the game. Hannah had simply picked a different way to win. The new position of the eight ball was no accident of a bad shot. It gently kissed the red ball hanging over the corner pocket. In every possible scenario of straight shots and bank shots, the eight ball would follow the red one into the pocket on the same stroke—and forfeit the game.

With resignation, Oren aimed his pool cue.

"Wait." Hannah's voice carried a slight tone of alarm.

Her left hand was raised high, and he followed the point of her finger up to the ceiling—where nothing was happening. He winced. He had not fallen for this ploy since he was ten years old. When he looked back at the table, he saw what Hannah's right hand had been up to. The eight ball had vanished, leaving him with an easy shot and a win.

"It's a miracle," said Hannah.

Sure. He laid down his stick, and lifted his beer.

"Don't you want to win?"

"No, I don't think so. Miracles take all the fun out of pool." He turned his eyes back to the table, where the eight ball had reappeared beside the red one. In what split second of distraction had she managed that? Hannah's sleight of hand reaffirmed his theory that, in her distant past, she had been a magician or a pickpocket.

"Some things in life just have to play out," she said. "If Josh hadn't died that day, it would've happened some other time. You *know* why he died."

Oren was not ready to have this conversation yet. He pretended interest in his empty glass. "And your next trick?"

"You'll see. It won't be long now." She held up her half-finished beer. "My capacity isn't what it used to be." Hannah happened to be facing the door when it opened, and so it appeared that Mrs. Winston had walked into the Endless Bar on cue.

Sometimes the whole is not greater than the sum of its parts. This was the thought of the barmaid in the lounge of a hotel on the coast highway.

Twenty-two men were gathered in front of the television set, and she counted them all as one creature. Her hope was that this angry buzzing thing would take itself out the door before it turned ugly. The barmaid looked up at the TV screen above the shelves of bottles and glassware. The news story of Sally Polk and her suspect had run over and over in short clips of commercial teases. Now it played out in full length for the late evening news.

The drunks were enthralled. Polk was their leader, their queen, though the CBI agent hardly said three words in this updated news story. Celebrity experts and an anchorman now put the words in the woman's mouth.

One studio guest, a man with a book to sell, said to the camera, "This is how Agent Polk will profile the killer. If he's handicapped in some way, his only outlet for sex is prostitutes—and children." The screen image changed to a photograph of a tender boy with a comical smile. And the next shot focused on a man with a rollicking limp and a cane.

The drunks hated the crippled man. They jeered and yelled at the television set.

The barmaid sensed that the thing of many parts was about to swarm as twenty-two faces turned in unison.

So creepy.

They moved toward the door as one giddy insect with many feet. The barmaid reached for the phone, planning to give the driving public a sporting chance to live through the night. But then she recognized a regular at the bar, a man with bleached highlights. This was the sheriff's deputy, the one who took his beer in a coffee cup when he was in uniform. Tonight, dressed in blue jeans, he drank from a glass, drained it and walked to the door.

She could hear the sound of many engines starting up outside, the whooping and hollering, the spin of wheels and the spit of gravel. The barmaid walked to the window and watched the deputy climb into a pickup truck. He followed the *thing* out of the parking lot.

No need to call 9-1-1.

Though the dim light of the Endless Bar was kind to the champagne blonde, that beautiful face was showing damage, and it was more than the ruin that came with age. Mrs. Winston was no longer the calm center of grace in every crowd. She had a startled look about her, eyes turning everywhere.

On the lookout for enemies?

That was Oren's thought, as he racked up the balls for a new game—as if Hannah's next game had not already begun. "You knew Mrs. Winston would be here tonight. I guessed that much."

"Keep your eye on the man tending bar."

The bartender never acknowledged Mrs. Winston, who sat down three stools away from him. He lifted the first hinged mahogany plank to leave the service station, a wheel within the wheel, and then he lifted the second plank to step off the revolving bar.

"That towel over his hand," said Hannah. "It's covering a brown paper bag."

Oren watched the man walk out the front door. A

moment later, the bartender returned with his towel draped over one shoulder. Back at his station, he served Mrs. Winston, who must be a regular, for he never bothered to ask for the lady's order. He set her glass on a cocktail napkin and walked away without a word.

"Sarah will only stay for one drink," said Hannah. "She'll leave a hundred-dollar tip under her glass. Then she'll go outside and find a bottle in a brown paper bag sitting on the front seat of her car."

"Okay," said Oren, "that's illegal as hell. Maybe this is a stupid question, but—"

"Why break the law? You wonder why Sarah doesn't just go to a liquor store—much cheaper, no risk. Well, no store in this county will sell her a bottle. Addison saw to that. He likes to control her liquor supply."

Hannah looked down at her wristwatch. She always wore a watch these days. When had time become so important to her?

"Right about now," she said, "Ad and Isabelle think she's passed out upstairs in her room." Hannah looked up at him and smiled. "You can learn a lot from a séance. Evelyn tells me that the Winstons' maid shows up at the cabin once a week, and that girl really appreciates a sympathetic ear. She hates Addison, bad-mouths him all the time."

Mrs. Winston slowly circled in and out of his sight as the bar revolved. When Oren saw her face in a shadowed profile, there was Josh's patron and friend, the most beautiful woman ever to set foot in Coventry. Revolving into better light, she became an aging barfly.

Hannah lined up another shot with her pool cue. "Sarah lost her license years ago, drinking and driving. Keep one eye on her glass so you'll know when she's leaving. That bottle waiting in her car? She'll try to empty most of it on her way back home. That means jail if she gets stopped by the law tonight. Or worse—she'll wrap her car around a tree."

"So we're going to offer her a ride home, is that the plan?"

"Well, not quite—but close. On your way to the Winston lodge, you'll stop at the turnout on Bear Creek Road. That'll be Sarah's idea, not yours. A lady shouldn't have to drink alone, so mind your manners. Don't forget to wipe the bottle after you take a swig. With any luck, Isabelle will never hear about the nice long talk you're going to have with her mother."

"Wouldn't it be easier if you just told me what Mrs. Winston was going to say?"

"You haven't heard a word I said tonight."

"You bet I have. You don't miss a thing, Hannah, and that's a gift I could use right now. So just spell it out for me."

"I tried that once with the judge. It didn't work so well."

"When you told him to send Josh away?"

"If I'd never warned him, he would've grieved for a while and then moved on. And he would've had one boy left to raise. You never should've left town, Oren."

"He *sent* me *away*."

"And now that old man lives with guilt. He thinks he

could've saved Josh . . . if he'd only listened to me. He would've been better off if I'd just kept my mouth shut."

"How did you know Josh was in danger?"

"Same way you did. That boy had a dangerous hobby, catching secrets in a camera." Hannah laid down her pool cue. "I heard you yell at him one day out in the yard. You tried to make him stop, but that was never going to happen. If the judge had sent him away, Josh would've died in some other town, and the old man would *still* blame himself. I should never have interfered, but I was more arrogant then."

"You were right to try, Hannah."

"No, I should've let life play out the way it was meant to." She lightly squeezed his arm. "If you'd stayed with Josh that day, it would've happened some other time. Your brother was fated to die when no one was around to save him. Cold logic, Oren. A murder can't happen any other way." She stared at the revolving bar. "Sarah's almost done with her drink. Almost time."

"Do you know who killed Josh?"

"What do you take me for? A damn psychic?" Hannah plucked the car keys from her pocket. "I'm going home. Now you can tell Sarah Winston that you're stranded without a ride. She'll let you drive her car, and she won't die—not tonight."

The BMW was a beautiful machine, bright red with a black ragtop—the stuff of dreams in his teenage car-crazy days. Oren watched from the distance of two parking spaces, confident that the lady would never be able to thread her key into the car's ignition.

He walked toward the convertible, calling out, "Ma'am? Mrs. Winston?" Stepping up to the driver-side door, he said, "You might remember me."

She looked up at him with a smile that was warm and wide. "Oren Hobbs. You still look so much like your brother."

"I wonder if I could get a ride as far as your house?"

"Of course you can. Get in, and I'll drive you all the way home."

"I noticed you were having a problem starting it. Could be the ignition. Want me to give it a try?"

"How gallant. An officer and a gentleman."

"I'm not with the Army anymore."

"So I heard, and there's nothing wrong with my ignition, but you'd never insinuate that I was drunk. Henry Hobbs did a good job of raising his boys."

The lady stepped out and did her best to walk in a normal fashion as she rounded the BMW to the passenger side. Oren followed and leaned in to open her door. Mrs. Winston smelled of whiskey and roses. Her daughter had been wearing that same rose perfume on the day she had kicked him in the shin. Keys in hand, he slipped behind the wheel, and they were off.

They had traveled no more than a few miles when he saw a pair of high beams coming up fast in the rearview mirror. The car behind him was weaving all over the road as it gathered speed, and there was no turnout in sight. Around each blind curve was the chance of a wreck with an oncoming car, but the vehicle behind him was a sure thing—close to climbing up the BMW's back end. Oren pressed down on the accelerator and rounded a hairpin turn with only two wheels on the ground.

"Don't be scared," he said to Mrs. Winston. But she was slow to understand what was happening. In the rearview mirror he caught sight of more headlights behind his pursuer. When he made a sharp left onto Bear Creek Road, they all followed him.

Up ahead, he saw the generous turnout carved into the shoulder. He pulled into it, slamming on the brakes and shooting out one hand to keep Mrs. Winston from hitting the dashboard. At least twenty vehicles whizzed past them to careen around the next curve.

"Ma'am? I don't suppose you have a cell phone."

"No. You'd have to drive twenty miles before you found a town with a cell-phone tower."

So much for their long conversation over a shared bottle of liquor. A caravan of drunks posed the problem of sudden death for anyone in their path tonight. He put the sports car in gear. "We have to find a phone."

The reporter's rental car was the last vehicle to travel up the driveway.

Dave Hardy sat in his pickup truck, counting money, five hundred dollars. He should have asked for more. An exclusive tip like this one was worth an easy thousand. One ear cocked toward his open window, he listened to the innocent racket of crickets and night birds. It made him smile to think that he'd been paid something for nothing—a better deal.

After a short stop at a gas station, the sheriff's office had been alerted to a runaway pack of drunks on wheels. And the smell of gasoline on a summer night was almost as sexy as the rose perfume.

They were under way again, Oren and Mrs. Winston, and there was not another car in sight. The road belonged to them. The convertible's top was rolled down, and the sky was banged with stars. The lady's hair was flying in long blond tangles, and the radio played vintage rock 'n' roll at the top of the volume dial.

Oren smiled, and then he laughed. Life was hard.

The night was ending all too soon, and he pulled into the Winstons' driveway with some regret. After parking the car in front of the lodge, Oren assured her that he did not mind walking home from here. "I'm not that far down the road."

"Maybe I'll drop by sometime. I haven't seen Hannah and the judge for a while. And I've always wanted to see Josh's photographs from the woods." She seemed puzzled by Oren's surprise. "You've never seen his nature shots? I used to run into him on the trails from time to time. He always had a camera with him."

"No, ma'am." Oren's hands tightened around the steering wheel. So Josh had been stalking Mrs. Winston, too—a woman who had shown only kindness to his brother.

"That boy was a born mimic. I'm the one who taught him birdsongs." She leaned toward him, surprised again. "You didn't know? He never mentioned that?"

It would have been awkward trying to explain the language of brothers: a nod of the head to say that he had understood what remained unspoken; a hand on his brother's shoulder to ask, *Hurt much?* There had been a million gestures to replace a zillion words, and, best of all, they had known how to be silent together—except for that last day in the woods.

Mrs. Winston rested one hand on his shoulder. "The grief is all new again, isn't it? . . . Now that you've found his grave. Your brother was the dearest boy I ever knew." She held up her hands in a gesture of helplessness. "I've lost the threads. What was I saying? Oh, of course. Photographs. My favorites are the pictures of my birthday balls. You stopped coming when you were how old? Twelve? Well, you must come to this one. I'm sure Isabelle's forgiven you by now."

"No, ma'am. I don't think it's safe yet. Maybe next year."

She laughed with high bright notes, almost music.

Was this how her daughter laughed? He was not likely to find out anytime soon. The front door flew open. Isabelle Winston had caught him in the act of conversation with her mother. She was one angry redhead, hands on hips in fair warning that a lethal weapon could be had at any moment. Oren said a hasty goodbye to Mrs. Winston. As he left the car and marched toward the road, a bullet in his back would have come as no surprise.

Near the end of the long driveway, he stopped to listen. The wind had changed, and it carried the sound of angry voices from the direction of Paulson Lane. He peered into the woods and saw fragments of bright light through the leaves.

A scream came from the lodge. He whirled around to look up at the tower. Sarah Winston stood on the deck and pointed the way for him. Oren plunged into the woods with no thought of getting lost tonight. He was guided by the lights, the shouts and the sounds of breaking glass.

With a sidelong view of the mob and the house, he could see William Swahn moving across a lighted room, limping badly as he dodged bottles, rocks and shattering glass. The telephone by the man's front window might as well be on the moon.

Moving toward the house by way of sheltering trees and deep shadow, Oren stopped beside a cluster of large trash receptacles and ripped one lid from its rubber hinge. The driveway and turnout were jammed with vehicles. As he moved forward, the headlights blinded him. He raised his rubber shield and shaded his eyes with his free hand.

The front door opened and William Swahn hobbled outside to the confusion of his enemies. The catcalls subsided. The drunken silhouettes in the headlights stood very still—deadly quiet. Leaning against a marble pillar and squinting into the light, Swahn raised his cane, and his voice shook with anger. "Most of your rocks hit my house instead of the windows! You morons throw like little girls!"

Break time was over.

They answered him with a fresh volley. Most of their missiles went wild. Only by sheer numbers, two struck home. A rock drew blood on Swahn's face, and a beer bottle slammed into his bad leg. He slid down the pillar to lie flat upon the marble slab.

And Oren came running.

Dave Hardy saw headlights slowing down in his rearview mirror. He had stayed too long on Paulson Lane—and the story was no longer exclusive to the reporter who had paid him. A van with a news-show logo pulled up beside his truck, and he could hear the static chatter of a police scanner. Swahn must have called for help. Highway Patrol cars and deputies in jeeps were en route from all quarters of the county.

The van's passenger door opened, and a man's head and shoulders appeared over the roof. His camera was aimed at the pickup truck.

Dave sank down low in his seat.

I'm so screwed.

No matter what road he took, he would run into the law in oncoming traffic.

The van's driver leaned out the window and extended a microphone. "I almost didn't recognize you out of uniform. You're a deputy, right?"

Inspiration.

"Yeah, I'm the first responder." Dave gave the man a short salute, then started his engine and put his pickup truck in gear.

Gaining the portico, Oren knelt down beside the fallen William Swahn and whispered, "Close your eyes. Don't move." He called out to the anonymous shapes who stood before the lights. "He's dead! You *killed* him!"

Here and there, rocks and bottles thudded to the ground.

Oren understood the ugliest things about mobs. This one had just lost its reason for being. Cohesion was dissolving as some edged away from the pack, a sign that self-preservation had trumped herd instinct. But the mob might rise again as one body, one mind—in seconds. The window for action was small.

The time was now.

He picked up Swahn's cane and held it high as he walked toward the lights. "I'm the law!" he yelled. "And now I'm gonna start cracking heads, and every man I mark is going to jail!"

Though blinded by headlights, his eyes were wide open as he walked into the fray with the slow resolution of a tank. Swinging the cane in wide circles, he connected with flesh and bone. Beyond the bright lights, car doors were opening. One engine starting up and then another. Twin balls of light were backing away, men walking away, and some were on the run.

Squinting now, blurred sight returning, his cane hit a man's skull and felled him, and this one crawled away. Other men were frozen, some of them weaving, easy targets. One stood before him, witless. Oren made a mighty swing to bring him down. A tight group of figures were moving toward him—the resurrection of the mob, though a smaller pack, a tinier brain. He turned on them, using the trash-can lid to fend off rocks. His shield and lance were ripped away, and their hands were on him.

Above their heads was a flash of gunfire and a shotgun blast. Standing atop the cabin of a pickup truck, Dave Hardy yelled, "Nobody move!"

And now the last of them scattered, feet running, engines revving, wheels spinning.

All gone.

Broken bottles and a trampled baseball cap, scattered rocks and a lost shoe were lit by the headlights of official vehicles, county and state. Reporters had been corralled at the other end of the driveway, where they screamed about their freedom of the press as their cameras were confiscated. And three men sat on the steps of the portico.

Dave Hardy sacrificed the last two beers in his six-pack. He handed a bottle to William Swahn and one to Oren, apologizing because it was no longer cold. "But it'll do for medicinal purposes. You know you're bleeding, right?"

Swahn, still dazed, was slow to lift one hand to his face, touching the wound to his cheek. And now he stared at the blood on his fingers. "I suppose it's bad form to mock people while they're chucking rocks and bottles."

And by a nod, Oren agreed that this was so.

Dave Hardy grinned at the bleeding man. "You did that? Well, good for you." He turned to Oren and jingled his car keys. "The sheriff's gonna be here any minute. I gotta go. If Cable catches me driving drunk one more time, I'm toast."

When the deputy's pickup truck had rolled off down the driveway, Swahn lifted his beer to clink bottles with Oren.

When Sarah Winston was sober, the tower room was only a circle. On toward evening, it was a wheel, spinning, spinning, taking her nowhere and leaving her with motion sickness. She straightened picture frames on the sections of wall that were not made of glass. It had taken courage to hang photographs and drawings on the walls of a house that rested upon a planet spinning madly while revolving round the sun.

She walked out onto the deck and looked up at the

stars. They moved for her. She had that combination of insanity and patience that allowed her to follow their trek across the sky. Spreading the sleeves of her robe on an evening breeze, she reached out to them.

No, not yet. Not tonight.

Sarah lowered her arms, as a bird would fold its wings. It was an act of will to stay when fear argued for leaving, when she need only let go of the earth and let the ether take her. The notion of flight, like the motion of stars, was seductive. She wrapped her arms close about her body, though not for comfort, but to save her own life—for the sake of Isabelle, who came softly rapping at the door, calling, "Mom?"

"Yes, Belle. I'm here." Still here. By an act of will, she stayed.

"Maybe she'll feel more like talking in the morning," said Addison Winston. "Sarah's a bit shaken up."

"Not surprising," said Cable Babitt. "You'd never expect a thing like that to happen in Coventry." The sheriff donned his hat as he walked to the door. "Mr. Swahn said to thank your wife for calling it in." And now he tipped his hat to Isabelle. "Lucky thing Oren Hobbs happened to be in the neighborhood tonight."

"Yes, very lucky." She stopped smiling after closing the door on the sheriff.

Oren's luck was about to run out.

She opened the hall closet and ripped her jacket from

a hanger. She intended to make dead certain that he understood the instructions attached to the birder journals. He was not to go joyriding with her mother one more time. It was going to be so satisfying to hear Oren Hobbs scream in high soprano notes when she—

"Does your mother have another bottle up there?" Addison was facing the staircase.

Isabelle crept up behind him, saying softly, "I know what you did."

He turned around, startled for the split second before he recognized this old routine begun in her childhood. Addison had taught it to her, and most often he had been the one ferreting out secrets with those same words. He glanced at the jacket in her hand. "I'd rather you didn't go down to William's place tonight. I might need help with your mother."

"I know Mom started drinking the year Josh Hobbs disappeared. The other night—after dinner—were you joking when you wondered if she had an affair with Oren? It's so hard to tell with you, Addison. You've got such an ugly sense of humor."

"If I'm supposed to be making a connection here, shouldn't you—"

"From the back, Oren and Josh looked a lot alike. Same kind of clothes, and they even had the same walk. Oren was taller, but if you came up behind his brother—alone—in the woods . . ." She let the rest of her accusation dangle unspoken.

He laughed. He *roared*. He showed her *all* his teeth—

wide smile. "Why don't you ask your mother about Josh? She's the one who buried the boy."

Isabelle's jacket fell from her hand.

Addison picked it up from the floor and returned it to the closet, still grinning as he arranged the garment on a hanger. "So you'll stay. Well, good."

Twenty-five

William Swahn refused an ambulance ride to the hospital, and a paramedic led the man indoors to patch his wounds. Oren sat alone on the front steps, watching the show as he nursed his beer.

Men and women in troopers' uniforms bagged the empty bottles found outside and inside the house. Every glass surface was a fingerprint examiner's wet dream.

A few yards away, Cable Babitt stood beside Sally Polk, saying to her, "Your guys are welcome to all the bottles they can carry. I don't need them. I've got the whole damn thing on film."

"I like a nice tight case," said the CBI agent. "The beer bottle I'd most like to have has a set of prints that might surprise you. Oh, and that film? That's mine now."

In answer to Cable's sputtered, "You can't do that!" Sally Polk explained that, yes, she could—now that she had charged a Los Angeles TV producer with conspiracy to incite a riot via some creative film editing.

"You can't make that stick," said Cable. "That's ridiculous."

"Oh, dear. You think I overstepped my authority? Well, maybe you're right. But it's gonna take a while to sort out the blame. Meanwhile the scope of the case extends across county lines." She surveyed the crime scene brightly lit by lights on poles. "And all of this belongs to me."

Oren decided that he liked Sally Polk.

Morning came with the smell of furniture polish and the sound of a vacuum cleaner. Oren woke up on a couch in the front room of the house on Paulson Lane. Every shard of broken glass was gone, and glaziers stood on long ladders to replace the broken windowpanes.

Swahn's cleaning lady was the mother of one of his old classmates, and now Mrs. Snow reintroduced herself as she worked around his stretched-out body. "What a night," she said. "What a mess." As he rose from the couch, she brushed him down with a whisk broom. "Can't have you tracking glass splinters through the house."

Pronounced clean, she released him, saying, "Hannah's upstairs in Mr. Swahn's room." As he climbed the steps, she called out, "Second door on your right. He's been through a lot, so don't you tire him out."

"No, ma'am, I won't."

When he came to the open door of the bedroom, he hung back to watch Hannah changing a bandage on William Swahn's right cheek, exposing a patch of skin that was red and raw. This fresh injury paled the older damage to the other side of his face. Oren backed away from the door and lingered in the hall to listen to a conversation of two old friends, who called each other Miss Rice and Mr. Swahn.

"Well, that paramedic did a real nice job cleaning the wound."

"Will I look more symmetrical now?"

She laughed. "When the swelling goes down and the bruising fades, you won't have another scar."

There was a third person in the room. Oren saw the CBI agent reflected in the mirror over Swahn's bureau.

"This'll cheer you up," said Sally Polk. "I got film of a reporter chucking the first rock, and I got his prints on a beer bottle, too. I figure he was just priming the pump—didn't want to wait around all night for his big mob scene. But the whole thing started with a nasty piece of editing on the evening news. I'm gonna bring down a TV network just for you, Mr. Swahn. Won't that be fun?"

"What about the mob? Did you get them all on film?"

"No, maybe half. But the two Oren Hobbs laid out are awake and talking. They gave up three of their friends, but they didn't even know the rest of those guys. A barmaid gave us a few more names. And then we got a slew of fingerprints off the beer bottles they tossed through your windows. Idiots. I can promise you I'll get 'em all."

The CBI agent said her goodbyes and stepped into the hallway, where she met Oren with a friendly smile.

He was certain that she would seem equally friendly on the business end of a gun. "Nice work," he said. "I mean the way you stole this mob case from the sheriff."

"Well, thank you. And when I get six minutes to catch my breath, I'll find out who killed your brother."

"Will that be *before* or *after* you wind up an investigation of the sheriff's office? I know you're using Josh to get close to Cable Babitt."

Her smile was still holding, but she was stalling. Weighing the odds? Would a lie well told beat whatever cards he was holding? Her shoulders squared off, and her feet were firmly planted. The lady was waiting for proof of this theory of his.

Oren nodded his understanding. "The CBI has a field office over in Shasta. But here you are in *my* county, camped out with the Highway Patrol. So I know you're not investigating them. That leaves the sheriff's office. And the investigation has to be department-wide, or you wouldn't need a gang of troopers for backup."

Sally Polk adjusted her purse strap, preparing to leave him now. "If you give the sheriff a heads-up, I'll cut your balls into little pieces and feed 'em to the hogs." She said this with such warmth, such cheerful goodwill, that she left him smiling.

Oren entered the bedroom, an austere place with no personal items on display. There was a light rectangle on one wall, where a picture frame had been recently taken down, the sign of an extremely private person—or a man with something to hide. That missing picture, once positioned opposite the bed, would have been the last thing Swahn looked at when he put out the lamp at night and the first sight of each new day.

Swahn's brow furrowed as he, too, stared at that empty space, no doubt recognizing his error.

And, of course, nothing got past Hannah. She held a roll of adhesive tape in one hand and, in the other, a pair of closed shears that might pass for the lance of a tiny knight. She hovered over her patient, prepared to take on all comers—even Oren. There was conflict in her eyes, and it pained him to see it. After pulling a chair close to the bed, he turned to her. "Hannah? Give us a minute?"

"I just gave him a sleeping pill. Can't this wait?"

"It won't take a minute," said Oren. "I promise."

Hannah bent down to William Swahn, laying one hand on his shoulder, and they held the silent conversation of friends for life. She asked by a worried look if she should stay and defend him. Swahn smiled in assurance that there was no need to fight for him—but thanks.

When the housekeeper had quit the room, Oren said, "I've got a question about those pictures of you in the post office. Josh caught you passing an envelope to the librarian. You dropped it into her tote bag. If it was addressed to Mrs. Winston, I can see why you couldn't just mail it. Half the gossip in town comes from the postmaster."

Swahn closed his eyes and turned his face away. The interview was over.

When Oren came out of the bedroom, he found Hannah sitting on the staircase. She reached up to hand him a prescription. "That's for his pain. Could you have it filled at the drugstore? Your father will be here by the time you get back. So there shouldn't be any more questions about those pictures of Mr. Swahn and Mavis."

"Eavesdropping, Hannah?" He sat down beside her.

"Mr. Swahn's a gentleman. He won't tell you what was in that envelope. But I will. The judge used to do the same thing for years. The line at the post office was the best place for it. Before we had rural delivery, Mavis always picked up her mail at the same time every morning. Coventry didn't have anything as grand as welfare, and Mavis hadn't seen a paycheck for a while. You may have noticed—no one goes to the library anymore. Officially, it was closed for years. But Mavis still showed up for work every day."

"A creature of habit."

"Right. And crazy. I'm sure you noticed that, too. So, once a month, people with money—like the judge, like Mr. Swahn—they'd slip her some cash on the sly. It was done that way so she wouldn't have to thank anybody. The envelopes were labeled as donations to the library, and that was to save her pride. I know Addison was generous, too. His envelopes were the thickest ones. It took the judge a long time to force the town council into reinstating Mavis so she could get regular paychecks. But back then, she was the town charity."

Hannah shook her head, slowly, sadly. "Josh and his collection of secrets. Hanging that one out in public made your father so mad. Only a handful of people would've understood what was going on in those pictures, and maybe a year passed by before any of them caught on to what the boy had done—exposing a sick woman that way. The judge was the first one to notice. I remember when he came home from the post office—so angry. His last conversation with your brother was an argument. After that, they didn't speak for days. And then Josh was gone—dead."

Oren stopped on the sidewalk outside the drugstore. Down the street, Alice Friday stood on the verandah of the Straub Hotel. The psychic was keeping watch on the judge's Mercedes. Well, if she wanted a word with him, the feeling was mutual. He had read her old interview with the sheriff and memorized every line:

ALICE FRIDAY: I know that boy is dead. Only the dead speak to me.

SHERIFF BABITT: Josh went missing a year ago. So that's hardly a revelation from the great beyond. Did the Ouija board tell you where to look for his body?

ALICE FRIDAY: The dead don't care about such things. I can tell you he's not at peace. Josh's death was violent.

SHERIFF BABITT: Lady, if you know something about that kid, you—

ALICE FRIDAY: He's my spirit guide. Now I came here today because I have a question for you. Josh keeps asking me all the time. What about the other one? Josh says you'd know about that. Now what does he mean?

SHERIFF BABITT: If you were a real psychic, you'd know I'm planning to boot your bony ass out of my office.

Oren walked toward the Mercedes. He was about to open the door when the psychic noticed him and waved. Evelyn Straub came outside as Alice Friday ran down the steps and crossed the street, yelling, "Young man!" When she had closed the distance, she stood before him, thin arms folded, her stance resolute. "You shouldn't have walked out in the middle of my séance. You have to come back. Your brother isn't done with you."

He was distracted by the speeding car, a standout in the crawl of Coventry traffic, and now Alice Friday also stared at this unusual sight. A redhead sat behind the wheel and aimed her automobile at Oren. He pushed the psychic into a space between parked vehicles, and then he rolled onto the trunk of the Mercedes. The nose of the black sports car almost kissed his rear bumper.

Isabelle Winston had looked right through him as if he were not there, as if—

"That woman tried to *kill* us." Alice Friday's words were hushed. Her eyes were startled and wide.

"No," said Oren. "She tried to kill *me*."

This distinction was lost on the stick-thin woman. She reached into her purse to produce a small notebook and a pen. "Not to worry. I got a good look at the license plate." After jotting down the numbers, she saw the stout hotelier crossing the street, and she yelled, "Evelyn, go call the sheriff!"

"Not a good idea." Evelyn Straub walked up to the smaller woman. "Cable's got enough to deal with this morning."

Alice Friday grabbed Oren's arm. "That woman tried to murder him with her car."

"No," said Evelyn, "that's just how they say hello."

The glazier's truck was gone, and the cleaning lady's car had also departed. Oren was surprised to see the yellow stray standing at attention in front of William Swahn's door. The animal must have followed the judge down the road to Paulson Lane.

Addison Winston sat on the hood of his Porsche, dangling his legs as he engaged in a staring contest with the wary stray, trying to win over a dog with his professional smile. The lawyer shrugged and turned to Oren. "I've got a great lawsuit to pitch to my client. Did you see those news broadcasts? He can get millions from the TV station *and* the California Bureau. But Hannah won't let me inside."

"The CBI agent had nothing to do with what happened last night."

"Sally's interview incited the—"

"That was no interview. That was an ambush."

"Why let the truth get in the way of a tasty lawsuit?"

Oren climbed the steps to the front door and leaned

down to pet the yellow stray. "Don't press your luck with any more cops. That bogus settlement in L.A. might come back to bite you."

"We had a deal, Oren."

"Your client is the wild card. I think he's putting it together all by himself. When Hannah barred the door, she probably did you a favor."

News of attempted vehicular homicide traveled fast.

The judge and Hannah were sitting at the table when Oren entered William Swahn's kitchen. Their conversation suddenly stopped.

That was a clue.

His father winked at the housekeeper, and then looked up with a pretense of shock. "I heard Belle Winston tried to run you down."

Hannah smiled. "Never dull, is it? I *love* this town." She rose from the table to fetch another cup and pour him some coffee.

Oren thanked her when she set it down in front of him, and then he let the two of them sit and wait. The judge was foiled by his own policy of never asking an obvious question, such as why would the Winston girl try to kill him? Oren sipped his coffee—slowly—and slowly he set down his cup to gaze out the window and watch the clouds roll by—while listening to his father's tapping foot beneath the table.

Finally, he said to no one in particular, "Alice Friday moved to Coventry a year after Josh disappeared. She knows Mrs. Winston, but she didn't recognize the daughter."

"Well, Belle's only been back for a few months," said Hannah. "I guess she's never been to one of Alice's séances."

"But over all these years . . ." He splayed his hands to ask how this lack of recognition was possible in a town the size of a postage stamp.

Hannah countered by holding up three fingers. "In all that time, Belle's only made three visits home that I know of. And I don't think the girl ever stayed a whole day."

So Isabelle Winston had been another exile. Had she also been sent away after Josh vanished? Or had she run away?

Cable Babitt's jeep rounded the last curve on the way to his house. He spotted the CBI agent's Taurus parked in the turnout just beyond his driveway. Her black sedan slowly pulled into the road and drove off.

That bitch! She had *waited* for him. She *wanted* him to see her.

He left the jeep's door hanging open and ran to the back of his garage. The cordwood was still neatly stacked against the rear wall, and there were no signs of disturbance among the individual logs. But he had to know for certain if the knapsack was still there, or he would get no sleep tonight. One by one, he pulled down the logs and flung them away. At last, he uncovered the bright green canvas wadded up inside the plastic bag. Perhaps it had been a mistake to move it from his former hiding place in the toolshed.

The cellar would be better, safer from Sally Polk. She'd never get in there without the proper paperwork, and that woman had burned her bridges with warrants in this county.

Half an hour later, he opened the storm doors that led him up to the light of his backyard, and he emerged from the cellar a satisfied man. Josh's knapsack was safe in its new resting place under piles of storage cartons and suitcases.

"Oh, goddamn."

He caught sight of the wind-whipped hem of a flowery dress, just a flash of material from behind the back wall of his garage.

That bitch!

He rounded the corner and there was Sally Polk, standing in the middle of his cast-off firewood. The logs he had strewn all about the yard now advertised something once hidden in the woodpile and removed with great haste—and fear.

But the damn woman only made cheerful small talk while he sweated on a cool morning.

Twenty-six

The judge sat in a wooden armchair beside Hannah's empty porch rocker, and the yellow stray stretched out at his feet. The man and the dog had been napping in the sun. But now the animal raised his floppy ears, and his eyes opened. Henry Hobbs also heard the sound of a car's engine.

The CBI agent parked her black Taurus in front of the house. She stepped out of the car with a wave of hello. The dog pronounced her harmless when he laid his head down on his front paws and closed his eyes. The judge was not so charitable in his view of this woman.

Harmless indeed.

Sally Polk approached the porch, and the judge stood up, as he would for any woman, lady or sociopath. And his tone was civil when he addressed her. "So you've come to vandalize the rest of my house."

"Oh, no. Today I'm on best behavior." Slinging her purse strap over one shoulder, she climbed the steps and paused to glance at Hannah's rocking chair. She waited for a nod from her host, and then she sat down. "Judge, I know you pulled the strings to take those homicides away from me."

"You don't know anything of the kind." And now that he had called her bluff, he matched her smile and made his wider. He remained standing, a pointed suggestion for a short visit.

She settled her handbag on her lap, a sign that she was not leaving anytime soon. "I *know* you've got a vested interest in a backwoods investigation."

"You mean Cable? He's the one with jurisdiction. The state of California has no interest here. My son's grave is on private land—a county matter."

"Only because Mrs. Straub's government lease was rescinded. I hear the paperwork to kill those old mineral rights went through in one day. Well, let me tell you—that gave heart attacks to a pack of bureaucrats down in Sacramento. They've never seen paper fly so fast. I'm guessing that's thanks to you. Oh, and Addison, too. He seems to be everybody's lawyer this week."

"I'm sure the sheriff will make a competent investigation."

"We both know that's a lie." She opened her purse and pulled out a photograph. "Maybe you forgot. Your son shared that grave with someone else." She held out the picture, leaving him no choice but to take it. "That's Mary Kent. A common name—easy to forget."

He looked down at the face of a girl—so young—with long blond hair, immortal when she smiled for the camera, smiling down a long hallway of doors opening, life unfolding. At this frozen moment, she could never have imagined her death.

"That's an old passport photo," said Sally Polk. "She was in her mid-thirties when she died."

"But you thought this photo of a youngster would make a much better inducement for cooperation."

"No, that's not it. I couldn't find any family albums with a more recent picture. There's no family. No close friends, either. So you got lucky, Judge. No one's gonna care if Cable Babitt screws up this case. Mary Kent's got nobody to fight for her."

He handed the picture back to Sally Polk, but the CBI agent waved it away.

"No, sir. You keep that." She settled back in Hannah's chair, rocking slowly, and the floorboards creaked. "The County Sheriff's Office has a team of investigators, but Cable's working this case on his own. That's the way you wanted it, right? A bumbling idiot in charge? That smells of collusion. It *reeks*." She looked out over the meadow, rocking, rocking. "What pretty wildflowers." In the same harmless tone, she said, "I think you're protecting Oren. I've seen his Army record. He's more than just a world-class cop. That boy *knows* how to kill."

The judge lowered his eyes. "Oren loved Josh more than his own life."

"I believe that. Oh, did you think I was accusing him of murder?" The rocking stopped, and she leaned toward him. "While you've still got one son left, you better hope I solve this case before Oren does."

The judge shook his head. Despite the military record, he could not see his son taking human life by choice—not on Josh's account. Twenty years of sorrow had a tempering effect. With great care, he had watched the returning soldier for signs of unraveling, and he had waited with his safety net to catch the boy when he fell. But Oren had come shining through, his character intact—if not his heart. And the pride of Henry Hobbs was enormous. "You can depend on my son to do the right thing."

"You mean act like a cop?" Once more the floorboards creaked beneath the chair's rockers. "When a child is murdered, cops always look at the parents first. I wonder if Oren took a hard look at you. Does he know what you did in the Korean War? So many medals. You were a damned death machine. As a soldier, you killed more people than I've arrested."

"I'm a pacifist. I sickened of killing as a very young man." And now the judge felt the need to sit down. He settled into the chair beside hers. "I did not murder my son."

The dog lifted his head, awakened by the inflection of pain in an old man's voice.

"I'd like to believe you," said Sally Polk. "But you can see my problem, can't you? Most parents—the innocent ones—they want a case solved. They want justice for the dead child. But you don't." The rhythm of the creaking floorboards was faster now, as if a rocking chair could take her somewhere. "That only makes sense if you already know who killed your son. Rumor has it you're an atheist. So I know God's not telling you to leave the vengeance to Him." The rocking stopped. "If you know who did this, *tell* me."

"Vengeance is thine, Sally Polk?"

"You bet your sweet ass, old man." She reached out to tap the photograph in his hand. "Mary Kent's skull was caved in with a rock. She died quick. The killer spent more time with Josh. It was hands-on torture. No other way to say it. Broken ribs, a fractured jaw, cracks in his leg bones, breaks in the arms. And then there's the damage to Josh's hands. My expert says one trauma can't account for all the broken fingers. They were snapped like twigs—one by one. The boy's pain just went *on* and *on*."

The judge looked down at the dog's brown eyes, wells of solace. "I don't know who murdered my son. If you find out, don't come back here expecting thanks. And I won't thank you for that litany of Josh's suffering—those terrible pictures you put in my head. Now I can *see* his fear—I can *feel* it. I can even hear the bones break-ing . . . my child crying. Is this what you wanted?"

He turned to her with all his pain, all his sadness, and it drove her away.

"I'm not an invalid." Swahn waved off assistance as he settled down on the couch in his library. He reached out to an end table and picked up a stapled sheaf of papers. "This is the final report on the bones."

"You didn't get that from the sheriff." Oren sat on the

floor and prowled through a box of food delivered by the cleaning woman. He pulled out two roast beef sandwiches and handed one to Swahn. "Who sold you the coroner's report? Dave Hardy?"

"No, I never paid a dime." Swahn bit into his sandwich and nodded toward the box. "There should be a carton of beer in there. And I've got better sources than the deputy. I know Dr. Brasco. He's the anthropologist they called in to examine the bones. I may have misled him. He thought I was consulting on the case. So he faxed me his own results. He also passed along his condolences and regards. Dr. Brasco tells me the two of you go way back to the mass graves of Bosnia. He said you were an uncommon man—his highest praise. He couldn't understand why you left the military. Especially now when—"

"Good job. I found it." Oren pulled out the six-pack of beer cans. "What was Brasco's finding?"

"The female victim died quickly. Josh's death was more drawn out." Swahn reached down to accept a warm beer and popped the tab. "That makes your brother the most likely target. The woman was probably a witness."

Oren could think of other scenarios, but he said nothing.

"That kills the theory of a murder for hire," said Swahn. "A professional would've been more . . . efficient. The killer's violence toward Josh suggests immaturity, control issues."

"Like somebody who knocks his wife around?"

"I wouldn't rule out spousal abuse. Your brother's

killer *might* have a history of violence, but he certainly had something to hide. Find the secret, something photographable—that's the motive. It's most likely a shameful thing, and that's where the rage comes in."

Oren set down his beer can. "I don't care about a perp's motivation or how he was affected by early potty training. I just collect the evidence, and then I catch him. So simple."

"But you seem to favor abusive husbands. Maybe a jealous husband? You think our killer might've mistaken Josh for you? We could narrow down the suspects if you gave me a list of all the married women you slept with— just the bleach blondes. According to my sources, the female victim was identified as a—"

"We're not partners," said Oren. "You give. I take. It's like that." And now he could rule out any tie to Evelyn, whose hair had been tawny brown, the color of a lion's mane.

"Dr. Brasco said you loved your work. Hard for him to believe you'd ever leave it. He also said you were a moral man. What happened? Were you asked to do immoral things? Is that why you left? Did your shining military code fall apart on you?"

Oren wiped his hands of bread crumbs. "I'm still looking for those missing prints from Josh's last roll. Hannah says she doesn't have them, and I know they weren't left at the drugstore. So that leaves you."

"Unless she lied. . . . But I would never believe any bad thing of Miss Rice, even if I knew it to be true." He looked down at the cartons, the papers and pictures that covered the rug. "You've seen everything I have. If those photographs aren't here—"

"Maybe you missed something. I'll just take a look around upstairs." Oren moved toward the open doors that led to the foyer and the staircase. He glanced back to see Swahn reach for his cane and rise to a listing stand.

Oren slowed his steps near the foot of the staircase, where he listened to the closing of the elevator door in the room behind him—and now the *whirr* of the slow-rising cage. This was an odd race of dragging feet. He heard the cage door open on the floor above. He climbed upward and paused near the landing to watch William Swahn hobble into a room at the top of the stairs.

Oren gave the man enough time to find the thing he most wanted to hide. Then he opened the door to a room of filing cabinets and other furnishings of a private office. Swahn was not holding papers or pictures. He was secreting a pair of binoculars in the top drawer of a desk.

Interesting choice.

Obviously, the cleaning woman had never ventured into this room. Only one windowpane had been washed, and there were repeated patterns of twin circles in the dust on the sill. Oren took the binoculars from the open drawer and turned to the one clean window, training the lenses on the only thing in sight that was not a cloud or a tree. The binoculars were already focused for the tower of the Winston lodge. Below the roof of bright copper shingles, half the wall was made of glass—a voyeur's dream. He watched Mrs. Winston pacing back and forth like a captive in a giant's jewel box.

"You were right about one thing," said Oren. "I never wanted to work on my brother's murder. Personal involvement screws with judgment." He returned the binoculars to the desk drawer—and slammed it. "That's what blindsided *you*." He stared at the ruined side of Swahn's face. "You still think you got that scar because the other cops in your precinct thought you were queer?"

Swahn looked wary, but curious, too.

Oren walked toward him. "That *A* carved into your skin doesn't stand for AIDS. Nobody heard that rumor until *after* you were attacked." He stood toe-to-toe with Swahn. "I think you believe that now. You're not even gay, are you? Even that was a scam. Back in L.A. when you were a cop, how many married women were *you* screwing? Was Mrs. Winston one of them?"

Swahn's gaze was fixed upon the window, the view of Sarah Winston in her tower. He closed his eyes.

Isabelle Winston reached over the paddock fence to feed a slice of apple to the horse, Nickel Number Two.

In her early childhood, Number Two had been her name for Addison. Legally, he was her father, the only one she had ever known. But once there had been another father, a natural one. What was his name? She had carelessly forgotten. Beyond a tie of blood, her sole connection to that other man had been an old photograph in her mother's wallet. After a time, the wallet had been lost, and the photograph had not been missed.

If only Daddy Number Two could fade away so easily.

Addison stood beside her, making a great show of looking around in all directions to be certain that they were not overheard. His lips close to her ear, he spoke in a stagy whisper. "Don't you have any curiosity? You never asked me about the day your mother buried Josh in the woods."

"I don't believe you."

"Sarah buried something else. Evidence of murder. I could show you where to dig."

Twenty-seven

A lerted by the cowbells on the judge's bedroom
doorknob, Oren took the stairs two and three at a
time, bare-chested, barefooted and zipping his
jeans on the run.

His father stood before the front door, shod in sandals
and wearing a sweatshirt pulled over pajama pants. Frustrated by three dead-bolt locks, he scratched on the wood
with a clawed hand. The sleepwalker's imaginary box was
cradled in one arm.

Oren gently turned him around and held him by the
shoulders.

There was anguish in the old man's eyes when he said,
"I need another miracle."

"You and me both." Oren embraced him and held
him close. Out came the words he could only say when
the old man was asleep. "I missed you. God, how I missed

you." He breathed in the tobacco scent trapped in his father's beard. This moment was the homecoming he had ached for, and he did not want it to end.

The judge began to cry.

Hannah appeared in her purple bathrobe. "This is my fault. I forgot to drug his whiskey."

"Get the key," said Oren. "Unlock the door."

The housekeeper shuffled off in fuzzy purple slippers to return minutes later, wearing sensible shoes and holding the key, two jackets, Oren's cowboy boots and a whiskey bottle. "First aid," she said, by way of explaining the bottle. She wrapped one jacket around the judge's shoulders.

After pulling on his boots, Oren unlocked the door and placed his father's hand on the knob so the old man could open it by himself.

Once outside, Hannah pulled two small flashlights from the deep pockets of her robe. Guided by these beams, she and Oren followed the sleepwalker down the porch steps. They woke the yellow stray in passing, and now they were four. The dog made no sound as he trotted along at the judge's side, only lifting his snout, sniffing for a scent of change in the air, something odd and maybe dangerous.

Inside the garage, his father became anxious again. The Mercedes was locked.

The housekeeper folded her arms. "I'm not giving up *that* key."

The judge let go of the door handle. Two by two, Oren and Hannah followed the old man and the dog.

They left the garage and walked down the driveway to the road. After a hike of ten minutes, the small parade turned onto a dead-end street with only one address. The grave-yard gate was open, no locks to thwart Henry Hobbs on his mission, but there were many obstacles, small marble stones to trip over and large monuments to collide with.

"Don't worry," said Hannah, reading Oren's mind again, annoying habit. "This part of the cemetery hasn't changed at all. Whatever year the judge is walking through, he'll do just fine. It's probably daylight in his dreams."

The judge neatly skirted every headstone along his path and came to rest before the Hobbs family plot, which held a hundred years of generations. He unlatched the small iron gate and stepped inside to sit down by the grave of Oren's mother. The yellow stray sprawled on the grass beside him.

"Compared to Horatio, that dog is a freaking genius," said Hannah. "He knows when to be still."

Oren entered the gated plot and sat down tailor fash-ion. By the light of the moon, he watched his father's face. The judge woke from the dream to see that it was not day but night, and he wore the same shy expression Oren had seen at the close of the last episode. The judge stared at his wife's headstone and then discovered his son seated beside him. This time, there could be no retreat into sleep and forgetfulness.

Finally, wits gathered, the old man said, "When will they give Josh back to us so we can have a proper funeral?"

"It won't be long," said Oren.

"I guess you believe me now." Hannah stood behind the judge, arms folded in a pose of *I told you so*. "You were walking in your sleep."

"I suppose that would explain a lot." The judge fished through the pockets of his jacket.

Hannah ended this search by producing two cigars and a pack of matches from thin air. After handing over the whiskey bottle, she further amazed them by opening her hands to reveal a tiny glass standing on each palm. All of the housekeeper's clothes had deep pockets, the props of her best magic act: producing what was needed at the moment, be it bandages for a boy's skinned knee or shot glasses.

Oren took a proffered cigar from his father and unwrapped the cellophane. "I've never smoked one before."

"Nothing to it." The judge bit off one end of his own cigar, and his son did the same. He struck a match and lit both stogies, warning, "Don't inhale, boy. Just let it run around your taste buds, and then let it out." He opened his mouth to blow a perfect smoke ring in the still air. And then he blew a ring within a ring, a thing that had once delighted his son.

And it still did.

"Hannah can do three," said the judge. "But she never upstaged me in front of you and Josh."

"You talk in your sleep, sir." Oren filled his mouth with smoke and exhaled it with his next words. "You asked for another miracle."

"Well, that can't be right. I'm opposed to all things mystical. I most particularly do *not* hold with miracles." The judge looked around to see that Hannah had wandered away to visit the gravestones of old friends. He poured whiskey into the shot glasses and handed one to his son.

"Sir, you asked for *another* miracle."

"But there never was a first—" The judge, lost in thought, stared at his wife's gravestone. "No, I'm wrong. There *was* a miracle—more like a joke. The miracle of the rain—it happened right here. I know you remember the Reverend Pursey."

"Yes, sir, I do."

"Anointing you as a teenage archangel—that wasn't the craziest thing he ever did. But I had a few words with him over that." The judge smiled at this memory. "That loony old bugger. Oh, but what a showman. He packed his church every Sunday. One time, he accused Ad Winston of being the devil himself. Addison was so pleased. A lawyer can't buy advertising like that."

"Sir? *You* went to church?"

"No, I never do. But I'm not your typical atheist, either." Henry Hobbs absently stroked the dog's fur, and the animal loved him back, nuzzling his hand. "The way I see it—it doesn't matter if God invented man or man invented God. It's a done deal, and you might as well try to *un*invent the isosceles triangle. But a bona fide miracle defies logic in both camps. A man-made god precludes miraculous acts. And a true god wouldn't allow them.

Why shake man's faith in sweet reason? Take the Reverend Pursey. He was shaken witless by the miracle of the rain."

Oren exhaled a blue cloud and sipped from his shot glass. In faraway places, this was something he had imagined time and again, sharing smoke and whiskey with his father and listening to the old man's oral history of family and town.

The judge slapped the ground with one hand. "Pursey's miracle happened right here on this very spot. It was the day of your mother's funeral. Well, the sky's clouding up. The rain's coming any minute, and everybody knows it—umbrellas at the ready everywhere you look. And the Reverend Pursey's building up to the high point in his eulogy. Then the first raindrops fell. Oh, how that pissed him off. He looks up at the sky, a real nasty look like a warning. Then it begins to pour—a solid wall of rain. Well, Pursey's drenched, and people are surprised he doesn't drown when he opens his mouth. His eyes roll up toward heaven. He shakes one fist and yells, 'Knock it *off*!'

"And the rain—just—stopped.

"Damndest thing, a rare thing, but not unheard-of. You see, the rain didn't taper off. It was more like a giant faucet in the sky got *turned* off." The judge snapped his fingers. "That quick. So the miracle of the rain figured into a lot of church sermons after that. And then it became the punch line to a joke on a crazy old fool. Every time it rained, you'd see people stop on the street to shake their fists and yell at the sky and *laugh*—how they laughed. Now, if that's a miracle in your book, I'd have to say your standards are really low."

Father and son smoked cigars by the light of the moon and shared the whiskey for as long as it lasted.

Addison Winston aimed his flashlight beam at a patch of ground behind the stable. He held out the shovel to Isabelle. "Shall we dig it up?"

"*You* put it there."

"Ask your mother who buried it. Oh, that's right. You can't, can you? It might send her poor fragile mind right over the screaming edge. Belle, you have a first-rate brain, and this is simple logic. If I had evidence to hide, why would I bury it on my own land? I would've thrown it into the sea. But your mother's clearly an amateur in all things criminal. Or maybe her mind wasn't working right the night she buried it."

Isabelle sank the shovel a few inches into hard ground. "All right—*logically*—it shouldn't still be here." She used one foot on the metal edge to sink it deeper. "Why didn't you dig it up and get rid of it?"

"Well, it helps if you think like a lawyer. It's evidence that goes to your mother's state of mind—insanity. I thought it might come in handy if, by some miracle, Cable Babitt ever got to thinking like a real cop. He might wonder why you'd fake an alibi for Oren Hobbs. I wondered about that myself when you were sixteen. There's two ways to look at it—from the law's point of view. Either you killed Josh and you needed an alibi for yourself—or you knew for a fact that Oren didn't do it . . . *because* you *knew* who *did*. Sorry I can't help with the digging or the disposal. That would make me a material witness. I wouldn't be able to represent your mother if it comes to a trial."

"Mom would never hurt Josh." Isabelle lifted a shovelful of dirt and then another. "They were friends."

"Her friendships end badly. Look at poor William. After you left town, he'd drop by for dinner at the usual time, and your mother would lock herself in her room. No apology, not one word of explanation. That was shabby."

The shovel clinked against a metal object. Isabelle knelt down to scoop the dirt away with her hands. She could hear her restless horse moving in his stall on the other side of the stable wall.

"And now," said Addison, "back to your phony alibi for Oren Hobbs. How could you know he was innocent? You must have seen your mother when she came home from the woods that day—the day Josh disappeared. She was all sweaty and exhausted. Burying a corpse is hard work. You might recall all the blisters on her hands."

Discarding the shovel, Isabelle lifted a camera from the hole. It was crusted with dirt, and the metal was pitted like a sponge. Every mechanism was jammed. She set it on the ground and wiped her hands. "I can't open the back."

"Looking for a roll of film? You think maybe the boy had time to snap a picture of your mother?" He handed her the flashlight and stooped to pick up the shovel.

"Good thinking, Belle. No telling how long film might hold up." He made a swing with the shovel and brought it crashing down on the camera.

Now it was easy to lift the broken back, but there was no roll of film inside. Isabelle aimed the flashlight beam at the open compartment. A small piece of torn film was snagged in the spool. "My mother didn't kill Josh. Mom knows how to operate a camera like this one. Somebody else ripped out the roll—and botched it."

"A prosecutor will argue that she panicked."

"Addison, did you ever try to rip something like this, a piece of plastic or a negative? It's not easy." She stared at the mangled snatch of film, all that remained of Josh's last roll. "This was a violent act. And the killer knew nothing about cameras."

"Like me?" He squatted down beside her. "Burying the body—that's what made the blisters on Sarah's hands. Remember how beautiful her hands were?" He pointed to the camera. "Your mother brought home that little souvenir the following day. She waited for the cover of night to put it in the ground. Sarah was drunk by then, and she couldn't find the key to the toolshed. No shovel. She dug the hole with a spoon and her bare hands. That was just hell on her manicure. You remember the broken fingernails? You even asked her *how* she broke them. Is it all coming back to you now?"

Isabelle dropped the camera back into the hole.

"What are you doing? Belle, this is the time to get rid of it. If we wait too long, your mother might dig it up herself. She's coming apart. Throw it into the sea."

Isabelle shook her head. "Bad idea."

"All right, here's a better one. The grave in the woods. There's no one guarding it anymore. And now that they've closed up the hole, it's the perfect hiding place."

"No, Addison, I don't think so. That would be tampering with evidence. So you'd better hope I never testify in court. I'd have to say that I saw you smash the camera with this." She took the shovel from his hands and steeped it into the pile of loose dirt. "It was all so long ago. I can't say I remember seeing blisters on Mom's hands," she lied, "or broken fingernails."

She filled in the hole and tamped it down with the flat side of the shovel. "And the camera's buried on your land, isn't it? What a crazy thing to do. And you knew where to dig. You led me right to it."

Isabelle handed him the shovel. "If this ever comes back on you, Addison, you can always plead insanity."

And that plea might ring true.

She picked up the flashlight and switched it off, not wanting to see his face. Was he grinning in the dark?

Twenty-eight

He stood at the door to the attic darkroom, unable to cross the threshold. The tools of his brother's art were arranged in the same old way. The chemicals in the bottles must have degraded by now, but no dust had been allowed to settle here. Josh might have walked away only an hour ago to have his breakfast downstairs in the kitchen.

Oren was afraid to go inside that small room. He might get lost in there, and a search party of a thousand townspeople would not be able to bring him back this time.

He heard wooden clogs on the attic stairs and turned to see Hannah pause on the top step.

Her eyes were on the darkroom's open door. "I told you, that's the *last* place I would've put those old pictures."

He nodded absently. Inside the room, only inches away, was a drawer that he might search, but it was too far to travel just now.

Maybe tomorrow.

"I had your black suit dry-cleaned," said the house-keeper.

"I'm not going to the birthday ball." Hannah's clogs were coming up behind him, and he could hear determination in every step.

"The judge wants you to come with us. Come—just to make your father happy for one night."

"He thinks I killed Josh."

The wooden clogs came to a halt. "You can't believe that."

"That's why he sent me out of town. He was right to blame me. Josh and I had a fight in the woods that day. He wasn't just stalking strangers. Sometimes it was people we both knew, and I called him on it. The last time I saw my brother, I was chasing him down, and I was angry."

Josh had shown him a photograph of two lovers on the porch of Evelyn's cabin—one captured instant of a slow kiss. Oren had torn this picture to shreds. And then he had reached for his brother.

"I know he was afraid of me. He ran off. I followed him. I *hunted* him all day long. And I would've found him if he was only lost . . . but he was hiding from me. He was scared."

Each detail of that day into night was so clear. The judge and Hannah had waited dinner, though the hour was late. They were sitting at the kitchen table when he came banging through the back door, out of breath and sweating—and bleeding, his face badly scratched by low-hanging branches after sundown.

The judge had been surprised to see him this way—and alarmed—and slow to ask him where his brother was.

That was the first time Oren had felt fear. He felt it now, standing in the open doorway of the darkroom—a time machine. Josh might still be wandering the woods, only missing his supper. The judge must be worried. It was so dark outside.

Hannah was shaking him back into the solid world, where it was morning.

A truck larger than a moving van caught Sarah Winston's attention. What now? All the flowers and the rented furniture had already been delivered, and the caterer's vehicles had arrived an hour ago.

She drank her breakfast slowly, for this single glass was the only alcohol she would be allowed all day. "Happy birthday to me."

The rear door of the giant truck was rolled up, and two large men climbed inside to stand among tall blocks of ice. They slowly moved one of the blocks toward the edge of the truck bed and onto a waiting forklift. This small yellow machine and its massive cargo turned and rolled across the grass, then up a wide plank and through the open doorway of the lodge.

As she followed the forklift inside, she felt the cold

chill of air-conditioning cranked to Arctic temperatures. Awaiting the ice block was a standing army of men and women with chain saws and more traditional carving tools. Addison was in their midst, talking to a man with a clipboard.

Delighted, Sarah called out, "Ice sculptures!"

Her husband whirled around and smiled, as if he had not seen her for years and years. He walked toward her. "Not to worry, Sarah. These artists work very fast. They'll be done hours before the first guest arrives." He put one arm around his wife's shoulders and guided her through the doors to the foyer. "It's too cold in here, I know. Can't have the ice melting before the ball. But there'll be at least a thousand candles lighting this room tonight. That should take the chill off." He closed the doors behind them. "Promise me you won't go in there again. I want the sculptures to be a surprise."

She kissed his cheek and climbed the stairs, glass in hand, sipping her way toward the tower room, where she had found a new hiding place for contraband. If she were to turn around right now, Sarah knew she would see the maid close behind her. Hilda must find it miraculous that her employer's wife could nurse one drink all morning. And the legend of the bottomless glass would grow into evening.

"It never fails," said Hannah. "Guilt always comes with a death in the family." The housekeeper pointed Oren toward an old trunk in a silent invitation to sit down.

She stood over him, hands on hips and great concern in her eyes. "This is how I remember the day. Josh asked me to make him a sandwich for his knapsack. But not you. So I know it was a last-minute idea—you going into the woods with your brother. You were keeping close tabs on him in those days. I bet Josh was the one who started the fight."

When Oren hesitated, she leaned down to peer into his eyes and smiled, liking what she saw. "I'm right. That boy meant to ditch you from the moment you set out for the woods. He had plans of his own that day—plans you wouldn't like."

She paced in front of him, hands behind her back and talking in the listen-up mode. "Your life started going off the track long before that day. I lay the blame on your mother for dying young. If she'd lived, she would've taught you how to dance and talk to little girls. You would've had an actual conversation with Isabelle Winston. The two of you should've had four kids by now. Incidentally, it's not too late for that. I realize that Belle seems a bit harsh, maybe even homicidal—"

"There are no pictures of my mother." As a child and a teenager, he had never questioned the loss of her. Other boys had mothers, but he and Josh had Hannah. "No photographs. I can't remember what she looked like."

"Of course there were pictures," she said, "dozens of them. The first time I walked into this house—uninvited—well, you know that old story—I saw your mother looking back at me from every wall. The judge cried all the time in those days. He couldn't walk into a room without seeing reminders of her. So, a week or so after her funeral, real late at night, I collected them all and brought them up here."

Hannah pulled a trunk away from the wall to get at the boxes behind it. "The next morning, the judge woke up, looked at the walls, then took a deep breath and got on with his life. We never talked about it." She opened a box and pulled out framed photographs, handing them to Oren, one by one. "You can see how pretty she was, but that's not what people remember best. You ask and they'll say she loved to dance."

The housekeeper picked up a small wooden chest. "This is why I came up here." She lifted the tiny latch, opened the lid and pulled out a frayed teething ring. "This was your stuff. Nothing of Josh's. You two weren't so much alike when you were small. He was on the frail side, but you always looked like a little man in training." She plucked a picture from the box and held it up to him.

He stared at the snapshot of a baby no older than two. Hannah placed the small chest in his hands and backed away a few steps as he pored through the contents. There were a few small toys, a lock of hair tied by a ribbon, and photographs of husband and wife taking turns with the camera to picture themselves with their first baby.

"That's the judge's invisible box," said Hannah, "the one he carries around when he walks in his sleep. It's the only box in the house that opens with a latch. You saw the way he opened it in the kitchen the other night. I told you I'd seen it before. Last night, he carried it to the cemetery to ask for a miracle. Do you get it now?"

He shook his head.

She threw up her arms. "That first time in the kitchen, he said to your dead mother, 'Our child is lost. I need another miracle.' You're the lost child, Oren."

"No, that was Josh. The judge blamed me for—"

"He never did."

"He sent me away. He couldn't stand the sight of me."

She silenced him with one finger pressed to his lips. "After a time, the judge came to terms with the idea that Josh was dead. But not you. You just would not give him up—always tearing around those woods—days at a time. There was a danger that you might die out there, half starved, no water. Maybe there'd come a day when we couldn't find you and bring you safe home. Your father sent you away to finish school in a place with no trees—so you couldn't get lost again. It was your idea to stay away—to join the Army. That mystified him, and it hurt him, too. That old man loves you beyond reason, and he missed you every single day that you were gone. The reason he kept the house like a damn museum—that wasn't on account of Josh. He wanted everything to be the same on the day when you found your way home."

Isabelle had spent half the morning in bed, using a pillow to muffle the sounds of workmen inside the house and out in the yard. She had spent most of the night reading the more recent birder logs written years after the disappearance of Joshua Hobbs—her mother's obsession.

The town had become smaller and more claustrophobic on each succeeding page. Some birds had eyes that glowed in the darkness as they traveled single file up the mountainside, and these were the witchboard people.

Showered and dressed, she unlocked her bedroom door. Last night was the first time she had ever thought to lock it. But she had gone to bed with no fears for her mother. She had believed Addison when he professed to love his wife—madly.

Isabelle's fear had come later, page after page of it.

When she smoothed out the bedding, she found a journal in the folds of the sheet. This was the one that had given her nightmares. She held the small book in one hand, weighing the consequences of its destruction. This one might be more dangerous than the journals she had left in the care of the judge. One day soon, she and Oren Hobbs must talk, but not of this. She planned to fling it into the sea.

This journal began with a séance in the woods. Wings spread, a young lark hovered over a table ringed with monsters, and it sang for them, "Oren, help me. Find me. Take me home."

Twenty-nine

On the night of Sarah Winston's annual birthday ball, the lodge is more dazzling than the Sun King's Palace. Strings of bright lights outline every beam, every window and wall; they run along the rooftop and upward to describe circles around the high castle tower.

So wrote Ferris Monty many years ago when these were all the details he could glean firsthand as an outsider looking in. And tonight—oh, *tonight*—he piloted his yellow Rolls-Royce up the winding driveway, fairly bouncing on the front seat, giddy as any ten-year-old with Cinderella dreams.

The car keys were handed off to a valet, and Ferris approached the lodge, resplendent in a new suit of red velvet, his nose held high. He was drunk with anticipation as he stood before the doorman, a large thug in a tuxedo, and handed over his personal invitation from Isabelle Winston—a true princess. The thug stood to one side, and Ferris was allowed to enter. Crossing the crowded foyer, he was accosted by a waiter bearing a tray of champagne flutes. Glass in hand, Ferris sauntered into the massive front room and the babble of conversations riding below the music of an orchestra. The bandstand was next to a gigantic window with the view of a second ballroom under the stars. Beyond that outdoor dance floor was a parking lot of luxury cars and ancient wrecks. Ferris wondered how many trees Ad Winston had killed to accommodate the vehicles of more than a thousand guests.

A tourist in fantasyland, he saw the most amazing sights looming over him, a flock of birds, gigantic and fanciful, carved in ice and presiding over platters piled high with lobster tails and giant shrimp. The cold air rising from these sculptures warred with the heat of a chandelier lit with hundreds of electric candles. It was like staring into the sun.

The walls were lined with real candles in sconces, with tables for two, and others had chairs for six. The orchestra changed its tempo to a livelier beat and the floor quickly filled with people. All around him, designer finery danced with secondhand clothes. Outlaw movie folk and grafting politicians commingled with store clerks and construction workers. A pedophile rock star danced past him. Oh, and there, bald as a cue ball, was a famous model—a killer drunk driver—in the arms of the post-master.

When the newspaper syndicate tired of the story about a lost boy's bones, here, swirling round him, was enough material to provide months of columns and television interviews. And somewhere in this gathering was an ending for his book.

His pen vibrated in his pocket.

Oren pulled out a chair to seat Hannah at the table reserved for the judge's party.

"Odd," she said, looking up at the ice statues. "They're less scary when they're monster size."

"I don't think our hostess agrees with you." The judge nodded toward the solitary figure only a few yards distant, a woman with pale upswept hair, glittering combs to hold it, and a long gown of that same champagne shade.

Sarah Winston stood frozen at attention before one of the giant birds, like one piece of art regarding another. The ice sculptures were all recognizable from her private journals, and now she stared at each of them in turn, astonished and clearly viewing them for the first time.

"This is Addison's work," said Hannah.

Apparently the lawyer had also read the lady's journals and selected these images from the darker pages. All of the giant birds had fangs. Shaken, Mrs. Winston reached for a drink from the tray of a passing maid, who defied her employer, lifting the wineglasses high and carrying them out of reach.

Oren realized that, more than anything on earth, Mrs. Winston wanted that drink, but all the gold bangles on her wrists would not buy it. And this was also Addison's work.

Alice Friday stopped by the judge's table and leaned down to Oren. "Look over there!" She pointed to the far side of the room, calling his attention to Mrs. Winston's daughter. "That's the woman who tried to kill you."

Oren turned to catch Isabelle staring at him, and she quickly looked the other way.

"No need to dive under the table." Evelyn Straub, an imperious figure in a long blue gown, sailed stately past him on her way to the caterer's bar. "The girl doesn't have a pocket to hide a gun—not in *that* slinky dress."

Ferris Monty had surmised that the woman in the maid's uniform was not one of the caterer's people. She was Sarah Winston's warden, a snatcher of drinks, a spoiler of fun. The maid's head turned in all directions, and there was panic in her eyes. Her employer's wife had vanished.

He smiled with the secret knowledge of Mrs. Winston's hiding place, for he had witnessed the lady's disappearing act. Ferris rounded a screen of potted foliage and saw two women standing on a small, secluded terrace, their heads close together in conversation.

Friends? Well, this was the mismatch of the century.

Mavis Hardy was so altered, he hardly knew her. She was a bare-armed amazon in sequins. And she was barefoot—the only outward sign of a mind gone awry. The madwoman had forgotten her shoes. Ferris was oddly touched by this, and he regarded her dirty bare feet as wounds.

As a gossip columnist extraordinaire, he had only to glance at that gown to recognize the designer, and that particular fashionista had died years before the close of the last century. However, even secondhand, this dress was well beyond the purse of a librarian—but not Sarah Winston, her companion and, no doubt about it, her benefactor.

One problem—the gift of a used dress would hardly fit the style of a multimillionaire.

And now he realized that the ballgown had been given to Mavis Hardy long ago when it was new, for here were all the signs of a reunion. The women embraced, drank wine and wept.

William Swahn returned Isabelle's wave. The black strapless gown was out of character for a woman who seldom wore lipstick. And the thigh-high slit was daring. So grown-up.

He missed the little girl, the shy redheaded wanderer always looking for love and a safe place to catch her breath. As a child and a teenager adrift among strangers—and only one old friend—she had always come to his table, demanding asylum. Tonight she resumed this old custom and sat down with him again. She stared at the giant ice sculptures. They worked an unnerving effect on her.

William lifted one hand to flag down a waiter bearing wineglasses. "I saw Oren Hobbs come in with the judge and Miss Rice."

Isabelle pretended not to hear this as she lifted two champagne flutes from the waiter's tray.

"There's a law against what you did, Belle." He had intended this as a tease, a friendly rebuke for her recent streak of violence against a certain young man. When she turned to him with guilty surprise, he decided upon a different tack, an older offense. "You lied to the sheriff— that alibi for Josh's brother. I know you had a crush on Oren Hobbs when you were a child, but that was—"

"I never did."

"Of course you did. But I can't believe it lasted five years. You were sixteen years old when you gave him that fake alibi."

So why the lie to save Oren Hobbs? Had she known the boy was innocent? Did Isabelle have a suspect of her own in those days? If so, it must have been someone close to her, someone she would never give up to the sheriff.

William Swahn sat well back in his chair, pushed there, as if revelation had punching power.

Later, at the keyboard of his computer, Ferris Monty would describe his companion as a vitriolic hamster who drank a lot. The town councilwoman accepted his invitation to sit down at his table.

"I don't gossip," she said.

But they all said that.

In answer to his question on the out-of-town guests, the hamster replied, "Those are Addison's clients. Don't you read *Rolling Stone* or *Forbes*? Criminals, every last one of them." When queried on the history of the ball, she told him that this very table had once been reserved for the late Millard Straub. "Mean little prick. He sat here with his oxygen tank, and no one said a word to him all night. But his wife danced every dance and had a high old time. There she is now."

Ferris turned to see Evelyn Straub standing at the caterer's bar, a grande dame in midnight blue and pearls.

"Back in the day," said the hamster, "Evelyn was a showstopper."

He nodded in agreement, for he had known her then, but having been barred from every ball, he had never seen Evelyn dance. "Her husband died suddenly, didn't he?"

"Not sudden enough. It's no wonder his wife took up with that boy, Oren Hobbs."

"And everyone knew?"

"No, not till the day Oren came home. I got that story from a guest at the Straub Hotel."

Ferris was bent over his notebook, jotting lines, when the hamster said, "Could you write down that *I* killed Millard Straub? That used to be my fantasy."

"You think he was murdered?"

"Oh, no, he died of old age—passed away peacefully in his sleep. There's no justice in this world."

My mother married him for his money," said Isabelle. "You were the one she loved."

William Swahn shook his head more in wonder than denial. Why was she so insistent on this revision of history? "Your mother was very much in love with Addison. She told me so before the wedding."

"She should have married you."

"I was a child," said William, reminding her for the second time in as many days.

"You loved her."

"I was smitten. I'll admit to that much. . . . And then I grew up."

"You were so handsome in your policeman's uniform."

"Belle, you never saw me in a uniform. Years went by before—"

"Mom has a photograph of you. It was taken the day you graduated from the police academy."

William well remembered that ceremony and also the picture he had posed for with Sarah by his side. He had his own copy of that photograph, and he treasured it. It had been displayed on his bedroom wall for years—and recently hidden in a closet. But how did this old souvenir figure into Belle's false recollections—why this artless attempt to bind him to Sarah?

"You still love my mother. I know you do."

"I'll always be her friend . . . and yours." This was true. Over the past two decades, Sarah had not said more than a handful of words to him, but he was constant.

"And you'll always watch out for Mom, won't you?"

"Yes, Belle." She had extracted this promise from him days ago. It had caused him worry then—and now.

When Isabelle had left the table, he looked for Sarah in the crowd. He saw her standing on the fringe and far away, feet moving to the music, and she was a little unsteady for the wine.

He whispered, "Don't fall."

A bottle of beer—his beverage of choice—was set down on the table alongside his untouched glass of wine. "Thank you," he said, looking up at Oren Hobbs, who played the gentleman tonight, waiting for an invitation to sit down. William nodded to the empty chair.

Hobbs turned the chair around and straddled it as he tipped back his own bottle. "I wasn't the only kid in Coventry who was shipped out of town." He stared at Isabelle's retreating back. "She was sent away before I was."

William sipped from his bottle, buying time to think, and then he sighed. "Cold beer on a summer night. You've won my heart. Does that scare you?"

"Relax," said Hobbs. "She never made my short list. She's got the killer instinct—I can vouch for that—but her style is piss poor. I'm still alive." He insisted on a toast to Isabelle, the most incompetent of assassins, and the two men clinked glasses. From any distance out of earshot, they might be taken for the best of friends tonight.

Addison Winston stood a short distance away—watching. A guest was speaking to him, but he seemed unaware of this, so intent was he on Oren Hobbs.

Jim Web, the postmaster, sat down at Ferris Monty's table. "That story I told you about Oren and the little Winston girl? Well, this is where it all began—the very first birthday ball."

Ferris's pen was at the ready, poised over a fresh page in his notebook. "What happened?"

"Lots of people would still like to know. Back then, Belle Winston was only eleven years old, skinny and shy." He pointed to the other side of the room. "She was trying to disappear into that row of potted trees. Oren was over by the bandstand. They were twenty feet apart when it happened. Ever see two children struck by lightning? It was a thing to behold. The two of them just stared at each other, circling around like little foxes scouting the territory.

"The band started playing, and people were pairing off for a slow dance. Belle was standing there, waiting so patiently. Oren couldn't take his eyes off her, but he hung back. Then the girl made it easy for him, though it cost her a lot to do it. Like I said, she was shy. She walked out on the dance floor all alone. Well, four mules couldn't have held that boy back. He moved toward her. Heads were turning everywhere. People stopped dancing to watch them. Then the crowd made a circle around those two kids when they met at the center of the room.

"The little girl smiled and lifted her hands to take Oren as her partner. He was only inches away. The boy stared at her for a second or two, and then I guess the girl just didn't make the cut. He walked right past her, left her standing there all by herself. I remember Belle looking down at her patent leather shoes—while everyone else was staring at her. A few kids were laughing. Oren kept walking—walked right out the front door. One kid in the crowd shouted out an unkind joke. And that little girl just stood there for the longest time, trying to figure out what had just happened to her . . . and why.

"When I showed up for the next year's ball, I saw her sitting on the staircase out in the foyer. I think she was still waiting for Oren, but he never came back."

By trade, Ferris Monty was a cheerleader for every sort of catastrophe, but tonight, he surprised himself. He found that he could relate to the public humiliation of an eleven-year-old girl. "Why did he do that to her?"

The postmaster smiled and shrugged. "It's a mystery."

Evelyn Straub looked up at a towering ice bird that stood guard over the seafood platters. She filled her plate with shrimp and scallops, while reminiscing with the small woman at her side. "I guess Oren was sixteen when I asked him what happened that night. He told me he got to within a foot of the little Winston girl, and that's when—"

"He remembered that he didn't know how to dance," said Hannah.

The judge had not come down from dancing people. The housekeeper had never learned how, and neither had the boys and girls of Coventry in those days. Children had no formal lessons until they reached the age of prom night, when the school took them in hand for ballroom classes. Hannah had not foreseen the lack of dancing lessons as a life-altering threat to a twelve-year-old boy.

Addison Winston avoided looking at his client. He stared at his glass, as if the details of William Swahn's old case eluded him. "No, I don't believe I ever saw the dispatcher's sworn statement. What of it?"

"Oren Hobbs said the woman disappeared before the police could question her. So that's true?"

"It hardly matters. I'm sure there would've been logbooks or tapes to back up what happened to you that night."

"You don't *know*? You never asked for the tapes?"

"William, when you were in the hospital, you didn't want to hear any details. And I don't recall you ever asking how I got you all that money."

"I'm asking now."

Addison loosened his tie. "Your settlement hung on

the evidence that the police *didn't* produce, things they didn't want in a public court record. That's why they put your deal on the table so fast. It was all about silence and the domino effect. The LAPD had so many lawsuits pending for corruption and brutality, and they stood to lose all of them because of you. You were the poster boy for police-conspiracy theorists. I hate to admit this, but a chimpanzee could've won that damage award."

"Then Hobbs was right. My case was never investigated."

"I'm sure it was." The lawyer swirled the dregs of the wine in his glass. "But that would've ended after the non-disclosure agreements were signed. When I do a deal, contract law trumps criminal law. They couldn't go forward with an investigation, not without breaking the agreement. They would've had to pay you triple damages."

"Did you think the cops were guilty?"

"It didn't matter to me," said Addison. "But you thought so. Maybe you don't remember—what with all those drugs the doctors gave you to dull the pain. The only time you were halfway lucid was in the recovery room after the surgery. You wanted revenge, and not just against the officers who left you to die that night. You wanted to nail every cop in town. Tall order, but I totally screwed the LAPD. I *gave* you what you asked for."

"I want to reopen the case."

"Can't be done, William. Breach of contract. You'd have to give back all that lovely cash." Addison moved his hands up and down in the manner of scales. "Justice," he said, his right hand rising. "And money." The other hand sank like a stone. "Not a tough call."

"No it isn't," said Swahn. "I want to reopen the case."

The lawyer laughed. His client did not.

Addison felt a pain in his chest and slipped a pill into his mouth. Within seconds, the medication had done its work, and he was immortal again.

Evelyn took Oren's arm, and he led her to the judge's table. When he pulled out a chair, she settled into it with a grace that chiseled away the pounds and passing years. She nodded to the company around her and then surveyed the crowd.

"This room is ready to *dance*." She slapped the table. "But that music is boring. I'll have to do something about that."

She rose from her chair and crossed the dance floor for a word with the orchestra leader. Before she left the bandstand, the tempo had changed to a Latin rhythm, and she seemed lighter on her feet as she headed back to the table. Twenty years ago, her hips would have swayed. Tonight she simply stepped in time to the beat of a drum and horns, turning gracefully full circle, and then continuing on her way. Many couples on the floor seemed stalled in place, not knowing where to put their feet this time. Addison Winston waved his arms, trying to catch the orchestra leader's eyes, but the man with the baton only smiled for Evelyn Straub, a woman who knew how to spread her money around.

"That's better." Evelyn sat down and leaned toward Oren. "The next dance will be a tango. Are you up for that?"

Henry Hobbs rested one hand on his son's shoulder. "We're not tango people."

"Speak for yourself," said Evelyn. "I taught him that dance when he was sixteen." Turning back to Oren, she said, "If you could do it naked, I guess you can manage well enough with your clothes on."

The judge spilled his wine and used a napkin to dab at the puddle. "Evelyn, you must find the statute of limitations very liberating."

Rising from the table, Oren held out one hand to her. "Would you like to dance?"

"No," said Evelyn, though she was clearly pleased by the request. "I think it's high time you settled accounts with the Winston girl. And here's the best part. You won't even have to say hello."

Oren crossed the floor, his eyes on Isabelle Winston, and he was not worried that she might turn him down. He had no plans to ask for this dance. That was not in keeping with the spirit of the tango, a dance of love and war. He grabbed her roughly by the wrist and joined her to his hip, then pushed her away.

And she came back.

They owned the floor.

The music was louder, more passionate. Faster, then slower, the notes almost shy and then—*vavoom*. The music wrapped around them and stroked them up and down. They moved apart. He grabbed her arm and yanked her back again.

So close.

He smelled the wine on her breath, and then, with a turn of the head, the flower scent of her hair, and now her sweat and his. Lips close, almost a kiss, but no. She backed away, a tease with no remorse.

He would make her pay for that.

They set out to destroy each other in every move they made. She lifted her face to his, he looked away. She returned the insult. He flung her across the floor, and Isabelle came crawling back to climb his body. Oren pressed down on her shoulders, and she sank to her knees. Rising to a swaying stand, she moved in close. Her leg rode upon his hip for an embrace.

And so they danced with perfect understanding, anger and contempt, sex and longing. Her nails dug into his neck. He left impressions of his fingers on her bare shoulders.

Apart, together—heat, incredible heat. And always the rhythm kept time with two hearts pounding. Bone against bone, grind and sway, down and down, lower still, he laid her on the floor and then pulled her up by one hand, not caring if he tore her arm off.

The Latin tempo was climbing the walls and thrumming in the floorboards.

Forced down to her knees again, she clawed her way

up his legs, and he allowed it. Long fingernails raked his breast, buttons went flying, and a small spot of blood appeared on his white shirt. All around the room, breath was sucked in and moans expelled. The two dancers tangoed on. The music reached a crescendo as Isabelle slapped his face—and he *loved* it.

The song ended like sudden death.

The dancers turned their backs on one another. Oren walked toward the terrace, and Isabelle walked toward the caterer's bar.

Applause rose up like thunder.

"**Well, that was different,**" said the judge, raising his voice to be heard above the clapping hands, the stomps and whistles. "I don't think I've ever seen blood drawn on a dance floor."

Hannah looked upon the bloodletting as progress in a somewhat stalled relationship. "I bet those two get married."

The judge doubted this, offering recent evidence that Isabelle would rather kill Oren than wed him. And Evelyn Straub ventured that Isabelle could do both. "I don't see a conflict."

"Ma'am?" One of the caterer's people stood by the table, looking down at a saucer that had been used as an ashtray.

When asked to put out her cigarette, the grande dame of hoteliers looked up at the waitress, a young girl who could be easily killed with a word or two. Yet Evelyn did

nothing to harm her. Instead, she took her smoking cigarette outside in search of some small dog that she might
kick.

Approaching her golden years, she found pleasure in
small things.

The couple on the terrace stood close together, sheltered by the low-hanging branch of a tree and the privacy of darkness. They never noticed Isabelle Winston
in the open doorway. She held two wineglasses, one of
them a peace offering for Oren Hobbs, but he had
found other company.

Eleven years old again, shy again, dying of it, Isabelle
left them a gift of two champagne flutes abandoned on
the terrace wall.

Oren bowed to his companion and gently took the
lady's hand to lead her out of the shadows. He pulled her
to him, and they moved to the strains of slow music waft-
ing out from the ballroom. The dancing partners closed
their eyes. Oren Hobbs held a slender woman with long
brown hair the color of lions, and Evelyn Straub danced
with the boy from the moon.

Sally Polk was never far behind the sheriff as he made his
way through the crowd, shaking hands and flashing his
politician's smile. He had yet to notice her, but she was
a patient woman.

Ah, now Cable Babitt was turning her way. He saw

her, and the effect was electric—a bit like a cattle prod to the private parts.

Apparently, her new party frock made quite an impression on him, though it was nothing stylish, just something grabbed off a rack in haste, and chosen only for its color. Maybe her bright green dress reminded him of some errand left undone, for now he was moving toward the door. She walked after him, taking her own sweet time, yet relentless in the click of high heels dogging him.

Can you hear me coming, Cable?

Thirty

A suitcase lay open on the bed, and two more stood by the door. Isabelle slammed a bureau drawer and opened another. "This is because of *him*, isn't it?" Her hands balled into fists as she turned to her mother. "It always ends like this!"

The hired car would be here any moment—so little time left. Sarah Winston stood by the window, dividing attention between her child and the driveway below. "Belle, you can't stay here and watch over me every minute. I want you to have a life of your own."

Isabelle held a blouse in her hands, absently twisting it into a rope. She dropped it into the open suitcase. Eyes full of tears—finally—for these tantrums always ended with tears, she crossed the room, reaching out to her mother.

Sarah opened her arms to an embrace and kissed her

daughter's hair. Turning her eyes to the window, she saw the approaching headlights of the limousine. "The car is here. I'll tell the driver you're almost ready. You'll be back in London soon."

Isabelle would not release her hold. "Don't make me leave. *Please*, Mom. I won't fight with him anymore. I'll be good."

Sarah held her daughter tightly. So little time—this moment only. Better to be stabbed with a knife, better that than to hear this old refrain from the first time she had sent Isabelle away—and the second time—and the tenth. Both mother and child knew all the words to this ritual parting and how it must end.

"I love you," said Sarah. "It's time for you to go."

The caterer's staff had been sent away and told to return in the morning. The lodge was still dressed in its gala finery. The debris of a thousand guests, their glassware and dishes and even their rented chairs, remained. Only the ice sculptures had been removed, taken outside to melt on the grass.

Addison Winston stood before a glass wall in the tower room. No need for a telescope tonight. He watched the headlights turn into the driveway down on Paulson Lane. The twin beams vanished under the boughs of trees and reappeared at William Swahn's front door. Time was allowed for the man to limp into his house, more time for a slow elevator ride upstairs to the study. There a lamp was switched on in keeping with habits of the past few nights. Addison counted off the usual ten seconds, long enough for Swahn to fetch a pair of binoculars from a desk drawer. And now that distant light was extinguished. Sarah's devoted sentry preferred to keep watch on the tower from a darkened room.

Addison never heard the barefoot steps behind him; he heard the clink of ice cubes in Sarah's glass as she entered the circular room.

The lawyer's smile was in place.

Showtime.

He turned around to face his wife, who seemed startled to find him in her sanctuary at this time of night. "So Belle is gone?"

"Yes." She closed her robe and belted it in an act of modesty, as if they had never been married, never shared a bed. Sarah tilted her head to one side, regarding him as a stranger here in Birdland, this other country at the top of the house. She took a long draught of her whiskey glass, draining it as she sank down in a chair.

"I'm not surprised that Belle left in such a rush." Addison uncapped a bottle he had discovered tucked behind the journals on the bookshelf. He leaned down to pour more whiskey into her glass. "You'll need this. Someone we know has been digging behind the stable." He picked up his wife's hand and kissed it. "Belle found Josh's camera." He stared down at his wife's shattered eyes, and he caressed her face with one hand. "Don't worry. She put it back in the hole and covered it up again. What a good girl. She'd never have done that to protect *me*."

Sarah shook her head, unable to make sense of this. And then she closed her eyes. She understood.

"That's right," said Addison. "Belle knows you're the one who buried that camera. I can only imagine what's going through her mind right now. Maybe she's thinking that I'm not the *only* monster in Birdland."

William Swahn held the binoculars to his eyes and watched Addison feed more booze to his wife. This could be construed as the slow poisoning of an alcoholic, nothing as graphic as battering, but just as deadly. Sarah was clearly pained by something her husband was saying.

William did not underestimate the killing power of words.

The telephone rang, and he knew who the caller would be before he picked up the receiver. "Hello, Belle. . . . Are you crying? . . . Yes, I'm watching her now."

By their poor connection, he realized that Isabelle was calling from a cell phone, and that would place her well outside the town. "Where are you? . . . You're leaving? . . . What about the maid? Is she still in the house?"

The call ended in the middle of a word, and he guessed that Belle's cell phone had failed her in this corner of the world where wireless lines of communication were hit and miss.

He resumed his watch on the tower room. Though he disliked the idea of spying, a promise was a promise. He had never been able to say no to Isabelle.

Sarah was more pliant when she was drunk, and Addison almost preferred her this way. When he took her hand, she obediently rose from the chair. How he loved her—he loved her to death. He led her to the sliding door that opened onto the deck.

The night was warm and all the winged rats had gone to sleep—so quiet now, only the soft applause of leaves slapping one another as the wind rushed through them. Man and wife were about to pass through the open door when Addison turned to the opposite wall of glass and smiled for his audience, the watcher in the dark. He waved.

William Swahn was startled—a voyeur caught in the act. He watched Addison kiss his wife. It appeared that the man was sucking air and life from Sarah's body. She went limp and staggered onto the deck, supported by her husband's arm about her waist. The two of them disappeared behind a solid portion of the circular wall.

This stroll in the sky would certainly make their watcher anxious, and so Addison was slow to lead his wife around to that part of the deck that could be seen from Swahn's window. The lawyer, a showman and consummate actor, delighted in dragging out the other man's tension. As they walked, he said to Sarah, "I saw you bury the camera . . . *and* the Hobbs boy."

She stopped, but failed to make a stand.

He led her onward, for they could not keep Swahn in suspense all night. Around the deck they went, and now they were in full view of the house on Paulson Lane. It was time to jack up the fear in Sarah's eyes. "When I borrowed one of your journals—I needed the sketches for the ice sculptors to copy—I couldn't help but notice that some of them were missing from the shelf. They covered the year when Josh died. Did Belle take them with her by any chance?"

"No." Sarah turned her head toward the ocean view, perhaps looking there for inspiration. And she found it. Her eyes were too bright when she turned back to him, saying, "I threw those books into the sea."

"Excellent." Did he believe her? Of course not. But he had read every one of her birder logs and pronounced them all insanely delusional. "So you just tossed them off a cliff. Now why couldn't you have done that with Josh's camera? Why drag it home and bury it behind the stable? What were you thinking?"

Was that the day your mind snapped?

Easier to recall that night when he had lain awake, waiting for his wife to come to bed. He remembered the sliver of light under their bedroom door. He had seen the shadows of her footsteps pausing there, then moving on to make her bed elsewhere.

Dating back to early days at eastern boarding schools, Isabelle Winston had spent most of her life grieving over a death that had not happened yet. And tonight she was still longing for a ghost mother who had not yet—not *entirely*—died.

The limousine driver pulled into the local airport. The commuter plane could be seen near the small building that passed for a terminal. Soon the aircraft would be loading passengers bound for San Francisco and connecting red-eye flights to points all over the world.

The ticket to ride was in her hand.

Every time she left her mother, all but pushed out the door, Isabelle felt the same sense of fear; it always escalated to panic when she saw these airport lights. And each time she had reached a distant shore, all she had ever wanted was to go home again.

A lifetime of longing.

Enough.

She leaned toward the driver and said, "Take me back!"

Addison took Sarah's hand and twirled her in the turn of a waltz step until she was dizzy and in danger of falling. "I know you still have that photograph of you and Swahn."

She could only stare at him.

He prompted her recall. "It's been a while—more than a quarter of a century. The picture was taken back in L.A.—at a graduation ceremony for police cadets."

Sarah nodded. "I ordered that print from the photographer. When it came in the mail, I showed it to you. And you *knew* I was going—"

"To see an old friend. So you said. The boy in that photograph was barely twenty-one—hardly an *old* friend, Sarah."

He held her at arm's length, and together they whirled around the deck, faster and faster, in and out of the sights of Swahn's binoculars. They stopped once again to stand on that portion of the deck overlooking Paulson Lane. Still in the dancing mode, Addison dipped his partner over the rail, her long hair dangling, her face contorted in fear. He turned his head to smile for the man who sat in the dark.

"Yes!" William Swahn yelled at the civilian aide who had answered the phone at the sheriff's office. "*Yes,* it's a damned emergency!"

"I don't think I like your tone." The girl's voice was painfully young and slightly bruised. "Why didn't you call nine-one-one?"

"The operator would've sent a deputy from Saulburg. The sheriff's house is right here in Coventry." But Cable Babitt's home telephone was unlisted. "You have to call him and—"

"What is the nature of the emergency?"

Oh, bloody Christ. He imagined her reading lines from a script. He gripped the telephone receiver tighter, and he was calmer when he said, "Call the sheriff's house. Tell him I think Ad Winston is going to murder his wife."

"You *think* he's gonna—" The girl paused for a second or two. There was sarcasm in her voice, a touch of payback when she said, "So no one's been injured. You just *think* somebody *might* kill his wife."

William yelled, "*Tell* him!"

"You kept that photograph all these years," said Addison Winston.

Sarah turned away from her husband and gripped the rail, off balanced by dancing and liquor, dizzy and sick. "I *told* you about the graduation ceremony. I always told you about every hour of my day—*where* I went, *who* I spoke to."

Behind his wife's back, ever mindful of their audience, Addison mimed the act of stabbing Sarah with a knife. For his next performance piece, he left her standing at the rail, holding on tight. He flattened up against the glass wall, and then, with both hands raised, as if to push her off the deck, he rushed forward, stopping short of touching her back. He lowered his hands and laughed out loud, imagining that he could hear Swahn screaming in the distance—in the dark.

Yet his voice was tender as he stood behind Sarah, holding her by the shoulders and nuzzling the soft skin of her neck. "I know you kept one of his letters, too."

She turned around to face him, uncomprehending. "What letters? There was only—"

"Only one left. I know. I suppose you burned the others, but this one was special. Every now and then, I dig it out of your keepsake box and read it again. All these years later, I still find it very powerful. I can understand why you kept that one."

He stepped back a pace to regard his wife. So this was what a stunned cow looked like after it had been hit between the eyes with a baseball bat—the prelude to slaughter.

Taking Sarah in his arms, Addison danced her past the open door. Her bedside telephone rang, and the answering machine played a message from a man in deep distress, an anguished paramour pleading for Sarah to come indoors. "Hold on!" Swahn yelled from the little box. "I'm coming! I'm on the way!" On this note of hysteria, the call ended.

Perfect.

William Swahn stepped out of the elevator cage and crossed the room to another telephone for one more call. Once he reached the lodge, he would be helpless. Its grand staircase was insurmountable for a man with a ruined leg that could not support him in a climb to anywhere.

His mere presence in the house might be enough to end the madness, but he could not count on that. William made a call for help from another quarter, spending precious seconds to listen to a tape recording telling him that there was no one there to hear him, no one home. He left a message and then limped toward his front door. Haste caused him pain.

His pills were upstairs on the desk in his study. No time to get them.

He left the house hobbling, aching.

Addison held her very close. "I followed you the night you dug up the boy's skull. Why did you have to do that? Guilt, Sarah? After all these years? Everything was going so well. But now you and Swahn are becoming more unstable every day. He's putting it all together. If he doesn't know already, he'll figure out that you were the cause of his mutilation. Well, you can see what you've done."

Sarah was looking down at the headlights rushing along Paulson Lane.

"He's coming," said Addison. "Almost here." He wrapped both her hands around the deck rail. "Don't go anywhere without me." He gently turned her face to his and softly kissed her lips. "I'd love to stay and dance all night, but I have to go downstairs and greet our guest."

Father and son walked up the driveway, and the yellow stray trotted ahead of them. Henry Hobbs was in good spirits and slightly tipsy when he tossed another stick, and the dog fetched it back. "Remember doing this with old Horatio?"

"Yeah," said Oren. "Those sticks kept whizzing past him. He never figured out what they were for."

The judge's happiness was complete. Fine wine and a warm summer night—these things were truly gifts, and best of all was a walk down a country road with his son. He held his watch up to the light of the porch and squinted at the dial. "Hannah should've been home by now. I'd better go inside and check the answering machine."

"Give her a little more time." Oren leaned down to scratch the stray dog behind the ears. "She must've been the designated driver for half the town tonight."

"Well, Hannah does love to drive."

"Odd that she never got a driver's license . . . but she'd have to produce a birth certificate to get one." Oren stood with his back to the porch, taking advantage of deep shadow to conceal his face. The judge was exposed, lit by a yellow bug light glowing brightly.

Oren sat down on the bottom step. "You still pay her wages in cash, right? I always wondered where Hannah kept her money. I know she can't put it in the bank. She'd need a Social Security number to open an account."

This posed an unsettling problem. There were rules to be observed, and Oren was breaking them with impunity. Henry Hobbs had invented this game to teach his boys the art of conversation, instructing them not to trivialize it by injection of the obvious. Oren was taking the contest to a new level, using lost points for bait.

The judge threw up his hands, feigning confusion and misunderstanding. "Don't you worry about Hannah.

She's well provided for in my will." He clapped his son on the back as he moved past him to climb the porch stairs.

Turnabout.

Now it was Oren's face that was bathed in light, and there was grave suspicion there. "Without any kind of identification, I wonder how she's going to *prove* that she's Hannah Rice—so she can *collect* from your estate."

Henry Hobbs forced a smile. "You're my executor, boy. You won't have any problem identifying her."

"Won't I? I don't even know if Hannah's her right name—and neither do you."

In his haste—as much haste as a cripple could manage— the late-night visitor dispensed with the custom of knocking. The great oak door to the lodge swung open, and the man entered the foyer walking ungainly, almost comic with his awkward limp.

Addison paused half the way down the staircase to lean against the banister. "Good evening . . . again."

Swahn advanced on him, hobbling, listing to one side, and every step threatened to tip him over. He came to a halt at the bottom of the staircase. "Where is Sarah?"

"William, my wife is too tired for any more entertaining tonight. I'll give her your regards."

Swahn shouted, "Sarah, I'm *here!*"

"Stop!" Addison held up one hand in the manner of a traffic cop. "Keep your voice down. My wife is quite drunk. I don't think she could handle these stairs any better than you. We don't want her to fall and break her neck, do we?"

Swahn placed one foot on the bottom step. The weight on his bad leg caused a wince of pain. He was slow to gain the next step, and the next.

"Well, I can see this might take a while." Addison danced past him down the stairs. There was time enough to enter the front room and fill two glasses at the caterer's bar. When he returned to the foyer, Swahn had fallen. Reduced to crawling, he had abandoned his cane to drag himself up four more steps.

"Good job," said the lawyer. "Only forty to go." He bent down and offered Swahn one of the glasses, but he was rebuffed. "No? None for you? Ah, well." He settled one champagne flute on the carpet beside the crawling man. "Just in case you get thirsty."

Six steps above his guest, Addison sat down to watch the man's slow, painful progress. "I can see that you're still totally preoccupied with my wife. Have you figured out Sarah's part in the death of Joshua Hobbs?"

Swahn's brow was beaded with the sweat of exertion. He gave up his struggle and laid his head on one arm. "That's insane."

Addison tipped back his glass, then wiped his lips. "I know you met with Sarah in the woods every Saturday at precisely twelve noon."

"That never happened."

"Don't interrupt." Addison lightly stepped down the staircase to retrieve the cane that had been left behind as dead weight. He raised it over his head and brought it down on the man's back. Swahn moaned.

The lawyer resumed his smile, always a gracious host. "I even know *where* the two of you met. With a telescope, I could always find Sarah's car on that bald section of the mountain. Of course, she knew I'd be watching, but you were cagey, William. You must've parked your own car under the trees—that turnout close to the clearing—easier to hobble into the woods from there."

"You're deluded."

This time, Addison had only to raise the cane, and his well-trained guest fell silent.

"One day, I decided to catch Sarah in the act. Hours before my wife left the house, I set out on foot. I took the old hikers' trail. Not far past Evelyn's cabin—that's where the bodies were. I had no use for the woman's corpse, but that dead boy was a gift. Sad, really. Poor Sarah had so few friends—just you and her little protégé, the fledgling photographer."

"You killed Josh?"

"That has nothing to do with my story." Addison brought the cane down on Swahn's hand. The blow was hard enough to break the skin and, hopefully, a few bones as well, but the man did not cry out.

A small disappointment.

"Pay attention, William. I dragged the boy's corpse up the trail to the clearing, and then I went to work on his face with a pocketknife. Sarah and I had a lack of communication in those days. So this was how I talked to my wife, through mutilation."

"Like mine?" Swahn raised himself up to lean upon one arm, and his fingers lightly grazed his old scar. "The woman they found in Josh's grave—was that the missing dispatcher from L.A.? Is that why you—"

"Oh, no, no, no." Addison shook his head in an exaggerated loss of patience. "You're muddling my crimes. Why would I kill the dispatcher? She had no idea where her bribe money came from. Her only job that night was diverting you to a surprise party—during a tour of duty—an insignificant crime. When you called in for backup and the dispatcher heard the shots and screams—that's when she realized what kind of a party it was. And she ran away. I'm told she didn't even finish out her shift."

"The dispatcher never called for help? *She* was the one who left me to die?"

"Yes. I couldn't have planned for that to happen. However, I am a creature of opportunity. Shame to waste the makings of a good lawsuit. But that woman I found with Josh—well, I have no idea who she was. And who cares?" He raised the cane and punctuated the beats of an admonition with strikes to Swahn's shoulders and his head. "She has *nothing* to *do* with my *story*."

Addison tossed his hair and tilted his head to one side. "Where was I? Oh, yes. I was carving up the face of a dead child. And then I found myself a good hiding place in the trees. I wish you could've seen Sarah's expression when she walked into the clearing and found Josh lying there. It was marvelous—insane, yet sympathetic, too. She screamed. She wept. I wondered if she would recognize my handwriting in that bloody scar I carved into the boy's skin. It was an *A* just like yours."

A cut above Swahn's eye half blinded him, drops falling to the carpet as if he cried blood tears. The unobscured eye had the glaze of shock.

But the man *was* paying attention.

Addison continued. "She started digging his grave. That surprised me. I thought she'd run—but no. Sarah knelt down beside the boy and tried to scratch out a grave with her bare hands. Well, eventually, she came to her senses and gave up on that idea. She went home and came back with a shovel. Much more practical for gravedigging. I assume she met you on the road and warned you off."

"I was never there."

This time, Addison rained blows on the man's damaged leg, saying all the while, so calmly, "It's—*rude*—to—*inter*—*rupt*."

Swahn cried out.

So satisfying.

Sarah Winston stared at the flagstones of the terrace below. Her grip on the rail was tenuous.

She looked up to the sky, asking heavenly bodies if she should stay or go. She interpreted the blinks and winks of planets and the ponderous movements of stars. Yes, they were all in agreement. It was time to leave the earth.

———

"**The grave Sarah dug** was much too shallow," said Addison. "I came back later and dug a deeper hole, a wider one—so I could bury the woman's body, too. When I was done, you couldn't tell there'd been any digging at all. I scattered the excess dirt so as not to leave an obvious mound. And I spread leaves to complete my camouflage. One last touch—and this is delicious. I left Josh's camera to mark the grave for Sarah. I knew she'd come back. How I wish I could've seen her face when she found that camera. It must've driven her wild."

"You can't kill Sarah. She's an innocent."

"It doesn't look that way. I'm speaking as a lawyer now. She tried to hide the evidence of a murder, and I think we both know why. Given that big bloody *A* carved into the boy's face, the sheriff would've knocked on your door first. Cable Babitt's a plodding dolt, but he could hardly miss *that* connection." Addison leaned in close. "She must've loved you very much. And now I need to hear your confession." He looked toward the ceiling, as if he could see through it to the tower room above. "I don't think poor Sarah's up to it. I want every detail of your affair with my wife."

"She was my friend," said William. "I never touched her."

"Liar."

A small voice called down to them, "It's true." Sarah stood at the top of the stairs. Her words were faint, and both men strained to hear her. She looked down at her husband's upturned grinning face. "Mavis Hardy was the one I met in the woods every Saturday, when she closed the library for lunch. We went birding together. You didn't want me to have any friends . . . so I never mentioned her. But after I saw what you'd done to Josh . . ." Her voice trailed off to whispers, and she spoke to the air above their heads. "Bad things happen to my friends, so I stopped seeing Mavis. . . . And how could I ever face William again?"

She could not face him now. Her eyes were vacant, seeing nothing. Sarah was gone even before she turned around and left him lying there. William stretched out one hand, as if he could reach her that way. He struggled to climb the next step. "She's going back to the tower. Addison, stop her. She's in a dangerous state of mind."

"Stop her?" The lawyer pressed one hand to his breast in mock surprise. "Don't you believe that the bird queen can fly?" He fished his wallet from a back pocket. "Ah, well, maybe you're right. She might need a little help, a gentle nudge in the right direction. But *can* she *fly*? That's the question." He opened the wallet and pulled out a bill. "I've got twenty dollars here that says she drops like a stone."

"She never cheated on you, Addison."

"Lies." He laid down the cane to pull a folded sheet of paper from his inside pocket. "I've got the proof—one of your old love letters." The paper was falling apart in the creases, having been read too many times by a madman. He opened it and held it up and pointed to the bottom line. "That's your signature."

Hannah rolled up the driveway and parked in front of the house. Stepping out of the car, she said to the judge, "The engine's sputtering some. Maybe we should have it looked at."

"Here's an idea," said Oren, with the mildest sarcasm. "Why don't you guys buy a *new* car?"

"I suppose it's time," said the judge. "But you know this old Mercedes runs fine. It's probably just low on gas." He turned to Hannah. "That's what happens when you spend the night playing taxi driver for every drunken man, woman and child in Coventry."

She marched up the stairs and into the house. The screen door slammed behind her, a message to tell him that she was in no mood for criticism tonight.

The judge called after her, "We'll get a new car, all right? We'll get *two* new cars."

"I called the sheriff's office," said William Swahn.

"And they laughed at you, right? You told them you saw a man dance with his wife? Something like that?" Addison Winston tapped his temple with one finger to illustrate a mind at work. "I anticipated you." Theatrically, he cupped his ears with both hands. "Do I hear sirens in the distance?" He lowered his hands. "No, I'm afraid not."

"I made another call."

Isabelle's limousine was headed homeward, but only moving at the legal limit. She renewed her quarrel with the chauffeur. "Yes, you *can* go faster. It's late, and all the state troopers are asleep by the side of the road. I *promise* you won't get a ticket." She reached through the opening in the glass partition and emptied her wallet on the front seat beside the driver.

The limousine sped up, but not fast enough, and she had no more money to buy another twenty miles per hour.

The screen door was pushed open so hard it banged against the porch wall, and Hannah came flying out. "Mr. Swahn left a message on the answering machine. There's trouble at the Winston lodge. No idea when he called, but he said to come quick."

Oren snatched the keys from her outstretched hand. When he slid behind the wheel of the Mercedes, the engine would not turn over.

"I misspoke." The judge turned to Hannah. "The car's not low on gas—it's *out* of gas."

Oren never heard this remark. He was running down the driveway.

"Ah, William. Intrepid fellow." Addison slowly climbed the stairs beside the crawling man, grinning with encouragement, pausing to beat him with the cane every now and then when he thought his guest's attention might be flagging.

"Great joke on me, isn't it?" The cane rose again and came down. "It just keeps getting *funnier* and *funnier*."

Swahn rolled onto his side, shot through and through with pain. "You can't get away with this."

"Of course I can. My wife has a history of slashed wrists and sleeping pills. And you're going to shoot yourself." Addison sat down on the steps, a brief respite from his labors—the heavy work of inflicting agony. "There's only one conclusion that our idiot sheriff will draw—that old cliché of unrequited love. If you can't have my wife, then no man can. So you pushed her off the deck and then—Oh, allow me one more cliché. You're going to *eat* your gun. That's the time-honored method for an ex-cop's suicide. I thought you'd like that part—a cop to the end—literally."

Addison wagged one finger at Swahn. "Don't tell me. I know what you're thinking. Those bruises on your body. They'll be blamed on the mob, all those flying bottles and rocks. And the cuts—the blood from your open wounds? Well, of course I tried valiantly to defend my wife, but then you pulled a gun." He reached behind his back and under his coattails to retrieve a revolver from his waistband. "Unregistered, untraceable. Finest kind. And they say nothing good can come of consorting with criminals." He took a handkerchief from his pocket and cleaned the surface. "Your prints will be the only ones found. And I have all the proof I need to back up my version of events." He waved the yellowed sheet of paper. "Your love letter to Sarah."

The lawyer laid the weapon on a step beyond Swahn's reach. "The revolver has to be in your hands when it goes off—just in case the sheriff remembers to test for residue from gunfire. This works best if you're unconscious when I put the barrel in your mouth. So you'll understand why I have to put you to sleep." He picked up the cane and raised it high for another strike. "Good night, William."

"That letter's going to destroy you. Any document expert can use it against you."

The cane stopped mid-swing. "I hardly think so. It's your handwriting. And the wording—so obsessive. Psychotic, I'd say. Love is insane, isn't it?"

"But I only wrote one letter to Sarah. It was the year she left school to marry you. She was twenty-four, a grown woman. I was barely fourteen years old." With his bloodied right hand, he pointed to the letter. "That's only the lovesick ramblings of a *child*."

Conviction was lacking in Addison's voice when he said, "You'd say anything to—"

"I was only her friend." Swahn rested his head on the stairs and left blood there from his wounds. "It would never occur to her that I killed the boy. You heard what she said—bad things happen to her friends. Sarah's own words." He touched the scar on his face. "When she saw this *A* carved into Josh . . . that's when she knew you were the one who did this to me."

The cane dropped from Addison's hand. He felt a constriction within, a vise that gripped his heart. From without, an invisible force was bearing down on his chest, pressing, pressing.

"I think she knew you were crazy long before that," said Swahn. "She was sending Belle away to boarding school years before Josh died. She did her best to keep her child away from you. But Sarah could never leave you."

Addison sank down on the stairs and gasped for air.

"I was at your wedding." Swahn dragged himself up one more step. "You might remember me as the pimple-faced little boy in the first pew. I'll tell you what I remember—the vows, old ones, so traditional. She vowed to stand by you *'in sickness and in health, for better or for worse.'* So she sent her child away because she was afraid for Belle. But Sarah stayed. Crazy as you are, she stayed to keep you company . . . and she even went insane with you." Swahn gripped the staircase carpet and dragged one useless leg behind him as he climbed the steps. "She buried Josh's body to protect you. She did it for love."

Addison leaned back against the banister.

So hard to breathe.

Pain radiated outward from his heart, traveling upward to his neck and his jaw. Soon the nausea would be upon him; he knew all the symptoms. Bile was rising in his throat. His face wet with cold sweat.

Swahn was impervious to all these signs as he dragged his ruined body upward. The man's face was turned toward the next flight of steps, the next round of agony that would lead him to the tower room.

Only Addison saw Sarah's body falling past the window. His wife did not cry out. It was Addison who screamed—or thought he did. His mouth opened wide, but he could only manage a hoarse whisper of her name. For one insane moment, he believed that he could call Sarah back before she fell to earth.

Would that she could fly.

Oren pushed open the front door and entered the foyer. Addison Winston sat alone on the staircase, tie undone and clutching the breast of his dress shirt. His face was ashen. The lawyer was orating to no one. His mouth only moved in dumb show.

Using the telephone in the foyer, Oren called for an ambulance. "It's a heart attack," he said, last words, as he hung up on the 9-1-1 operator. Joining Addison on the stairs, he picked up the gun on the step behind the man. And then he saw William Swahn's cane. There was blood on the silver handle, but none on the lawyer.

The lawyer's gun in one hand and the cane in the other, he traveled up the stairs to the second-floor landing, following a trail of small bloody dots and long smears. Swahn had collapsed on a second staircase, a narrow one. Oren laid down the cane, freeing one hand to roll the man over and check for a pulse. It was there, weak and thready.

Swahn's eyes opened.

"Ad Winston did this to you?"

"I have to get to Sarah." Swahn pointed to the top of the narrow staircase, and then his hand dropped. His eyes closed.

Oren climbed the stairs to enter a circular room, where

he found a shattered cocktail glass and melting ice cubes on the floor, but no sign of Mrs. Winston. A smashed answering machine lay on a rug beside the bed. He passed through an open glass door and crossed the outside deck to look over the rail. Her body lay sprawled on the terrace below, and a blood pool spread around her head.

"Sarah," said Swahn, weak and whispery, as Oren walked past him on the stairs. "I promised to—"

"Lie still," said Oren, though he doubted that this man would ever move again. "An ambulance is coming."

He ran down the stairs, skipping every second step, passing by the lawyer, who was laughing at some private joke that he had told himself. Oren sprinted across the front room and rounded the line of potted trees that hid the terrace doors. He opened them wide, and there she lay, animated by the wind lifting long strands of pale hair and playing with them, but the former soldier could not be fooled.

He would know death anywhere.

This time, the journey was longer as he made his way back up to the top of the lodge. The fallen man was no longer lying on the tower staircase. He had underestimated Swahn's mission to get to Mrs. Winston. There was no one inside the circular room. Once again, Oren stepped out onto the deck, and there lay the cane.

The man was gone.

The corpses were in body bags when the coroner's team carried them from the back terrace to the front of the lodge. They were laid on the ground side by side. This strange reunion of Swahn and Mrs. Winston was the first thing Addison saw when his gurney was carried out the door.

The circular driveway was choked with police vehicles, and a path was being cleared for the imminent flight of the ambulance. Its lights were spinning and the engine running. The rear doors hung open, awaiting the coronary patient.

A civilian vehicle was parked a short distance away. Hannah sat in the backseat of the limousine, breaking the sorry news to Mrs. Winston's daughter. As if by explosion, the car door flew open, and Isabelle touched ground at a dead run, aiming her body like a bullet and streaking up the driveway toward the gurney that held Addison Winston. The lawyer wore a maddening grin as he lifted one hand to wave to her.

Though the redhead was slender, one burly deputy was not up to the job of thwarting her forward momentum. She was only slowed down a bit when she stopped to send her knee into the man's crotch.

On the other side of the yard, Oren winced in sympathy and wisely elected to stay out of her way.

Isabelle's assault on the deputy bought Hannah time to close the distance, and now she stopped the younger woman with only one leaf-light hand and a few low-spoken words that did not carry. By some trick of flashing ambulance lights and body language, tiny Hannah seemed to grow larger in Oren's eyes, and Isabelle became smaller and smaller, shrinking to the ground in tears. The housekeeper's arms enfolded her, and Oren moved closer to hear Hannah say, "Patience, child. It won't take long."

One of the paramedics left the ambulance and ran to the sheriff. The coronary patient, earlier pronounced stable for transport, was now dead.

Spooky Hannah.

And there was no question of bringing Ad Winston back to life. The medic held one hand pressed to his own heart, illustrating his story of a body part broken beyond repair. "The second attack hit him like a bolt of lightning. The guy had to be in agony, but I swear he was laughing when he died. Weird, huh? Like he thought the pain was just so damn funny."

Cable Babitt was beyond the reach of his jeep radio, though he could hear the faint static of chatter behind him. By flashlight, he made his way to the grave at the center of the clearing. The crime-scene tape had been removed, and the hole had been filled in. He dropped the large plastic bag at his feet, needing both hands for the digging. When he steeped his shovel into the earth, he was blinded by a brilliant flash of light.

Sally Polk's voice came out of the darkness. "Can we take that picture again? I think you moved."

The next photograph caught him with one hand protecting his eyes.

Flashlights clicked on to illuminate two of the largest state troopers Cable had ever seen. Or maybe it was his fear that made them into giants. One of them relieved him of the shovel, and he heard the metallic click of locks as the other one cuffed his hands behind his back.

Sally Polk was still wearing her party dress, but she had traded her high heels for hiking boots. She bent down to pick up the plastic bag and opened it to pull out a bundle of canvas. "What a coincidence. It's the same color as my dress. Bright green. Cable, isn't that how you described it in that old missing-person report?" She placed one arm around his shoulders to pose for a photograph with her trophy suspect. "Well, Josh's knapsack gets around, doesn't it? First your toolshed, then the woodpile. Oh, and thank you so much for moving it off your property. I don't think there's a judge in this county who would've given me a search warrant for your place."

"I know this looks bad," said Cable.

"Bad or stupid—one of those things." Sally Polk said this without much conviction for either case. She held up the green knapsack. "You couldn't just throw it away, could you? No, you had to keep a souvenir."

Thirty-one

Ferris Monty polished his final column for the tabloids that paid his wages. Soon the lost boy would disappear from the headlines, and so would the author's byline. His last contribution to the scandal sheets was a story of love and death one night in a castle made of logs.

> *Two bodies were found on the terrace, a man and a woman lying close together. It is said by a highly placed source that William Swahn and Sarah Winston were lovers who died in a suicide pact, a common enough event. Even the beauty-and-the-beast aspect does nothing to electrify this tragedy. Only one thing places the story beyond the pale, almost beyond credulity: A third victim, a lawyer, died of a broken heart.*

He reread the words, and none rang true, though his source had been none other than Isabelle Winston, who had stopped just short of alluding to Rapunzel in her tower. However, fairy tales often passed for journalism, and he owed Isabelle this favor, this lie. In deference to her, he had scratched out the best line, stolen from the Rolling Stones, his expression of sympathy for the devil.

Done with this drivel, he turned to his unfinished book, an exercise in humility and an act of devotion to a young artist, who had felt nothing but revulsion for his biographer. The thick manuscript on his desk only needed a proper ending—the truth.

At the sound of a *rap, rap, rap,* he parted the drapes to look out the window. How prescient of Sally Polk to pick this moment to come knocking on his door.

Oren pulled the evidence carton from the trunk of the black Taurus. He carried it up the porch steps and set it down at the feet of his visitor, Sally Polk. The cardboard box was clearly stamped with the initials of the agency that owned it, the California Bureau of Investigation.

"You owe me," said Agent Polk. "I got all the bodies released for burial." She sat down in the rocking chair and settled a purse on her lap. "And I loaned Miss Winston a state trooper to get her through this day. That boy has orders to shoot reporters on sight."

"Thank you," said Oren. "I didn't think she'd want any help from me." He ignored the mystery box that sat between them.

Sally Polk rocked slowly, and her words were unhurried. "The judge came in to claim the remains of Mary Kent. Him and me, we had a nice chat."

"You've been feeding my father brownies?"

"Lots of them. It was a nice *long* chat. He's worried about you. He says you have a penchant for taking on blame that doesn't belong to you." She opened her purse and pulled out a small notebook. "I got a pathologist's preliminary finding on William Swahn." She flipped to a page of neatly printed lines, ripped it from the spiral and handed it to him. "Massive internal injuries that didn't come from the fall. That man was as good as dead before you got to the house."

"I would've been there sooner if I'd checked the answering machine when we—"

"Hindsight should be against the law." Sally Polk said this in a tone that would brook no contradiction. "You're not at fault. One of Cable's deputies called him at home last night. He was only a few minutes away from the lodge, plenty of time to save those people. But he thought I was behind it—a trick to get him out of his house so I could search it. And, of course, Isabelle Winston blames herself."

Oren nodded his understanding. Lessons from Hannah—guilt always followed a death in the family. "I heard you arrested Cable."

"But I'm not sure what to charge him with yet." Tired of waiting for Oren to take an interest in her carton, she bent down to open it and retrieved a large plastic evidence bag. Inside it was a wad of bright green canvas. She pulled it out and spread it on the lap of her flowered dress. "Can you identify this knapsack?"

"It can't be Josh's. It doesn't look twenty years old."

"It's been in Cable's toolshed all these years. He kept it to back up your alibi—or so he says. He told me Mrs. Straub made a statement to account for your time that day. And her story places Josh on a trail by himself."

Oren kept his silence and waited for Evelyn's old lie to come unraveled.

Sally Polk folded the green canvas into her evidence bag. "The sheriff says he found this knapsack not too far from her cabin. But I've only got his word on that. He's been up half the night, running his mouth. Oh." She paused for a quick smile. "And he gave you up."

"He told you I took the red folder."

"With Mrs. Straub's statement."

In lieu of a lie, Oren shrugged this off. "If that's all—"

"Well, no. He said there were other statements in that folder. Isabelle Winston gave you a *second* alibi. So one woman's story saves your ass, but two of them can hang you. It's lucky the sheriff kept the knapsack to back up Mrs. Straub. Too bad he never vouchered it as evidence." She lowered the evidence bag into the carton at her feet. "He also spilled his guts about leaving Josh's bones for your father to find." She picked up another evidence bag, a smaller one. But then she put it back in the cardboard box and closed the flaps, as if having second thoughts about showing it to him.

Yeah, right.

"Let's say the bones were left for bait," said Sally Polk. "That's one way to get you back here—so Cable could draw a target on your chest. Well, then Mrs. Straub's statement and that knapsack could be worth something. You think the sheriff was planning to sell them to your father, maybe to pad out the old retirement fund?"

Oren admired the lady's logic, but he shook his head. "Ever hear of Hanlon's Razor? It goes like this—never attribute to malice that which can be put down to stupidity."

"Amen," she said. "Cable Babitt's got a long history of stupidity." With a slap to the arm of the rocker, she said, "Okay, we'll go with that. But I'm still investigating the sheriff's department. It'll take quite a while to clean up all his messes." She opened her purse and dipped in one hand, then looked up to give him a slow-spreading grin. "I need an outsider as interim county sheriff—just till the next election." She pulled out an envelope and handed it to him. "That's from the Justice Department. You've been drafted."

"I don't want the job."

"But you'll take it." The clasp on her purse clicked shut. "My ace card is Hannah Rice." Her eyebrows arched to say, *Gotcha*. And now she waited for his reaction.

She would wait forever.

He had known this day would come; he had that much faith in Sally Polk. Hannah was his only weakness, and he worried over this tiny hostage, but he would never let it show.

"It's a colorful town you've got here." The CBI agent

looked out over the meadow. The chair rocked. The clouds rolled by. "A girl couldn't ask for more suspects. Like your housekeeper for instance. She's been flying below the radar all her life. No driver's license, no Social Security number. Housework is probably the only kind of job she could get. Sounds like a fugitive to me. I could look into that . . . or not."

"Nobody in this town would believe anything bad of Hannah—even if it was true. And you're running a bluff."

"Okay, I lied." She said this with the shrug of one shoulder, giving in way too easily. "I already did a background check. There's no record of any woman born under that name. It's an alias. I bet you didn't know that. . . . Your father didn't."

"And he didn't care, did he?"

"Don't you want to know what she's done?"

Seconds ticked by in silence, and then Oren was declared the master of the waiting game, the staring contest, and he also won for the widest smile.

"Okay, there's no warrants out on your housekeeper." The CBI agent put up both hands in a show of good-natured surrender. Once more, she bent down to open her carton. "Lucky for me, I always palm two aces." She pulled out the second evidence bag, the small one. The metallic object inside was partially obscured by paperwork. "Cable thinks Ad Winston killed that lady tourist and your brother. So we know that's gotta be wrong." She handed the bag to Oren. "My people found signs of recent digging behind the Winston stable. That was in the ground."

The small bag was heavy. When Oren turned it over to see what the documents had hidden, he was looking down at a ruined camera, corroded and crusted with dirt.

"There's damn few legible markings," said Sally Polk, "but I know it's an old Canon FTB. When I send it to the lab, they'll raise the rest of the serial number. The stamp that imprints the metal goes deeper than the corrosion. But you knew that. You're a cop." The agent opened her purse and pulled out a county sheriff's badge. "*My* cop." She polished the gold star with the hem of her flowered dress.

"And the digging was recent," said Oren. "So you think this was planted behind the stable?"

"Could've been moved there from some other hole." She held up the sheriff's star to admire its shine. "You can see that camera's been in the ground for a long, long time. I took it to a photographer. Famous guy—he's got a summerhouse right here in Coventry. He couldn't read much off those little numbers on the lens, but he had enough to work out the—what do you call it?"

"The F-stop?"

"Right. The F-stop was low. The lens was wide open, and the number for the shutter speed was as high as a pro could go without a tripod. Thanks to corrosion, every moving part on that camera is frozen in place. Assuming nobody screwed with the settings, Josh was in a shadowy area when he took his last shot."

"Deep woods," said Oren. "Not the clearing. And the knapsack puts him on the trail near the cabin."

She nodded. "The focus of that lens places the boy within a few yards of what he was aiming at."

And his brother only took pictures of people.

Sally Polk took the evidence bag away from him. "I've got more." She opened the carton flaps wide to show him a stack of photographs clipped to sheets of paper—Swahn's collection. Atop a pile of file folders was a thick manuscript bound by a rubber band. It bore the name of Ferris Monty, and there were many Post-its for page markers.

She closed the flaps. "I could have a real good time with this stuff. All I need now is a suspect—and that red folder."

Oren had finished ransacking his brother's darkroom. Next, he planned to tackle the other side of the attic, where trunks and boxes were stacked up to the rafters. He hunkered down to open the seal on an old storage carton, and then he heard the bumps on the steps. Rising, he walked to the stairwell to see Hannah climbing upward and dragging his trunk behind her.

"You're a lot stronger than you look." He descended the stairs to relieve her of this burden. He found the trunk surprisingly light now that she had unpacked his civilian clothes. It only contained twenty years of his life, a dress uniform, his decorations and the only personal items, Hannah's letters from home.

"What are you doing up here?" She reached the top of the stairs and stared at the mess on the other side of the open door to Josh's darkroom. "You're still looking for those missing pictures? Any luck?"

He settled the trunk on the floor. "I'll never find them, will I, Hannah?"

She deigned not to hear this. "I hope you're not planning to upset the judge with—"

"No, this is between you and me."

"Good." Bending low, she grabbed a leather handle and dragged the trunk toward the shadows on the far side of the attic.

To hide it?

"What's the hurry?" he asked. "That could've waited another day."

She stood upright, arms folded. "Tell me something, Oren. How much do you miss the Army?"

He hesitated for a moment, and then he fashioned the softest lie that came to mind. "No one misses the Army, Hannah."

"Then we'll put all these old memories away." She stooped low to grab the handle once more.

"Wait a minute." He crouched beside his trunk. "There's one little thing I keep forgetting to check." He opened the lid and sorted through the contents until he found a packet of envelopes addressed in the house-keeper's handwriting.

"You kept my letters," she said. "How sweet."

"Not all of them, just the most recent ones . . . but you already knew that."

He smiled, and she smiled. And now they had a game.

Oren leafed through the packet, reading every postmark. He pulled a letter from its envelope to scan the opening lines. "This is the one. This is why you couldn't wait to stash my trunk up here."

The woman could hardly hide it—as she had surely hidden the pictures from Josh's last roll of film. Letters missing from this trunk could not be easily explained away. He waved this one like a flag. "It's the letter you wrote to call me home."

She shook her head, as if confused—as if Hannah could ever be confused. "That was a while ago, Oren. I remember it took a bunch of letters to get you here."

"This one was mailed *weeks* before the first bone was left on the porch." Oren held up the envelope to show her the postmark, his proof. "It can't be a coincidence that you asked me to come home when—"

"Oh, *that*." She smiled. "I wrote that letter after Sarah Winston's daughter came back to town. It looked like Isabelle planned to stay awhile this time. Well, she wasn't married, and you weren't married—"

"Hannah, don't even *try* to tell me this was all about matchmaking."

"All right, I won't." Indignant, she marched to the attic stairwell, and her wooden clogs made more noise than necessary as she descended to the floor below. Then she put on some speed—and she was fast. Oren was lagging behind her as she made it down the next flight of steps to the ground floor.

And there the interrogation of Hannah Rice ended.

The judge sat in the front room, fitting the yellow stray with a collar. He looked up at his housekeeper, saying, "We'll have to come up with a name for this dog. Any ideas?"

"I got an idea," she said, and the old man never raised an eyebrow as the little woman dragged the stuffed carcass of the late Horatio out of the room and down the hall, heading for the back door.

Oren was pressed into offering his father a few suggestions for likely names, and then he caught up to Hannah down by the garden shed.

She handed him a shovel. "Let me know when the hole's deep enough."

The housekeeper raced back up the path. *So* fast. Oren had to run to catch her, and now he held her by the shoulders. He stood behind her, bending down to whisper in her ear. "Hannah, you *know* who killed Josh. I can even name the hour when you put it all together. It was the night of the séance . . . when you went back up there for a talk with Evelyn. She told me about the tourist in the yellow slicker, a woman with pale blond hair. The one who stopped by her cabin on the day Josh—"

"Evelyn shouldn't have done that."

"You told her not to tell. You were afraid I'd lose my alibi, and you worked so hard to get it for me. Well, it's gone, Hannah. Last night at the ball, I tore up Evelyn's statement and gave it back to her. So now there's a lot riding on those old photographs—Josh's last days. He went to some trouble to hide them—so they were important. I *need* them. Where are they?"

She was helpless to answer him, hands flailing, words failing her.

Custom of the house forbade the obvious question: *Hannah, what have you done?*

Thirty-two

Evelyn Straub escorted her visitor into the crawl space beneath the cabin, where two ancient television sets had been running for a day and a night, scanning years of séances.

The back wall of shelves had once been filled with videocassettes. Now there were wide gaps where some of the tapes had been pulled out and stacked on the floor between two wicker chairs. Evelyn held one in her hand, hesitating to play it. The younger woman's grief was only days old—still raw. "Are you sure you want to see this?"

Isabelle nodded.

Evelyn fed the old cassette into the slot below a TV screen and then depressed the play button. The two women sat down to watch the image of Sarah Winston taking a turn at the Ouija board. Sarah had been the first of the players to raise a question of murder.

"Any day now," said Evelyn, "Sally Polk will get a search warrant for this cabin. I thought you might want the tapes of your mother . . . to keep them . . . or burn them."

Late last night, Oren Hobbs had stressed the option to burn this evidence of guilty knowledge, and Evelyn had wondered why. "Just being tidy," he had said to her then. And what else had he done to thwart the CBI agent's investigation?

Isabelle leaned closer to the television set, as if to climb inside the glowing box with her dead mother. Her fingertips touched the barrier glass.

On screen, the late Sarah Winston was crying as she posed a question for the lost boy. "Did you suffer?"

Isabelle waited out the string of letters chanted by the players around the table, and she strung them all together to whisper Josh's reply. *"All day long."*

Over the rims of coffee cups, Hannah and the judge discussed the long-overdue burial of Horatio. They turned to the kitchen window as Oren rode by in the open cab of a small yellow tractor. Extending out from this noisy machine was a long metal arm with a mechanical elbow and a dangling bucket with jaws and teeth.

Henry Hobbs frowned. "I believe that backhoe belongs to the cemetery."

"I'm sure he'll give it right back," said Hannah.

"Remember the good old days—when we buried our

pets with shovels?" The judge kept his eye to the window. "Where's the boy going with that thing?"

"I thought we'd bury Horatio down by the garden shed. And Oren's not a boy." She smiled at the yellow stray waiting in the open doorway, still hesitant to enter any room except by invitation. "Why don't you name the *dog* Boy?"

"Come here, Boy," he said, and the dog ran to him to be petted and scratched behind the ears and to lick the old man's face. "Boy it is." The judge looked out the window, following the backhoe's progress toward the shed. "That grave should be on higher ground, closer to the house. The water table rises after spring rains."

"I'll mention that to Oren." The housekeeper handed over the car keys. "Can you drive to the bakery in Saulburg and pick up a special-order cake? It's got Horatio's name on it."

That made him smile. "Nice touch. I'll be back in an hour or so."

Oh no, you won't.

"There's a few more things I need." She tacked on a grocery list for the Saulburg supermarket and other errands that guaranteed long waiting lines.

When the judge's car was safely down the road and the noise of the backhoe had also died off, she made a telephone call. Then, after taping a note to the front door, she went down to the garden shed, where the dead Horatio had been waiting patiently these past two days.

The backhoe was nowhere to be seen and neither was

Oren. The opening in the ground was roughly squared. She would judge it to be maybe three feet wide, a tad more in length—and insanely deep if one only wanted to bury a dog. The mound of excavated dirt was almost as high as she was tall. Hannah looked over the edge of the hole to see her muddy reflection at the bottom. But Oren had not struck underground water; a garden hose with a dripping nozzle lay coiled by the shed.

The yellow mongrel padded down the path to join her. He stood by her side and licked her hand in a show of worship for the giver of food. Dog and woman raised their heads at the sound of the approaching vehicle. It rolled up the driveway and disappeared behind the house. The engine died. The driver would need time to climb the porch steps and read the note on the front door. Hannah watched the second hand crawl around the face of her wristwatch.

The dog was also waiting—anticipating—every muscle tensed, sniffing the air, sampling a breeze and catching the scent of a man.

The deputy rounded the side of the house. This was his day off—no uniform, no star, no gun. "You weren't real clear on the phone, Hannah." Dave Hardy was unshaven and surly for being called out of bed on a morning when he had planned to sleep late. Eyes hidden behind dark glasses, he walked down the path and stopped at the edge of the freshly dug hole. "What're you up to?"

"Oh, I thought we'd bury Horatio today."

He turned toward the two animals, the red Irish setter,

the dead one stuffed in a pose of sleep, and the live yellow dog drawing close to Hannah's side. Dave inclined his head to look down at the gaping hole. "You could toss *ten* mutts down there."

"It *is* deep. That surprised me, too." She cocked her head to one side. "Now that I see it, I think maybe Oren dug this pit for you."

The deputy stiffened. Like a man made of wood, all of one piece, he turned around to face the house, no doubt checking the back windows. He slowly revolved to take in the meadow and the surrounding woods. When he looked her way again, the housekeeper could see herself, two tiny Hannahs reflected in his dark lenses.

"Oren *knows* you killed his brother." And now she repeated the words she had said to him on the telephone. "How fast can you run, Dave?"

The man forced a smile. "The way I heard it, Josh died because he saw Ad Winston murder that lady tourist. Ad just killed the wrong woman is all—a woman with the same color hair as his wife."

In the spirit of a helpful correction—no anger—she said, "*You* murdered the wrong woman." Her hands dipped into the deep pockets of her denim dress, and her fingers wrapped around old photographs. "Millard Straub paid you to kill *his* wife."

Dave stood up a bit straighter and rolled back his shoulders. "Nobody could've mistaken that tourist for Mrs. Straub. Her hair was the wrong color."

"That tourist could've been bald for all it mattered.

She wore a yellow rain slicker. The hood covered her hair when you came up behind her and caved in her skull with a rock."

The deputy's head snapped back, as if she had slapped him.

Hannah pulled a photograph from her pocket. It was only an old shot of Horatio in his puppy days, but it would do for a prop. She stared at this image and focused on the memory of another photo destroyed long ago. And then she told her first lie. "This is a picture of you, Dave."

He removed his dark glasses, wanting her to see his eyes, and there was a warning note in his voice. "Don't tell me that came from the film in Josh's camera." Oh, no, said his smirk—he knew better.

"You mean the roll Josh shot in the woods—the day you killed him? No, you ripped out *that* film. You had to jerk it free from the spool . . . and you tore it."

He lost his smirk. The sunglasses dropped from his hand.

The yellow dog was deadly quiet, lips drawing back to show his fangs.

Hannah held up the photograph, only showing Dave the back of it. "This one's from a roll Josh finished *before* you murdered him. I found it hidden in his sock drawer. Oh, that boy and his secrets."

Dave stood on the lip of the pit, legs bent, ready to jump it, but the dog crouched low to change his mind. Then Hannah startled him with magic, the minor trick of a second picture finding its way out of a pocket to materialize in her free hand. "This one's a shot of you following Evelyn Straub at a street fair." She fanned out the back sides of three more photographs, and—more magic—the three became one. "Here's a picture of you turning around to see Josh with his camera pointed right at you. And don't you look mad? The boy was following you. So you couldn't kill Evelyn then. Not that day."

With no sudden movements to set off the dog, Dave edged along the side of the pit to get at her. His sunglasses were crushed underfoot. His right hand was on the rise.

To rob her or beat her?

The deputy froze. His eyes were on the crouching dog, its bared teeth. So quiet. There would be no bark of warning. "Hannah, I was just a kid that summer. Nobody's idea of a hit man. Why would—"

"You were perfect for the job, a bully all your life. And there's nobody in this town who hates women more than you do. Who would know that better than Millard Straub? You worked in his hotel every day after school. He was a lot like your father—the meanness, the cruelty—almost like a second daddy."

"I hated that old man."

"But you *loved* his money. He paid you to spy on his wife, didn't he? That's how he knew she was cheating on him. But Millard never tried to cut Evelyn out of his will. No need. He just hired himself a killer—a boy who'd work cheap."

"Nobody paid me to—"

"I bet you would've done it for free, but you were

paid. Millard kept a wad of cash in the hotel safe. That money disappeared when you left town. Evelyn thought you stole it, and that's what she told the sheriff, but Millard dropped the charges that same day."

More pictures appeared in her hands, and Hannah spread them like playing cards. She stared at them but did not see them. She was calling up memories of other photographs. "Here's one Josh took in the locker room the night you went after him. *My*, you look angry. You didn't want him following you around anymore. You had places to go, a woman to kill."

Dave folded his arms. His smile was twitchy. "Hannah, those pictures are worthless."

"You think so?" She shook her head. "The first time I saw them, I wanted to burn them." And she *had* burned them—all but Oren's homecoming present. She had not been able to part with the photograph of the two brothers. "It's all here," she lied, thumbing through her pack of props like pages in a book. "Like a story. The boy only had one reason for following people. Josh wanted a shot of your secret, and that's all his brother ever needed to know. When Oren was a boy, I was so afraid he'd see these pictures and beat you to death. He almost killed you back in high school—that fight in the gym."

She stuffed the photographs in her pocket and sighed. "Well, the damage is done. He's seen them all . . . and now he's crazy dangerous. I tried to warn you."

"Hannah, where is Oren?"

"Behind you."

There was no time for Dave Hardy to turn his head. A shove to his back sent him sprawling, arms waving, falling.

He landed on his feet, crouched knee-deep in water, shoes sloshing and sliding. The close sides of the pit were slimed with mud. Dave reached up to grab a wet tree root, and it slicked through his fingers. Footing lost, he slumped down a muddy wall, legs folding until his kneecaps were higher than his chin and poking out of the brown water. His clothes were soaked, his face and hair splattered. Looking upward, all he could see was a crude square of blue sky, and he yelled, "I could've broken my damn legs!"

Oh, God, the water was cold. His teeth clicked, his body shook.

Rising to his feet was slippery work in this dank, narrow space, and the wet blue jeans weighed him down. Twice, his shoes shot out from under him before he managed to stand. Flattened back against a wall, he craned his neck. All he could see was the high mound of earth piled near the hole. He stretched out both hands but could not reach the top. He jumped for the edge, and the mud sucked off his shoes and socks. But he had glimpsed the back of Oren Hobbs as the man steeped a shovel into the dirt pile.

Hannah's head leaned into the bright blue square above, and her voice was fearful. "You should've run. I *warned* you." She drew back as a spade of earth rained down on him.

"Hey!" Dave brushed loose dirt from his clothes. The rest turned to mud in his wet hair. He raised his face to yell again, and another load from the shovel filled his mouth with soil. He spat it out and wiped his eyes. "Knock it *off!*" Hands raised to ward off the next spray, he had his first look at Oren's face—so cold. What lifeless eyes—eyes of a machine that could lift a shovel and—

Ploff.

The deputy lost his barefoot traction. Sliding down the slick wall and landing hard on his backside, he clenched his teeth on grit. Shaking—so cold—he hugged his knees and lowered his head when the shovel appeared in the sky-blue opening. Dirt crumbled down from his hair to melt in the water when he lifted his face to the light and yelled, "Hannah! Call him off!"

Or turn him off. Switch off that *thing* with the shovel.

"I tried." She reappeared, head and shoulders, to lean over the hole. "No use." Her fingers curled over the edge. "Oren knows that Josh and the tourist died close to Evelyn's cabin."

"What? The grave was in the *clearing*. Nowhere *near* that cabin." Dave saw the shovel too late to duck his head. He gagged on the dirt, and his breakfast beer came stealing up his throat for a second tasting. Above him, the mute shoveler worked with an easy rhythm. Steep and lift, and *ploff* went the dirt.

"Josh and that woman died on the old hikers' trail."

Before he could ask how Hannah knew this, she read his mind and said, "Oren told me. He's been watching videotapes of the witchboard people—all day, all night—no sleep."

Dave looked up at her, his eyes wide in a mask of mud. "The *witchboard* people? Are you *crazy*?" More dirt hit his face to blind him and fill his mouth. He vomited up his last liquid meal, and the hole reeked of beer and bile. When his eyes were wiped clear, Hannah was gone. "No!" he called out to her. "Don't *leave* me!"

Don't leave me here with Oren, crazy Oren.

Scrambling to raise himself, Dave braced his ice-cold hands on the slippery walls. He could see her standing beside the man with the vacant eyes, lunatic Oren, who worked like a robot to fill his hole. Steep and lift and—

Hannah squinted, as if trying to see the mechanical man more clearly and from a great distance. "I don't think Oren can hear me anymore."

Ploff.

She hunkered down at the edge of the pit. "The witchboard people knew everything—bits and pieces here and there. Oren put it all together."

"Help me!" A downdraft swept his wet body with cool morning air. His teeth clicked. His hands trembled. "Hannah, I know you don't believe in that séance crap."

"Oren does." She looked down at him with such pity. "He *knows* you went up to the cabin that day. You waited awhile—just to make sure Evelyn was alone. It was raining when you saw a woman leave by the back door—a woman in a yellow slicker. You thought you were following Evelyn." She backed away and disappeared as more dirt came down.

"Hannah!" he screamed.

"Josh was following you." Her voice was behind him now. He whirled around, bare feet slipping in the muddy water. His fingers raked grooves in the wall of dirt as he was falling—*splash!*—into freezing water. He looked up to see Hannah's face framed in the square of blue sky.

"Josh saw you kill that poor woman. But Oren says the boy didn't take a picture of the murder. Is he right, Dave?"

The sound of shoveling stopped.

Hannah crouched low to peer at him, as if her answer might be written on his face. And then she nodded in a knowing way. "You didn't know Josh was behind you— not yet. The boy could've backed off and saved himself and run. My Josh could run so fast. You *never* would've caught him."

Dave twisted his head to look behind him. Above the edge of the pit, he could see the handle of the shovel as it was lodged in the mound of dirt, and there it stayed. Oren, the robot, was also listening to Hannah.

"It took time for Josh to set up the perfect shot," she said. "The boy was so quiet while he looked down at his camera to line up the little numbers on the lens. And then he looked up to focus, and he waited. . . . You rolled the body over . . . and saw you'd killed the *wrong* woman. The look on your face, a rock in your hand, the dead woman's eyes staring back at you. Josh just couldn't help himself. It was his nature to catch that moment. No power on earth could've stopped him. . . . You heard the camera click."

Ploff. Steep and lift. *Ploff.*

Dave's voice was pleading, breaking. "Hannah, call for help." Where was she?

Oh, Christ, don't leave me.

She came back to him and leaned over the edge. "I told you—Oren's seen the witchboard tapes. The year you came back to Coventry—that's when you went to your first séance in the woods. Everybody in town went to at least one. At the time, I didn't think anything of it."

"The sheriff sent me out there to check up on the psychic."

"That's what Evelyn thought—just Cable's silly idea of an undercover cop. But Oren says you didn't act like one. You never joined the players. You stood at the back of the room, hiding in the dark, listening. Were you scared that a message from a dead child would give you away?" Hannah smiled, but there was no mistaking her expression for happiness. "Scared now?"

Ploff.

"Hannah!"

"I tried to help you," said her disembodied voice. And then her face appeared again, but her eyes were raised to stare at the madman with the shovel. "You should've run. Oren knows that Josh died slow." Hannah lowered her gaze. "You dragged out that child's pain all day long." She drew back from the edge.

"Hannah, don't *leave* me!" He struggled to gain his feet. Half bent, he held up his arms to ward off the next shovelful of dirt. If he could not stand, he would die in this stinking hole. Every shovelful of earth thickened the water, and he could not climb upon mud to save himself; he could only sink. How long would he be able to lift his feet before they were encased in mud? He screamed, *"Hannah!"*

The walls seemed closer now, suffocating, and he looked up with the mad idea that the square of blue light was growing smaller—farther away—closing up. Mud from his hair dripped into his eyes. The light went out.

The yellow dog looked over the edge, ears flattened down and snarling.

Oren smelled piss and shit and vomit. The dog smelled fear.

The man in the hole rallied, rising to a stand and reaching high to grab the tree root. His bare toes dug into the muddy wall, scrambling, frantic for purchase. Dirt caved in all around the root, and the deputy fell, legs folded under him and covered over by the small avalanche. Dave Hardy raised his head and rubbed his eyes. He looked down at the place where his limbs should be. Oren watched the deputy twist and strain, but Dave Hardy could only free his arms; he could not move his buried legs. Panicked, manic, as fast as he could scoop the dirt away, Oren piled on more.

Ploff, ploff, ploff.

He lowered the shovel and stood back as Hannah leaned over the hole.

"My memory is long," she said to the deputy. "The proof was in your hands. Your knuckles were red and raw . . . from doing murder in the woods."

"That happened in a fight with Oren." Dave's voice was weaker, and his words came out like a whine. "You *saw* it, Hannah. You were in the gym that night."

"Oh, I'll never forget it. Every punch belonged to Oren. All those people in the bleachers—they all remember Oren's bloody fists . . . your bloody face . . . not one bruise on your knuckles. But Cable Babitt got the story secondhand. He didn't see that fight. If he had, he would've arrested you twenty years ago."

Ploff.

The dirt from the caved-in wall had thickened into mud all around the deputy's body, and he ceased to struggle. He only shivered, and his words were half-hearted. "Make him stop? Please, Hannah?"

"I'll try." She stole a glance at Oren, and then turned her face down to the deputy. "But he's got this idea in his head that you raped his brother before you murdered him."

Oren lost his rhythm with the shovel. He turned to stare at her.

"No, no, no!" Dave's voice was breaking, his head shaking. "I wasn't queer for Josh. I never—"

"You broke that child's bones. His jaw, his arms—half his ribs." There was no recrimination in her voice, only sadness. "And then . . . his fingers. . . . You broke them one by one. . . . Oren says only sex perverts do sick things like that."

"I'm no *pervert!*"

"You hurt that child all day long." Hannah's voice faltered and cracked. "And then when Josh was broken and helpless, you took off his—"

"I'm not a *pervert!*" Dave's voice was growing stronger, louder. His hands were raised fists when he yelled, "I killed the woman for *money!* The *wrong* woman, all right? But what I did to Josh—that was *payback!*" His fists slowly lowered. He was deflating, losing air and will. In a smaller voice, he said, "Payback for that beating I took from Oren . . . that night in the gym . . . the whole town watching."

The shovel dropped from Oren's hands. His head moved slowly from side to side, lips shaping the word *payback*, and his eyes rolled up to the sky. *Payback*.

The door of the garden shed creaked open. Oren turned around to watch the CBI agent retrieve a microphone from the ferns near the hole. He had not agreed to that.

Sally Polk nodded to him and mimed the words, *Good job*.

Their deal was done, the bargain kept—on his end. He had broken a suspect without using his fists. That had always been his way, and once it had been a source of pride, but not this time—not for a long time.

The voice from the pit was faint. "Make it stop," Dave begged, as if dirt still rained down on him.

Agent Polk led Oren out of earshot and then opened

her purse to pull out a small recording device. "My tape starts with the splash—him falling into the hole." Smiling, she shook her head. "That clumsy boy. So all I've got is his voice and Hannah's. Nothing to prove you were ever here."

"You can't use that tape." He had agreed to break Dave Hardy, to take him naked to a place where posturing was ludicrous—half the battle, only that and nothing more.

"I need this." Her hand closed on the recorder. "You laid out a good case, but it's all circumstantial evidence and hearsay. Though I did like that part about the money missing from the hotel safe. Now, just in case his lawyer gets picky—when I get the deputy cleaned up, will I find any defensive wounds—anything to back up a fight?"

"You can't use a coerced confession in court."

One hand on her hip, she nodded toward the pit. "You call that *coercion*?"

No. He would call it torture. He always called it by its name. Over the past few years, he had, once or twice, thought to look down at that line he would never cross—as if he could still see it. He could, at least, remember it, but now the only salvage of any value was this one rule of evidence—a law that he could keep.

"Erase the tape," said Oren. "It'll come back on you if you don't. That's a promise."

The set of her jaw and the pugilist stance told him she was taking this as a threat. *Good*.

Oren turned around to face the pit. "After you pull Dave out of there, when he's wearing dry clothes and drinking tea—when he's chewing one of your damn brownies—that's when you tell him you'll drop the charge of assault on a child. And word it just that way. Then offer him a deal—one count of murder for hire. He'll grab it—even if you get him a dozen lawyers. But I don't think he'll lawyer up—not today. Dave's ready to talk, and he'll write it all down if you like. Today, a ten-year-old girl could get his confession."

Any female would do.

Dubious, the CBI agent walked with him to the edge of the pit and called down to the man below. "Dave Hardy? It's me, Sally Polk." Now she remembered to speak her only line, one final lie. "Hannah called me to come get you out of there."

Down in the hole, a mumbling of nonsense words turned to convulsive sobbing. Dirt was piled up to the deputy's chest. Mud caked his face and covered his eyes. Despite his old hatred of all her kind, blindly, Dave reached up to her—like any crying child seeking comfort from a woman—like every man who believed, at his core, that a woman could save him.

The CBI agent hefted the recording device in her hand.

Weighing its value?

"You'll get a *legal* confession." Oren said this as an order, wanting no misunderstanding. He was not *her* cop.

This past hour had cost him dearly. Hannah, too. The tiny woman sat on the ground, rocking her body, her head bowed low. She had played her part so well, and now she was spent and crying and sick at heart.

Sally Polk held up her tape recorder and pressed the erase button. "I'll look after Hannah. You should be gone before the troopers get here."

Oren obliged her and walked away.

On the far side of the meadow, he was swallowed up by dense woods. For the love of Josh, he was a staggering man, feeling every wound to a child's broken body. He traveled farther into the forest, only stopping when he was certain that no one would find him this time.

Birds flew up from the trees in a whirlwind of spread wings and songs of panic, as though they had heard the bang of a bullet. On the ground, other creatures gave a wide berth to the man with a lost look about him, who sat with a gun in his lap all that day.

Night fell.

Thirty-three

A new Mercedes was parked in the driveway, but Henry Hobbs was on foot today. Striding across the meadow, he was heading for a promising trout stream with his rod and reel and a yellow dog.

The old man never walked in his sleep anymore.

Oren was on his knees, cutting flowers from the judge's enduring garden. He was nearly done with his term as interim county sheriff. Would he run for election—or lay down his gun like his father before him?

Did it matter?

He had once had a darker idea for that weapon, but he was now trapped in the inertia of life ongoing, one empty hour chaining into the next. Some days, he envied Dave Hardy, who had hung himself on the eve of sentencing.

Shading his eyes from the noon sun, Oren looked up at the tower of the Winston lodge. Birds on the wing circled their old sanctuary with gliding rises, dips and rolls, hungry for seed. After a year of abandonment, someone had begun to feed them again.

No birds sang in the cemetery. There was only the sound of footsteps crunching gravel on a path that wound around headstones and marble angels. Oren stopped before a fenced-in plot of ground where kith and kin were buried, and he laid a profusion of yellow blooms on Josh's grave.

In answer to an old question once posed by a Ouija board, he said, "I still love you."

Half his flowers were saved out for Hannah Rice. He placed them at the foot of a marble stone that dated her death to the previous summer, when every last question was answered.

Early on an August morning, he had found her on the porch, sitting in her rocking chair, eyes closed, but not in sleep. Pills had spilled across the floorboards, and the label on a fallen bottle had been his first clue to her cancer. More had been read into the smaller print, a date of origin for her prescription. It matched up with a postmark on an old letter, the first of many that Hannah had written to call him back to Coventry. She had seen death coming, on-rushing—with only enough time left to bring him home.

That morning on the porch, Oren had sat down beside her for the last time, and they had passed a quiet hour, the living and the dead. Nothing could have stemmed the flow of his tears—easier to stop the rain.

Armed with an old photograph of her and a notion that she hailed from Tennessee, Oren had used all his skill to find a date of birth for her gravestone. He had located her only official document in the records office of a small town, where he came to understand why she had never cared two cents for proof of her identity: Originally, her name had been a plain one, given to her by the state— after being abandoned in a trash can on the day she was born.

She had renamed herself with no one's permission and vanished from the public record. A pilgrim without papers, all that Hannah had ever asked was to be taken on faith alone. Respectful of that, Oren had stolen the birth certificate and burned it. Now, her only proof of life on earth was this stone—these flowers—this man who kept her secret.

"Hannah, I'm lost," he said, as if expecting one more parlor trick to fix him and make him whole.

Retrieving a yellow dahlia from her grave, Oren carried this flower to Miss Rice's good friend, Mr. Swahn. In the absence of farsighted generations and a family plot, the Winstons and William Swahn had been buried in the last available section of land, a far corner of the cemetery, and a triangle was played out in the position of these three monuments.

He laid Hannah's flower down.

A bouquet of common weeds sailed past his feet to

smash into Ad Winston's headstone. Without turning around, Oren knew that Isabelle had returned to Coventry.

The pretty redhead showed more decorum when she placed red roses on her mother's grave, and she also gave flowers to Swahn, laying them down next to Hannah's yellow token.

Oren and Isabelle stood in silence, side by side. He had yet to hear the sound of her voice.

And then she said, "Last summer, Hannah told me that we were always meant to get married and have four children."

He might have known that this first conversation could not begin with a simple hello. At least, Isabelle had not tried to kill him. "In all my life," said Oren, "I only loved one woman, and it wasn't you. But we could have dinner sometime."

She kicked him in the shin—hard. *That* had been predictable.

Isabelle walked away, pausing once on the gravel path to look back at him, just a brief taunt thrown over one shoulder, a smile for the damage she had done.

Echo of a tango.

Oren's wounded shinbone hurt like mad, and he chased that redhead down with the ghost of a limp, running for his life. He grabbed her by the hand and held on tight, despite that gleam in her honey-brown eyes that promised him more pain. He held on.

Penguin Group (USA) Inc.
is proud to present

GREAT READS—GUARANTEED

We are so confident you will love
this book that we are offering a
100% money-back guarantee!

If you are not 100% satisfied with
this publication, Penguin Group (USA) Inc.
will refund your money!
Simply return the book before
January 3, 2010 for a full refund.

To be eligible for refund, please mail the book, along with a
copy of the receipt, your address, and a brief
explanation of why you don't think this is a great read,
to the address listed below.
We will send you a check for the purchase price and sales tax
of the book within 4–6 weeks.

Great Reads Guaranteed/ATTN: Dept RP
Penguin Group (USA) Inc.
375 Hudson Street
New York, New York 10014

Offer ends January 3, 2010
